Conceived the morning after VE Day in 194[...]
educated in London. He worked for Rolls-Royc[...]
thirty four years, becoming the internationally r[...]
field of subsonic air-breathing missile propulsio[...]
turn of the century, and following a period of consultancy for HM government,
he now writes full time while living in a village between Bristol and Bath.

Following the success of *an unknown soldier* published in 2017 and
random consequences 2018, these two volumes of *recurring echoes* mark his third
and fourth publications with SilverWood Books.

Also by Peter Morse

an unknown soldier
random consequences
recurring echoes (part one 1940–1942)

recurring echoes
a narrative of war

part two
1943-1945

peter morse

SilverWood

Published in 2024 by SilverWood Books

SilverWood Books Ltd
14 Small Street, Bristol, BS1 1DE, United Kingdom
www.silverwoodbooks.co.uk

ISBN 978-1-80042-280-3 (paperback)
Also available as an ebook

British Library Cataloguing in Publication Data
A CIP catalogue record for this book is
available from the British Library

Page design and typesetting by SilverWood Books

for my mother:
Ivy Edith Rimell
10 February 1914–14 September 1997

History, with its flickering lamp stumbles along the trail of the past, trying to reconstruct its scenes, to revive its echoes, and kindle with pale gleams the passion of former days.

W. S. Churchill
November 1940

1943

62

Soon after new year, John had taken the train down to Bath and then a taxi to the farm. The train had taken ages, double the normal time, and he had arrived tired and irritable. Invited down by Marjorie, it was an opportunity to deliver their Christmas presents and to recover his car. With luck, Celia also might manage a visit.

He'd spent two weeks there being constantly fed, and occasionally cosseted by Marjorie. Towards the end, Celia had come up from Hamble to join him.

One afternoon he had driven the two of them into Bath for the January sales, spending a couple of hours in a tearoom while they went shopping.

John was their main topic of conversation. Both were concerned.

"He looked absolutely dreadful when he first arrived," commented Marjorie. "And thin. He's lost a lot of weight."

Celia too had noticed that.

"How is he sleeping?"

"Reasonably, I think," replied Celia. "Though he's twitching a bit. His leg aches at night, needs movement."

Marjorie was trying on a new pair of shoes, waggling her toes.

"What worries me most," continued Celia, "is that he's lost some of his sparkle. I think he's more tired than anything. No, not tired, more bone-weary. Malta took a lot from him. You don't get awarded the DSO for nothing. Then the wounds and the illness."

Marjorie purchased the shoes and they began to wend their way down Milsom Street deciding where to go next. Winter sweaters were the next target, if they managed to find any.

"One thing is certain though," said Celia. "He won't be made operational for quite a while." She thought of his leg. "If ever again. Flying at altitude, and the cold, his leg will be very uncomfortable."

They talked some more. "I've insisted he stays at the flat when he goes back to London. That way I can keep an eye on him and so can Elizabeth." Marjorie suddenly laughed. "And, of course, regular food parcels."

John had managed to stay awake in their absence though by now he was awash with tea. Unusual cakes were being served which, it appeared, mostly consisted of carrot. Surprisingly good.

He felt better for his afternoon out, watching normal people do normal things. And Celia and Marjorie seemed to have enjoyed themselves.

The drive back to London was as tedious and even longer than the journey down. Leaden January sky, unrelenting. Such was the amount of vegetables Marjorie had insisted he take – it took three trips from the basement car park up to the flat using the service lift. He feared he might tire of vegetable soup after a while.

***

Soon after breakfast, Luke trudged over to the mechanical engineering laboratory to see how his experiment had worked out.

A couple of days before he'd sat in on a meeting at the Royal Aircraft Establishment at Farnborough, deputising for Henderson who, with a heavy cold, had taken one look at the weather and declined the invitation. It had snowed and although Hampshire is reasonably close to Oxford, the journey had been fraught: three hours there and even longer to make his way back in the dark. Lunch, too, had been pretty dire, served by some slow moving, aged retainer who'd probably been there since the place was originally built in 1912.

The meeting itself had been unremarkable and the notes Luke had taken for Henderson had been brief. However, he had come away with a prize, and a valuable one. It was a new form of adhesive known under the name of 'Redux', a contraction of research at Duxford where it had been developed. It was an epoxy resin, coming in two parts which, when mixed in equal quantities, allowed not only metal to metal, but metal to wood bonding. No other adhesive could do this – it was unique, and was the secret of de Havilland's Mosquito construction. Wood to metal junctions had always been fraught with difficulty, chaffing and fretting under load. No longer. The strength of the joints was phenomenal and Luke had seen the test figures to prove it. Now he wanted to see the results for himself. The compound, previously exclusive to de Havilland, had now been released for general use.

The adhesive's components, a phenolic liquid and a polyvinyl powder, came in two separate containers. Such were the quantities now being produced

8

Luke had come away with a half-gallon tin of each. Taking a scrap piece of steel gauge plate he'd found lying around the lab, he'd cleaned off one end and roughened it up with a piece of emery-paper. Mixing the adhesive in equal proportions he'd glued the plate to a piece of four-by-two pine, wrapped the joint in a piece of greaseproof paper and secured it in a vice to set. Twenty-four hours was the approved curing time and now it was up.

Luke had left a do not disturb sign hanging on the vice and this had caused a few comments from the other inhabitants. After he had released the vice, a small crowd gathered to see the results.

The joint had a faint odour of fish. Getting the greaseproof paper off was the first job for it had become stuck. After some laughter he trimmed it off with a knife. The epoxy had cured to a very pale green, faintly tacky to the touch. Now, time to test the bond.

Clamping the free end of the gauge plate tightly in the vice he pushed on the wood, using it as a lever, to break the joint. It held. He invited the others to try. It was like something out of a fairground. None could break it. Hitting the wood with a hammer had no effect. It was only when some enterprising student swung at it with the back end of the fireman's axe from the corridor did they get any effect, and that was merely to splinter the wood. The joint itself held. The glue was most impressive and Luke was careful to take his test piece and his two precious tins back with him to his rooms.

As he walked, he thought. Luke's knowledge of advanced chemistry was pretty thin. It would be a topic of conversation with Allegra at the first opportunity.

Since the epoxy, once set, was impervious to water and acted as an effective electrical insulator, and being readily moulded while liquid, it was going to find a host of other uses besides being a wonder glue. He could think of several already.

It was time to make some telephone calls. The Toyshop and the Wheezers would be top of the list.

***

After months of pestering and an appeal to the admiralty, there was to be a press demonstration of the MGBs. Two boats were detailed to take them out for an hour, plough around at full speed for photo opportunities, weapon demonstrations and the chance for the visitors to have an appreciation of the operations of small, high-powered boats at sea. A good show was expected by their lordships.

The order had been greeted with a certain amount of mirth, though tinged with regret that they couldn't lose one particularly annoying reporter at sea. Mark, as correspondence officer, was tasked with arranging it all.

A couple of days later, boats selected, everything organised, Mark advised the commanders concerned. Naturally, he'd included his own boat.

That done he had a quiet word with his own commander, Lieutenant Harris.

"I wondered if I might make a request, sir."

Harris looked at him suspiciously. "And what might that be?"

"I wondered if I might bring along a guest on this thing?"

"Did you now. Anyone in mind?"

"A Wren lieutenant from Landguard Fort."

Harris looked at Mark, registering his expression.

"Most irregular." Day trips for girlfriends, he thought. MGBs were not pleasure boats.

"So is an outing for the press, sir."

Harris laughed and looked again at Mark.

"She is to come in full uniform. If anyone asks, she is a liaison officer. Be sure to tell her that."

"Yes, sir. I will. Thank you, sir."

"And what is her name?"

"Bridget Whittaker."

"I'll try and remember."

"Thank you, sir."

Harris smiled as he watched Mark hurry away to make his phone call. He must be going soft. Though he'd been wondering how he might get a trip out for his wife. She'd never make this one, and she was a civilian. That would be tricky. Harris laughed to himself as he thought of the idea of a family day. Or a supporters' day. There was a village inland that had adopted the flotilla, knitted them things, invited them to dances. It could be a thank you to them. He would broach it at a suitable opportunity.

Immediately Christened 'Operation Junket' by all and sundry, Mark was encouraged to get the press demonstration over with as soon as possible. With preparations well in hand, and checking that the weather would be favourable, he summoned the press for noon two days hence. The admiralty had commanded that they put on a show and Mark was determined that it would be a good one.

Rising early, Mark was at the berths well before eight. The boats had been thoroughly cleaned the day before and the final preparations were well in hand. The ratings looked cleaner than normal; hair had been carefully combed. A suggestion that they might get their photographs taken and their names in the papers more than sufficient encouragement.

Mark had arranged for a couple of rafts to be lashed up, empty five-gallon oil drums and copious lengths of four by two, eight drums to each float. Mounted in the centre were a pair of high-sided boards, slanted together rather like a sail, this to act as a target for the guns. He watched as the rafts were manhandled on board, resting on the depth charges at the stern of each boat.

It only remained to make a final confirmation of the running order with Lieutenant Harris and the other boat's captain and they were ready to go.

Mark had told Bridget to arrive early and she duly did. Smart in her best uniform and suitably made up, she caused quite a stir amongst the crews. The story that she was some sort of liaison officer had fooled no one and Mark got a number of knowing looks from the ratings. Albert, their coxswain, took rather a shine to her and invited her to join him at the wheel. Mark left her to it as the press arrived, all wearing raincoats as suggested.

There were six of them in all, including two photographers. Mark split them three to a boat with a final reminder that they were there to observe and not to touch anything unless invited.

The two boats eased out of the harbour and then, when the engines were warmed, accelerated to full speed. Three miles out they began to follow the coast, running parallel to each other, the huge plumes, like rooster tails, trailing behind. This allowed the photographers to photograph each other and get the desired shots of the boats travelling at high speed. They charged up and down for twenty minutes executing tight turns until everyone was thoroughly wet.

They dropped the rafts and then ran back in line astern allowing the guns their moment. The rafts erupted very satisfyingly under the combined fire of the Lewis and Oerlikons, finally disintegrating when the pom-poms started up. The depth charges were left to last. Rolled off the aft of the MGBs, exploding about a hundred yards astern. First the instantaneous circular shock wave on the surface of the sea and then, moments later, a great geyser of water erupting upwards, hundreds of tons of water thrown several hundred feet into the air.

After a pause to collect a decent haul of stunned fish, they cruised back to the harbour with the final entertainment of the Holman Projectors, each of the boats firing potatoes at each other, a competition for the most hits.

The pressmen had a wonderful time. They were all soaked to the skin but it didn't seem to matter. There were much effusive thanks. While the officers politely declined the offer to be taken to the pub for lunch, the ratings had no such inhibitions. They wouldn't see most of them for the rest of the day, but it was a duty of a sort.

Bridget, make-up still intact, hat still secure, handed back the oilskin the coxswain had dressed her in and said goodbye to Albert. She gave him a little kiss on the cheek for looking after her. Mark had never seen him blush before and the size of that smile was new.

She joined Mark on the quay looking remarkably fresh.

"Did you enjoy that?"

"I absolutely loved it," she replied, smiling broadly.

Glancing around she gave him a quick kiss.

"You really know how to impress a girl."

Harris came up behind them.

"Well done, Forbes, good show. I rather enjoyed that. I expect we will get some really positive coverage out of that."

He looked at the two of them, reminded of himself and his wife in earlier times.

"Now, I suggest you take Lieutenant Whittaker for a well-deserved lunch."

***

1943 had brought no change to Matthew's daily round, an afternoon in 3 Commando's office in Largs after his morning workout.

The physio department had almost become Matthew's second home such was this routine. He spent so much time there, every morning the regime of exercises and manipulation. They'd given him another small rubber squeeze ball to exercise his left hand and his fingers. He kept it in his tunic pocket, carrying it around, using it whenever possible. Occasionally, in frustration, he bounced it off the wall, throwing it with his right arm. Trying to catch to rebound had an unexpected consequence. Throwing the ball to rebound towards his left side prompted an involuntary, reactionary movement from his left arm. Encouraged, he developed it into another exercise regime using one of the squash courts.

The regrowth of nerves was exceedingly slow, measured in millimetres over weeks. Anything that fooled the brain to develop alternative pathways was to be encouraged. He was beginning to move his arm on command. Not much yet, but enough to be able to pick things up. It was a beginning.

63

John read the letter from his solicitor for the second time, more slowly, taking it in. In his absence his house had been requisitioned by the American Army for the duration. There was no appeal. His tenants, meanwhile, their hand forced, had chosen to return to London. The house was to be used as an HQ location for a US division moving into the area. Other accommodation was to be erected in the grounds. Once the war was over and the Americans had no further use for it, the house and grounds would be restored to their previous state, and his furniture returned from storage. It was likely that a full refurbishment and redecoration would ensue.

The tone of the letter was apologetic since, as explained, the solicitor was powerless in these circumstances, though the rental offered by the American Army was particularly generous.

John penned a short note thanking him for his continued efforts on his behalf and apologising for his delay in replying.

As regards the house, in truth, he didn't really care. He'd not thought about it in months and he had no use for it and wouldn't until the war was over. And that, assuming he survived. Those considerations were too far away to even think about. That it would be returned assumingly pristine was an advantage, but beyond that, John had no other thoughts. He had more pressing things to concern him, including his recovery.

He was definitely getting stronger, improving by the day. Soon he might be judged fit for duty, though when he would be cleared to fly again was more problematic. Two years ago, when he'd been in this position before, he'd been able to apply a degree of subterfuge. He didn't have that advantage this time.

John was enjoying staying at the Kensington flat. He was immediately available should Celia find her way to London and, failing that, Elizabeth could mostly be relied upon to supply him with entertainment should he need it. But it couldn't last forever.

John washed up Elizabeth's breakfast things, made himself some tea and, by the watery light of the early February morning, settled down with the morning paper she'd left out for him. It was Celia's birthday soon and he wondered if she could contrive to get to see him as she had for his a couple of weeks before. He also wondered about a present. Never easy.

As his eyes flicked between news reports his mind drifted back to pondering what he might do or, more likely, be called upon to do next. A return to Training Command held something less than appeal. Fighter Command was a possibility but, with Leigh-Mallory still at the helm, that seemed unlikely. Being now a confirmed Park man, he did not anticipate favour. Old rivalries and antipathies ran deep in the RAF, blighting many a career and sometimes enhancing the mediocre. The politics was all, and while John had done his best to ignore it, he knew he was tainted. It was an advantage that he didn't care.

Whereas Park was halfway human, Leigh-Mallory was austere, something of a martinet, and a political animal with grudges; too conscious of himself and vainglorious. It was not, to John's eyes, an attractive combination.

Perhaps he was not helped by the shadow of his more famous brother, George Mallory, the alpine mountaineer who had died on Everest in 1924. Another strange character, though considerably less inhibited than his surviving sibling. Mallory, reputedly, had been asked once why he climbed mountains. He had replied, "Because it's there." The quote had become famous, considered witty; it had been much used in many contexts, and had fallen into the language almost as a catchphrase. But, as one of their masters at school had explained, it had been completely misunderstood. What Mallory had meant was that he found 'it' there. Whatever 'it' was.

John thought he knew what Mallory meant. Occasionally when flying he'd experienced an 'it'. Something of a deeply intense, almost spiritual nature, totally different from anything else and impossible to describe. It was one of the reasons he flew. Celia, he knew, had it too.

Perhaps Leigh-Mallory, unlike his brother, had never found his 'it'. It would explain a lot. Not that any of this would help John. Common to everyone else in the country, he was not in charge of his own destiny. He would just have to wait and see.

As the mood took him, John had begun to write up his official pilot's logbook. Contrary to official guidelines, he kept two: the working copy, written on a day-to-day basis, aircraft, flying hours, task, success or otherwise; and another, a more considered version, enclosing the odd photograph and a few pertinent notes. Occasionally, the odd reflective paragraph.

The working copy, something of a scrawl, was the minimum necessary. Invariably, he'd been too tired for anything else. Likewise, he didn't keep a diary. The closest thing to that were his letters to Celia. A diary, especially on Malta, would have made dull and repetitious reading. "Got up. Went to fly. Killed a few enemy, or not. Went to bed." Just like a schoolboy's tedious entries.

He thought about keeping one now. He had ample time. All he lacked was the inclination. "Got up. Read the papers. Listened to the radio. Fretted."

Maybe not.

Wet, cold and miserable, February was a tiresome month at the best of times. Confined to the Kensington flat for most of the time, waiting for his body to heal, John's days had slipped into a predictable routine. He read the papers, listened to the radio and read the odd book. An afternoon walk to the park, a greeting of familiar dogs, a nap to follow. A five-bob meal at one of the local hotels in the evening. Then whisky and bed.

Due another medical board several weeks hence, he got his paperwork in order. His logbook still needed attention and he spent another morning on it bringing it up to date. Sorties flown, flying hours and dates, individual aircraft used, outcomes and scores. Totting them up he had twenty-nine confirmed aircraft destroyed, split almost equally between fighters and bombers. Over thirty probables, at least four of which he was certain had gone down, scores of damaged. It was, by any measure, an impressive tally, considerably ahead of the average. And he'd been lucky. Very.

A sharp pain from his left leg caused him to get up and move around the room before settling back into another of the chairs. He lit a cigarette and watched as another squall lashed the rain across the windows.

He suspected his days as an operational fighter pilot might be over. There was no shortage of pilots now or the aircraft for them to fly. The various training schemes were churning out pilots at a prodigious rate comfortably in excess of the losses. He looked again at his tally, double underlining the numbers. They could be his final score. The future was something of an unknown.

That was the trouble with being inactive – it gave too much time to think.

**

Luke could think of better ways of starting a week. A telephone call from Henderson at seven in the morning instructing him to be in his rooms by nine.

The early February weather had been cold, wet and miserable. Now, there was the threat of more snow. Luke hurried between the lees of the buildings trying to keep out the way of the wind.

Henderson greeted him with coffee and sat down opposite him.

"Casablanca," he said, brightly.

Luke thought of the newsreels and the pictures of Churchill and Roosevelt enjoying the sunshine.

"Morocco," he replied absently. "Better weather."

Henderson laughed and lit his pipe. Luke waited until the inferno died down and the last of several matches were tossed into the ashtray.

"I saw the newsreels."

Henderson nodded. "As you know, the meeting was held to agree, finally, a long-term strategy for the prosecution of the war. It would appear that our view prevailed over the American one. All that preparatory work paid off. So, it will be Germany first, Japan second. Finish North Africa, then Italy, then western Europe, in that order. At last, we have a coherent and agreed forward plan."

Henderson relit his pipe.

"Now, the directives are starting to come out. Ignoring the Mediterranean theatre, they are securing control of the Atlantic to ensure that the uninterrupted supply from the Americas can be maintained and increased. Achieve air supremacy over west and central Europe. Meanwhile continue to destroy the German capability to wage war. And finally to make a successful invasion of mainland Europe, occupy Germany and destroy all German forces. The terms of the surrender will be unconditional."

Luke drained his cup and put it back in the saucer. He thought of all the arguments that had gone before, giving silent thanks that Norway did not get a mention.

"Atlantic, destruction of the Luftwaffe, bombing, invasion," he repeated. The task was immense.

"So now we have our priorities," continued Henderson. "Whatever we do from now on must be directed towards these aims."

He gave a broad smile. "At long last I think we're moving in the right direction."

Later that morning, and with a clearer head, Luke sat looking at his notes, allocating activities to objectives. He began to appreciate what Henderson had meant. Whilst the Casablanca directives didn't change fundamentally anything he was doing, it did help to have clarity, and a defined sense of purpose.

But, as he'd discussed with Allegra over several gins the night before, there were years more to go. The real question was how many.

There was another outcome of the Casablanca conference, perhaps the most significant and far-reaching: the Allied declaration that Germany would have to submit to unconditional surrender. As Henderson had commented wryly, this time, no compromises.

The fighting would be long and pitiless, devastating. Little of Germany would remain. And few would care.

Henderson's original intention for the focus of their activities, though inflated over time, had proved surprisingly durable. The proliferation of secret departments, organisations and specialist sections within all the services, combined from those from industry, were now legion. By Luke's estimate, there were upwards of two hundred of them now. Henderson's idea of cross-pollination was even more relevant.

From necessity, and his own sanity, Luke had devised a comprehensive index card system. It detailed each of the organisations he'd had contact with, their location, their specialisations and key personnel. His system had grown – four wooden boxes housed in the bottom of his second safe.

During his regular visits to the various key establishments and their offices, he would compare and contrast and then casually suggest a contact that might prove useful. Within a couple of days he would follow up his suggestion with a letter giving a name and telephone number. Luke was always careful never to give any information as to what organisation they belonged or where they were located. Neither did he give any indication of what their particular projects were. The jealousies and personality clashes within this community were rampant, needing no encouragement. Luke's discretion was recognised and appreciated, resulting in degrees of openness that might otherwise not have been forthcoming.

Now, it was not unusual for Luke to receive requests for suggestions and contact details to solve particular problems. Putting X in contact with Y to get from A to B. And all with the minimum of fuss or external interference. It was, Luke thought, one of the more satisfying aspects of the job.

*

18

It had been a difficult night. As he walked back to his rooms, Henderson pondered, ruminating. A colleague's marriage had foundered in rather spectacular circumstances and through the evening, over a bottle of one of the better college brandies, the whole sorry tale had unfolded. It had been a sad story though not, he suspected, dissimilar from many thousands of others.

Theirs was a generation that didn't speak of emotion, confide their feelings. Thought of on occasion, but rarely spoken. To witness this sudden torrent from what had obviously been many years of suppression was as shocking as it was tragic.

His own experience of marriage and subsequent female relationships was, at best, chequered. And though his personal affairs had settled into some form of equilibrium, an awareness of his previous failures was not lost.

He turned a corner, missed his footing on a kerb and narrowly avoided falling into a puddle. The brandy. He'd not been this pissed for a long time. Unsteadily, he leant against a wall, lit his pipe and paused for a few moments. Not much further to walk. He would tackle his stairs by leaning forward and not stopping. Remember to drink water.

There was something once said to him years before by one of the wise and aged dons. Peeling himself off the wall, he struggled to recall it.

"The tragedy of marriage is that women think that a man will change, but he does not. While men assume that a woman will not change, but they do."

64

February had passed through March and had now reached April. The London weather, stubborn, continued to be mostly foul, occasional days of promise unfulfilled. John's mood seemed to reflect it: mostly poor, leavened by the occasional visit from Celia. His medical board had been inconclusive; though his improvement had been noted, it was not judged sufficient for a return to duty.

John recalled a word from his youth that perfectly described how he was spending his time: schlep, as in schlepping about. Yiddish, a word much favoured by an old Jewish barber Marjorie had despatched them to as boys. It meant mooching, meaningless activity. Not improved by definition.

The enforced inactivity was beginning to wear him down. There was a limit to the number of books one could read, newspapers browsed, radio programmes listened to before the heavy veil of depression began to descend. That his next posting, whatever it might be, was unlikely to be a flying one, weighed on his mind. It was likely to be some kind of staff appointment, no doubt of some value, but nevertheless flying a desk. The thought held no appeal. Meanwhile, the war continued, with or without his active participation.

The morning's post had delivered another food parcel from the farm and a letter from Marjorie. Quiet domestic news from the countryside south of Bath, comments on the activities of the others and encouragement to himself. Plus the usual pleas to Elizabeth to take care of herself.

John would reply to her letter in the evening. He wondered whether to motor down to see them in a few days. He had an ample stock of petrol coupons. He could even take Elizabeth with him if she was around.

He carefully unpacked the cardboard box. Eggs, butter and a few more jars of preserves together with a couple of loaves of Marjorie's farm baked bread wrapped in greaseproof paper. Breakfast for the next two weeks.

Mid-morning the telephone rang. Wearily, John reached for a pad and pencil before he answered it. Elizabeth's answering and message service. A group captain of whom he'd never heard invited him to lunch. A hotel off Kensington High Street behind Harrods, a ten-minute walk away.

Setting off before the appointed hour, John found the group captain already waiting for him, sitting at a corner table, studying the menu. A man in his late forties and, judging by the medal ribbons, a veteran of the Great War.

He stood up as John approached and introduced himself.

"Good afternoon, Buchan. Group Captain Henry Baker. Good of you to come."

"Good afternoon, sir. Thank you for the invitation."

Lunch passed in general service conversation. John's experience gained in Norway, the Battle of Britain and his more recent activities on Malta and how the situation of the island had changed so dramatically in the last few months. Their conversation ranged further, other theatres of the war, how it had broadened in the last eighteen months to become a truly global war and how the involvement of the Americans had utterly changed the dynamics of the conflict. John gained the impression he was being rather subtly interviewed, being assessed.

With the lunch completed and the debris cleared away, Baker ordered coffee and then sat back in his chair and lit up a pipe. The restaurant was now empty and they had the room to themselves. John lit a cigarette wondering what would happen next.

Baker had appeared to have come to a decision.

"You have been aware of the Casablanca Conference in January?"

"Churchill and Roosevelt? I read about it, of course. And I saw the newsreels."

"Quite so. One of the major agreements of that meeting was the formal decision to invade western Europe next spring. There was also the recognition that the organisation to begin the planning of such an enterprise should be put in place as soon as practicable. That has now been achieved. What we are embarked upon now is the next phase, to lay the groundwork for a full-scale invasion."

Baker put down his pipe, resting it carefully on the edge of the ashtray.

"The invasion, by its nature, is a combined operation involving all the branches of the three armed services from the outset, and from all the armed forces of what President Roosevelt has chosen to call the United Nations.

Predominantly, of course, it will be a British–American exercise, the higher echelons of which it is recognised will need to be fully integrated for the venture to succeed."

Baker gave a rueful smile. "No small task in itself."

He picked up his pipe again, examining its contents.

"My task here today is to invite you to join me and the, so far, small RAF contingent."

John paused before he answered, staring at the remains of his coffee.

"Thank you, sir, I'm flattered by the invitation. But I'm not sure that my areas of expertise are completely relevant." He shrugged. "I know nothing of invasions."

Baker nodded. "I know that. But at this stage that could be seen as something of an advantage. What we are attempting to do is to draw in a mixture of personnel with a wide range of differing experiences. This is to avoid us all singing from the same hymn sheet, as it were.

"At all costs we must avoid the dismal, and frankly disgraceful failures of some of the previous operations. Dieppe, for example, a fiasco. If ever there was a template of how not to organise and conduct an opposed landing, that was it."

August 1942, John had been in Malta, but he remembered the few reports he'd seen. A so-called reconnaissance in force by a frontal assault on a German-held port in France, resulting in the slaughter and capture of thousands of Canadians and with it the loss of a good many aircraft, ships and equipment. Fiasco didn't begin to describe it.

Baker was relighting his pipe and John took the opportunity to light another cigarette as he made up his mind. It was not, he realised, an opportunity to be missed.

"Well, sir, on the understanding that I have not the faintest idea of what this job entails, and whether or not I can do it, I would be delighted to join you."

Baker smiled and then let out a hearty laugh. "Well put. Welcome aboard."

"A couple of questions if I may?"

"Ask away."

"Presumably there is a headquarters building somewhere to report to and it might help if I knew who is in overall charge."

"Indeed. We're based in Norfolk House on St James's Square just off Piccadilly. Walking distance, as I did myself to get to this hotel."

John immediately thought of his leg. It would be a test – he would try, comforted by the knowledge of ample buses, the tube, or even a taxi should he fail.

"As to your second question, our ultimate head is Lieutenant General Morgan. Frederick Morgan. You will like him. A thoroughly good chap, very sound, very capable with an excellent background in the planning process. He also has a very good rapprochement with the Americans which is going to be important. He is an ideal appointment and, most importantly, he comes with Churchill's full backing. He has a reputation for innovative thinking, not least in his recruitment policy. Having made his senior appointments, he allows them to appoint their immediate subordinates and so on down the chain. The best people in the right place throughout the organisation."

"So far," commented John, smiling.

"General Morgan's full title is Chief of Staff to the Supreme Allied Commander – Designate."

Baker smiled. "Something of a mouthful."

John nodded.

"For that reason, and to give a degree of misleading anonymity, he's chosen to call his organisation after the initials of his appointment. So, Buchan, welcome to COSSAC!"

John walked back to the Kensington flat a mite bemused. He had no idea why he'd been approached though he suspected Park's hand somewhere within it. Leigh-Mallory was now in overall command of Fighter Command who themselves would be deeply involved in any invasion. Knowing their animosity, perhaps Park wanted his own man on the inside. Who knew? Neither had he any idea whether he'd be up to the job. That someone thought he would was of limited comfort.

The only thing he did know was that he was due to report at Norfolk House at nine o'clock the following morning.

John laughed as he recalled the date. Today was 1 April. Somehow it seemed fitting though – there were precedents. The Royal Air Force had come into being on 1 April 1918. They hadn't fared too badly since.

Though it had rained overnight, the weather had dried up and the sun had come out. John had given himself a good hour for the walk to St James's Square which, even accounting for several stops along the way to rest his leg, had proved more than adequate.

Norfolk House was a large imposing four-storey structure on the eastern side of the square with one of those private gardens, protected by railings, so typical of London, across from it. The railings had long since gone for munitions leaving only the gate, still locked against its post. Ridiculous and curious.

With time to spare, John stepped across the grass and sat on a wooden bench taking the opportunity for a quiet cigarette or two. The sparrows, in profusion, chased each other around the bushes while a pair of grey squirrels ran up and down the trees. John had been wondering who would have the job of sorting out all the paperwork for this new job, and the medical Board. With luck, he wouldn't have anything to do with it. Looking at his watch, he stood up and flexed his leg. Those 'first day in a new job' feelings.

An army private, with rifle, stood guard at the entrance. John gave his name to the sergeant lurking behind him and gained admittance. A reception clerk at a desk just inside the entrance had his details and directed him to his office on the second floor. The lifts had been commandeered for furniture so he was forced to use the stairs. A lot of them.

The office, partitioned off with half glazed panels, stood in the corner of a large room with windows running the length of one wall. It contained two desks, two chairs, four filing cabinets and two telephones, one each for internal and external use. Neither were connected. A small rectangle of carpet lay in the centre of the floor. Both desks and all the filing cabinets were empty.

John rearranged the furniture. One desk he placed to the side of the door, the other for his personal use he placed behind the carpet in the far corner, the filing cabinets in a row alongside it. He took the best of the chairs, the one with arms, put it behind his desk and sat down to watch the activity in the main office. A constant inward flow of furniture and office equipment. He went in search of a waste basket and an ashtray and was rewarded with both.

Group Captain Baker appeared, two orderlies in tow, laden with files and reports which they dumped on the desk inside the door.

When they'd departed, Baker pulled up the spare chair and waved a hand at the files.

"That, Buchan, is the accumulated wisdom of Combined Operations on projects associated with a cross-channel assault. You'll also find a host of detailed reports on the Dieppe Operation including the formal report on the air operations by Leigh-Mallory."

Turning his head again towards the files, he continued. "Your task for the next few days is to read that lot and absorb the content. Once you've done that, write me a few relevant notes."

John stared at the files: two piles, each about two foot high.

"Yes, sir, understood."

"Good. In the meantime, I have some dockets you need to sign."

John signed where indicated including his new, temporary pass.

"Oh yes, I mustn't forget this."

It was a plan of the building, the location of all the offices and services. The mess was on the top floor.

Baker smiled at him and stood up. "I'll leave you to get started."

"Thank you very much, sir."

Having watched him go, he sat for a couple of minutes, staring at the piles of files, wondering what he'd got himself into. Then, slowly, he stood up.

Daunted, but determined not to be intimidated, John sorted through the files and decided to read in two-hour sessions. He would then take a break to stretch his legs, wander around the building with his map learning the layout while taking the opportunity to grab a cup of tea from the mess being established on the top floor.

One file, discovered early on, gave a broad-brush explanation of the concept of combined operations and the particular problems they generated. It was a useful primer. While he concentrated on the air aspects of the proposals and actual experiences of previous assaults, he also began to keep notes of the naval and army aspects as well. Combined Operations were interdependent. It would be prudent to have at least a degree of understanding. For an invasion to be successful, it would need to be won in every dimension; on land, on the sea and in the air.

Before the invasion of western Europe could even be contemplated, certain crucial prerequisites had to be satisfied. The first was the complete command of the sea – not only the Channel and the North Sea, but crucially the whole of the northern Atlantic. Without control of the Atlantic by nullifying the U-boat threat, the convoys from the USA and Canada with their loads of war supplies and troops could not reach the UK. Enormous tonnages were going to be needed. The second criterion was the command and control of the air over western Europe by the defeat of the Luftwaffe. While the third requirement was the complete control of the whole of the intelligence aspects related to the invasion, which itself would require the development of a fully integrated and coherent deception plan. None of these crucial prerequisites had yet been met and their achievement was going to require a tremendous and continuous effort sustained over many months.

But even that paled when compared to what would be required for a successful invasion itself. The size of the enterprise was simply enormous. To John's uninitiated eye, the figures quoted for the armies' logistics, manpower and equipment and supplies, were staggering. Quite extraordinary, measured in the hundreds of thousands. And all to be safely conveyed across the English Channel. If nothing else, one thing became immediately obvious from only an initial reading: the invasion, in the primary stages, would be principally a naval operation.

Naturally, the army would form the bulk of the manpower. After what might be expected to be an uncomfortable and unfamiliar voyage across the Channel, they would land on an enemy held coast and, after the initial assault, gain a lodgement onshore to allow for the landing of all the follow up forces and their equipment. But, once ashore, they would then be fighting on the land in much the same way as they had for millennia.

Likewise, the air forces of the UK and US would be required to conduct a variety of tasks; heavy bombing, fighter protection, reconnaissance, tactical interdiction of specific targets, but these were all within the normal *rôles* they were trained for and executed in the normal course of the war.

It was the navy that would carry the greatest burden. It was they who would have to supply and man the thousands of purposefully designed ships to facilitate the landing. Seamen who would have to be specifically trained to operate this type of craft. By their very nature landing craft were not much use for anything else and in consequence the navy did not contain a wide pool of ready trained manpower. The provision of the vessels and their crews was going to be a prodigious task in itself.

A successful invasion would prove the famous dictum that the sea ruled the land.

John took a late lunch: tea and a variety of sandwiches. Hot meals were not yet available in the mess but were promised for the following week. Privately he was rather pleased with that prospect – it would solve all his cooking and catering problems in the evening.

Returning to his office he began to collate all his notes from six hours of reading, making additional comments, forming the basis of what he would present to Group Captain Baker. Then he tidied the office. Files read in one filing cabinet, those to come in another, his own notes in a third.

Tomorrow he would begin on the specifics, starting with a study of the reports from Operation Jubilee, the Dieppe Raid, in August 1942.

65

Mark's heavy cold had developed into bronchitis. Coughing, wheezing, the occasional sneeze, a constant battle to constrain the expunging phlegm from the papers on his desk. He observed his evolving symptoms with a clinical detachment. To begin with, everything he drank seemed to pour straight from his nose; it was if his body had become one great mucus factory. Then the bronchitis. A possibility of pneumonia to follow.

Unfit for sea, he'd been reduced to dealing with the flotilla's ever-mounting backlog of paperwork. While days of effort had shown signs of progress, he was sick of it, not helped by the knowledge that it would be at least another week after his symptoms improved before he would be allowed to return to sea duty.

Described as saturnine and cruel, the cold grey waters of the North Sea had made it a long winter. Wet, miserable and monotonous. Whenever the weather allowed, the coming of night found the MGBs on patrol. As the long nights progressed, a pattern to their missions began to be established, spread over three main types.

Bread-and-butter activity was to accompany the flotillas of mine laying MLs as they lay their patterns off the German-held coastlines of Holland, Belgium and northern France in the path of the German coastal convoys. These mining operations had proved to be a great success with many sinkings recorded, resulting in a sharp reduction of convoy traffic, the Germans now preferring to move their iron ore imports from Sweden by the more secure method of rail. What convoys remained moved only at night and were heavily defended, two or three merchantmen surrounded by three times as many warships. Interceptions were short and vicious affairs with the lightly armed MGBs unable to inflict much damage unless attacking in combination with torpedo-carrying MTBs.

E-boat hunting continued along the so-called Z line, a notional demarcation zone some seven or eight miles east of the British coastal convoy routes. Groups of MGBs would gather to either lay static or cruise slowly on silenced engines towards a likely interception point.

Intelligence on E-boat operations and their detection had improved considerably in the passing months. Shore radar, shipborne radar from the destroyers escorting the convoys and particularly from the intercepted E-boat radio traffic monitored by the Y-Station listening posts now strung along the length of the east coast. Copied from the RAF practice of listening to all Luftwaffe RT signals and using VHF direction finding equipment, it was now possible to plot and track the E-boat positions and movements using cross bearings and triangulation. The Y-Service now employed hundreds of trained Wrens, many with knowledge of German, and was manned twenty-four hours a day.

Once a fix was obtained and verified, the information was immediately passed to the MGBs and MTBs out on patrol together with any aircraft airborne on anti-ship patrols within reach of the area. The successful interdiction of the E-boat patrols had increased accordingly and a steady, if gradual, attrition of their numbers was being achieved.

Potentially, the most spectacular of their operations were the joint patrols with the MTB flotillas operating out of Felixstowe. The standard technique once enemy shipping had been sighted was for the MGBs to launch diversionary attacks by circulating a convoy at high speed and blazing away with every available weapon. While the weight of fire from the MGB's restricted calibres was not great, there was certainly plenty of it.

If freed from navigational duties, Mark would position himself lying flat on the top of the boat's whaleback with a stripped-down Lewis, firing as many pans of ammunition as possible. For some reason it always reminded him of the old western movies where the Indians surrounded the wagon train, except in this case the US Cavalry and their bugle calls were not about to ride across the waves.

With the German's attention fixed firmly on the circling MGBs, the MTBs would sneak in unobserved, closing the range to launch their torpedoes.

While considerable success was on occasion achieved, damage from returning fire was invariably incurred on the MGBs with a commensurate level of casualties.

The seventy-one-foot six-inch MGBs were a great improvement on the previous designs but they were still under armed. A lightweight twin Oerlikon mounting as devised by Beehive at Felixstowe was still subject to admiralty machinations as was a long-standing request to trial the fitment of a pair of lightweight eighteen-inch torpedoes.

While through a combination of better tactics and better intelligence the MGBs were holding their own against the E-boats, better, more appropriate weapons would enhance their capabilities considerably. The apparent reluctance of the admiralty to allow such advancements was a cause of considerable disenchantment amongst the crews of the flotillas, Mark included.

At the beginning of the war, no one in authority had known what to do with the fledgling MGBs. Now they had proven their worth beyond question, but they were still being hidebound by admiralty intractability. Even Cinderella had eventually got to go to the ball. There was a limit to what could be achieved by vague and distant promises.

Bad news travels fast: shocking, dreadful news travels even faster. Hichens had been killed.

Four MGBs on a routine operation to escort a group of mine laying MLs had been off the Dutch coast. With the sortie completed and the MLs returning home, the MGBs went to investigate the sighting of a dim blue light seen travelling inshore along the coast. Finding a trawler with a small gun coaster as escort, Hichens had immediately engaged. Directing the attack from his customary position standing on the top of the whaleback with his arm around the communications mast, Hichens was hit by fragments of a 20mm shell and killed outright. The trawler was left burning as the boats immediately broke off the attack.

The news of Hichens's death was broadcast in plain text during the return journey, as the boats drew towards their berths the whole dockside was lined by every man and women of the base in tribute. Most of the Wrens were in tears, as were a good many of the men. Complete silence as his body, placed on a stretcher, was carried from the boat, up the steps, and onto the quay.

Hichens's death, given wide publicity including a broadcast by the BBC, was mourned throughout the service. No more so than at HMS Beehive and Felixstowe.

The effect on morale was shattering and the mood within the Sixth Flotilla was very subdued. Soon, the flotilla was redirected to Dartmouth to work up a batch of new boats, but Mark, still recovering from his illness, did not go with them. Many changes in personnel followed in quick succession as staff took promotion and replacements flowed in. Hichens's death marked the end of an era.

While remaining at Felixstowe, Mark continued to process the paperwork for the flotilla. With cruel irony soon all the improvements to armaments – larger calibre guns, the provision of torpedoes, all that Hichens had fought the Admiralty for over the winter months – were approved. The Sixth Flotilla MGBs were to be redesignated as MTBs to become the First MTB Flotilla.

Hichens was the most highly decorated member of Coastal Forces with two DSOs and three DSCs. After his death there were strong representations that he should be recommended for the Victoria Cross. In the event only another mention in dispatches was granted, the only other award available posthumously.

This decision did not sit well within the flotilla. The award of a VC was no more than Hichens deserved, it would have acted as a fillip for the Coastal Forces as a whole and his flotilla in particular. And, of course, it would have been gratefully received by his wife and two young sons.

The denial was a mean, small-minded decision, and again it did nothing for Felixstowe's morale.

Mark had now been based in Felixstowe for over two years. By now, heartily sick of the sight of the North Sea, beyond Bridget he had no reason to stay.

Gifted from an ancient relative who, since the basic petrol ration for private cars had been abolished, had no further need of it, some weeks before Bridget had acquired a car, a small bull-nosed Morris, old but sound.

Irrespective of its lineage, the car had immediately become a real asset. Opportunity and petrol supplies notwithstanding, their time together was no longer limited to the confines of Felixstowe. They could travel out to places where they were not recognised and have time together in peace. Just like private, normal people.

Over the course of one of their nights away in the country, he talked it over with her. Their conclusion was simple. Mark would seek a transfer somewhere away while Bridget, in due course, would attempt to arrange a posting to be closer to him.

66

The reports and files delivered from Group Captain Baker on the Dieppe Operation were many and various. Every aspect of the action had been formally reported on, and narrative accounts had been compiled for each of the three services. Unusually, for completeness, a final file of contemporary newspaper accounts was included. There was a considerable amount to read and it had taken John the best part of two days to work his way through it. It was a depressing way to begin the week.

Mid-1942 had been the nadir of Allied fortunes. After almost three years of fighting, Britain and her Commonwealth were yet to register a single significant victory on the field of battle. They had been driven back to Egypt by the Germans and Italians in the Middle East; America and Britain were rapidly retreating towards Australia following the Japanese onslaught in the Pacific; while the Russians were being forced even further east by the continuing advances of the Germans. In a now truly global war, nowhere were the Allies holding their own. Not one single theatre. Bleak midwinter had become a bleaker midsummer.

Nowhere was the situation more serious than in Russia. While the perilous state of the Red Army had improved since 1941, 1942 was showing only marginal improvement as they continued to lose vast areas of both territory and men. Stalin was making well publicised and increasingly desperate demands for immediate assistance. Massed public rallies in London and New York had called for the immediate opening of a 'second front' in western Europe to relieve the Russians.

Whilst a second front, as such, was beyond the capabilities of the British and Americans, and would be for some time; it became obvious to Churchill and the British chiefs of staff that something had to be done to retain, or even increase, the numbers of German divisions based in France to avoid them being diverted to the Russian campaign. If Russia was lost, the Germans would join up with the Japanese, sweep further through the Pacific and the far east, and the war would be over. Lost.

It was against this backdrop that an amphibious assault on the port of Dieppe on the Channel coast was conceived. There was also another, unpublished and covert reason for the raid which arguably overcame the obvious objections and supplied the final excuse to proceed.

In early 1942 the Germans had changed their naval Enigma encoders to a four-rotor system from the previous three. Thereafter, Station X at Bletchley Park were unable to decode and read the German Navy's radio traffic, in particular, that of the U-boat fleet deployed in the north Atlantic. Allied shipping losses rose accordingly, to a point where they threatened to become unsustainable. If the convoy supplies to the UK from America were denied, the results would be catastrophic.

The Dieppe raid was seen, therefore, as an ideal opportunity for a 'pinch' operation. A small contingent of specially trained Royal Marine Commandos were to penetrate the German Naval Headquarters in Dieppe to seize and remove whatever secret material, code books and Enigma machines, they could lay their hands on.

Resurrected from a previously planned assault that had been abandoned due to serious doubt and appalling weather, Operation Jubilee to assault Dieppe, and described as a reconnaissance in force, was put together with some speed, and approved and executed in haste without being subject to the normal scrutiny applied to offensive operations.

And, in common with any venture of this sort, there was a political dimension. Mountbatten, vainglorious at the best of times, and much disliked by the upper echelons of the British military who considered his promotion beyond his competence, was eager to demonstrate the prowess of his combined operations command in a large-scale engagement. Likewise, the Canadians, idle for two years since reaching England, were desperate to make a contribution, whatever it was.

The selection of Dieppe as the target had been made more for convenience than any real tactical consideration. It was the nearest reasonably sized enemy-held port to England's south coast and thus easily reached. It was not an ideal choice. A narrow, deeply shelving shingle beach backed by high cliffs with projecting headlands either side.

The attack plan called for an assault at eight separate points along a fourteen mile stretch of coastline with Dieppe harbour positioned in the centre. It was an ambitious and elaborate plan requiring precise sequencing and timing.

The action was to commence before dawn with groups of Commandos attacking the coastal gun batteries either side of Dieppe and capable of ranging on the main attack force. 3 Commando were to land eight miles east of Dieppe to make a pincer attack on the battery at Berneval, while 4 Commando would make a similar styled assault on the battery six miles west at Varengeville. It was essential that these coastal batteries of 150mm guns be neutralised before the main assault on Dieppe itself could begin.

The principal assaults, using four battalions of Canadian troops, was to land in four separate locations. On each side of Dieppe at two fishing villages, Puys to the east and Pourville to the west, and timed half an hour before the final assault. Their task was to disable the defensive guns and machine gun emplacements that overlooked the central landing beaches.

The main frontal assault, timed soon after dawn, was to land on the two beaches immediately in front of the town. Some four thousand men supported by twenty-eight tanks were allocated to this frontal assault.

To avoid casualties to the French civilian population, there would be no bombing of the town and neither was there to be a preliminary naval bombardment. It was considered that stealth and surprise would be sufficient to overcome what was adjudged to be a lightly defended port.

Once the flanking and frontal attack areas were made secure and consolidated, the battalion from Pourville would link up with the troops and tanks coming in from Dieppe to then push inland to the aerodrome at Saint-Aubin-sur-Scie. From there they would advance to Arques-la-Bataille, about four miles from the landing beaches, to ransack and destroy the German Divisional Headquarters. Once achieved, a phased withdrawal would follow thereafter. The whole action was timed for less than six hours.

Overnight, on 18–19 August 1942, an armada of over 250 ships approached the French coast. 6,000 soldiers supported by another 3,000 sailors with air support to follow, a combination for the largest amphibious assault of the war so far.

At first things went well. The sea was relatively calm and the voyage across the Channel proceeded without incident. Some of the ships, particularly the landing craft, suffered mechanical failures, but otherwise there was no other drama.

This changed dramatically when at 0345 the flotilla carrying 3 Commando, positioned on the port beam of the main armada and still about eight miles from the French coast, ran slap bang into a German coastal convoy, itself heavily protected by armed escorts.

Though the landing craft had a steam gunboat along for protection, the navy had not supplied a defensive screen to either of the flanks of the assault ships. The resulting battle with the German convoy escorts was distinctly one sided. Pleas for help were misinterpreted and no destroyer support came to their aid. Of the twenty-three landing craft allocated to 3 Commando, four had already retired due to engine trouble. From the remaining nineteen, only seven reached the coast of France, four of which were promptly sunk. The naval engagement was a disaster for the landing craft, unarmed and unarmoured and packed with troops.

The landings, such as they were, either side of the battery at Berneval, were thirty minutes late, made in full daylight and with all surprise lost. They were immediately engaged by the German defenders. Heavy machine-gun fire and mortars. Outgunned and outmanned, it was impossible to overrun the battery. Instead, the Commandos resorted to sniping which fortunately proved to be surprisingly effective at keeping the German gunners inoperative for the duration of the action. 3 Commando had done the very best they could, but it was small consolation for the loss of one hundred and twenty men, over half of the attacking force.

By contrast, the assault on the western battery at Varengeville by Lord Lovat's 4 Commando was the complete opposite of that on the east. Undetected, 4 Commando's two groups of landing craft touched down in the right place at the right time. Attacking from two sides in a classic pincher movement, 4 Commando executed their attack plan to perfection destroying all the guns in the battery and taking a heavy toll of the defending troops. Though the fighting was vicious at times, with much use of the bayonet, casualties were light. The mission completed, the Commandos withdrew in good order to be re-embarked as planned. It was a copybook assault, exemplary, pressed with vigour resulting in a complete success.

Alas, it was the only high point of an otherwise appalling day.

The landing at Puys, to the left flank of the main assault, faced considerable obstacles. A narrow self-contained shingle beach, a fifteen-foot-high sea wall topped with dense barbed wire, with exit step ways and a slipway similarly blocked top to bottom. In addition, substantial pill boxes were sited at both ends of the sea wall while others had been built into the cliff faces on either side.

It had been recognised that without a preliminary bombardment, the only way these defences could be breached was by surprise. That essential element was completely lost by the interception of 3 Commando. The Germans were ready and waiting for them and, as the Canadians approached, a fearful weight of fire was brought to bear upon them.

Within seconds the attack collapsed as the assault troops began to be slaughtered. Only a very few managed even to reach the shelter of the sea wall. Further advance was suicide and an immediate evacuation was ordered.

Fighter aircraft strafing the defences proved of limited value as the landing craft attempting to lift the troops off the beach were either sunk or damaged beyond use. Attempts continued throughout the morning with more craft lost. Eventually, sixty men were evacuated from an initial force of over five hundred. The remainder were either killed, wounded or captured, with a quarter of the force killed outright. The Germans suffered two dead and nine wounded.

The assault at Puys had been an horrific fiasco achieving absolutely nothing but death and loss.

Of the four Canadian assaults, the landing at Pourville on the right flank was the most successful. Here the Germans were caught by surprise and did not begin to react until the second wave began to come ashore. The relatively wide beach was divided by a series of breakwaters leading into the sea upon which the Germans concentrated their fire, apparently in a pre-set pattern. Under the cover of smoke, the Canadians chose to pass in the space between the breakwaters and were able to clear the beach. Here they split into companies to then advance towards their individual objectives.

While one company pressed towards the radar station behind the west Dieppe headland another stormed Pourville itself and, after a brief intense fight, took the village including a fortified house which overlooked the landing beach.

The remaining two companies passed through the village and moved forward to reach the bridge over the river Scie. Positive leadership ensured this was taken, but the attack was stalled by a string of pill box defences on the far bank impossible to penetrate.

The follow up troops had by this time broached the cliffs to occupy a wood inland of Pourville village. Here they were supposed to meet up with the tank contingent coming up from Dieppe and then together advance towards the aerodrome and the German HQ.

With the tanks failing to materialise, further advance was pointless and the troops began a fighting withdrawal back towards the beach. The re-embarkation was successfully achieved in good order, over six hundred men being evacuated from the thousand or so that had landed.

The assault, in itself, had been a failure insofar as the final objectives had not been realised. But considerable damage had been inflicted on the enemy and several of the secondary objectives had been achieved. The price had been high – forty per cent of the attacking force did not return.

From a topographical perspective, there were few locations on the French coast less well-suited to an assault from the sea than Dieppe.

The beach, where the main attack was to be directed, is in the form of a natural amphitheatre. A wide flat esplanade bounded on each side by cliffs rising some two hundred feet. Limestone cliffs, honeycombed with numerous caves, which the Germans had exploited by turning them into a labyrinth of gun positions. Artillery pieces, heavy and light machine guns with mortar batteries interspersed, all carefully sited to enfilade the beach expanse from either end.

The beach itself, well over half a mile wide, consisted of deep pebbles backed by a sea wall up to ten feet high the top of which was heavily wired. Behind this were several semi-submerged and well-concealed observation and fire direction points with a clear view seaward.

Along the promenade, several hundred yards back was a line of hotels and associated buildings, all of which had been fortified. East of the beach was the dock complex fronted by a large tobacco factory, and the western end, another large building that had once been a casino which the Germans had reconfigured as a fortified strongpoint. Dieppe, far from being the lightly defended target it was supposed to be, was instead the exact opposite.

As one of the reports that John had studied had poetically stated: the beach at Dieppe was a stage, the sets erected and dressed, and the actors primed to enact an ignoble tragedy. Except, there is no poetry in wanton slaughter.

The beach was to be assaulted simultaneously at both ends. Again, there was to be no preliminary bombardment, though as the landing craft began their final run in, five squadrons of cannon-armed Hurricanes were to strafe the cliff and hotel defences, supported by the four destroyers offshore firing high explosive and smoke to obscure the landings.

The strafing proved totally ineffective at surprising the defences, while the fire from the destroyers was too high, the guns not sufficiently depressed to hit the cliffs. Nine Cromwell tanks, Britain's newest, were scheduled to land with the first infantry assault but due to navigational errors, they landed fifteen minutes late. By then, the damage had been done.

Enfiled from the cliffs by machine guns and mortars firing on pre-set patterns, heavy cannon fire plus a four-inch howitzer from gun pits near the casino, the first assault waves were simply obliterated. The follow-up waves, close behind, piled into the first, just adding to the carnage, though their tank support did manage to land on time. Men dead, men dying, men about to die. From a total of twenty-eight, only twenty tanks made it to the shore of which thirteen got off the beach, to be then immediately halted by an array of anti-tank obstructions. They fought where they stood until destroyed. Of the others, they were either lost in the shallows, the crews drowned, or they bogged down on the beach, the deep pebbles stripping the tracks. Incredulously, the suitability of the beach for a tank assault had been judged solely on the inspection of holiday snapshots and postcards from before the war.

More assault waves landed intended for the eastern flank but, because of a strong westerly tide race, landed on the west bank directly under the cliffs. It was a hopeless position though by accident it did create a diversion which allowed some of the troops to get off the beach in the confusion.

The casino was stormed and taken while a few troops and sappers managed to move into the town destroying a gas works and a few German guns. In the meantime, direct fire from a destroyer had set the tobacco factory ablaze.

Communications with the destroyer acting as the control ship offshore were vague at best, at worst utterly misleading. Upon learning that troops were off the beach, some three hours after the initial attack, the decision was taken to send in the floating reserve of Royal Marine Commandos.

As their landing craft emerged from the smoke screen protecting the ships offshore, they ran straight into the same dense walls of fire as had the preceding waves. The Germans, now convinced that this was a major invasion, had brought up all their reserves of heavy mortars and artillery pieces.

The Marines' commanding officer, leading from the front and recognising straight away that the situation was suicidal, had stood on the forward deck of his landing craft desperately signalling with his white gloves, attempting to turn them back. He was immediately killed. Six landing craft did turn back but the majority did not, to merely swell the numbers of dead and dying on the beach.

After four hours of this, the withdrawal was finally ordered, and for another agonising hour landing craft ran in and out of the beach under continuing fire rescuing what men they could find. The tide had now ebbed resulting in the width of the beach widening considerably. An open killing ground for the Germans. Over a thousand men were brought off, but that was only a quarter of those who had landed. The losses could have been greater. Perhaps the Germans just got tired.

As it was, the final casualty figures were simply appalling. Devastating. Of the five thousand Canadians who took part in the raid, only two thousand two hundred returned, a quarter of whom were wounded, many seriously. Of those left behind, nearly a thousand were killed, the rest captured, again many wounded amongst them. German losses were slight.

The raid was a tactical disaster, a complete débâcle, a tragedy, and should never have been attempted. Many young lives sacrificed for no tangible result.

Saving it to the last, John read Leigh-Mallory's account of the air aspects of the Dieppe operation carefully. It was very thorough. Apart from listing all the squadrons used during the action, he even detailed the ammunition and fuel stocks accumulated within 11 Group beforehand. Very large numbers: 1,454,400 20mm cannon rounds with belt links, 9,959,200 rounds of .303 and 712,000 imperial gallons of 100 octane petrol. John was impressed by the precision of the numbers, though he thought them to be a totally unnecessary inclusion. Leigh-Mallory was nothing if not pedantic.

Having described the intentions and preparations for the raid at some length, together with the tasks allocated to the air contingent, he then took the usual narrative approach to describe the actions of the day, and the vigorous response of the Luftwaffe.

That done, his conclusions were surprisingly brief. Direction of all air activity from the ex-Fighter Command, now renamed Home Defence Fighter Organisation HQ at Uxbridge, augmented by the two forward air control ships, had worked well, though there had been times when target requirements were inadequate. Close support by the Hurricane cannon attack fighters was insufficient against well protected defensive positions. Allied aircraft suffered considerably from anti-aircraft fire from naval ships due to poor recognition skills, resulting in damage and losses. All tasks allocated had been achieved satisfactorily.

Whatever the failure of the raid, John sensed Leigh-Mallory was distancing himself from it. Self-interest and self-preservation; the classic plea of 'not me guv'.

The RAF had lost a little over one hundred aircraft to all causes, whilst it was estimated the Luftwaffe had lost around the same.

John had learnt to halve the claims of shot-down enemy aircraft. Even with gun camera footage, over-estimation at the time was inevitable. It was only much later, and after careful analysis combined with intelligence from other sources, were accurate figures compiled. It was true of every air battle.

On this basis, the Allied losses were about double that of the Luftwaffe. Though they could ill-afford these losses, their air assets in western Europe being now only a fraction of those available to the Allies, the Luftwaffe would have celebrated this as a comfortable victory on the day.

Appended to Leigh-Mallory's report was a further commentary on his conclusions, illustrated by examples, and a list of recommendations for awards for conduct during the battle. It was long and comprehensive. John gave the list a wry smile. He remembered Matthew's comment after St Nazaire. The greater the failure, the bigger the crop of medals awarded.

Cynical, but true.

Dieppe had involved the combined strength of seventy-five squadrons, forty-eight of which had been Spitfires. Forty-eight. At a standard full squadron strength of eighteen, that was over eight hundred and fifty aircraft. John was astonished by the numbers. He couldn't help but think that some of this vast fighter resource would have been better employed on Malta. What they would have given for a few more Spitfire squadrons in August 1942.

The final file contained the press cuttings. It was an eclectic mix. Not only British, but American and Canadian together with some German translations and stills from a German propaganda film.

The coverage was predictable, though none were particularly accurate, especially from the Allied side. The heavy hand of censorship had seen to that.

The photographs were appalling. Deeply disturbing. One showed a narrow strip of beach, shattered tanks, scattered equipment and dead Canadian soldiers piled upon each other, with more washing in on the tide. Grainy black and white images of unimaginable horror.

John didn't linger long with them. He'd read quite enough.

67

John had read the Dieppe reports with a mounting sense of sorrow and anger. That the raid had subsequently acted to persuade the Germans to increase their forces in France and thus relieved, to an extent, the pressure on the Russians, seemed a poor recompense. The Torch landings in North Africa the following November, prompting Hitler to occupy Vichy France, had made a greater contribution.

After finishing with all the files, John had taken a break to clear his mind, an evening to contemplate and then a night's sleep. It wasn't until the following morning he'd begun to write up his observations.

He attempted to keep his notes short and concise. Their implications, however drastic they might be, was not his immediate concern.

Firstly, it would appear to be an impossibility to capture an enemy held port without an unacceptable level of casualties. And even if it was, the Germans would, as a last resort, destroy it to render it useless.

The assault plan for Dieppe was over-elaborate and too rigid for what it was. Too dependent on sequencing and exact timing that, when disrupted, had no flexibility or capacity to respond to changing circumstances.

Intelligence provided prior to the raid was appalling, inaccurate and hopelessly out of date. What was suggested as a lightly defended target proved to be anything but.

There had been no dedicated headquarters ship allocated to the raid. Instead, the army commanders had been accommodated on one of the destroyers accompanying the raid, which itself was overstretched with naval duties. The results were predictable. They only received inaccurate and conflicting reports of the battle, so instead of exercising clear command and control, they were reduced to the position of mere bystanders.

The training of the Canadians assault forces had been totally inadequate. They had never undergone realistic battlefield indoctrination exercises using live ammunition such as the Commandos had since their inception. Though not their fault, with a few exceptions, the Canadian troops had not performed well under fire. Their first inclination had been to lie down on the beaches with a disinclination to get up again. While this may be a natural enough instinct, it is, alas, the wrong one. Enfiled from either side they had been slaughtered where they lay.

The deliberate decision not to inflict a massive and sustained bombardment before the assaults had been a grave mistake. Strafing from fighter aircraft supplemented by a few destroyers was totally inadequate. Massive and sustained bombardment should be an absolute necessity, and should be continued up to a point where the assault troops were seen to be about to advance off the beach.

Special equipment for amphibious beach assault must be developed. Both for the beaches themselves and the obstacles the real intelligence reveals must be overcome. Judging the suitability of beaches for tank assault by simply examining old photographs and holiday postcards was ridiculous, and frankly, criminal.

John finished his report with a few more pithy comments and then passed it out to his secretary to have it logged and typed.

He'd received Baker's response later that afternoon. Favourable and complementary. Whilst none of John's observations had proved to be original, unsurprisingly, he had managed to cover all the salient points. His appreciation of the finer aspects of amphibious operations was being honed, as was his understanding of the magnitude of the task before them.

After a short conversation covering mostly admin and housekeeping issues, Baker then presented him with another substantial document headed 'Skyscraper'.

This described in some detail an assault plan for the invasion of France, and it was recent, dated 18 March 1943, less than a month ago. It had been produced by a planning staff under General Paget, Commander-in-Chief British Home Forces.

Noting the date John commented on it.

Baker gave a rueful smile. "Alas for General Paget, it's been overtaken by the formation of COSSAC with its emphasis on Anglo–American integration. And it was not well received by the chiefs of staff. Rejected on the grounds of being too general, impractical in terms of resources required and to be viewed of academic value only. Pretty damming, faint if any praise."

Baker lit his pipe. "To my eyes, as an outsider, that seems overly harsh. My understanding is that it does provide a useful, and substantial benchmark for our undertakings."

He smiled again. "Read and absorb as they say. And, in the meantime, give me your initial thoughts on the air dimensions and their implications."

John dutifully carried the 'most secret' report, the broad red diagonal cross on the cover, back to his office. Skyscraper, what a bloody silly name. He could only hope the content was of better quality.

John recalled something he'd read on his first morning. So elegant and precise had he thought it he'd have kept a copy in his desk.

It was the Alan Brooke test. General Alan Brooke, a tough Ulsterman, chief of the Imperial General Staff, Britain's most senior military appointment and Churchill's right-hand man.

A test applied to every new operation. Where will it be? Can it be done? Who will do it? Are there enough forces? Equipment? Training? Support? As a list it was formidable and required every criteria to be satisfied.

This, in essence, was COSSAC's initial task. Find a positive answer to every question.

As it is in life, so it was when planning military operations: there is always a choice of approaches. In considering the invasion of western Europe, there were two. The first could be described as the utopian approach. This is the task, make a plan of how to do it, and then determine the resources for it to be done. The second was the more realistic, real-life approach. These are the resources, this is the task, make a plan to suit that resource. It was a bit like buying a house; to wish for a multi-roomed mansion was pointless if all you could afford was a one-bedroomed flat.

Skyscraper, on which work had begun in mid-1942, had never been given any clear guidance on what level of resource would be committed to it. They had, therefore, no choice but to adopt the first approach. To formulate a plan for a successful invasion while assuming an appropriate resource commitment. It was a hiding to nothing, and John could see why the plan had been immediately rejected. The resources it required were simply too great for the British Army to supply.

COSSAC on the other hand, formed on an Anglo–American basis from the outset, was not so constrained. And further, the resources to be made available were to be stated from the start.

The Skyscraper plan, though unsurprisingly army centric, was a very considerable document and, to John, with his growing awareness and understanding of amphibious operations, quite fascinating. Not only did it give the answers, but it also showed the workings and none more clearly than the choice of the invasion site: the Caen beaches and the eastern beaches of the Cotentin peninsula in Normandy.

From quite early on, the planners had determined that there were only two locations on the French coast where an opposed landing could be seriously contemplated. The first, and certainly the most obvious, was the Pas-de-Calais. It was the shortest route, air cover would be at a maximum, and the shipping would have the shortest route and the quickest turnaround. It was, however, where the Germans expected the invasion to come. Consequently, it was the most heavily fortified section of the, so-called, Fortress Europa or Atlantic Wall. Here was the greatest concentration of German army divisions stationed nearby and was also the focus of the Luftwaffe's air defence system in France. It was the enemy's strongest point on the whole of the continental coast.

There were other drawbacks as well. Beyond the port of Calais, itself not large, major ports were not plentiful along that stretch of the French coast. Major incursions would have to be made as far away as Le Havre or even Antwerp before sufficient landing capacity could be secured. Landing on the coast was not the end of the operation, but only the beginning. Much thought had to be given to the campaign to be waged once a successful landing had been achieved and a lodgement consolidated. Calais to Berlin was, once again, the shortest route, but a direct drive towards the German capital would expose both flanks of the Allied Armies. It was not a strategy that would succeed.

Normandy contained a number of advantages the Pas-de-Calais did not, the first of which was the shape of the coast. The weather in the English Channel is notorious, rarely is the sea calm and storms can arise with little or no warning. The Bay of the Seine, off the Normandy coast, is bounded on one side by the Cotentin Peninsula with Cherbourg at its head to the west, and to a lesser extent by the headland containing Le Havre and the mouth of the river Seine to the east. It was an area of coastline, some fifty miles wide, completely sheltered from the predominately westerly weather and would provide a secure anchorage.

Compared to the Calais region, the German defences were considerably reduced, both on the beaches themselves and further inland. And there was the question of topography. The Norman beaches are wide, deep and flat. There were few cliffs of any significance and the hinterland immediately behind the beaches is similarly flat. Beach exits would be critical. It was essential that once the landings were made, a lodgement area was established as quickly as possible to enable the follow-up forces, with all the essential stores, to be unloaded and allocated at speed to ensure a rapid advance. An invasion battle fought purely on the landing beaches is a battle lost. Normandy offered significant advantages as to rapidly securing a sufficient area of land for the build-up prior to a breakout and the subsequent capture of Cherbourg and its port facilities.

John had read the Skyscraper report and its accompanying documentation with great care and with a growing sense of admiration. The reports deserved close scrutiny and rewarded the effort.

As he read through the various estimates of manpower, equipment and shipping requirements, one thing became abundantly clear. The invasion was to be the greatest amphibious military operation the world had ever seen.

Now, it was for the fresh eyes of COSSAC to examine all the questions and all the options afresh. Persuaded by what he had read, John wondered if they would come to the same conclusions.

Physically, it was not one of his better days. John more fell into his chair than sat on it. There were a lot of stairs to his office on the second floor from the map room, a distance away on the ground floor. Though the lifts, or elevators as the Americans called them, were now available, he preferred to use the stairs, reasoning the exercise would be better for his leg as well as his general fitness. He did the same at the Kensington flat, but at least there he could pause and sit on the stairs should he need to.

Norfolk House, this undistinguished, plain brick four-storey building was, until appropriated for the war, the headquarters of Lloyds Bank and was, coincidentally, the birthplace of George III, he who had lost the Americas; very ironic in the current circumstances. The building, relatively empty for the first week, was becoming fully occupied.

The first of the American contingent had begun to arrive and in so doing had brought an immediate and unexpected benefit. So appalled were they at the standard and quantity of the food on offer, they had immediately begun to ship in their own. And such were the quantities arriving, all were catered for. Already, John had eaten his first hamburger, very filling, and drunk his first Bourbon whisky, a little sweet.

And American cigarettes, Camel and Lucky Strike. John was developing a taste for the latter. Toasted tobacco, whatever that was, vaguely Turkish. Though contained in thin paper packaging rather than the British cardboard, allowing them to crush too easily, their price, a mere thruppence for a pack of twenty, compensated. Even cheaper when purchased by the carton of two hundred.

And it wasn't just the goodies the Americans brought. They brought an energy, uncomplicated by experience. Gratifying to witness.

They made for interesting comparisons, the Americans and the British. The tired cynicism of the later, the brash confidence of the former. The old world and the new. The characteristics were stereotypes, simplistic, but there was some truth in the observation. The old world and the new, united in purpose.

68

War is a full-time occupation, a seven-day-a-week business. In common with the rest of the population, sometimes John was hard put to say what day of the week it actually was.

Saturday morning and General Morgan was due to address the whole of the COSSAC staff. With all the doors secured, denying either entry or exit with only the guards on duty outside, they gathered in the large room used for the NAAFI – Navy, Army and Air Force Institutes – coffee shop on the ground floor of Norfolk House. It was quite an assembly. There were around three hundred people on the staff of COSSAC by now and all, without exception, were here. From the humblest kitchen staff to the most senior of officers.

After a brief introduction of himself and his senior staff including his deputy, Brigadier General Barker of the US Army, General Morgan began his address.

"I have called you here, all together in one place, because I think it is fair and just for you all, of whatever rank or position, to know exactly what we are setting out to do.

"At this point, I should also remind you from the outset, that the work we are about to undertake is of the utmost secrecy. Any suspicion of any leakage of any information to anyone not of our number will in all probability cause catastrophic disaster in the cause of the United Nations. You are upon your honour never to divulge any information outside of Norfolk House.

"What we are about, quite simply, is the biggest operation of the war. The invasion of France and the complete defeat of Hitler's Europe.

"I want to make it clear that, although the primary object of COSSAC is to make plans, I am certain that it is wrong to refer to it in any way as a planning staff. The term planning staff has come to have a most sinister meaning – it implies the production of nothing but paper. What we must contrive to do somehow is to produce not only paper, but action.

"In spite of the fact that it is quite clear that neither I nor you have by definition any executive authority, my idea is that we shall regard ourselves in the first instance as primarily a coordinating body. We plan mainly by the co-ordination of effort already being exerted in a hundred and one directions. We differ from the ordinary planning staff in that we are, as you perceive, in effect the embryo of the future Supreme Headquarters Staff. I do not think I can put the matter any better to you than by quoting to you the last words of the Chief of the Imperial General Staff, who said, 'Well, there it is: it won't work, but you must bloody well make it.'"

There was general laughter at this point, more nervous than humorous, and Morgan waited until the room was quiet before continuing.

Quoting from a couple of sheets of foolscap in his hand, he read them the directive to COSSAC as jointly drawn up by the British Chiefs of Staff and their equivalents in Washington, the American Chiefs of Staff.

In essence, they were to prepare plans simultaneously for three possible operations. The first was an elaborate camouflage and deception scheme extending over the whole summer with a view to pinning the enemy in the west and keeping alive the expectation of large-scale cross-channel operations in 1943. This was to include at least one amphibious feint with the object of bringing on an air battle against the Luftwaffe employing the Metropolitan Royal Air Force and the US Eighth Air Force.

This John presumed was a way to demonstrate to the Russians the support their western allies were continuing to give, while also alleviating the German strength in Italy.

The second plan was for a return to the continent in the event of German disintegration at any time from now onwards with whatever forces may be available at that time.

Memories run deep in the military. Germany had disintegrated suddenly and rapidly towards the end of 1918. John thought history was unlikely to repeat itself this time. Under Hitler, Germany was a different beast than it had been under the Kaiser.

Their third, and major task, was the planning for a full-scale assault against the continent in 1944 and as early as possible.

Morgan closed his address with a couple of rousing remarks, wished them good morning and good luck and then rapidly left the room.

There was, as he intended, a buzz of excitement. John had attended a good many briefings in his time, indeed, had given them himself. But none of them had been as assured as Morgan's. The feeling in the room was buoyant. Morgan had engendered an admirable *esprit de corps*.

Making his way slowly up the stairs to his office, John was overtaken by Group Captain Baker. They discussed Morgan's address and then he handed him a slim docket.

"That fleshes out the three operations a little." Baker gave him a smile. "We're going to be busy. Glad you joined?"

John laughed. "Wouldn't dream of doing anything else."

At this early stage of its creation, COSSAC was grouped into three main branches: operations, administration and intelligence. John was in the intelligence group. It was a wide remit covering huge swathes of material. Reports on information gleaned from every conceivable source were landing on his desk with increasing frequency. Busy indeed.

Back in his chair John lit a cigarette and read though what Baker had just given him. It wasn't much, though it did give him the code names of the three operations. Starkey was the deception plan; Rankin was the sudden return to the continent; while Overlord was the name for the full-scale invasion.

Not for the first time John wondered where these names came from. Someone, somewhere deep within the War Office was no doubt responsible, allocating them from some pre-prepared list. Starkey meant nothing to John, Rankin he remembered with an E on the end as a temperature scale. Overlord though met with his approval. Suitably grandeur with implied success.

He glanced at the map of western Europe, the Channel and southern England recently attached to his office wall, Morgan's words coming to mind. The eventual invasion of western Europe and the defeat of Hitler was going to be the greatest military endeavour the world had ever seen.

For reasons both mental and physical, John habitually took a walk sometime around mid-afternoon before tea. It took his eyes away from the papers and the work scattered all over his desk and the floor either side, and physically, it stretched his leg, the ache becoming irritating after a couple of hours of inactivity.

The last few days had seen him end his stroll in the large map room. Upon General Morgan's order, a huge map was being constructed of the whole of Europe, completely dominating one wall. The coverage stretched from the Arctic to Africa, from the Atlantic to the Mediterranean. It was a mosaic made up of the map sheets of the RAF, a small army of airmen on stepladders busily employed.

What most interested John was the perspective and the projection. Practically every map he had ever seen had been drawn north-south, with north at the top. This huge mosaic, however, was being constructed east-west with the British Isles at the foot. This alignment gave a bird's eye view of the whole of Europe from somewhere over the English Midlands.

It created an astonishing effect. Whereas previously the British Isles could be seen as some mere excrescence off the north-west coast of Europe, shunted into the Atlantic, the east-west perspective demonstrated with startling clarity that these same islands lay in the concavity of an arc of a circle on whose circumference lay Finisterre at one end and the North Cape on the other. From this standpoint, Britain was affectively surrounded to the east, with the Atlantic to its back on the west.

John found it fascinating, and the more he saw of the map's construction, the longer he spent looking at it. It focussed the mind wonderfully.

To his eye, one thing was blindingly obvious. To invade western Europe, one would not begin in Norway, scenic though it is; the so-called Operation Jupiter, an idea being bandied about in some circles lately. The map made an immediate nonsense of that. Logistics alone would be a mockery. It was going to have to be France; the only question was where.

John remembered the old adage: while wars are about geography, battles are about topography.

Amongst other things, COSSAC was subject to a stream of suggestions from Mountbatten's outfit. His Combined Operations Headquarters in Richmond Terrace contained a disparate group of characters. A charitable description would be eclectic. Mountbatten himself, sometimes known as the Master of Disaster, especially after Dieppe, had assembled a staff in excess of three hundred. As someone had memorably described, in addition to numerous officers from each of the three services, it also contained a fair degree of self-appointed experts, charlatans, certifiable lunatics and, amongst the civilian staff rather worryingly, a good many members of the British Communist Party. Russia may be a valued ally now, but until June 1941, it had been anything but. The enemy of my enemy is my friend might be the sensible pragmatic view, but it did not mean they were to be trusted.

And there was more. Given Mountbatten's social connections through his royal association, Richmond Terrace had also drawn in various personalities from the arts including several notable movie actors, both British and American.

Unsurprisingly, Combined Operations HQ was looked upon with some scepticism by the rest of the military establishment, as were their ideas. While a few had merit, most did not, and some were downright bonkers. Light relief if little else.

69

Henderson was occupied by a telephone conversation when he arrived. Judging by the acerbic comments he overheard, Luke thought it prudent not to interrupt.

Glancing around the room for something to occupy himself he noticed that one of the bookcases had undergone a change. A small, framed picture had appeared, propped up between two piles. Luke picked it up. It was not a picture one might immediately associate with Henderson. A horse climbing a steep mountainous road, hauling a heavily loaded cart. The expression of the horse weary, resigned, devoid of sense – it was easy to imagine the interminable plodding tread.

There was a little plaque at the base of the frame, French: *Cheval-vapeur* – Horsepower.

Luke was still holding the picture when Henderson, finishing his call with a final flourish of invective, joined him.

Luke went to put the picture back, but Henderson took it from him.

"I found this the other day. I'd almost forgotten I had it. Nineteenth century. An allegory for life, perhaps."

Henderson gave a short laugh and replaced the picture.

"*Cheval-vapeur*, literally, horse vapours."

Luke followed him back to his desk.

"Cvs are the French measure of horsepower, though it's different to ours. Eighteen hundred cv is equivalent to 1,775 imperial hp. 542-foot pounds per second compared to our own dear 550."

He laughed again.

"Must be something to do with the oats."

From somewhere, Allegra had acquired a small box of tinned food – seven cans in all. Alas, all lacked labels. Luke had volunteered to try to determine the contents without opening the tins.

Ideally, he would have weighed them, but lacking immediate access to a set of scales, he first decided to determine whether they contained liquid, like soup, or something more solid. There is always a void in a tin. When placed on its side the contents would form a meniscus, a shallow crescent on the surface.

Due to inertia, when the tins were rolled the more liquid the content the greater the meniscus on the surface. The greater that meniscus, the centre of gravity of the whole would move further back from the rolling centre of the tin. When the rolling came to a halt the tin would roll backwards a short distance as the contents settled. By calibrating that distance, he could reasonably estimate whether the content was a liquid or something more solid. So much for the theory.

Luke found a tin of baked beans and a can of soup to act as controls. Rolling them along his desk on a sheet of paper he carefully marked the amount of backward roll. As predicted, the soup rolled back further than the beans.

He then turned to Allegra's mystery tins, rolling each one in turn. He repeated the process several times with much the same result. There was a limited backward movement in all cases, but it was similar if not identical for each one. Apart from concluding the contents were more solid than liquid, as to what the actual content was, he was none the wiser.

He reported his results to Allegra that evening.

She listened patiently while he made a demonstration.

"Doesn't help much, does it?"

Luke nodded agreement. "You're the chemist, clever clogs. What's your suggestion?"

She didn't answer, instead picking up the tins and shaking each one to her ear. Then, she repeated the process with the tins in his little storage cupboard. With a look of triumph she took a slip of paper, wrote something on it and put it under one of the tins.

"I know, sure of it. Open one up and we'll see if I'm right."

Luke did as he was told. Bright green processed peas. Allegra was clapping, waving the piece of paper proving her guess.

"Ta-da!"

Luke congratulated her.

"We need some fish," he said.

***

COSSAC had received a supplementary directive from the Joint Chiefs of Staff. Resources for Overlord and a date. The date was 1 May 1944; the resources:

twenty-nine divisions for the assault and immediate build-up; of these, five divisions to be loaded for the initial assault plus two in the follow-up, plus two airborne divisions.

It was not enough. Inadequate. There was much wringing of hands around COSSAC and a certain amount of dissent. Morgan was quick to quell it. The gift of resources was not in their hands. Bellyaching was pointless. They had the task; they had now been given the tools. It was for them to plan the job, cutting their coat to suit.

Fairly quickly, and for much the same reasons as before, the invasion site for the Overlord landings had become a straight choice between the Pas-de-Calais and the Bay of the Seine in Normandy. Each had their own fervent supporters and the debates between them had become quite fierce. To resolve the tangle General Morgan had instigated a formal comparison within COSSAC to resolve the issue. Effectively, he had formed two competing teams. The Army Operations Section of the US Army were tasked to produce an outline plan for an operation centred on Normandy, while their British Army counterparts were ordered to do likewise for an operation aimed at the Pas-de-Calais. Meanwhile, the naval and air staffs had been directed to participate, without favour, in support of both teams.

Faced with a plethora of paperwork, questions for which he had no answers, answers in search of a question, John's mind was overloading. Frustrated, and in need of diversion, he buttoned up his tunic, pocketed his cigarettes and walked down to the map room. Vague, unspecific staring at maps has its own particular type of solace. Sitting on a chair he lit a cigarette and gazed at the English Channel, his mind drifting.

How narrow that little strip of sea between Dover and Calais, twenty-two little miles, so often England's salvation, never more than now.

John favoured the Normandy option. Why attack where the enemy expected you and the defences were at their strongest? It lacked both logic and sense. As he stared at the map something remembered stirred and he looked more intently. A thought. With it now foremost in his mind, John stood up and sauntered in the direction of the naval section and a captain he'd spoken to a couple of times.

A similar office, heaps of reports and charts, a recognisable worried frown.

"Tell me," asked John brightly, "what's the usual separation for naval vessels at sea?"

The naval captain eyed him suspiciously.

"It varies a good deal. Class of ship, sea state, tides, the wind, weather, visibility. What do you have in mind?"

"Destroyers, landing craft and the like. A mixed bunch."

The captain eyed him again. "Well, the general rule for a minimum is about a cable, six hundred feet in your language. It'll be less for some, greater for others, but as I said, it depends on a considerable number of factors. Why do you want to know?"

"Oh, I don't know," replied John casually. "I've just been wondering about sea room, how much space a large collection of ships takes up."

"Like an invasion fleet?"

John smiled. "Just like an invasion fleet."

The captain nodded and gave a small smile. "Good of you to take an interest."

It wasn't a sarcastic comment, confirmed by the next, accompanied by an enquiring smile.

"Not just a pretty face then."

John didn't respond.

"Two hundred yards then?"

The captain nodded. "Tenth of a nautical mile."

"Thank you."

"Anytime."

John wandered back to his office. He'd got the information he wanted and, he suspected, something else besides. Pretty face! Bugger off chum, as it were.

Unlike the police who considered it the most heinous of crimes, the services had a pretty relaxed and tolerant attitude to sexual mores and homosexuality in either sex. Though officially taboo and discouraged with explicit threat, as long as it was not blatant and kept exclusively private, it was given the blind eye. It may have been an innocent comment, if an odd one, but somehow John doubted it. As a child, blond hair, blue eyes, face of an angel, he'd had his share of approaches. His antenna had become fine-tuned at recognising the signs. John had never seriously considered it and neither had any of the others, though there had been a little of it at school.

He would have to warn Celia she had a rival, or something. He laughed to himself as he remembered Churchill's once reported observation. The Royal Navy, a tradition forged by rum, sodomy and the lash.

It was a childishly simple sum. Using the figures from the raid on Dieppe as a template, John made a few simple calculations. For Overlord there were to be a total of seven divisions afloat. A division of troops was typically twenty thousand men giving a total of, say, a hundred and fifty thousand. Comparing this to the six thousand at Dieppe gave a ratio of twenty-five. Scaling up the Dieppe fleet by twenty-five suggested a grand total of six thousand five hundred ships. It was a very large number.

John considered it for a while, pondering whether or not to reduce it. Bigger ships, different types of ships would no doubt be used for the invasion, special ships. Not least, those used for the bombardment of the landing areas before the troops hit the beaches. However, with no idea of what these might be, he decided to leave the total unchanged.

In search of a rectangular area, John guessed at a core frontal assault of twenty-five miles. This equated to two hundred and twenty ships using the cable spacing and making the depth of his rectangle about four miles deep.

The sums were right, but the more John thought about it, the logic seemed wrong. What was the formation of an invasion armada and, importantly, he'd made no allowance for manoeuvre. He thought about an equivalent number of aeroplanes all flying at the same altitude. It didn't help.

Taking more advice from an expert on ship movement in another part of the building increased the depth dramatically by an order of magnitude, over forty miles, and that figure took no account of formation and assembly areas from the demarcation ports.

It didn't matter. He'd proved his initial suspicion. There was simply not enough sea room facing Calais to accommodate an invasion armada, or at least, not without seriously compromising it.

Though only too conscious this was not his concern, John pondered what to do with this piece of information. The three services were very protective of their areas of operation and meddling would win him no friends. He wrote a short memo to Baker explaining his findings and the basis of them. He would know where to float it.

Every time John thought about it, he worried. And every time he worried, he brought the subject up at one of the weekly joint services meetings. And every time the answer was the same. They were to work within the resources they had been allocated. It didn't help. And while he recognised the instruction, it didn't solve the problem.

COSSAC's task was to prepare detailed plans for the invasion of continental Europe: Operation Overlord, 'The Mighty Endeavour'. To this end they had been allocated specific resources. In John's view this was backwards. Surely the logical way was to determine the scope and dimensions of the enterprise and then calculate the size of the force required. An architect, when designing a new building to a loose specification, does not begin with a fixed number of bricks.

The subtleties and niceties that operated in the upper echelons of the British and American military were, for the most part, a mystery to those of John's relatively junior rank. These were ways of doing things seemingly written in stone. It was the way COSSAC had been formulated, the very initials; General Morgan's appointment. Chief of Staff to the Supreme Allied Commander (Designate). It was that word 'Designate'. As yet they didn't have a Supreme Commander. And that was the nub of it.

Planners are charged with making the best plan possible from the means specifically allocated to them. A commander on the other hand is in a position to insist on greater means.

The master plan was due to be submitted to the Chiefs of Staff in mid-July. The memorandum to accompany it would suggest a substantial addition of resources. For the time being John would have to content himself with that. And wait.

The invasion of France could not partially succeed. Their plans must be either totally successful in every way, or fail completely. It could not be a draw. This wasn't a game of cricket or any other game.

70

The choice between the Pas-de-Calais or Normandy for the site of the invasion was proving to be impossible to resolve within the confines of COSSAC. Morgan's two opposing teams had now become fiercely partisan, seemingly unable or unwilling to decide between themselves. That one was British, the other American, only added to the intractability.

The British, more experienced and used to mounting operations with the minimum of resource, were confined to a more traditional approach; whilst the Americans, with their vast potential of men, materiel and capacity, were less hidebound and constrained. Their way to solve a problem was to simply crush it by weight of force. The British, more subtle, preferred incisive, carefully directed engagement.

Debates had ended in acrimony, where pride became the enemy of reason and rationality suffered accordingly.

A decision by a higher authority would have to settle the matter and, importantly, leave no lingering resentment which might remain if the final decision was made in-house.

Recognising this, General Morgan had approached Mountbatten at his Combined Operations HQ in Largs for help. A six-day conference was rapidly convened where the whole subject was to be thrashed out in minute detail.

John thought this a shrewd move by Morgan. Rancour ran deep in the military, old enmities rarely forgotten. An independent arbitration should allow all to accept the final decision.

Morgan, all his senior staff and a good many others, including Group Captain Baker, had decamped to Scotland in late June. John had stayed at Norfolk House never far from a telephone. There had been a good many calls, mostly clarification of minor points.

In the end, when every aspect of the invasion had been examined in detail, war gamed and scored accordingly, the decision had become self-evident. Overlord would land in Normandy.

John was both pleased and much relieved by the decision, matching as it did his own preference. It further confirmed the choice determined by the earlier Skyscraper plan. Calais, meanwhile, where the Germans expected the invasion to come, could now become the logical focus of the deception plan.

The Largs conference had wound up on the Sunday, coincidentally, 4 July, American Independence Day. Since the US were to provide the bulk of the resources for Overlord, it seemed to John a good omen.

John was finding that staring at a map had benefits beyond mere geography. While one part of his mind observed, another would consider related problems. Such was his concentration he failed to hear the footsteps behind him, and the sound of a voice made him jump.

"I wonder how well the Germans know English history." It wasn't a question, more of a statement.

Recovering his composure, John turned to find a senior army officer standing close behind him.

"I've no idea," replied John. "What do you have in mind?"

"Edward III."

John's knowledge of medieval history was, at best, sketchy.

"Remind me," he said, and smiled.

"The beginning of the Hundred Years' War. England's first invasion of France."

The officer's eyes narrowed as he thought. "1346 from memory. Edward landed at Normandy. The Battle of Crécy followed soon afterwards."

He thought again. "Ten thousand French dead, English three hundred."

"Encouraging precedent," suggested John.

The officer smiled. "Let us hope so."

Recalcitrance: obstinacy in opposition; John had looked it up – it was exactly the right word. Days of it. His head, metaphysically bruised from banging on walls, had left him bloody minded and not a little vengeful.

There were strict protocols within the services for communications with senior officers or with any branch outside one's immediate ambit. One used the chain of command, a conduit supposedly passing up and down, though in practice more akin to a spawning salmon and a river.

John had been rather spoiled with his direct access to Park in 1940 and 1942, while General Morgan's approach, encouraging input and ideas from anyone and everyone, was in a similar vein to Park's. So, while he could gain access to everybody within COSSAC, John's communication with anyone outside had to go through the interminable 'channels'. It took days instead of minutes and attempts to circumvent the system rarely succeeded and were likely to be counterproductive.

Whilst he was   developing his contacts within the Air Intelligence Branch of what had been Fighter Command, together with a few other potentially useful sources, it was still taking a bloody long time. It didn't help, of course, that he couldn't be explicit in his interest.

With Normandy now confirmed as the place of invasion, John had been drawn back to the problem of fighter coverage during the initial stages of the landing.

The early air assessments on Allied fighter coverage over the Pas-de-Calais or Normandy beachheads had concluded that while Calais was the easiest option to reach, it would also meet with the greatest opposition since the Pas-de-Calais region was the focus of the Luftwaffe fighter groups in France.

Normandy, on the other hand, was further away but could be covered adequately by Spitfires based close to the Channel coast. The opposition, based where it was, could be expected to be lighter and, by the time of the invasion, more of the Luftwaffe's assets would be based in Germany rather than France, defending their airspace from the Allied bombing offensive.

So far, so good. With Normandy now chosen, John began to scrutinise these assumptions on fighter coverage more closely.

The accepted range for a Spitfire IX, operating in still air, was a radius of action of 175 miles, which included an allowance for ten minutes combat. Using his earlier map as a basis, John drew a series of semi-circles centred on every available operational airfield in southern England. Coverage was adequate, but could not be described as generous, and sortie rates would have to be high to maintain continuous coverage.

Obtaining similar information from the Americans on their fighters, the P-47 Thunderbolt, 230 miles, and the twin engine P-38 Lightning, around 250 miles, improved the situation though not entirely.

To optimise the performance and fighting strength of the three types of aircraft they would operate at different altitudes. The Spitfires at the lowest level, the Thunderbolts above as top cover, while the Lightnings would range over the whole of the ship armada.

This still left the Spitfires as the weakest link. From his own experience of longer missions, he knew there were occasions when the pilots spent more time looking at their fuel gauges than they did looking for the enemy.

Remembering the sums he'd done on long-range fuel tanks for ferrying Spitfires direct from Gibraltar to Malta the previous autumn, John produced another set of sums equating additional fuel carried to increased radius of action and time on station. He then drew a couple of little graphs to illustrate the results.

And there was more. If Spitfires could carry a bomb under each wing, then they could carry a fuel tank. And, to negate the argument on the effect on combat performance, these could be made as disposable drop tanks to be jettisoned at the first signs of the enemy.

John wrote a short report to Baker and then went to see him.

Baker listened to his arguments, asked a few pertinent questions and then lit his pipe.

"What I suggest is you talk to Supermarine down in Southampton to check on the feasibility. I've got a number somewhere. Assuming there's no unforeseen complications and the idea holds, write me a short discussion paper that I can pass up to General Morgan's staff."

Once John had managed to locate the appropriate technical department, Supermarine were very helpful. John learnt there were proposals to add an additional fuel tank to the Spitfire fitted in the rear fuselage which should be in general service before the end of the year. And, they too had thought of drop tanks but had not received any instructions to proceed.

There was an art in getting a report noticed in the right quarters, and then acted upon. It was twofold. First was the circulation: the official nominees were relatively straightforward – the art was the so-called 'blind copies', an unofficial distribution to interested parties. Second, and essential, was the need for a cogent and concise summary of no more than half a page.

John stared at his notes, re-reading what he had written; correcting, adding, deleting.

"For Overlord to succeed, air supremacy, not mere superiority, is essential. Interdiction by the Luftwaffe of the invasion forces either at sea, on the beaches or the close inland, will jeopardise the whole operation and imperil success.

To negate interdiction an impenetrable air umbrella must be maintained at all times, above and beyond the invasion forces. Until such time as this screen can be supplemented by secure continental-based air operations, UK-based fighter aircraft will have the exclusive responsibility.

This report demonstrates the range restrictions of the umbrella operation and the bearing it has on the invasion."

John spent the following morning producing a fair copy of his discussion paper, included a page of illustrations, and had it on Baker's desk by mid-afternoon. For once he felt he'd produced something really useful, and he lingered in the bar that night allowing himself a private celebration.

One of his opposite numbers from the US contingent was also there and they fell into conversation. Pilot's talk, never difficult, particularly fighter pilots. A convivial half an hour with much laughter, educational to both.

Somehow the subject of drop tanks came up and the American, after a pause, asked him to wait a few minutes while he went to fetch something.

"I'm not sure you should see this, but I guess it won't do no harm."

He handed John an extract from a report prepared by a certain Robert A. Lovett, Assistant Secretary for Air in Washington, who'd recently conducted an inspection of the US Army Air Force's bombing campaign against the continent while on a tour of the UK.

As the American pilot explained, "He's real well connected – I mean to the President himself. What he says gets done, and real quick."

There was a list of recommendations, some of which meant little to John, but two of them certainly did.

The first stated the absolute necessity of increasing the production of auxiliary drop tanks as swiftly as possible to enhance the range of all US aircraft operating in Britain. John almost cheered.

The second recommendation was the most intriguing. Great urgency should be given to the development of long-range fighter escorts. The Merlin-powered P-51 Mustang being the most promising option.

The B-17 Flying Fortress operations had recently suffered grievous losses in daylight raids over Germany. Unescorted, the Luftwaffe had taken a terrible toll. It was a lesson Bomber Command had learnt to its cost in 1940 and why, now, they bombed almost exclusively at night.

John began commenting on the recommendations but his new-found friend began to get a little nervous.

"Maybe you'd better keep all this stuff to yourself for a while."

John smiled reassuringly. "Of course. I wouldn't wish to embarrass you."

They parted on good terms with John giving further assurance on his silence.

He caught the bus back to Kensington feeling quietly pleased – something at last to be cheerful about. Finally getting somewhere. There hadn't been many days lately where he could feel that. And it wasn't just the Bourbon.

As part of the support planning for Overlord, someone had conducted a statistical analysis of the total resources available to the Germans on the one hand, compared to that available to the British and Americans, together with the Russians, on the other. It was a detailed paper describing both the methodology and the presumptions made. However, what could have been a dry academic paper was transformed by the summary which preceded it. Reducing the whole of the research to a single graph, it suggested that while the Allies were on a continuous upward slope, that of the Germans had already begun to descend. Extrapolating the graphs forward indicated the lines would cross, with the Allies ascendant, by early 1944.

By mid-July COSSAC had completed the outline plan for Overlord. The landing of three assault divisions on three separate Normandy beaches ahead of Bayeux, and then to secure a lodgement within twenty-four hours on a line between Grandcamp-Maisy and Ouistreham. From there would follow an advance towards Caen. In addition to the forces coming from the sea, two airborne divisions would be dropped ahead of the seaborne landings to secure the flanks of the invasion force.

General Morgan formally presented the plan to the Joint Chiefs of Staff on 15 July. His covering letter, while stressing the need for adequate force build-up by the use of artificial anchorages, warned of the danger of making direct comparisons between Operation Husky, the successful invasion of Sicily mounted a few days before, and Overlord.

John read Morgan's penultimate paragraph carefully, admiring its lucidity.

"In 'Husky', the bases of an extended continental coastline were used for a converging assault against an island, whereas 'Overlord' it is necessary to assault from an island against an extended continental mainland coastline.

Furthermore, while in the Mediterranean the tidal range is negligible and the weather reasonably reliable, in the English Channel the tidal range is considerable and the weather capricious."

The target date for the Overlord invasion was set for 1 May 1944.

***

Luke, a rather indifferent glass of bitter before him, stared at the surface of the river. The occasional rising of a fish, a heron, perched motionless on a branch of an overhanging tree, watching.

He was meeting Henderson at his preferred pub by the river. He was early and Henderson was late.

To his right, beyond the pub garden, was a boathouse. Swallows were nesting in its eaves, the parents constantly back and forth with beaks of insects. A swoop to pause on a nearby branch, then a dart inwards to the nest to feed the chicks. Continually back and forth, unceasing, while Luke watched them. Occasionally they paused and sat alongside one another, preening. Playing with loosened feathers, dropping and catching, sometimes one to drop and the other to catch. Playful.

Constantly vigilant, the marauding kestrels and magpies were given short shrift. The swallows chasing them, arcing around their wings at amazing speeds, so close they seemed to touch. And then, when all was safe, returning to the relentless feeding of the chicks. There would be four of them, Luke knew, or if flies were plentiful possibly an exceptional five. And when they reached adulthood and began to breed in their turn, they too would return to this same spot to do so. The barns on the farm accommodated families of breeding swallows year after year, and always a great flat pancake of bird shit on the floor beneath the nest as a remnant.

Glancing at his watch he lit another cigarette, watching as the smoke rose to mix with the gossamer seeds floating by on the evening air. Should Henderson be much longer he would have to go and get another pint.

71

A new document had appeared in the map room and was causing quite a stir. Intrigued, John walked down to see it. A piece of treasure.

Over ten feet long and about thirty inches wide it reminded him of a strip of wallpaper. And the writing was on the wall. It was a German document, a blueprint from the Todt Organisation for the construction of the Normandy coastal defences. The Todt Organisation was Germany's slave labour force for civil engineering, its manpower taken from the countries they had occupied.

The blueprint covered the whole Normandy coastline from Honfleur to Cherbourg. With typical German thoroughness, every blockhouse, barbed wire entanglement, minefield and machine gun emplacement was indicated. Every gun to be sited was detailed, it's calibre and its arc of fire. The detail was astonishing: while, naturally, all in German, a complete translation into English was mounted on the wall beneath the original.

Incredulous, John sought out the officer in charge of the map room.

"Where the hell did this come from?"

The officer smiled, used to the question. "Bit of a coup, isn't it. The French resistance came by it last year. Nicked it from some office or other. Then they sent it over to us."

"Is it genuine?"

"Oh yes, it appears so. They're building it now." He laughed. "Or rather trying to. We get regular progress reports. It appears they're running way behind schedule." He laughed again. "Those dams your lot blew up are diverting most of their materials."

617 Squadron's breaching of the Möhne and Eder dams the previous May led by Wing Commander Guy Gibson, using Lancasters modified to carry special bouncing bombs, had made headlines around the world. The aerial reconnaissance photographs of the raid's success had been particularly spectacular.

John had not forgotten it, gratified that his colleagues in Bomber Command had finally received the recognition they so rightly deserved.

That the raid might eventually weaken the Normandy defences was an unexpected consequence, but nevertheless welcome.

The Overlord plan, as presented to the British Chiefs of Staff, had been revised to incorporate an increased level of resources. This would take the form of an accelerated rate of force build up after the initial assault, the idea being that it would allow for a more rapid expansion inland; first to the west and then to the east.

Coincidentally, the next meeting between Churchill and Roosevelt was scheduled in Canada for early August. The Quadrant Conference in Quebec. Morgan and his staff duly travelled over on the Queen Mary with the Prime Minister, and presentations of Overlord were given to the President and the US Chiefs of Staff in Washington, followed by further discussions in Quebec.

Morgan returned in early August and immediately convened another meeting of the whole of the COSSAC staff in Norfolk House. The room was more crowded than the last time reflecting how the staff numbers had increased in the meantime. Nearly a thousand people packed themselves into the room.

Morgan's address was another tour de force. He began by announcing that the outline Overlord plan had received the full endorsement of the Prime Minister and the President together with that of the nation's Chiefs of Staff. The green light was now shining brightly. In addition to Overlord, and to ensure the Germans continued to keep their forces in the west, the deception plans were to be given a greater impetuous. A plethora of code names followed. Under an overall title of Operation Cockade there was Starkey, Tindall and Wadham, various deception plans for western Europe, plus the addition of Jupiter, a full-scale assault on Norway.

Another outcome of the Quadrant conference was the commitment that the invasion of western Europe was to be the major activity of the British and US Forces in 1944. All else was secondary. Italy, and more importantly the US campaign against the Japanese in the Pacific, would become a second priority.

As Morgan commented, the summer would not find them idle.

He concluded his address by announcing a change in the status of COSSAC. Henceforth, not only were they required to elaborate the plan for Overlord, COSSAC was now charged with making the preparations to put the plan into effect. Pending the appointment of the Supreme Allied Commander, or his deputy, Morgan was to be responsible for carrying out all the planning duties of said Supreme Commander and taking the necessary executive action to implement those plans approved by the combined Chiefs of Staff. Gradually, COSSAC would evolve into an operational staff with all that implied.

John wandered back to his office feeling cheerful. Morgan, it would seem, had got all he wanted and all their work since April had been ratified. Now, the real detailed effort could begin.

As he sat at his desk, he remembered a comment made by one of the senior naval officers a few days before. When developing any project, ninety per cent of all the mistakes were made in the first ten per cent of the time. With three months gone, COSSAC was well past the ten per cent mark. With less than ten months more until Overlord's target date of 1 May, John could only hope that whatever mistakes had been made were small.

Ninety per cent of all American resources were to be directed towards Europe, the remaining ten per cent to the Pacific theatre. The US attitude, now confirmed, was that Hitler and Germany were the real threat, the Japs they could take care of in their own good time.

That the deception plans were to be given more impetus suited the British contingent very well. Espionage, counter-espionage, deception was something the English excelled at. It was a game, a competition without rules or regulations and one played for the highest stakes of life and death. But the English brought a peculiar, unique talent.

Most of the world's sporting games had been invented by the English. Cricket, football, rugby and a host of others. And even if not originally invented here, they had been adopted and then re-imagined and codified. There was something in the national psyche, an aptitude for games.

And so it was for deception. Perhaps it was the almost infinite subtlety of cricket, taught from childhood: a long sometimes interminable game, needing patience and concentration but capable of sudden unexpected drama unlike any other sport that had honed the skill. Whatever it was, the English excelled at deception.

***

Celia was spending a few days at Hatfield delivering Mosquitoes. She had grown to love de Havilland, their ethos and inventiveness. It was, of course, biased since it was they who had originally taught her to fly. Though not exactly like this. Executing a final barrel roll she began to laugh. It was amazing what could be done with a few sheets of ply and balsa wood, imagination, epoxy resin and a pair of Rolls-Royce Merlins.

She was enjoying herself. Levelling off from a rolling loop she throttled back to an economical cruise of 180 knots, re-harmonised the two Merlins and trimmed the Mosquito to fly hands off. Checking the compass, she set course for Lincolnshire, under an hour away. The Mosquito was an absolute delight to fly – de Havilland's finest aeroplane, powerful and responsive. Not quite so exciting as a Spitfire, nothing could surpass that, but the Mosquito ran it close and this was a particularly sweet example. Funny how aeroplanes, even if they were supposedly identical, all had their own subtle characteristics.

Relaxing, she looked around her, checking for other traffic. At ten thousand feet she was above the moderate cloud base and her view was unimpeded in all directions. There was something behind her, at similar altitude, coming in from the starboard beam. Celia watched it carefully as it became more visible. A four-engine heavy, American Boeing B-17.

Since it was obviously intent on formatting alongside her, she throttled back a little to make it easier while she examined the Boeing bomber with interest. She'd not seen one in the air before. The so-called 'Flying Fortress'. It looked purposeful enough, but with all the lumps and protuberances on the fuselage she thought it a rather ugly aeroplane, not helped by that enormous tailfin. It reminded her of something with warts.

She could see the pilot now, waving an arm in the air. No doubt the driver was some young American hot dog pilot of about nineteen. As any American was only too eager to tell you, all their flyers were hot dog pilots. It went with the nationality. Celia got the distinct impression she was being challenged to a race. You must be joking. She smiled and then she laughed, considering how she might respond.

First, she took off her flying helmet and shook her hair free. The sudden sight of long blonde hair sent an obvious message – immediately she could see more faces at the windows. Then, keeping perfect station on the B-17, she feathered the starboard propeller while opening the throttle on the port engine. The Boeing's engines began to smoke more as the throttles were opened to the maximum.

Celia waved to the crew, blew them a kiss and then rolled to port, levelling off inverted. After a few seconds of that, she opened the throttle of the port Merlin to maximum and, laughing, pulled rapidly away.

That would give them something to think about. She laughed again, imagining their reaction. OK hot dog, pick the sausage out of that.

***

Lying around in the mess John had found a document entitled 'Instructions for American Servicemen in Britain'. He took it back to his office to read as light relief. Seven pages of close typescript printed on rather poor-quality foolscap.

John was quite impressed. Whilst most of the advice was obvious, like don't ever criticise the monarchy, and the view of Britain was, perhaps, over generous, it would serve well as a general introduction. The War Department in Washington were to be congratulated. Though he did wonder if there should not be a reciprocal publication to explain the Americans to the British. Now that would be interesting.

72

Soon after his discussion with Bridget, Mark had requested a meeting with the base commander. Whilst he was sympathetic to Mark's concerns, he requested he stay his hand for three months until things had regained some kind of equilibrium.

With the three months now served Mark had requested a formal interview with the base commander. Again, he received a sympathetic hearing, the commander almost fond with his concern.

A Wren brought in some tea and there was a pause while pipes were lit.

"Any thoughts on where you might go?"

"No, sir, not yet. I thought I'd wait until I got your reaction."

The commander smiled. "You'd prefer to stay in the UK presumably? I know of your attachments here."

Mark blushed and then smiled a little boyishly. "It would be more convenient."

"Quite so."

The commander rummaged through the paper and dockets in his in tray and extracted a folder.

"A request has come in from a London-based organisation for a competent coastal forces navigation officer. Language skills an advantage. I know no more than that. Interested?"

A few days later, Mark was summoned to an interview with a Commander Slocum at his offices in London.

Rather reminded of being in the headmaster's study for some misdemeanour, Mark sat awkwardly in his chair as Slocum read through his file. Asked to outline his experience – Mark described his work at Felixstowe and some details of the navigation tasks.

"And you have some knowledge of French?"

Mark nodded. "Yes, sir, a working knowledge."

"How good is your French?" asked Slocum suddenly, in French.

Mark paused and then replied in kind. "Not as good as it was, though I'm sure it would recover with a little practice. I was reading modern languages before the war started."

"And German also?"

"Not as good as my French."

Slocum smiled, reverting to English. "Both may prove useful."

He closed the file and leant forward on his desk looking directly at Mark.

"You have already been vetted and security screened and, subject to you signing the Official Secrets Act, I am prepared to offer you an appointment as a Navigation Officer."

"Thank you, sir."

Slocum smiled again. "In the light of your previous service, a promotion to full lieutenant would seem appropriate."

"Thank you, sir," repeated Mark, unable to conceal his surprise. "Thank you very much."

"Not at all, young man. Thank you. I think you will find the work rather interesting, different, though no less dangerous than you are used to."

Commander Slocum was Deputy Director Operations Division (Irregular) or DDOD (I), responsible for all covert and clandestine sea transport to occupied France. Mark was now part of the secret 15th Flotilla of Coastal Forces, based at Dartmouth.

***

The prodigious quantity of documents that found their way to Professor Henderson's rooms never failed to amaze Luke. There were reports by the dozen, confidential briefings, minutes of government meetings and summaries and conclusions of all the Churchill–Roosevelt conferences as well as those including the Russians, and Stalin. How he came to be privy to all of this Luke never asked – he wouldn't get any straight answers in any case. What most concerned him was the amount of additional work it brought with it. How much Henderson actually read was unclear. There were few notes in the margins; but he was expected to read all of them, and then produce a one-page summary.

Out of necessity, Luke had developed a method of rapid reading. Although it required great concentration, he could now process a page in under ten seconds. Eyeing the latest heap sent across for his attention, Luke made himself comfortable in the armchair and began to read.

The first file was a summary report on the conclusion of the fighting in Africa, the complete defeat of Rommel's Afrika Korp in May and the German surrender in Tunis. There had been more than two hundred and fifty thousand prisoners, including twelve generals. Not that a head count had been immediately taken – it was an estimate based on the acreage.

A few days later after dinner in hall, Luke had sat for a while, pondering. Returning to his rooms held no particular promise, with nothing on the radio he wanted to listen to, the temptation to work might prove too great.

He'd spent a couple of days with the Americans, a meeting to discuss specialist beach assault weapons for the eventual invasion of Europe. Their attitude had puzzled him. Whereas the British were keen to explore all sorts of weird and wonderful contraptions for the task, the Americans were reluctant to consider anything other than the raw weight of sheer numbers of troops. Their suspicion of anything they hadn't thought of themselves, and their inclination to immediately reject without any pause for reflection, had discouraged him considerably. Even the argument that special weaponry had the promise of significantly reducing casualties during the initial assault had failed to cut much ice.

It was an odd attitude and Luke had begun to look beyond the obvious to try to explain it. He'd begun to wonder if there wasn't something in their respective use of language that might be a contributory factor.

Idly, he began to compile a list of the Americanisms he could remember. The words were mostly long, multi-syllabled, and combinations of other words; ugly, lacking elegance or, indeed, eloquence. Others were just plain odd. Soon he'd covered a double page of his notebook. He stared at it wondering – beyond being an interesting exercise, it hadn't advanced his understanding.

An advantage of Oxford was that there was always someone to be found who was either an expert or knew someone who was on the most obscure of topics. It gave Luke access to an encyclopaedic array of knowledge of things not necessarily found in encyclopaedias.

There was an English don sitting not far from him and Luke enlisted his help.

"You've been spending time with the cousins, have you?"

Luke outlined his problem, and his suspicions, and showed him the list.

"You have a good ear." The don paused. "It might help if you understood a little of the origins of their language. There was a time when it was very mixed, a real mishmash. Indeed, there was a vote, alas I don't remember the date, to determine what was to be the official language of the Americas. English was adopted as the official language but only by a narrow margin over German. In essence, the way to understand the American language is to consider it to be seventeenth century English but with overlays of German syntax and word construction. Hence all the combinations. This leads to a weakness for long unwieldy words and phrases which frankly mostly mean nothing. They make verbs out of anything, and anachronisms litter the language like so much verbiage."

He smiled at Luke. "Brevity appears to be an unknown. I find reading some American prose tortuous. God knows what official reports must be like. You have my deepest sympathy if you have to do that." He smiled again. "Beware of irony – it is rarely understood. And, of course, though the vast majority of the words are identical, if not the spelling, they do have in many cases subtly different meanings. Oh, and one final thing. When they don't know the correct word, they invent one, or some spurious acronym. They are very fond of acronyms. The use of a dictionary appears to be rare."

He laughed. "So, young Luke. Does that help? I fear it may not."

Luke smiled at him. "I'm not sure. Interesting though. I'll let you know."

The don paused before he left him, leaning on the table.

"Sarcasm is completely alien – they interpret it literally as the tearing of the flesh and, beware their pronunciation. Invariably, though not always, Americans tend to put the stress on the last syllable. We, of course, the first."

He demonstrated with the name Gerard, the American with a hard and elongated 'ard'.

He touched Luke on the shoulder as he walked away chuckling. "It's a whole new world."

***

John liked women. It he'd had to choose between an evening spent solely with women, or alternatively with men, he would pick women every time.

Though he wouldn't pretend to understand them, he felt entirely at ease in their company. And he treated them with respect; summers on the farm, Marjorie's careful nurturing and Elizabeth's waspish humour had taught him that. And while he liked them, they seemed to like him in return. It made for easy working relationships with all the women he came into contact with. And particularly now when there were so many more of them amongst the support staff.

But there were boundaries. A compliment was rarely amiss, even a mild flirt, but an overt sexual comment was not. And never ever touch, whatever the circumstances.

One of the younger WAAF secretarial staff, though fortunately not the one he usually favoured since she could not readily decipher his handwriting, was becoming rather over familiar. Though initially flattered by the attention, John was careful not to play up to it. It was a complication best avoided, and he knew from previous observations how easily emotional entanglements could spiral. While he could easily have a word with her supervisor, that seemed unnecessarily heavy-handed. Something more subtle was required.

Photographs mounted on desks of one's nearest and dearest were common around COSSAC, and he thought to join the custom with a photograph of Celia. Judging the ones he'd carried with him since Malta were not entirely suitable, he requested some more in his next letter to her while giving the reasons why.

Within a week he received her reply. It was an amused letter, commenting on her rival and, semi-seriously, threatening retribution. It also contained a selection of half a dozen photographs for him to choose from. One of her fellow pilots at Hamble had a camera and Celia had prevailed upon her.

He'd chosen three. The first showed her in her ATA uniform, the second in her flying gear beside a Spitfire and the third sitting in the cockpit prior to take off, but yet to put on her flying helmet. Long blonde hair over her shoulders, smiling, turned towards the camera.

Unable to choose one definitive from the three, John decided on a triptych. A couple of sorties along Piccadilly secured a suitable folding frame. It wasn't cheap – silver, highly polished, but the shop mounted the prints for no extra charge.

It looked rather splendid positioned on his desk and placed in an obvious position. He found himself looking at it quite often, rather as one did a new watch. And it drew rather more interest than he'd anticipated, practically every one of his visitors enquiring as to who Celia was.

Most importantly, it succeeded in its primary objective. Celia was formidable opposition in her own right. Being an ATA pilot sealed it.

73

According to Allegra, Luke was looking pasty.

"Fresh air and sunshine. Sunday, picnic. I know the perfect spot a couple of miles down the Cherwell. Borrow a bike. I'll bring the food, you find something to drink."

Luke didn't argue. He could do with a day off. Pasty was a bit harsh though. He took another glance in the mirror. A touch pale perhaps, but it was the morning.

The weather had stayed fine. Allegra, the front basket on her bicycle supplemented by a picnic hamper strapped behind the seat, arrived soon after nine. With the aid of the college scouts, Luke had located his old rusting steed, oiled it and blown up the tyres. More importantly, he'd secured a bottle of red wine, provenance uncertain, together with a couple of bottles of pale ale. He'd added some lemonade as an afterthought.

As they set off, Allegra leading, a large black cloud obscured the sun. There were more, stretched in a line to the horizon. Allegra refused to be disheartened and Luke, recognising her determination, demurred.

Their behaviour together had slowly evolved into a pattern. Luke's formative experience of being ordered around by his older sister since childhood made it familiar. Allegra had taken charge of all their social arrangements: what they did, where they went, when they did it. Luke rather enjoyed it. Allegra had a rather definite personality and he found it less fractious to let her get on with it. Though it was within bounds insofar as she would pretend to order and he would pretend to obey. And there was another advantage he recognised. He didn't have to give any thought to their time together. All would be arranged. He could think about something else.

Having pedalled down the bank of the river for about half an hour, Allegra declared their arrival. It was indeed a perfect spot, a tiny bay set into the bank overhung by willow trees on either side. Within minutes, with provisions placed in the shade, they were stretched out on rugs enjoying the morning sun. She'd been right – the black clouds had passed, replaced by high white cumulus, breaking up as the day warmed.

They talked for a while and then, while Allegra settled down to her book, Luke lay on his back staring at the sky, trying to clear his mind. To forget what he'd been doing the day before and trying not to remember what he had to do tomorrow. Eventually, he fell asleep.

Allegra woke him up soon after one o'clock.

"Fancy a swim before we eat?"

He stared at her. "I didn't think to bring anything with me."

"Neither did I. But I've got a towel."

She laughed at his expression as she began to strip off, tying her hair back into a ponytail. "Come on, there's no one around to see."

Nude bathing was not totally unknown in Oxford's rivers. There was a stretch of the river Cherwell known as the Dame's Delight, where female students traditionally bathed naked.

Luke liked looking at Allegra naked. A pleasure not diminished by frequency.

"I bet the water's bloody cold," he said, following her.

It was. They stayed in the shallows by the bank avoiding the current of the main stream. A naked walk back along the riverbank was best avoided, even in Oxford.

Luke finished drying his hair and glancing at Allegra found her staring at him rather quizzically, her nose wrinkled.

"Naked men are somehow – oh I don't know – untidy."

Luke glanced down at himself, scrotum and penis somewhat shrunken from the effects of the cold water.

"Maybe. But not quite so untidy as usual."

She laughed.

"That's true. Come here and let me warm you up."

Later, Luke lay on his back starring at the sky. He watched clouds, passing birds, butterflies, his mind drifting. A pair of buzzards circling, steering with their tails; three wing flaps then a glide, effortless insouciance. But something was missing. And then he realised. The swifts were gone.

Arriving in May, confirmation of the spring, then leaving in late August, a reminder that summer was on the wane. A pair of butterflies, chasing one another, passed across his face. The sound of bees close by. It was sad to see the swifts go, melancholic; but summer wasn't over just yet.

***

Since his initial appointment in the North African campaign, Eisenhower had proselytised the equality between the British and the Americans. Any order from a superior was to be obeyed irrespective of whether it emulated from a British or American source. Despite his efforts, the British disdain for the perceived lack of professionalism of the Americans continued while American Anglophobia persisted in some quarters. General Morgan shared Eisenhower's ecumenical zeal and had insisted on its application throughout COSSAC. Further, any demonstration of dissent would result in immediate dismissal without recourse to appeal. Whatever the exaltations, unity required perpetual vigilance.

Meanwhile, as an organisation, COSSAC continued to grow organically and, like any expanding entity, it had begun to outgrow its original clothes. Norfolk House could no longer contain the whole. 80 Pall Mall close by was the first building to absorb the overflow, followed rapidly by other suitable locations within hailing distance. COSSAC's portfolio of real estate in the west end of London was becoming considerable.

Likewise, the air staff had grown also, but not appreciably within Norfolk House. There were a variety of reasons, not least availability of living accommodation in the area. The greater majority of the RAF fighter work was retained in-house at Stanmore while the bomber work continued to be conducted at Bomber Command's Headquarters in High Wycombe. The US air effort was similarly rapidly gearing up.

Personally, as COSSAC grew, John's *rôle* within it continued to evolve, widening considerably. Directed to attend numerous meetings and discussions as the nominal RAF representative, he was beginning to become something akin to a full-time liaison officer.

Inter-service appreciation of each other's strengths and weaknesses was not high. Sometimes, the level of mutual ignorance was startling. Knowledge was low and preconception dominated thought. There was much to unlearn before cooperation became automatic and truly effective.

Though this was task enough between the British services, it was to nothing when it came to the American involvement and integration.

From his own observations, John had concluded that there were two distinct types of Americans. The first liked Britain and the British and admired what they had achieved against the Nazis. The second group loathed Britain and everything it stood for. They considered the population aloof and standoffish, poorly dressed and poorly fed; the British military staff incompetent, reluctant to fight and fossilised in thought. All Britain had done since 1939 was to conduct a holding action and wait until the great USA turned up to rescue them as they had done the last time.

The first group were easy to work with, refreshingly open, eager to learn and share, thoroughly committed to the cause. The second group, fortunately in the minority, were obstructive, reluctant, sanctimonious, rude and downright unpleasant.

At a recent meeting a couple of weeks before, John had been harangued over the failure of some RAF fighter sweep or other that had failed to intercept a Luftwaffe attack on a group of unescorted US Army Air Force bombers on a mission over France. John had heard something about it but had no particular knowledge. It was likely that the Americans had been late to the rendezvous since invariably they were. While he did his best to deflect the criticism while remaining scrupulously polite, his attacker was having none of it, getting more and more angry, accusing the RAF of dereliction of duty and, eventually, downright cowardice. The room had gone ominously quiet.

Before anyone could intervene, John had raised a hand and asked, very calmly, as to the man's combat experience over France, or indeed, anywhere else. The answer had been as John suspected, minimal, practically non-existent.

John had been prepared to leave it there, but immediately one of the more supportive of the Americans had addressed his own question back to him. Areas of operation, combat flying hours, victories confirmed, medals awarded. The question had not been subtle in the extreme and not something John would dream of answering under normal circumstances. As it was, he chose to answer factually but in a casual self-depreciating manner.

The room had again gone very quiet, a silence broken by the most senior US officer present ordering the man from the room never to be seen again. Though John was gracious in accepting the apologies, dismissing the incident as something of no importance, it was not something he forgot.

Underlying all of this hostility was the very political stance of anti-imperialism, where the British were seen as the arch enemy. That the Americans had imposed their will upon, for instance the Philippines, taking the islands from the Spanish as recently as 1899 was conveniently ignored. And there were other examples. Irony with Americans did not feature highly, if at all.

The story of the meeting, the attack and John's response to it, was circulated within COSSAC aided by suitable embellishments. John had heard accounts with amusement but had kept suitably silent. The incident had done his reputation no harm, even admiration from the American contingent. He was becoming trusted by them, an important asset. Mutual trust between the Americans and the British was perhaps the hardest thing to achieve.

As his attendance at the various meetings increased, John had taken to having informal conversations with the various attendees beforehand. Initially it had been purely for his own education but gradually he realised that such informal briefings were rare. It gave him a broad and, specifically, non-partisan view which in itself was unusual.

For all the formal meetings there was a pool of official transcribers supplied by the central secretariat, who produced minutes recording what was said and by whom, akin to the Hansard Record for Parliament. Reams of paper sometimes perhaps most useful for historical reasons than practical working documents.

Again, beginning for his own purposes, John had begun to produce concise notes. An outline of the topics discussed, the problems identified, and the actions agreed to resolve them. Rarely more than two pages, his notes also doubled up as a briefing document.

John had also recalled the advice he'd been given by an army officer who had been a senior civil servant before the war. The trick with committees was never to have a vote but come to decisions by mutual agreement. And it helped to have written up a draft on the notes of the preferred solutions beforehand. It focussed the discussions and saved much time.

The more meetings he attended, and the more notes he produced, the wider the circulation became. It wasn't the *rôle* he'd originally envisaged for himself at COSSAC and, in a service context, it was pretty irregular. But, with the active encouragement and support from the upper echelons of the staff, he was directed to do more.

From a personal standpoint, John was only too willing. It gave him entry to a wide field of activity that would otherwise be denied.

One afternoon, over tea with Group Captain Baker to whom he still reported directly, John brought up the subject of this seemingly evolving *rôle*. Baker had been remarkably sanguine.

"Evolution, my dear boy. Evolution. We're all still feeling our way to a certain extent. I shouldn't worry about it. The work you are doing is valuable and I've received considerable comments, all favourable. So just carry on with it as you are."

Reassured, John thanked him, finished his tea and was about to leave when Baker called him back.

"Word has it that the Supreme Commander, whenever he is appointed, will be an American, while each of the air force, navy and army commanders will be British. Considering the American contribution, it makes perfect sense when one thinks about it. There is also, of course, the political dimension."

John nodded. There had become a certain inevitability – it was the consensus view.

Baker continued. "That being the case, I think it's odds on that Leigh-Mallory will get the air force appointment."

Baker looked at him questioningly. "Not someone you have the greatest amount of time for, as I understand."

John gave a rueful smile, and laughed.

"True. I'm not particularly enamoured. Too much service politics," he added, remembering the spats between Leigh-Mallory and Keith Park only too well.

"I'm happy to serve under him though," he continued. "Though I wouldn't expect any advancement from doing so. I suspect I've had my card marked as Keith Park's man for some time."

Though Baker agreed, he didn't immediately comment. John's file contained a letter from Park which was extremely complimentary, which rather proved the point.

"Be that as it may, I doubt Leigh-Mallory's appointment will have much bearing on you. As I said, just continue in the *rôles* you've been assigned until further notice. I can't see them changing in the near future, or indeed, if at all."

Dismissed by Baker, John walked down to the map room and stared at the latest additions to the walls and the partitions that had started to appear to give more hanging space.

On reflection, he was happy with what he was doing and gratified it was making a valued contribution. Though one thing was very clear. Should Baker be right about Leigh-Mallory, he was extremely unlikely to receive a flying appointment ever again.

He would think about that. In the meantime, he would have to make his own private arrangements to keep his hand in.

*

Eisenhower had broadcast the news on the BBC on the night of 8 September: Italy had surrendered. The belief, common in some quarters, that given an Italian capitulation the Germans would withdraw to the Alps in the north, proved to be false. Forewarned, the Germans immediately occupied the whole country in force and with all the same brutality they had shown to the other countries they had overrun. More so in some cases since Italy, once an ally, had changed sides and the Germans felt betrayed. Nevertheless, as someone at COSSAC commented: one down, two to go.

Napoleon's comment on Italy was that the country was like a boot and best entered from the top. The Allies, unfortunately, were entering through the foot. With the great majority of the available resource directed towards Overlord, what remained for the Italian theatre was to be never more than marginally adequate. John foresaw the conquest of Italy a just one long hard slog.

Malta was again on the newsreels. The remains of the Italian fleet, led by the Royal Navy, had sailed into Grand Harbour in Valletta to formally surrender.

Unsurprisingly, the ramparts had been packed to witness the event and the film had lingered over cheering crowds accompanied by a suitably rousing commentary. Meanwhile, Park had received a much-earned knighthood the previous July.

John watched the reports with mixed emotions remembering his months on the island. He wondered as to the supplies and the rations now available. With the war now effectively over for Malta, life, he assumed, would be getting back to normal. He thought of all those little cafés and restaurants, evenings spent overlooking the blue of the Mediterranean, watching sunsets. The heat. John did miss the heat.

John got a call from Baker requesting he pop into his office when he had a moment. The call was conversational enough, but something in his tone prompted John to go immediately.

"Ah, Buchan." The group captain waved a hand. "Take a seat."

"You wanted to see me, sir."

Baker eyed him over the top of his reading glasses.

"I hear you've been angling to get in some flight time."

John nodded. "I have made a few enquires, yes, though I haven't arranged anything. I wouldn't, of course, without your clearance," he added, perhaps a little too hastily.

"I should hope not." The tone did not convince. "Why do you want to fly? I would have thought you'd had enough by now?"

John asked for permission to smoke, received it and lit a cigarette.

"It's not that I want to fly operationally again, at least not immediately. It's more to keep my hand in. I've not flown the Mark IX Spitfire yet and from what I've heard, I'm missing something. It would be nice to get reacquainted."

Baker gave him another look, though not unsympathetic. He'd like to fly again himself sometime, even though it was unrealistic. He thought a little before replying.

"Well. I suppose it would be useful in some ways." He paused, staring at some point on the far wall. "There are provisos. We'll call these air experience flights for the moment. You are not to get involved in any operation of any sort whatsoever, and you are to limit yourself to overland. No little forays out over the Channel. Is that understood?"

"Perfectly, sir."

"Good. We cannot risk you being captured by the Germans at any cost. You know too much about Overlord."

The Group Captain suddenly gave a broad smile.

"In the event of you being captured I would expect you to shoot yourself forthwith. The best way I understand is to put the muzzle of the pistol in one's mouth. The old pressed-to-the-temple technique is not always reliable."

"Thank you, sir. I'll bear that in mind," replied John, a little startled.

"You do that," commented Baker and dismissed him.

He watched as John closed the door behind him and allowed himself a smile. Bloody fighter pilots. He scribbled himself a quick note and then called in his secretary.

74

Matthew and Kirsty had decided to marry. With Matthew recovered sufficiently to become a full-time demolition and explosives instructor, and with no likelihood of any immediate further overseas service, Matthew and Kirsty had bowed to an increasing undercurrent of family pressure. The ceremony was to be in a little church in Largs to the west of Glasgow followed by a small reception at Kelburn Castle nearby. John, nominated as best man, would attend with Celia, while Luke and Allegra would also travel up. Mark and Bridget though were unable to make it due to service commitments. With the date only a few days away, Celia had begun to consider her options.

Whilst obtaining a 48-hour pass to attend a wedding was relatively easy to obtain, getting to Scotland and back by train in such a time in wartime was problematic. It was not such a problem for John who could, no doubt, wangle seventy-two hours or more if needed. But there was an obvious solution for Celia: she could fly.

White Waltham on Salisbury Plain was the control hub of the ATA, organising the daily flight patterns and movements to over eight hundred UK airfields. Hamble, being one of the larger pools, had a direct line and being close by had a regular interchange of support staff. Celia had some good contacts there at the moment so it might just be possible.

It took some doing but, by a mixture of cajoling, charm and promises, Celia managed to organise an Anson for a ferry flight up to Glasgow for the day before the wedding, and a 48-hour leave beginning immediately on arrival, giving her the whole of the second day to get back by train.

The Avro Anson was something of the unsung hero of RAF aircraft. A small twin-engine multipurpose aeroplane developed a few years before the war, thousands of them now served in a host of support *rôles* around the country and abroad. They were stable little aircraft, rugged and reliable and the ATA used them extensively for communication flights and collecting pilots after their ferrying duties. If an aircraft could ever be a pet, then the Anson, known universally as Annie, was such an aeroplane. The version they used was the dual-control training model, stripped of all armaments with extra seats fitted in the fuselage. Though it cruised at a sedate 149 knots, it was relatively long legged with a range of around eight hundred miles.

Stretching out her flight map, Celia drew a straight line from Hamble to the airfield west of Glasgow, a distance of around four hundred miles. Taking account of exclusion zones, she plotted her waypoints adding another hundred and then a further reserve. Oxford was only a minor deviation to the right and that gave her another idea. The trick would be not to get found out. Later that evening she rang John.

A few minutes into their conversation she asked him a casual question.

"About the wedding – how are you proposing to get up to Scotland?"

John had toyed with driving, but it was impractical.

"Train, I suppose."

"I've had a much better idea. We fly up the day before."

She outlined her plan to him, laughing at his shock.

"Have you any idea what Luke and Allegra are doing?"

John said he didn't.

"Well, find out. There's no reason why I can't take them as well as you if they can get to the airfield. One thing though, and this is important. Everyone should be in uniform to make it look official, less suspicious. Do you know if Allegra is a member of anything?"

John had no idea.

"Doesn't matter what it is. Just something service looking. A greatcoat would do."

After he'd put the phone down, John poured himself a drink. It was a brilliant idea if they could pull it off, but there might be the most almighty bollocking if they got caught. Though Celia sounded confident enough and it wasn't as if other similar stunts hadn't been pulled before. The flight would be official, even if the passengers were not.

Then he thought about being flown by Celia. It would be an interesting experience to say the least. Should he sit beside her? Should he worry? Who knew?

He emptied his glass, poured another, and then put through a call to Luke.

After a cursory breakfast, Celia, with overnight bag in one hand and a smaller one stacked with Thermos flasks of tea in the other, made her way over to the waiting Anson. With her bags stowed in the rear, she walked around the aircraft making a visual inspection with the flight sergeant and signed the acceptance form. Coverall and helmet on, maps in hand, she climbed aboard and took the left-hand seat, buckled up her harness and started the engines one at a time.

It was a good day for flying. The weather was clear with only patchy high cloud and a light westerly wind. No rain was forecast en route. With the engines fully warmed up she taxied into wind and took off. She flew a climbing circuit of the airfield and checked the compass. Levelling out at three thousand feet she trimmed out the aircraft and began to think about the rest of the journey. It wouldn't be long before she reached Oxford. The adventure had begun.

John had taken the first train, had breakfast with Luke and Allegra and then they'd taken a taxi to the airfield. Luke was in his full RNVR uniform and a greatcoat as was John in his best RAFVR regalia. Allegra, wearing dark civilian clothes, was encompassed in a Wren overcoat borrowed from one of her student assistants. Each had an overnight bag while Luke also had a paper carrier bag full of sandwiches supplied by the college refectory.

It was a fairly small airfield much used for transit flights. While Luke and Allegra made themselves inconspicuous in a corner of the reception hut, John went to the control area to get an estimated time for Celia's arrival. Pulling rank and stressing the urgency of his journey without saying why, he ensured their collection would be made with the minimum of fuss.

It went like clockwork. Celia landed on time and taxied over to the reception area, then swung the Anson back towards the runway. With the engines still idling, they walked briskly to the aircraft, swung in the bags and climbed in. Celia shouted a greeting, waited until they were seated and strapped, then opened the throttles and taxied to the end of the runway. Clearance came immediately and after a final check Celia advanced the throttles to the stops and took off. John hadn't flown in an Anson for years and he'd forgotten how long the take-off run was compared to a Spitfire.

He waited until Celia had levelled off before releasing his straps and walking forward the few steps to the cockpit. Kissing Celia on the top of the head, he dropped into the co-pilot's seat to her right.

Dressed in a white coverall over her uniform, leather helmet clamped over her hair, she looked rather fetching.

"Good morning, darling," she said, grinning broadly. "So far, so good."

John settled back to watch Celia fly. Her touch was very light, almost imperceptible as she flew straight and level keeping a steady course. Totally without drama. She did this practically every day, he reminded himself. Indeed, she had far more hours on Spitfires alone than he had himself.

After about twenty minutes Celia glanced across at him.

"Would you like to drive for a bit? I'd love a cup of tea, and a sandwich wouldn't go amiss. Breakfast was a bit short this morning."

John had never flown a twin-engine aircraft before and said so.

"About time you did then."

John took hold of the control column and rested his feet on the rudder pedals while giving the gauges ahead of him a closer scrutiny and noting their readings.

"Ready?"

"Yes."

"You have control."

After a couple of minutes, Celia unbuckled herself and eased out of the seat.

"Just keep her straight and level and stay on that heading. How does it feel?"

"Fine."

It was a lie. Though attempting an air of insouciance, he felt anything but. The Anson was alien to everything he was used to. Slow, leaden responses, sluggish, a trundler. He told himself to get used to it. Just steer.

Standing behind him, judging his progress, Celia patted him on the head as one might a child, or a dog.

"There's a good boy."

"Bugger off."

"If anything happens, call me immediately."

"Oh, believe me, I will."

Although Celia had met Luke a number of times, this was the first time she'd met Allegra. Over a cheese and lettuce sandwich and tea, they sat and chatted.

Allegra had only flown twice before and Luke's experience wasn't that much greater. Indeed, the last time he'd flown had been with John in a Tiger

Moth shortly before the war. Both were excited by the flight which pleased Celia to no end.

John, concentrating on his flying with more attention than usual, could hear their laughter behind him. He looked at Celia's map and glanced at the ground beneath them. He didn't recognise anything, but neither did he expect to. Looking at her flight plan and comparing the instrument panel with his watch, he guessed they were coming up to a waypoint. He called back over his shoulder.

"Co-pilot to captain. Assistance required."

Celia dropped into the seat beside him and retook control, laughing at his relieved expression.

"At least I didn't break anything. I hope," he added.

Luke and Allegra were meantime having a splendid time in the back, staring out of the windows, getting excited as they spotted various landmarks, helped by Celia calling back to tell them what to look out for and where they were. They were like a couple of school children on a day out.

For Celia and John flying was a commonplace experience – the simple magic had long since worn off. Not so with Luke and Allegra. It was a reminder of something lost.

Their landing at Glasgow soon after two o'clock was completely without incident. Celia floated down to a faultless landing and taxied towards dispersal. There was quite a lot of other traffic and attention was directed to the other side of the airfield where something far more interesting was going on. It was easy for John and the others to slip off the aircraft on the blind side to the buildings before Celia swung around and switched off.

While she went to formally hand over the Anson, John looked around for their transport. It wasn't hard to find. Matthew had sent down a staff car, a huge pre-war American Packard, and soon they were away, heading west to Kelburn Castle.

From Matthew's letters Luke and John were aware of 3 Commandos connection to Kelburn Castle, and Lord Glasgow as well as his personal relationship with the family and his subsequent involvement with Kirsty. While Celia had met members of the nobility since she was a child, the others were not so practised.

"They're just like anybody else," she commented. "Good, bad and indifferent. Though their houses tend to be rather grander."

As the Packard turned into the long drive leading up to the castle Allegra chuckled.

"When I think of castles, and it's not that often frankly, I always imagine ruins. I think this one still has a roof."

Matthew bounded down the steps to meet them, and Lord and Lady Glasgow appeared soon after. Matthew immediately commandeered Celia and Allegra's bags and carried them inside. John, climbing the steps behind him, wondered about the state of his arm. While the left seemed less relaxed than the right, the effect was slight. Tea was served immediately as questions were asked as to their journey and answers given.

Celia was still wearing her flying coverall and excusing herself soon slipped out of the room for a few minutes. Reappearing in her uniform, hair brushed and fresh lipstick applied, she was joined by Lord Glasgow.

"Very enterprising of you to fly up."

Celia explained the reason and her 48-hour pass restriction.

"You're one of those ATA Spitfire girls. I've seen you on the newsreels and in the papers of course."

Celia laughed dismissively. "I wouldn't take too much notice of that. They make most of it up. You know what the press is like. We're just simple delivery drivers really."

They continued to chat easily, Celia asking about the castle and the family and the forthcoming wedding. Correctly suspecting that Lord Glasgow was intrigued about their journey, particularly how she'd managed to carry the others, she was careful to deflect any further questions. The knack was not to allow the conversation to flag and, of course, Lord Glasgow was too polite to enquire directly. After a suitable interval, Matthew was deputised to show them up to their rooms.

After they'd gone, Lord Glasgow turned to his wife and smiled.

"I wonder quite how many rules and service regulations they broke by flying up here?" He laughed knowingly. "We'll have to keep an eye on them while they are here."

In keeping with tradition Matthew and Kirsty were to be kept apart until the ceremony. For reasons of convenience, she was spending the night with her parents in a hotel in Largs. Meanwhile, Lord and Lady Glasgow were to host a dinner for the groom and his guests. It was a lively meal, conversation flowing freely with particular interest being shown in Allegra's research work and the exciting future being predicted for plastic polymers. The state of the war and recent developments were, for once, almost an irrelevance.

After dinner they retired to a very large withdrawing room for coffee, breaking into separate groups. The girls in one, the boys in another while the Glasgows entertained Matthew's parents.

Eventually, John enquired of Matthew the obvious question as to why they were getting married.

Matthew laughed. "I was wondering when you'd get around to that." He laughed again. "Well, it's not the obvious reason. I can confirm that Kirsty is not pregnant. It's more prosaic than that. Kirsty finished agricultural college in the summer, I'm now stationed permanently at Lochailort, so we've rather run out of excuses not to. And, of course, there was a certain amount of encouragement from Kirsty' parents. Not that they're prudes or anything, but the Scots do rather prefer their arrangements, shall we say, formalised."

"Where are you going to live?" asked Luke.

Matthew smiled. "Good question. For the moment Kirsty will stay on the farm – it's about thirty miles south of here, and we'll meet up at the weekends or whenever we can. It's not ideal obviously, but it will do. We're lucky compared to most other couples."

Matthew paused for a second. "And Kirsty comes up here to the castle due to the family connection, so I expect we'll meet here from time to time. They're very gracious, the Glasgows – offering to hold the wedding here is typical of them." He laughed. "Lady Glasgow has made all the arrangements. She enjoys weddings. All we have to do is turn up. You'll like Kirsty's parents too. They're not dissimilar to Marjorie and Richard. It's a good solid farming family."

Proprieties were to be observed. Luke was sharing a room with John, while Celia was sharing with Allegra. The rooms were a fair distance apart but at least they were on the same floor. By prior arrangement, around 2am Celia and Luke passed each other on the corridor, both trying to suppress conspiratorial giggles while feeling like naughty children.

Celia slid into bed alongside John.

"Hello," he said, and kissed her.

"This is a first."

"What is?"

"A night in a castle. Do you think it's haunted?"

*

Though it was traditionally expected, Kirsty did indeed look lovely. A close-fitting white satin dress with a short swirling train. She'd chosen to wear her hair loose and the deep red of it made a startling contrast draped over one shoulder. With Matthew, newly promoted to full lieutenant, in his full dress uniform they made a handsome couple.

Luke was surprised at quite how quick the actual service was; somehow, he'd expected it to be longer, though none the worse for that. It was all rather reassuring in its way with the mothers crying in all the expected places. Even the ever-present midges seemed less irritating than normal.

John discharged his none-too-arduous duties as best man without embarrassment. He delivered the ring when required without losing it and kept his speech at the wedding breakfast mercifully short. He read a string of telegrams from people he'd never previously heard of, a rather witty offering from Mark and Bridget and another from Elizabeth feigning mock disappointment. Marjorie and Richard had sent their heartfelt congratulations with an open invitation to visit.

Weddings are exhausting events and by the time Kirsty and Matthew's car arrived to take them to the station and their eventual destination, a hotel by Lock Lomond, the assembly was suitably sated. With Mr and Mrs Peterson seen on their way the party broke up rapidly as people drifted off to change and take the opportunity for a rest.

It was a bleary-eyed group who greeted each other the following morning. Lord Glasgow, watching them over the breakfast table, had no illusions as to the nocturnal activities of his younger guests while under his roof. Apart from remarking that he fancied he'd heard the ghost abroad in the early hours, he made no further reference, though there was a faint twinkle in his eye. Soon a car arrived to take them to the station and final farewells were made with invitations to return to the castle, should they be able, generously offered.

It was a long, tiresome journey and it was the evening before they reached Swindon. Here they were to split up. Celia to Southampton, John to Paddington and Luke with Allegra to Oxford. As someone remarked, it was back to the war.

It had been a hectic three days though somewhat to his surprise, John found himself behind his desk before eight on the Monday morning. There was a lot of work to catch up with and a new set of intelligence reports compiled over the weekend.

By lunchtime he could hardly keep his eyes open. He cleared a space and laid his head on the desk. Immediately he was transported back to infants' school. Their rest breaks, lying on their desks, listening to the sounds coming through the wood, deep and mysterious. He'd loved doing that.

Sound travels faster through denser mediums, wood rather that air, causing the frequency of sounds to drop. But the explanation didn't lessen the experience. Within minutes he was asleep, not waking up until his telephone rang sometime later.

75

With the need to relieve the Russians in the east still paramount, in early July COSSAC were tasked to devise a series of ruses, deceptions and exercises to keep the Germans interested and suspicious of forthcoming operations in the west. Further to that, plans were to be formulated to suit sudden and changing circumstances in western Europe should they ever transpire.

Under the overall code name of Cockade there were to be three component operations. Starkey, the most significant of them, was to convince the Germans that a large-scale landing in the Pas-de-Calais area was imminent. This, it was argued, would compel the Luftwaffe to engage in full-scale attritional air battles in circumstances pre-arranged to be advantageous to the Allies. Fighter forces, RAF and American, were to be pre-positioned and concentrated in the southeast of England to give a numerical advantage in excess of four to one. While the Luftwaffe might hastily reinforce their numbers, this force ratio might temporarily reduce to two-to-one in which case further reserves would be drafted in to allow for intensive fighting over a limited period.

While naval forces gathered for the feint assault and all the necessary support logistics moved into the south-east, intensive bombing operations in the Pas-de-Calais area would commence for a period of fourteen days prior to the supposed landings.

In the meantime, the second element of Cockade, Operation Wadham, was an American-led operation targeted at the Brest peninsular and timed later than Starkey to give the impression its execution was dependent on the success of Starkey. Forces for this activity were centred on Plymouth.

The final element, Operation Tindall, was a major deceptive threat to Stavanger in Norway and was designed to convince the Germans of the continuing Allied threat to Norway and thereby ensure they kept the large German Army garrison in the country undiluted. Suitable force projections centred on Rosyth were to be simulated.

Cockade was a complete interlocking plan and was played out from late July to early November.

In the event, the initial high hopes of COSSAC were not to be realised. Tindall suffered a severe shortage of resources and effectively petered out. Wadham, likewise, suffered delays, a dearth of aircraft, and much disruption due to bad weather which put an end to reconnaissance flights and bombing missions. Unsustained, it too fell away.

Starkey fell victim to the same malaise as the other two. Shortage of landing craft to simulate a full-scale assault was only resolved by the extensive use of dummies. A shortage of fighter resource, both from the RAF and the US Eighth Air Force, further complicated by a restriction on the number of bombing sorties on the Pas-de-Calais area prior to the feint assault. The Allies simply lacked the resources in the UK to embark upon such operations. Simulated radio traffic between fictitious army divisions could only achieve so much – by themselves they were not enough. For COSSAC it was a painful realisation.

Notwithstanding, Starkey went ahead on 9 September. Preceded by large-scale troop movements towards assembly and loading points, though the vast majority did not embark, the lead elements of an invasion force sailed from Kent and Hampshire accompanied by a full naval protection flotilla whilst an air umbrella operated above them.

Ten miles from Boulogne the convoys halted as planned. And then, nothing. The Germans refused to come out to play.

The shore batteries did not open fire, the Luftwaffe failed to put in an appearance and neither did any German naval craft. The convoys were simply ignored. With nothing left to do, the ships turned around and sailed back to port. Aircraft returned to their bases without a single engagement. In the afternoon the BBC put out an announcement that a full-scale amphibious exercise had recently taken place in the English Channel. It had been completed most successfully and valuable lessons had been learned by the services and civil authorities concerned. It was a poor return for all the effort employed.

Why had the Germans not reacted as expected? With Italy signing an armistice only a few days before, the Germans had concluded, quite rightly, that the Allies would concentrate their efforts in the Italian theatre for the foreseeable future. What alarms were raised by Starkey were immediately rescinded when the convoys stopped ten miles short. The bluff had failed. As someone commented, not so much Cockade as cock up. Whilst this was harsh, the general mood at COSSAC was certainly deflated and, particularly after the optimism of the summer, glum.

Morgan was quick to issue a note to all staff. Acknowledging that Starkey had not achieved all that was expected of it, he emphasised the credit side. Valuable experience had been gained by everyone on our side of the water, however remotely connected with the operation. And the battle, such as it was, had suffered zero casualties. Everyone involved had had a foretaste of what was to come later on. There was much more work to do. It was a case of onwards and forwards.

***

Luke had a general arrangement drawing of a fusing device spread out on his drawing board. GA design drawings showed all the various components of any mechanism assembled together and were accompanied by brief notes highlighting the major components. Reading drawings was an art, improving with practice.

It was a complicated device – to Luke's mind, too complicated, over-elaborate, and he was having difficulty differentiating where one component ended and another began; not conducive to understanding of how the thing was supposed to work. A twenty-minute scrutiny had left him none the wiser.

Making himself more tea, he lit a cigarette and reached for a box of coloured pencils. Purists might disapprove and it was a time-consuming occupation, but by colouring in each individual component, the colours chosen to sharply contrast with each adjacent one, the drawing became so much easier to read. It was the adult version of a child's colouring book.

Half an hour's effort yielded a full understanding, and a confirmation of Luke's suspicion of over-complication. There were better ways of doing this, simpler, less elaborate.

He spent the next two hours simplifying, redesigning the mechanism and halving the number of components.

***

Marjorie was struggling. She was, as the phrase had it, 'on the change'. Hot flushes, headaches, irritability. And she was tired – a constant fatigue worn like a second skin, draining, burdening.

Standing over the kitchen sink she began the morning's washing up, swirling the soap-saver around in the water trying to get a lather. The soap-saver broke, the clip on the little wire cage breaking, falling off, scattering all the little pieces of soap into the water. She scooped them up, squashing them back into the cage.

Washing up, elbows deep in soap suds, the draining board and the racks above slowly filling up; monotonous and, in this house, never ending. And then she dropped a cup.

In disbelief she stared at the shattered china on the floor at her feet. That had been one of the last remaining cups with a handle still on it. The last cup of the crockery set given to her on her wedding by her mother.

Leaning on the edge of the sink with her hands, she began to weep. Deep gulping sobs shaking her body.

***

It was nearing dusk before Professor Henderson and Luke had finished their discussion. Henderson had seemed grumpier than usual, irritated and preoccupied. Luke remarked as such as he gathered up his papers preparing to leave.

"What are you doing now? Next, I mean. This evening?"

Luke looked at him in surprise.

"Oh, I don't know. Going back to my rooms, getting something to eat, go for a drink. I hadn't thought."

"Fancy a walk along the Cherwell? I might even be persuaded to stand you a drink."

Luke gave him an enquiring look, but got no response. "Sure. Love to."

They walked in silence. It was some weeks since Luke had been down here. He noticed the difference from the summer. Nature was turning dark, shutting down.

Suddenly, from nowhere, a huge flock of starlings appeared above the trees on the other side of the river. Thousands upon thousands of them moving as one, complex patterns wheeling against the sky.

Luke stopped to watch, as did Henderson.

"Extraordinary. I've never seen that many together before."

They watched the changing patterns for several minutes, Luke delighting in the display, fascinated.

"Murmuration," said Henderson slowly. "A sign of winter forthcoming." He paused. "And a long and bleak one, I fear."

Luke had first heard it soon after Alamein the previous November, the victory that Churchill had subsequently called the end of the beginning and, so far,

God willing, so it seemed. Now, almost twelve months later, the phrase first heard then had become common usage: 'after the war'. Used as either a place or a time.

To Luke, who was more concerned with winning the war than its aftermath, the phrase seemed singularly premature. The latest estimates he'd seen suggested an end to the war with Germany by 1946 and that with Japan sometime in 1947.

He looked out of the window of the train as they clattered over some points. The rain, the wind behind it now, streamed down the glass. He'd been in two meetings that day in London and at both the phrase 'after the war' had been used. The context hadn't been particularly specific, but the usage had.

Already various individuals had started to position themselves. Avarice to the fore. Not for the first time Luke concluded that war doesn't change people but it exaggerates their traits, character weaknesses and character strengths; the extremities displayed, exposed without camouflage. The private became public.

It was not an edifying sight, unseemly, and it depressed him.

76

The night was oppressive, close, and Mark went up on deck to get some air before returning to his charts. The sky, dark, almost moonless, seemed to close around them. A tiny boat surrounded by the enormity of the sea.

He listened to the water as waves broke against the hull. They were travelling at fourteen knots, a good cruising speed but not great enough to leave a lasting wake. Occasionally, the sound changed, suddenly becoming softer before picking up again. This puzzled him and he looked more closely at the surface of the sea.

It took a little while before he realised what it was. Oil slicks – there were islands of them all around. There'd been an action around here not so long before. The oil drifting to the surface from the bowels of the sunken ships.

Eventually, the action of the waves and the wind would break up the slicks to then deposit the remains on the shoreline. Here the oil would stick on sand and rock leaving heavy black blobs of evil smelling tar. A sticky foul pollutant, destined to last for years.

Soon they were stationary. Mark was now an evader, not a hunter. There was an irony here, almost bitter to the taste, and it did not escape him. Standing orders were to avoid contact with the enemy at all costs. Clandestine operations, by their very nature, demanded it. There was no case to argue otherwise. But while Mark accepted it, it was the exact reverse of everything he had learned. When he had been at Dartmouth the year before with the Sixth Flotilla, they did nothing else but seek out the enemy. Two years he'd spent looking for the Germans, engaging at every available opportunity. Now, it was the complete opposite. Find and engage replaced by if found, avoid.

Though he knew the imposed restraint served a greater good, it rankled nonetheless. Opportunities forsaken that months before would have been eagerly seized.

They had lay stopped, drifting ever closer to the headland, for over twenty minutes. Nothing beyond the sound of the waves slapping against the hull and the muffled roar of the surf. Constant scanning with the night-glasses showed an unbroken horizon. Of the three E-boats there was no sign. It would have been a perfect situation for an attack. Coming in from their landward side they could have swept past all three guns blazing before they'd had time to react.

The engines were started and, at low speed, silently running they started on the voyage back. The passengers showed obvious signs of relief. So too did some of the crew.

Mark plotted the course. Barring any unexpected diversions, they would be back at Dartmouth soon after dawn.

***

As the COSSAC staff numbers continued to increase, the opportunity was being taken to replace certain personnel who were viewed as less than desirable. Baker had compared it to the weeding of flower bed. Some American officers, and indeed a few British also, had regarded their first enemy as their partner in arms rather than concentrate their efforts on defeating the real enemy, Germany.

As had been so ably demonstrated by the Allied experience in North Africa and Sicily, anything less than a total United Nation's approach was disruptive to the conception of unity and cooperation. Arguments based on purely national lines were neither tolerated nor accepted. It was to be together, or not at all.

Returning to Kensington, John sat on the top deck of the bus watching the rain lashing at the windows. The bus, crowded, lurched every time the driver changed gear. Every hopeful acceleration followed by an immediate deceleration, occasional sudden braking, the road pitted and broken, patched repairs from the numerous air raids. Smooth the journey was not. Wet clothes and warm bodies, the air moist, heavy with tobacco smoke. A fug almost as thick as the recent fog. Depressing in the darkness, an accompaniment to his mood.

John had been pondering on how much of his effort was just simply wasted. Circumstances and plans changed or discarded, new facts negating previous fond held assumptions. Whole new developments making earlier work redundant.

And not just for himself. His thoughts broadened to all of his companions at COSSAC, then to the whole of the services, and then finally to the whole of the population at large. So much effort wasted. It was a depressing thought, the dimensions of which he'd not had before.

In his previous life, John had been used to planning operations overnight and executing them the following day. Simple cause and effect. You succeeded and lived, or you failed and died. An instant judgement. The operational planning at COSSAC was the complete opposite. Grinding toil day after day with no discernible result.

On good days it felt like two steps forward and one step back; on bad days, distinctly the opposite. And today had been a bad day. That this was the nature of operational planning was of little comfort. There had to be a moving forward, something tangible to cling to.

Speaking to those who had more experience of these things, senior officers including Baker, suggested progress, on the whole, was very good and compared favourably with previous examples. John took some encouragement from that, though not enough for his own peace of mind.

Perhaps he was just tired. Perhaps it was the weather, the season; November, nights closing rapidly, a long dark winter to come. More discomfort from his leg.

Weary of war, weary of life: just plain weary. What he needed was some leave, somewhere to rest his mind.

And he'd started to dream again. Waking terrified, wet with sweat, some shrouded memory of combat, the aircraft burning, watching himself die. Not always the same dream, but always the same result.

A few days leave, frivoling, something frivolous and inconsequential. John wasn't sure if frivoling was a real word. Well, it was now.

***

Luke had received a package from MI5's counter sabotage unit. They were a tiny organisation, only three people plus a draughtsman, led by Victor Rothschild from the banking family. The Rothschild's had a long association with the British military – their banking dynasty had begun by financing Wellington's campaigns against Napoleon. The counter sabotage unit had been formed on Rothschild's own initiative and was funded from his own resources.

Over the past few months they had produced a manual of German booby-trap devices, written descriptions accompanied with a series of beautifully produced general arrangement drawings, sub-assemblies and exploded views. As the accompanying letter explained, the manual's intent was as an aid to those tasked with defusing them.

There was an incendiary device disguised as a Thermos flask, an explosive army mess tin and another concealed in a can of motor oil. There were also a variety of timing devices. Most lacked the ingenuity, subtlety and indeed wit of those produced at the Toyshop in Whitchurch for British special operations, but there were some similarities. A test tube filled with dried peas which expanded as they absorbed water to push a pair of electrical contacts together to complete a firing circuit reminded Luke of the Toyshop's dissolving aniseed balls and Alka-Seltzer tablets.

There was no distribution list included with the letter so Luke was unsure whether one had been sent to Whitchurch. He was overdue a visit and he made a note to take the manual with him on his next opportunity.

***

To an English eye, American production figures for munitions were truly astonishing. It had taken time to organise and tool up, but once begun it became unstoppable. John saw the weekly reports on deliveries to the UK from across the Atlantic. While these figures were impressive enough, the numbers predicted for 1944 were enormous.

By January the figures suggested that the combined might of American industry would produce a tank every five minutes, an aircraft every thirty minutes, and an aircraft carrier every week.

By mid-1945 it was forecast that the Americans would have manufactured over three hundred thousand aeroplanes. That was more than all the other belligerent nations combined. It would be a staggering achievement.

Paradoxically, it was not the dictatorships that conducted total war with complete ruthlessness and efficiency, but the great democracies. As Britain had done under Churchill in 1940, so had America under Roosevelt from 1942. Swinging powers had been introduced at tremendous speed to ensure a complete transformation of American capitalism to a war economy.

Maximum salaries were restricted to $25,000 after tax negating war profiteering at a stroke. Fixed farm and commodity prices, wages and rents controlled; rationing, credit, the function of the labour market and a host of civil liberties all suspended for the duration. Any form of industrial production that was not directly or indirectly in support of the war effort was forbidden. Penalties for transgression were draconian.

Considering the USA was previously the bastion of free-market capitalism, the transformation was all the more remarkable. Such had been the shock of Pearl Harbor; all had been achieved with practically no internal opposition.

True, the Russian economy was likewise militarised, achieving truly astonishing production levels, but Russia was neither a free-market economy nor a democracy. What Britain and particularly the United States had achieved, in so rapid a time, would be viewed by future historians in wonder.

That said, as John knew only too painfully from the appraisals and assessments he'd read, the weapons available to the Allied armies were in general inferior to those of the Germans.

While the aircraft and the ships were now mostly superior to the German, not so the weapons on the ground. There was no equivalent to the ubiquitous German 88mm gun and the Allied tanks, typified by the Sherman M4, were under gunned and under armoured, and as such no match for the Tigers and Panthers of the Germans.

Come the battle in Normandy, it would be the Allied quantities not quality, covered by total air supremacy, that would determine the outcome.

***

Celia had been back at the all-women's ATA pool at Hamble for the past few weeks. Seen as the prime posting and not far from Southampton, their task was to ferry factory fresh Spitfires from Supermarine's airfield at Eastleigh to wherever they were required. These were either the MTU units for the aircraft to be fitted out with radios and guns, or occasionally, if the need was great, direct to the operational bases.

It was work she really enjoyed – who wouldn't? Sometimes she flew as many as four individual Spitfires in a day. Never an aeroplane to tire of, even though the working routine was rigorous; thirteen days on, followed by a couple of days off.

But there was always the English weather to contend with. The official regulations limited them to an altitude limit of two thousand feet, the ground to be always easily visible. As such it made their operations particularly susceptible to cloud cover and ceiling heights. While a few of them, Celia included, had no qualms about flying higher to climb over the weather, this option didn't exist when the cloud descended over the airfield. And, being close to the south coast, this happened pretty frequently. Consequently, there was a fair amount of enforced downtime.

Sitting around ops' rooms and waiting areas could become tedious in the extreme. The amount of cards one could play, letters one could write, conversations one might have, palled after a while. Moods not improved, fractious arguments, general female bitching only too easy.

Celia, as an alternative, had decided to read – not magazines but books, serious ones, literature. She estimated that working her way through the classics of the English canon would take at least four years. By that time, she might have had enough of the ATA, or preferably, the war would be over.

Deciding on an author at a time, her first choice was Thomas Hardy. Pastoral, simple though not uncomplicated lives, beautiful descriptions of the Wessex landscape over which she flew. It was, she thought, an appropriate choice.

Celia lay in the bed in the room she'd been allocated and stared up at the ceiling. After a while she sat up, draped her uniform jacket over her shoulders and, lighting a cigarette, pulled back the curtains and stared into the darkness over the US base. Her body felt peculiar – not distressing, but odd and she couldn't put her finger on it.

Some of their pilots had received an urgent request to ferry a collection of aircraft to a US base in east Anglia, and Celia had flown in later with the Anson to pick them up for the return to Hamble. The weather had closed in, a sudden deep fog rolling in from the North Sea, making all further flying impossible and they'd been forced to spend the night.

The Americans couldn't believe their luck and had entertained them royally and everyone had had a jolly good time. A swing band had appeared from nowhere in one of the hangars and Celia, together with the other girls, had danced with anyone who asked her. It had been a triumph for Anglo–American relations. The amount of drink, and particularly food, they'd been offered had been truly staggering.

And then Celia recognised what it was she was feeling. Full up, stuffed to the gunwales. So used to being hungry as almost a way of life, it was a most peculiar feeling, and one she couldn't be sure if she liked.

77

Matthew watched as members of the latest batch of trainees returned. A two-day exercise and the hardest yet. There were none of the springy steps of the morning before. They came in ad hoc groups, some supporting others. Matthew looked on with professional sympathy. They'd be out again the following night.

It was a process being repeated all over the country. The training regimes and methods pioneered by the Commandos had now been adopted by the whole of the British Army. The Americans had followed suit. Battle inoculation.

Troops were marched insensible, deprived of rest or sleep; starved, frozen, soaked and then shot at. The process was repeated continuously until eventually they were pronounced fit enough to adventure into the comparative luxury of a battlefield.

Matthew had not forgotten his own experiences of training and those never ending, hideous route marches. But it worked.

Less than fifty per cent would finish the course to receive the coveted green beret of the Commandos. The majority would be returned to unit, RTU, the cruellest of initials for those who aspired to so much.

As an adjunct to his lectures on the theory and construction of shaped charges, Matthew had devised a series of demonstrations to illustrate their potency. He'd had a batch of copper cones turned up ranging in diameter from half an inch to two inches. Fitted inverted into thick-walled steel tubing of the appropriate size, a power charge and electrical detonator tamped in behind and sealed off with a screwed cap gave him a lethal collection of directional pipe bombs.

These he then taped end on the blocks of steel. Once detonated they gave a series of spectacular blow holes, punched right through the steel by the hypersonic slug of molten copper. The two-inch charge passed through an eighteen-inch rod lengthways without difficulty. But it was his final demonstration which was the most remembered.

Giving one of the students a block of gun cotton, Matthew asked him to carve his initials into it, but reading backwards. This done, he would place the block face down on a steel plate, apply a detonator and get them to place a large boulder on top.

After firing the student was sent to retrieve the steel plate. The surprise and delight never varied. There, on the plate, were the initials neatly indented. It was an elegant and simple demonstration and, as Matthew explained, how shaped charges were first discovered.

It was known as the 'Munroe effect', named after the explosives tester in a US Navy arsenal who had first noticed the effect in around the year 1900.

***

In preparation for its transformation into Supreme Headquarters Allied Expeditionary Force, SHAEF, COSSAC was being reorganised to a pattern that more closely resembled an American staff model. At John's level this made little or no difference to his day-to-day activities. He still reported to Group Captain Baker and, while Baker's reporting chain had changed, the affects did not peculate downward.

What these staff changes did do was confirm General Morgan's statement months before as to the eventual direction of COSSAC that it would evolve into an operational staff becoming the nucleus of SHAEF.

While the staff reorganisation was all very well and necessary, with the invasion planned for the following spring, there was a growing need to appoint the commanders for the operation, the leaders of all the individual services together with that of the supreme commander. Until that time, real momentum would be difficult to sustain despite General Morgan's efforts.

In a way, it was like buses. You wait and wait, and then several come along at once. And so it was with the appointment of the senior commanders for Overlord.

After much late speculation, Trafford Leigh-Mallory was confirmed as Commander-in-Chief of the Allied Air Expeditionary forces while Admiral Sir Bertram Ramsay was appointed Commander-in-Chief for all naval forces. Ramsay was the perfect choice – a magnificent organiser who amongst other notable achievements had been the driving force behind Operation Dynamo, the evacuation of the BEF from Dunkirk.

Soon after these announcements, the Deputy Supreme Commander was appointed: the British airman Sir Arthur Tedder. It was an inspired choice by the Joint Chiefs of Staff. It gave no offence to any of the interested parties while giving the necessary impetus to the air forces.

Only two appointments were now left unfilled: Commander-in-Chief Land Forces and that of the Supreme Allied Commander himself. Some wag in Norfolk House had attempted to open a book on it, but with everyone giving the same prediction, he'd soon abandoned the idea. Montgomery for Land Commander, Eisenhower for Supreme Chief. There was no other sensible choice.

In November at one of his many meetings, Roosevelt had asked as to what were the total armed forces available to Britain and the United States. The numbers were illuminating, as was their disparity.

Total US forces were ten and a half million compared to Britain's three point eight million with another million from her dominions. Of deployed forces only two and a half million US Army personnel had so far gone overseas. The bulk of the US Army remained in country.

To John, the implications were only too obvious. Whilst the levels of American and British forces committed to the initial stages of the invasion were roughly comparable, as the campaign progressed, the Americans would gradually predominate. The reasons were simple. While the British were reaching the limit of their manpower resources, the Americans were yet to deploy anything near their true potential.

As the war progressed in Europe the more it would become an American war of liberation. It was a fact best recognised early.

Whatever their faults, there was one thing the Americans were completely devoid of; John searched for the word, perfidiousness. That English thing of politely tolerating while actually excluding. Once the Americans were in, they were in, with all the youthful enthusiasm of the new world.

One of the younger secretaries had made a sudden departure. Found in the ladies' lavatory most mornings being violently sick, pregnancy was diagnosed. One of the orderlies had been named as the father. A rather plain girl as John remembered, very shy.

John felt rather sad for her. There had been others and no doubt there would be more. He remembered Fowler, *English Usage*, and his explanation of the difference between expect and anticipate. "A woman who anticipates marriage may find herself expecting."

With his appointment as Supreme Allied Commander for Overlord, General Eisenhower left Algiers in North Africa just before Christmas. He did not travel alone. Experienced now since the Torch landings, and only too aware of the sometime fraught relations between the British and Americans during the North African and Italian campaigns, particularly Sicily, he decided to bring the vast majority of his key staff officers with him. They would form the basis of SHAEF, Supreme Headquarters Allied Expeditionary Force, based in London. This in turn would absorb the COSSAC organisation. COSSAC had a staff of well over a thousand; SHAEF was projected to exceed three thousand.

With every available piece of office space in London now occupied, John wondered where this whole new staff was to be accommodated. A completely new site outside London needed to be found, and soon. And, assuming Norfolk House and the other office building were retained, secure communications channels between the new and the old established.

John wondered about this and particularly, what effect it might have upon him personally. He liked working at Norfolk House and living in the Kensington flat bestowed considerable advantages. He would be loath to move.

78

It had been drummed into Mark from the first. Security was all – the secrecy of their operations was such that nothing could be allowed to compromise it. To this end there was, by now, a well-established method for the mounting and execution of the 15th Flotilla's clandestine operations from Dartmouth across the Channel to Brittany. So well-practised had this become it had been formalised into a seven-stage procedure.

Initiated by Captain Slocum as Deputy Director Operations Division (Irregular) – DDOD(I) – in London, in conjunction with whichever of the secret intelligence services in occupied France was involved, the need for an operation would be agreed. A unique code name would then be allocated.

The next stage was to select a rendezvous position, a pinpoint, for the operation through radio contact with the agents in Brittany. An approximate future date suitable to all would be selected during a period of no moon which occurred for around ten nights each month. With the pinpoint agreed, every piece of relevant information on the location would be collected and collated. Ideally this would include details of German coastal shipping movements, coastal installations and defences and would, importantly, include recent photographs of the area from RAF reconnaissance shot at the various states of the coastal tides.

Stage III formalised the operation. As the selected date approached, London prepared detailed orders, both real and dummy should the MGB be intercepted and captured by the Germans. Recognition signals, ship to shore, and communication protocols if radio telephones were to be used.

Stage IV would allocate a boat to the operation together with a selection of personnel including the boat's commander, a conducting officer to oversee the landing party and a navigation officer. The MGB would be thoroughly checked and tested, defects rectified. Compasses, engines, communication systems, guns, echo sounders and the like, while equipment specific to the operation such as the double-bowed surf boats would also be carefully inspected, tested and equipped.

It was at this point that Mark, if selected as navigation officer, became involved. Hours of close scrutiny of charts and tidal tables. Sunrise, sunset, moonrise and moonset, detailed weather forecasts.

The 15th Flotilla's most senior navigator was David Birkin, as Mark, a lieutenant in the RNVR and, like Mark, to a degree self-taught. Birkin was a remarkable man in several respects. Meticulous in his preparation and totally precise with his navigation and this in spite of being severely hampered when at sea by constant violent sea sickness, sinusitis, a persistent cough with bleeding lungs, combined with double vision. That he managed to function at all was remarkable, and with such efficiency, even more so. Mark had accompanied him several times as his assistant and found him inspirational; a perfect pattern to copy.

To control his symptoms when at sea Birkin smoked a pipe continually: heavy pungent shag tobacco that reduced the air in the limited space of the chart room to a fetid fog. Mark's own use of a pipe was much less and with a lighter mixture. Regular doses of sea air were required when accompanying Birkin.

Stage V was the day of the operation. A couple of hours before departure all the officers would attend a final conference in the wardroom of Westward Ho!, their depot ship, where final intelligence reports of activity on the Brittany coast would be reviewed, particularly any German shipping movements. They would also be supplied with the German recognition signals for the day for response if challenged.

Once on board the MGB, Mark would settle himself into the confines of the chart room. Close below the bridge and connected by a voice tube guaranteed to leak, it was a space roughly six feet square with a low ceiling height requiring a constant stoop if standing. Bijou would be an estate agent's description, a misnomer for small and cramped. With him he brought and attaché case containing all the relevant charts and acetate sheets for overlays; two drawstring oilskin bags containing the tools of his trade: notebooks, pencils, standard and multicoloured chinagraphs, dividers and rules, two stop watches, speed calculators and a collection of bulldog clips to hold the charts down to the small collapsible table.

In his jacket pockets were stuffed with what Mark thought of as his survival kit just in case he became stranded on the other side. Survival ration packs, a basic toilet bag, two pipes and spare tobacco, spare socks and a Colt forty-five automatic with two spare clips. Should he need he had enough for a frugal week.

Once unpacked he would gather the boat's ratings on the mess deck to brief them on the operation and the procedures to adopt should they become marooned on the Brittany coast.

As the final preparations for sea were being made on the MGB, the last train would slowly wheeze its way, shrouded in steam, into Kingswear station. The gunboat's passengers would discretely disembark to be spirited aboard the MGB by the conducting officer while their luggage and any other stores for transit would be stowed on the open deck space ahead of the bridge.

Stage VI marked the commencement of the operation. At the exact time specified in the orders, the MGB would slip the mooring lines, the engines would be started and the boat would move slowly downstream. Invariably, in the best naval tradition, the boat's company would be standing to attention on the foredeck. Always a touching sight in the gathering dusk. Passing through the boom that guarded the river entrance, the boat accelerated, around Blackstone Point and the Combes heading south-west along Slapton Sands until they reached the aptly named Start Point. With guns tested, ready use ammunition checked, Start Point marked the beginning of the Channel crossing and the business end of the operation.

With an accurate fix and time from their departure point, Mark would begin to plot their speed from the engine revolutions and the QH position finding system for as long as the transmission strength held out. Mid-way across the Channel they would pass over the Hurd Deep, a depression running up roughly ninety miles from Alderney. The echo sounder readings would dramatically increase for around two and a half miles before returning to normal – another useful check on their position.

The crossing to the Brittany coast took on average about six hours. Fifteen miles out speed was reduced and the engines silenced. All available eyes were now on deck scanning the horizons for any German coastal traffic. If any of the Breton lighthouses were illuminated, however dimly, fixes would be taken. Five miles on they would alter course to counter the prevailing tidal streams while moving ever onwards towards the coast.

Mark would switch to his large-scale coastal charts, calling up to the bridge with fixes on the outlying rock formations, an eye continuously monitoring the echo sounder readings.

On reaching the rendezvous pinpoint engines would be switched off and the boat anchored. Now began the wait. Sometimes the shore party would already be in position but mostly they would not. They could wait for a maximum of four hours by which time dawn would be rising. Standing offshore at anything between half a mile and a hundred odd yards they were in a very exposed position and certainly within range of any coastal searchlights and gun emplacements. It was a tense time which passed very slowly as constant attempts were made to contact the shore party on the walkie-talkies while eyes strained to pick out faint-lighted signals from the shore.

The surf boats, launched onto the water soon after they anchored, oarsmen in place, had perhaps the most nervous wait. Either to be hauled back if they were detected or despatched once contact was established. Sat low in the water to the leeside of the MGB with only the whispered comments from above for company.

If and when contact was made, the passengers and their luggage were rapidly embarked and the surf boats, the conducting officer in the prow of the lead boat, struck towards the shore. It could be a hard row if the sea was rough. Reaching the shoreline the surf boats did not linger. Ten minutes was considered the maximum time onshore. Passengers and stores were unloaded, then the ever-important intelligence packages and mail were stowed in the boats together with anything up to twenty-five passengers for the return. Evading Allied airmen and intelligence agents, often with women and children, wet and frightened.

The surf boats and their cargoes were recovered back to the MGB and while the passengers crammed into the little wardroom, the anchor was lifted, the engines restarted and, still silenced, the gunboat would nose its way towards the open sea. Once well clear of the coast, throttles would be opened for the return across the Channel under a dawning sky.

Quite often from around mid-way they would be greeted by a pair of Spitfires flying top cover for their return. Always a sight to lift the spirits.

After a total mission time of anything between fourteen and sixteen hours the MGB would return to Dartmouth, the passengers would disembark, often to catch the first train out of Kingswear for London.

Mark would eat whatever he could of breakfast, make whatever notes were required for the operational report and then, after a quick bath, retire to bed. It was always a measure of how stressful the night had been as to how easily he slept. Had they been successful, he slept well. Had they failed and the mission aborted, his sleep was fitful.

1944

79

John had made a special effort to return to the flat before seven. Celia had secured a forty-eight-hour pass and he wondered if she'd be there to greet him. Being a well-known regular visitor, the concierge would have let her in his absence.

As he opened the door he heard laughter. Surprisingly, Elizabeth was there too.

He kissed Celia, greeted Elizabeth and asked what they'd been laughing about.

"Scissors."

"Scissors?"

"Scissors, and how bloody awkward they are."

John nodded as the penny dropped. Both Celia and Elizabeth were left-handed. Most items were indifferent to handedness though scissors were perhaps the exception, practically impossible to use left-handed. The right hand had to be trained to use them. He remembered this from his mother who had also been left-handed. He still recalled the muttered cursing when she'd been sewing.

"Wasn't your mother left-handed?" asked Celia.

"Yes, she was."

"I wonder if you are, naturally I mean. There are some things you do with your left hand that a natural right hander wouldn't."

"Like what?"

"Opening jars, catching things in your left hand when I toss them to you."

"Maybe."

John remembered something. So aware was she that it was a right-handed world, his mother was determined to make him right-handed. As she'd

111

explained to him years later, as a small child and asking for something, she would only offer things to his right hand.

"You could be right," he said, and related the story.

Elizabeth wasn't staying, just a flying visit, swapping over clothes, collecting laundry and her post. John knew she was spending a lot of time somewhere in Chelsea – he had a telephone number to go with all the others but was polite enough not to enquire about the circumstances.

"Are you sure you won't join us to eat?"

Elizabeth laughed. "Thank you, John, but no." She laughed again, a little knowingly.

"Stay overnight with you two? You make too much noise."

After Elizabeth left, they discussed what to do for the evening. A meal and the cinema perhaps.

"Then we can come back and make some noise," commented Celia, a twinkle in her eye.

It had been such a seemingly simple decision, a matter determined by some lowly bureaucrat in the War Office in early 1942. The question as to where to house the flood of US troops when they began to arrive in England.

At the time, with the British fighting and directing a war from southeast England, it made obvious sense to base the Americans somewhere else. The first American forces to land in the UK did so in Northern Ireland but, as their numbers and frequency of arrival began to increase, their accommodation was accomplished in the west of England. It made logical sense. The west of England was geographically closer to the United States, and it would avoid the complications of Atlantic traffic being mixed up with British naval operations in the North Sea and the central Channel. The third consideration was that the American command's preference to keep itself and its resources as concentrated as possible. Furthermore, it being neither conceivable nor desirable to combine the British and American systems of supply, keeping them physically isolated would avoid a great deal of unnecessary complication.

In the event, the original stroke of the bureaucratic pen had far-reaching and unforeseen consequences.

For Overlord, and the assault on the Normandy beaches, the Americans, reflecting their positioning in England, would land on the right, the western side, while the British and Canadians would be on the left, the eastern side. Cherbourg would be an early American objective, while Le Havre the equivalent British.

As the battle developed, the whole of the invasion armies would wheel to the half left, the British towards north-west Germany, with the Americans heading towards south-west Germany, supplemented by their forces advancing from the Dragoon landings in the south of France.

Thus, from such a seemingly simple decision on accommodation, the whole strategy for the reoccupation of western Europe had been determined.

***

In high summer, Westward Ho! might hold some charm, but not so on a cold and windy day in mid-January. A coastal spit of sand south of the Torridge estuary on the Bristol Channel, it faced almost due west towards the Atlantic Ocean. A practically uninhabited shoreline, it was a melancholic place at the best of times; a place where the land meets the full force of the sea and where the sea invariably wins. The inclusion of an exclamation mark in Westward Ho! was a mystery to Luke. Perhaps it was the surprise to find that, once having reached the place, one found so little there. Setting off well before dawn on the Wednesday morning, it had taken him the best part of six hours to make the journey from Oxford.

What Westward Ho! did have at low tide was broad open beaches, devoid of breakwaters, almost identical in terms of composition and gradient to those found on the beaches of northern France. As a consequence, the whole area had been requisitioned by the Combined Operations Experimental Establishment, known as COXE, as a trials and testing area for the various special weapons being developed for the forthcoming assault and invasion of western Europe.

Hitler's much vaunted Atlantic Wall, though by no means continuous, did contain areas of formidable defences, including stretches of reinforced concrete bastions ten feet high and seven feet thick. To broach these, a high explosive charge of at least a ton would need to be placed in close proximity to the base of the structure.

With target and solution thus established, the question then fell as to the delivery system for such a large charge. Not only would the explosive need to be placed with precision, but the system would also have to traverse an open beach, heavily mined and subject to continuous machine gun and mortar fire.

One idea, originating from Combined Operations HQ in Richmond Terrace and probably emanating from the triumphate known as the lunatic asylum, was a device resembling a giant Catherine wheel. Two large, spoked steel wheels, ten feet in diameter with a foot wide tread, connected in the centre by a broad drum hub within which was a charge of at least a ton of TNT. Around the periphery of each wheel were connected a series of slow burning cordite rockets mounted tangentially. The idea was that this monstrosity would be launched off the ramp of a landing craft, rockets burning, to then propel itself across the open beach, accelerating all the way, to then smash into the sea wall at sixty miles an hour. The steel wheels would collapse on impact, the drum of TNT would explode and the bastion would be destroyed.

The task to bring this concept to fruition was presented to DMWD in mid-1943 and taken up by Nevil Shute Norway, one of the more literary members of the Wheezers and Dodgers. Norway immediately christened it Panjandrum, taken from characters invented by the eighteenth-century writer Samuel Foote who had gunpowder running out of their heels.

Designed at Weston-super-Mare the prototype Panjandrum was constructed within a month at an engineering works in Leytonstone north London and then, in early September, transported at night and in great secrecy to Appledore in Devon where COXE had located its headquarters. Here the great security operation collapsed, for having rolled the Panjandrum off its transporter onto the beach, the security detail promptly abandoned it where it was immediately surrounded by local holidaymakers who took it for some new beach attraction provided for their amusement.

Transported the short distance around the coast to Westward Ho! and mounted at the head of the beach where a great pebble ridge ran parallel to the sea, the Panjandrum was prepared for its maiden run. To simulate the explosive charge, four thousand pounds of dry sand was loaded as ballast into the central drum and then sealed. This gave the whole contraption a total weight approaching three tons. Though estimates had been made of the rolling resistance both through the surf and across the sand, no one was sure how many rockets would be required to propel the device to the desired speed. It was to be a classic case of 'suck it and see'.

To ensure a continuous rolling motion, the rockets, each with a thrust of about forty pounds, were required to be fired in sequence, and with an adequate overlap, complicating the firing circuits. Sensibly, for the initial run, it was decided to fit the minimum estimated number of eighteen rockets and then measure the performance.

Enveloped first in clouds of smoke, then steam and trailing jets of flame, the Panjandrum charged off the ramp of the landing craft like something possessed and ploughed its way through the surf and up the beach with a thunderous roar. The course was reasonably straight until two of the rockets on one side failed to ignite causing it to veer off to one side. It then came to a stop after about two hundred yards. The speed had not been impressive – more rockets were obviously required.

Two days later, with the number of rockets doubled, a further eighteen fitted to the inside of the wheels, the test was repeated. The Panjandrum traversed around a hundred and fifty yards of shallow water without difficulty, but once it cleared the surf and reached the sand, its progress became increasingly erratic. Swaying from side to side and, as some of the rockets failed to fire, slowing to a stop after for hundred yards.

Two things were now clear from these initial trials. The Panjandrum was far too slow and there was a major stability problem. Further thought and a redesign was needed.

This process was to continue for the rest of the year. With the number of rockets again doubled to seventy-two, a third but smaller trailing wheel was added in an attempt to improve the stability. This failed spectacularly. The Panjandrum swerving back towards the sea immediately after launch, to then topple over on its side and disintegrate.

Abandoning the third wheel, another method of stabilisation was attempted using differential cables and a braking system used for barrage balloons attached to the hub of each wheel. Throughout November further trials failed to exhibit anything resembling consistency. Each test seemed unique to itself. Few attempts at steering achieved anything positive whichever way the brakes were applied. While the seventy-two rockets gave the required speed, directional control remained problematic. Given that the whole device would have to be operated under fire, the winch-man's position was not to be envied.

Following a further series of unsuccessful attempts which destroyed another prototype, trials were suspended until such time as another two vehicles were constructed. In the meantime, Combined Operations decided that absolute accuracy was no longer required negating the need for a steering mechanism.

These new, revised versions of the Panjandrum had almost reverted to the original design but for the addition of more propulsive rockets. These in themselves were not inconsiderable pieces of ordnance, weighing in at about twenty pounds each and producing forty pounds of thrust for a duration of forty seconds. They were also prone to severe vibration and while firing requiring substantial restraining clamps.

By now, the Great Panjandrum had become something of a *cause célèbre* amongst the Wheezers and Dodgers while poor Norway had become the butt of many a joke. Also, more seriously, patience was wearing thin. By mutual agreement of all concerned, the trials scheduled for early January would be the last. Unless successful, the project would be abandoned. It was these trials that Luke had travelled down to witness.

Long practised now at attending trials such as this, Luke had established a routine, particularly where to position himself to get the best possible view. Invariably these events were filmed so now he always stood as close as possible to the cameraman. It was a similar technique on taking scenic pictures at the seaside. The local photographers always knew the best local viewpoints. Examine the postcards on sale, and then try to replicate them. Since the trials cameraman would be well briefed, it was reasonable to assume he would position himself in the optimum position.

Luke had met the photographer before, one Louis Klemantaski, who'd made a name for himself before the war filming motor races. Now, he'd become the Wheezers and Dodgers in house photographer. They wished each other good afternoon while Luke promised not to get in his way.

They were positioned about halfway down the course allowing Klemantaski to film the whole sequence panning right to left. Close by were the remains of a concrete blockhouse affording a degree of shelter should it be needed. Further behind them, on the crest of Pebble Ridge, the great and the good had gathered. A group of perhaps forty senior naval officers including a couple of admirals and a bunch of equally senior army officers, generals amongst them. Luke wondered at the numbers and the reason. Perhaps it was the prospect of a day at the seaside that had tempted them out.

A test run in the early morning using forty-eight rockets had been judged a success, though again the speed had been disappointing. More rockets to the maximum of seventy-two had been added for this crucial run. To make the beach more realistic, two lines of mines had been laid and these were now detonated to form craters simulating the effect of an offshore bombardment. After the smoke from these had cleared, an army officer's dog, an Airedale with the appropriate name of Ammonal, had broken free from his owner and had charged past them onto the beach to be now seen scampering about excitedly. Whistles were blown. It wasn't only the dog who was excited.

Standing on the lowered ramp of the LCT the first rockets on the wheels of the Panjandrum ignited. Luke had made a bet with himself as to how many of the rockets would break free. They were never designed to withstand the lateral loads imposed by the rotation. He'd guessed at six.

At first, all went well. The Panjandrum trundled off the ramp to emerge in a stately manner from within the clouds of steam and smoke as it thrashed through the surf. Luke could hear Klemantaski's cinecamera whirring in his ear. As the Panjandrum began to accelerate a rocket broke free from its clamp, and then immediately, two more. By now it was moving fast, somewhere close to eighty miles an hour, running straight across the beach.

Reaching the first line of craters the right-hand wheel closest to the shore dipped ominously. The Panjandrum arced in a great curve and began to head straight towards them. A great thrashing monster belching fire and smoke. Luke was fascinated and though he estimated it would miss them by about thirty yards he moved closer to the slabs of concrete of the blockhouse.

There was pandemonium behind him. Glancing back, he saw Klemantaski with the others, legging it over to the far side of the ridge. Not the best idea – beyond the crest there was a mass of barbed wire in a ditch.

By now the Panjandrum had run into the second line of craters. This time the other wheel dipped sharply steering it in the opposite direction and back out to sea. The dip increased as the wheel bit into the sand. The Panjandrum turned sharply in on itself until it slowly toppled over like a drunken man, landing on its side, smothering the rockets beneath it in the wet sand. With those still firing, the ones on top began to break off, screaming across the open beach in every possible direction. Ammonal meanwhile was having a wonderful time, chasing after the rockets and barking his head off.

After a few more minutes the show was over. Luke and the others, some with their uniforms torn by the wire, trooped down to the seashore to inspect the remains. Twisted and blackened wreckage almost beyond recognition. It made for a sad sight as the incoming tide lapped around to submerge it.

The remains of the Great Panjandrum had drowned at sea, but no one could deny it had been spectacular while it lasted.

Luke wouldn't have missed it for the world.

***

Unlike England, where it is a relatively common, America has few occurrences of the name Bushey. This unfamiliarity was to have significant repercussions for the Normandy invasion.

With Eisenhower's appointment as Supreme Commander confirmed, the immediate question was where to physically locate his headquarters. With several hundred staff to accommodate, central London was not an option. Norfolk House was full as was every other suitable building. In the meantime, the locations of the other three service commands were scattered. Naval Command was exercised from Portsmouth while the Air Command was positioned at Stanmore, a dozen or so miles north-west of London. Moving either of them, particularly Stanmore, was not a practical proposition. Montgomery's HQ, meanwhile, was accommodated in the buildings of his old school, St Paul's in Hammersmith west London, close to the Thames.

It was thought desirable that the HQ of the Supreme Commander should be located as close as possible to that of the Air Commander. Leigh-Mallory certainly thought so. Events move quickly in the air; the shortest possible communication routes would be an obvious advantage. Accordingly, he suggested that Eisenhower's main HQ should be installed on Bushey Heath, close to his own at Stanmore, and where a suite of perfectly suitable office buildings already existed.

In late December, General Bedell Smith, Eisenhower's chief of staff, had arrived in England hot foot from Algiers to prepare the ground for his boss. Coincidentally, the US Army Air Corps, as part of their own reorganisation prior to the invasion, were about to vacate their previous HQ in Bushey Park, a huge area ten miles west of London in Kingston upon Thames next to Hampton Court. With the name Bushey firmly lodged in Bedell Smith's mind, this seemed the obvious solution, and perfectly timed. Immediately, US construction teams moved into Bushey Park to begin building at a prodigious rate working in shifts twenty-four hours a day. By the second half of January a complete, purpose-built headquarters complex was ready for Eisenhower's occupation.

Only later did Bedell Smith discover that Bushey Park was not Bushey Heath, but by now it was too late. There was no time left to effect a change.

John felt a degree of sympathy for Leigh-Mallory's position. To exercise effective command of the Air Operations he needed to be at Stanmore, but to exert personal influence he would need to be with Eisenhower at Bushey Park thirty miles away. John strongly suspected he would be unable to achieve either. The consequences for the future co-ordination of the air–land campaign could only be guessed at. The runes did not augur well.

One consolation was the US Eighth Air Force HQ, with its huge bomber force, had gone from Bushey Park to High Wycombe where RAF Bomber Command's HQ had been since 1940. At least their co-location could be expected to bear fruit.

80

On Monday, 17 January 1944, Eisenhower formally took command as Supreme Commander and COSSAC became SHAEF – Supreme Headquarters Allied Expeditionary Force. Whether COSSAC had become SHAEF, or had become totally subsumed by it, was a moot point. Eisenhower had retained Bedell Smith as his chief of staff while General Morgan, effectively demoted, had graciously agreed to become one of Bedell Smith's several deputies.

The number of American staff that Eisenhower brought with him totalled nearly a thousand; thus SHAEF doubled the size of COSSAC overnight, a number, once Montgomery's contingent was included, was expected to exceed three thousand by the spring. SHAEF was destined to be a sizable organisation. Bloat was a word commonly heard around Norfolk House, but lean was not the American way.

It wasn't only Eisenhower who brought his own staff with him. Montgomery too had insisted that the majority of his senior Eighth Army Staff accompany him to London.

Installed in Claridge's until his permanent accommodation was available, Montgomery had not been idle. Having read the COSSAC Overlord plan while still in Marrakesh, to then express his total horror at it, he immediately convened a three-day conference at St Paul's School between his own staff and COSSAC. With Bedell Smith representing Eisenhower, Admiral Ramsay for the navy, Leigh-Mallory for the air forces and with Morgan and Barker with other members of COSSAC, it was a meeting that was to have profound implications; not only for the invasion itself, but for the whole prosecution of the war in western Europe.

The COSSAC presentation, measured, earnest almost sombre in tone occupied most of the first morning. Montgomery then took to the floor. By contrast he gave a coruscating performance, demolishing the Overlord plan with a pitiless brutality.

In his opinion, and supported by Bedell Smith, the Overlord plan as currently envisaged had no hope of success whatsoever. It was a landing of too few troops on too narrow a beachhead. Further, the troop numbers were inadequate to contain the inevitable German counter attacks whilst the width the beachhead was too small for the landing of reinforcements and supplies to build up an adequate lodgement. Further still, the rapid capture of the port of Cherbourg was unlikely to be achieved by such an initial narrow frontage.

He instructed the planners to consider a much-enlarged beachhead to encompass the eastern side of the Cotentin Peninsula and parts of Brittany, and also to the western side of the Normandy coast towards Dieppe. The number of troops required for the initial assault would be at least doubled, while the implications for the navy, who would have to transport them, would be immense.

By the second day, the west of the Cotentin Peninsula and Brittany had been rejected since they fell within the range of the German heavy artillery batteries on the Channel Islands. But, with Montgomery still insisting on an initial invasion force of five divisions instead of the original three, the beachhead was extended eastwards along the Cotentin Peninsula. Such was Montgomery's conviction that unless his new plan was adopted, he was not prepared to command and would resign forthwith.

Since its inception, COSSAC had operated within the means specifically allocated to it by the Combined Chiefs of Staff. Eisenhower and Montgomery were not so constrained. As commanders of the operation they could insist and demand greater resources, whatever the consequences, and particularly at the expense of time.

By the third day of the conference the overall plan, Overlord II as it was now called, was agreed by all parties. The beachhead was doubled to a frontage of fifty miles, landing to the west of Caen and eastwards halfway up the Cotentin Peninsula. Five separate invasion beaches, two American to the east, two British and one Canadian to the west. In addition to the five assault divisions landed from the sea, there were four further airborne divisions, dropped either side to secure the flanks, while another twelve divisions would land by sea in subsequent waves. The ramifications for the navy were enormous. Over seven thousand vessels were going to be required including over four thousand specialist landing craft of all types.

The provision of sufficient landing craft had always been problematic. The vast increase now required by Overlord II meant not only a delay to the invasion, put back by a month to the beginning of June, but the cancellation of Operation Anvil. This was originally intended to coincide with Overlord, and had now been renamed Dragoon by Churchill, reflecting how he felt he'd been coerced into it. This invasion of the south of France from the Mediterranean would be conducted sometime in mid-August.

The outline plan for Overlord II landed on John's desk on the Friday. The enthusiasm it generated within Norfolk House was palpable and it was easy to see why. Assuming the navy could cope, a wider frontage and a much-increased assault force solved most of the inherent problems associated with the original plan. It was also familiar.

John had retained his copy of Paget's original Skyscraper plan from March 1943. He now compared Overlord II with Skyscraper. They were remarkably similar. The landing areas were practically coincident as were the levels of the assaulting troop numbers, though Overlord II had another couple of divisions afloat to follow up. John was suitably reassured. That Paget's plan had been immediately rejected out of hand as unrealistic as regards resources, while the Montgomery–Eisenhower Overlord II plan had been readily accepted, showed as nothing else could how things had changed between March 1943 and January 1944.

As a matter of policy, COSSAC had always excluded the French. De Gaulle's Free French, fractious, with a myopic leader, were no one's idea of a collaborative partner. There was nobody who'd had dealings with de Gaulle who felt enhanced by the experience. Furthermore, the security of the Free French was notoriously poor. They simply could not be trusted with anything.

SHAEF, in the form of Eisenhower and Montgomery, loathed de Gaulle as did Churchill and Roosevelt. There would, therefore, be no change in policy. No French.

De Gaulle and the Free French would simply be informed of the invasion; the date, the location and the details of their participation at only the latest possible time and in common with the other contributing Allied nations. By then it would be too late for them to interfere, however much they might protest.

As one American had put it in a typically robust phrase. Come the day, the French would be forced to be inside the tent, pissing out, rather than on the outside, pissing in.

***

Luke's three fingered typing method, though proficient enough, did have its limitations. After typing for what at times seemed to be the whole of his life, but in reality was little more than a day, he read through his finished report. A review of a dozen or so related weapon developments. He was rather pleased with it: his analysis was cogent and sufficiently detailed, the conclusions and recommendations mostly self-evident. The report ran to twenty pages topped off by a single page synopsis as a cover sheet.

That he'd recommended the cancellation of several of the projects was going to upset a few people. It was a characteristic of some of his fellow engineers to pursue an idea well beyond reason, insistent that they would somehow, eventually, get 'it' to work in the face of all the mounting evidence to the contrary. The Wheezers and Dodgers' Great Panjandrum was but one. Resources were not infinite and time, Luke knew, was getting short. Having signed the report only one thing remained. What security classification should he give it?

Beyond the most general and obscure overall guidance, the British way of classifying documents was to depend on the discretion and opinion of the author. It avoided the need of an all-seeing eye to determine the classification and it played to the vanity of the authors. The human tendency of always valuing their work of greater importance than it actually is resulted in over classification of practically everything. This suited the security bureaucrats perfectly who were inclined to consider even the time of day a state secret.

There was an array of rubber stamps before him, hanging from a rotating wooden rack, a choice of five official classifications. Protect, Restricted, Confidential, Secret, Top Secret. Ink pads two: one red, one black. Such was the bureaucracy imposed on security and, notwithstanding the documents, the stamps themselves were required to be kept under lock and key when not in use. Nothing was said about the ink pads. He had a box of triplicate forms to suit each classification and a reducing circulation list as the classification increased. He decided on Secret and began stamping away at the top and bottom of each sheet.

In truth, the most sensitive information handled by Henderson and himself never resorted to rubber stamps. They were single copy documents, unmarked, and handled by a select band of couriers. Read, initialled and returned on the spot. No notes to be taken.

Luke's recollection of these somewhat rare items were kept in a cardboard wallet file, in the bottom of his second safe, under the heading domestic affairs. That was his own secret.

God it was cold, bone cold. January, barely above freezing for days; snow upon snow, frost upon frost, unrelenting. Luke crouched in front of the gas fire for a few minutes warming himself and his hands before settling back at his desk.

A small wooden box, delivered that morning by one of the college scouts, lay on his desk. Nestled within a packaging of wood shavings, Luke found a collection of components wrapped in greaseproof cloth, a completed assembly and a technical report describing the device. This was an example of the newly developed and very secret proximity or variable, VT, fuse for anti-aircraft artillery shells now being manufactured in America based on earlier developments in Britain. Luke had been awaiting the delivery with a mounting anticipation. It promised to be something special and of huge significance.

Historically, aeroplanes had always been notoriously difficult to hit by artillery fired from the ground. High, fast-moving targets, varying speeds and altitudes. In 1940, such was the accuracy of anti-aircraft fire using time-fused shells, it was estimated that it took 18,500 rounds per aircraft destroyed. And that was in daylight. At night, the results were considerably worse. What was required was a method of detonating a shell near enough to the target to destroy it. The answer was a proximity fused shell that did not require a direct hit. But how to achieve it? The pursuit of such a device had become something of the Holy Grail of munitions.

During the 1930s various concepts were investigated including acoustic, thermal, electrostatic and magnetic, together with optical and photoelectric. None were found to be satisfactory. One idea, however, showed promise. Radar. In 1939 Marconi-Osram at their research lab in Wembley had produced a subminiature electronic valve about the size of a 0.38 revolver cartridge, an inch and a quarter long, that was rugged enough to be fired from an artillery piece. This little cylindrical glass valve acted as a miniature radar set, both transmitting and receiving, the idea being that once a returning pulse of sufficient strength was returned, detonation could be initiated.

This Marconi development, together with a host of other British inventions, had been taken to America by the Tizard Mission in 1940 following the agreement between the two nations to share scientific developments. The Americans, with their usual energy, had poured money and resources into the concept to bring it to fruition. The contents of the little wooden box contained the results.

Luke read the technical report, replete with diagrams and illustrations, with considerable care before he began to examine the components. He had the mechanical engineer's traditional suspicion of electricity and all things electrical and electronic. Electricity; once memorably described as 'fuck all in a hurry!' Luke's natural discipline and interest was fluid dynamics. Air, the working fluid, of which the composition was well known and easily described, was notoriously difficult, if not impossible to predict when in motion. Electricity on the other hand, itself difficult to describe precisely, was totally amenable to mathematical analysis and performed with an absolute certainty.

It was a teasing paradox. An engineer who understood, and had a thorough working knowledge of both disciplines, was a rarity.

There were four major components. The miniature radio transmitter–receiver combined with an amplifier and capacitor which, cleverly, used the body of the shell itself as an aerial; a battery; an explosive train using a thyraton tube switch, a gateway valve which discharged the capacitor when the return signal strength came into phase with the transmitter, indicating proximity to initiate detonation; and all the necessary safety devices.

Though each of the components were by necessity small, they were particularly rugged. They needed to be. An artillery shell typically experiences an instantaneous axial acceleration of 20,000g at the moment of firing and, spinning at somewhere between two fifty and five hundred revs per minute from the barrel rifling, another 5,000g of centrifugal force.

Luke found the battery solution particularly ingenious. About the size of a fountain pen barrel, it was a wet battery, the electrolyte contained in a glass ampoule at the centre of ninety stacked wafers, carbon on one side, zinc the other. Completely inert until firing and thus capable of long-term storage, when fired, the shock would break the ampoule and the centrifugal force would distribute the electrolyte between the wafers to initiate power from the battery. Clever.

The US had conducted lengthy and exhaustive field trials of the new fuse to prove its validity before ordering full production. Combined with radar-directed gun laying, only fifty shells were required for an aircraft's destruction under all conditions. Fifty shells compared to the conventional twenty thousand. Impressive indeed.

Luke held the assembled fuse in his left hand, barely four inches long, easily accommodated in the nose of a standard 3.7inch artillery shell. It was an amazing development and the Americans had ordered twenty million of them immediately. Over a hundred manufacturing plants, employing over a million people were now producing them twenty-four hours a day at a unit cost below twenty dollars. Staggering numbers. The total programme cost would exceed a billion dollars, an unprecedented industrial achievement.

Luke carefully repacked everything into the wooden box before putting it into one of his safes. The Holy Grail of munitions had been found. With the invasion of western Europe expected in the spring, the full deployment of this proximity fuse could not have come at a more propitious time.

81

Henderson, as an Oxford man, had a natural and automatic distrust of anything related to Cambridge; though, to his credit, he recognised this as the prejudice it was. Nevertheless, his critical faculties were always more attuned to anything originating from what he always thought of as that other place. Cambridge, a countryside of fens and marshland, endlessly flat with huge disorientating skies. Guaranteed to unhinge if not make mad. One such was a certain Geoffrey Pyke.

Pyke had an interesting history, encompassing a variety of diverse unrelated fields and, perhaps, one of the most unique minds in the country, and this combined with an ability to devise ideas that no one else would ever consider. Unfortunately, these prize abilities were coupled with a personality and temperament that alienated everyone he had ever met. Most considered him mad, others, more charitable, described him as his own worst enemy.

Through twenty years of mixing in left wing political circles of which Cambridge was merely one, he had built up a prodigious list of influential contacts all of whom he would bombard with long and detailed letters concerning whatever his latest obsession was. Eventually, like water dripping on a stone, he would get a hearing, his enthusiasm invariably infectious. Charm and guile to begin, and as each new idea failed, spite and anger to follow.

Appointed Director of Programmes at Combined Operations by Mountbatten at his headquarters in Richmond terrace, with Bernal and Zuckerman from Cambridge as scientific advisers; this trio were known as the department of Wild Talents by some, the Lunatic Brigade by others. Certainly, some of the more imaginative schemes to be deployed for the forthcoming invasion had originated with them. Fuel provision by pipeline under the sea and artificial harbours being but two, though it was left to others, and very many of them, to make these ideas practical prospects and bring them through to fruition. But there were other ideas, however original or brilliant, that were beyond the bounds of practicality, resource and particularly the timescales available to the Allies.

Henderson was reading the admiralty's final report on Habbakuk, a project named after an Old Testament prophet who had promised to amaze; a project finally abandoned after much expense several weeks before.

Conceived against the backdrop of the battle of the Atlantic, when losses against the U-boats were at their height, Pyke's idea was for the creation of a colossal aircraft carrier, at least ten times the size of normal, to be permanently stationed in the mid-Atlantic. From this it would be possible to mount standing patrols of long-range aircraft to nullify the U-boat packs. To build such a behemoth from steel was impractical, if not impossible. Pyke's revolutionary idea was to build it from ice.

Ice, in itself, is a brittle substance prone to fracture. However, as Pyke had discovered, when mixed with a small percentage of wood pulp, a material now named as pykrete, frozen water was transformed into a substance with similar physical properties to that of reinforced concrete but at a fraction of the cost. And there were other further important advantages. Apart from being naturally buoyant, the material was impervious to attacks from high explosives – bombs and torpedoes left but the merest dent.

So, a giant, unsinkable aircraft carrier moored in the mid-Atlantic. As a concept it was indeed brilliant, but, as trials to build a sub-scale berg ship on a lake in northern Canada demonstrated only too clearly, to bring such a concept to fruition involving as it did scores of refrigeration units and tens of miles of special pipe work, would take years. In the meantime, the Atlantic battle had swung in favour of the Allies. By a combination of new equipment, land-based very long-ranged aircraft and much improved tactics, the U-boat threat had been defeated.

So had Pyke. Embittered and feeling betrayed, his career with Combined Operations terminated and denied any further access, he became isolated, reduced to writing voluminous letters to *The Telegraph* and *The Times*, few of which were published.

Henderson finished the admiralty's report with a sigh and put it on the heap to pass on to Luke. Lighting his pipe, he stood up and walked across the room to a window, looking down to the comings and goings in the quad beneath him. Green sprouts from the bulbs planted in the borders were beginning to show through. The promise of a good show of daffodils and tulips soon.

He'd never met Pyke and for that he was grateful – their personalities were incompatible. But he felt a sadness too. He'd known his like before. Their endings were invariably tragic.

***

Bridget watched as the last of their balloons rose elegantly into the evening sky and then slowly began to drift eastwards. Illuminated by the slanting sun and starkly white, they were like so many rising moons in the dusk. Two hundred of them, heading over the North Sea and towards the continent and Germany.

The balloons, filled with hydrogen, would gradually rise to twenty-five thousand feet where a value would operate to bring them down in a slow descent to around a thousand as they approached Germany. On a pre-set timer, half of them would then deploy a long length of trailing piano wire to be dragged across the countryside with the aim of shorting out high voltage electricity transmission lines. On the other half, the timer would arm an incendiary bomb targeting the wide extent of German forests.

Operation Outward, this system of attacking Germany with free-flying hydrogen balloons, had begun two years before in 1942, but now it was coming to a gradual close. With the ever-increasing size and frequency of the heavy bombing raids on Germany, and the danger the balloons might present to the aircraft, the opportunities to launch were becoming less and less frequent. Following the invasion, they would be suspended altogether.

It would be the end of the two-year campaign. The two stations, Landguard Fort behind Felixstowe and Oldstairs Bay next to Dover had launched almost a hundred thousand balloons, often over a thousand each night. Results had been variable, but had been a source of constant irritation to the Germans, who had been forced to devote considerable resources to counter them. And Outward had been cheap – mass-produced the balloons cost little more than thirty shillings each.

Bridget had been stationed at the Fort since late 1941, but now she had the opportunity to move on. Her obvious destination was Dartmouth and the estuary. A huge build-up of activity was taking place there in support of the invasion offering ample opportunities and, of course, it was where Mark was stationed. Both professionally and personally the move made perfect sense.

By the end of April, she would be in Dartmouth as an ordnance officer servicing guns.

***

A young flight lieutenant from RAF Stanmore had brought down some papers John required. He could easily have sent a despatch rider but John suspected he wanted an afternoon off skiving in London.

John went down to meet him by the entrance to Norfolk House in the area they used to confine visitors who had no access to the main building.

John introduced himself and signed for the delivery. Handing back the chit he found the young man staring at him.

"I think we've met before."

John smiled without recollection. "Really?"

"I think we may have been at the same school."

He mentioned the school and John confirmed the suspicion.

"I was a few years behind you, and the others. We used to call you the Gospels. Matthew, Mark, Luke and John."

John smiled at that. It was a long time, a very long time since he'd heard that description.

"How are the others, are they still...?" The young man broke off.

"Yes," replied John hurriedly. "We're all still here." He gave a quick résumé.

The young man then began to regale him with the seemingly legendary exploits they had got up to at school and how they'd been looked up to.

After a few minutes of this John had cut him short, though not unkindly.

The flight lieutenant apologised for taking up so much of his time and, after shaking his hand warmly, disappeared towards Piccadilly Circus.

John climbed the stairs back up to his office smiling to himself. He'd include this little incident in his next batch of letters to the others. Then he laughed at himself. Oh, to be a hero.

Another long report read, absorbed and summarised to a page. And another bewildering string of acronyms and code names. The military spored acronyms and code names in ever-increasing profusion.

John had begun to compile two lists: one for code names and another for acronyms with a brief description of each to form a glossary. Given time and inclination, a rearrangement into alphabetical order would make it easier to use, but as yet he'd had no opportunity. A tiresome task, better suited for one of the typists to take up.

John ran his eyes down the lists. They ran to many pages with over five hundred separate entries and definitions. A fine job for some poor soul.

The debate had been particularly bitter but, eventually, the British view had prevailed. It was the correct one. It would save troops and it would save lives. Another example of the somewhat cavalier attitude to casualty numbers the Americans were prone to adopt unless checked.

John was reminded of a phrase supposedly attributed to Churchill. The Americans could always be relied upon to do the right thing, but only after they had exhausted all of the alternatives.

As part of the overall bombing campaign to reduce German industrial and shipping capacity ahead of the invasion, in late February, the US Air Force by day and RAF Bomber Command by night launched a series of heavy raids over a wide area of western Germany. Operation Argument, to John's mind a particularly ridiculous code name, and better known as 'Big Week', were the largest concentration of raids on Germany so far.

Results were, for the most part, satisfactory, some factories appearing to be totally destroyed. But the German's capacity to recover their production capacity was becoming depressingly familiar. Within a month, levels had returned to their previous volumes. For the Americans, the raids had been costly, approaching three thousand aircrew lost.

Coincidentally, during the same week, Churchill had made a statement in the House of Commons on RAF losses. Since the beginning of the war, thirty-eight thousand pilots and aircrew had been killed with the loss of ten thousand aircraft.

That evening, on the bus back to Kensington, John had made a few rough calculations on the margin of the evening newspaper. Using Churchill's figures as a basis, and taking account of the ever-increasing air activity in the months to come, he estimated the future size of the Allied losses. He didn't like the answers and did the sums again.

By the end of the European war with Germany he estimated total RAF losses close to a hundred thousand men with twenty thousand aircraft lost. Depressed, he ripped off the front of the newspaper and stuffed it into a pocket.

His figures took no account of the gradual degradation of the Luftwaffe and the ground defences. There was an office at the Air Ministry that specialised in these sorts of statistics and predictions. Perhaps their estimates were more encouraging. He would give them a ring in the morning.

*

The initial plan for 'Fortitude South' had been revised considerably. The original ideas had called for the construction of a considerable number of fake army camps coupled with large-scale displays of tank parks, equipment dumps and dummy airfields packed with inflatable rubber aeroplanes.

The new plan had rejected most of this as being over-elaborate and prone to detection. Considerable day-to-day activity would be required to maintain the pretence and neither were the Luftwaffe conducting a sufficient number of reconnaissance flights to justify the effort.

Active airfields are notoriously difficult to simulate. There had been a famous case earlier in the war when the Germans had constructed a dummy airfield in Holland made entirely of wood. So elaborate and time-consuming had been its construction that a daily PR flight had recorded the progress and once judged complete, a Wellington from Bomber Command had dropped a single wooden bomb on it.

Fake landing craft were another matter. Located on the coast they stood a good chance of being noticed by the Germans. There were two main classes of dummies. Landing Craft Assault and Landing Craft Tank. The dummies were known as 'wetbobs' and 'bigbobs'. John had read that with a wry smile. An Eton connection: 'drybob' was the slang for a cricketer, while 'wetbob' was a rower. It was a practice his school had studiously avoided.

Bigbobs were huge. Thirty feet wide, a hundred and seventy feet long, they were constructed from heavy canvas arranged over a scaffolding of steel tubes mounted on empty steel drums. With a total weight of five and a half tons and over a thousand components, they took around forty men to erect them in one overnight shift.

To support the FUSAG, First US Army Group, deception, closer to the date of the invasion, a whole fake dock and oil storage facility was to be built up the coast from Dover. Constructed by the set builders from Shepperton Film Studios it promised to be a sight when built.

John marked it down in his diary. There was to be a grand opening by the King with Montgomery and his staff in attendance. He would see if he could wangle an invitation.

82

Luke had been reading a report on the production difficulties of a munition considered essential for the forthcoming invasion. A lamentable tale of poor planning, failure to procure the correct machinery and tooling, and poor training. It was the blight of British manufacturing. That inbuilt reluctance to invest; the preference to somehow manage to muddle through. Not this time. Civil servants had moved in *en masse*, suspended the management, reorganised the machinery and tooling, trained the staff and got the production started while leaving a team in place to guard against slippage. The ammunition would now be available, in quantity, when required.

As the report had tartly concluded, borrowing one of Churchill's phrases, under the previous arrangements it hadn't been the case of "give us the tools and we'll finish the job", more like give us the job and we'll finish the tools.

***

Although the level of his workload showed no sign of diminishing, John had nothing pressing for the next couple of days. Their latest plans had been submitted for consideration and now awaited judgement. The map room had become particularly busy, a recent batch of intelligence photographs being displayed, and he spent a lot of time there. Any knowledge of the overall state of developments was never wasted.

On one of these visits, he fell into conversation with an army major. There was a detailed set of reconnaissance photographs of the Normandy landing beaches stretched across one of the tables. Shot from about fifty feet and taken parallel to the shore, they showed the steel girder constructions on the beach in stark relief. These were a recent addition. Erected on Rommel's order and known as Rommel's asparagus, they were in the shape of a cruciform with a Teller mine mounted on the top. Pilotage parties had been over at night to examine them and schemes were afoot to neutralise them. With their footings driven deep into the shingle they would pose a serious obstacle to shallow draft landing craft approaching the beach. Groups of German soldiers, working parties, could be seen running up the beach. The sudden appearance of a low flying Spitfire terrifying them. Their inclusion showed how large the obstacles were and their spacing.

As they studied the photographs, the major made a surprising suggestion.

"I'm going to a demonstration of some beach breeching kit on Thursday. Would you like to come?"

It was not an opportunity to miss and John eagerly accepted. Any diversion from his current activity would be welcome and it was a while since he'd been on an outing.

A huge olive-green Humber staff car collected him from the flat soon after 0800 and then lumbered out of London to the north-west. They were heading to Whitchurch, a village north of Aylesbury, home to the organisation known to all as Winston's Toyshop, formulated soon after he came to office as a centre for innovative weapon development. Not only was it the place that produced a variety of special weapons, but it also had extensive grounds, now used as firing ranges and proving grounds. It was an ideal location to lay on demonstrations for all and sundry.

Sitting in the back of the car with a cavernous amount of leg room, John and his companion engaged in intermittent conversation. The major's name was Jack Sheppard. Back in the eighteenth century, Jack Sheppard had been the most famous thief of his day; the original Jack the Lad. Stories of his exploits and escapes from custody were legendary. Thousands of sympathetic supporters had attended his very public hanging at Tyburn. Later, Dickens had used him as the basis for the Artful Dodger in *Oliver Twist*.

John Buchan and Jack Sheppard. They discussed the virtues, or otherwise of having a famous forebear, if only by name. Both agreed it could be something of a hindrance, something inherited that was not one's own.

The demonstrations were due to commence at eleven and to Jack's relief they arrived in good time soon after ten. Security was very tight. Their passes were inspected twice at two separate checkpoints before they were allowed in and, once inside, there were contingents of military police everywhere making spot checks.

A long line of armoured vehicles was lined up with their crews in close attendance to answer questions. All were based on either Churchill or Sherman tank chassis and all were part of the 79th Armoured Division.

As they walked down the line, Jack explained what each of them were. The first was a bobbin tank and it looked exactly that. A huge roll of reinforced canvas mounted on a giant spool to lay a track ahead of the tank to give greater purchase for the tracks on wet sand, mud or pebbles for vehicles travelling behind. Next came a flail tank, a rotating cylinder mounted ahead of a Churchill chassis to which were attached multiple heavy-duty chains with a large ball on the end. At the far sides of the cylinder were teeth with sharp-edged cutters. While the chain flails were designed to detonate mines buried beneath the surface, the cutters would chew through any amount of barbed wire.

Next came what had been nicknamed the 'flying dustbin'. A type of spigot mortar more accurately named a petard – a twenty-six-pound high explosive charge capable of being fired over two hundred yards to destroy hard points such as gun emplacements or protective coastal walls.

There was a bridge laying tank – a huge, concertinaed truss steel structure mounted on top that unfolded forward to then cantilever across obstructions such as streams and small rivers – and another variant carrying giant circular bundles of sticks, known as fascines, that would block and fill in anti-tank ditches, an idea borrowed from the Great War.

Most fearful of all was the variant known as the Crocodile. A standard Churchill tank, it's gun and turret still in place, but with the addition of a forward projecting flamethrower nozzle replacing the normal hull-mounted machine gun. A trailer connected to the tank carried four hundred gallons of a specially developed highly flammable petroleum-based mixture. There was a glass-topped tray of this stuff resting on a table. An almost colourless liquid with the consistency of thin jelly. The range of this terrifying device was quoted at over one hundred and twenty yards. John could only imagine the effect of it, both physically and psychologically, on enemy troops. Man has a primeval fear of fire and, as he knew from his experience with burning aeroplanes, it was a terrible way to die.

Last in the line were the amphibious swimming tanks known as DD for duplex drive. Connected to the main gearbox by a separate shaft they were fitted with steerable twin propellers at the rear for use in water reverting to standard track drive when beached. Above the tracks was a waterproof and sealed canvas screen erected on compressed, air-filled rubber struts which turned the tank into a boat, albeit an ungainly one, allowing the thirty-ton bulk of a Sherman tank to float and propel itself to shore. Launched off a beach they would swim at four knots and once landed would revert to track drive, collapse the canvas screens and be ready for immediate action. While they were not to demonstrate their aquatic abilities, they were to feature in the demonstration. There was also an array of Valentine DD light tanks that were being used for training.

The DDs were known colloquially as Donald Ducks to the tank crews. John wondered at their sea-keeping properties and how easily they might be breached in anything other than a calm sea. However, he did have one overwhelming impression. Used to the fine precision and light engineering of aeroplanes, John was initially taken aback by the agricultural nature of armoured fighting vehicles. It was the first time he'd ever been close up to a tank and he'd been surprised at the sheer size of it. They were massive, every inch of their thirty tons. No subtlety here, just simple brutal efficiency.

The whole event was being orchestrated by an energetic senior officer wearing oversized glasses. This was General Percy Hobart, the much-feared GOC of the 79th Armoured Division. Not for nothing were they known collectively as 'Hobart's Funnies'.

"He also happens to be Montgomery's brother-in-law through marriage," commented Jack. "It's a small family, the British Army."

Watching from a distance, Hobart somehow reminded John of a ring master at a circus. All he needed was the whip and, judging from the way his staff reacted to every order, it was as if he actually had one.

The great and the good were gathering. John and his companion distanced themselves some way off. Montgomery was already there, looking self-important as always, Churchill and others were expected later.

There were several film cameras set up to record the proceedings and John gravitated towards them. As he got closer, he spied a young, studious looking bespectacled RNVR Lieutenant with the emerald-green stripe of the Technical Branch on his sleeve.

John and Luke stared at each other in mutual disbelief, laughing as they shook hands.

"What are you doing here?"

"I might ask you the same thing."

John introduced Luke to Jack, explaining their connection. A light-hearted conversation between them then followed, mostly concentrating on what they were about to witness. The questions as to why they were there remained unanswered.

Whistles were blown and red flags were waved as the demonstration began. There was even a commentator equipped with a public address system to explain what was going on. A simulation of an opposed landing from the sea.

First the DD tanks, their canvas screens raised, advanced towards a row of concrete bunkers some two hundred yards ahead. They dropped their screens in unison and immediately opened fire. After a few rounds they pulled aside to clear the path for a couple of the petard mortars to launch their projectiles. Two enormous explosions demolished a pair of bunkers. Then, following in the wake of a row of flail tanks to clear the way, the fascines and bridge tanks forded an anti-tank ditch ahead of the bunkers. Finally, the Crocodile approached.

There was a rushing, gushing sound, then a vicious hissing from the nozzle. A golden wand shot forward and slapped on a concrete bunker immediately obliterating it in a sickening fire. Even from two hundred yards they could feel the heat – great clouds of evil smelling grey black smoke. It was over in seconds. No one needed a repeat performance.

Lunch came as a welcome distraction. An abundance of hot food and copious quantities of gin to fend off the cold. John had long observed the link between the British Armed Forces and gin. The two seemed inextricably linked.

Luke and John gossiped throughout the meal exchanging news of themselves, Matthew and Mark, happenings on the farm, and laughing about Elizabeth's latest exploits. Luke had learned not to worry about his older sister, though having John living at the Kensington flat was an advantage should anything untoward occur. A view, he knew, shared by his parents.

With the lunch completed, and the coffee drunk, Luke offered to give them a tour of an exhibition hut showcasing the establishment's creations.

John was intrigued by Luke's knowledge of each of the devices on display, and how readily he answered the questions from Jack without any hesitation. The use of an aniseed ball as a timing device dissolving under water simply brilliant. He had wondered what Luke had been up to these past few years but, of course, had known not to ask. Now he had an inkling. Luke was certainly well known here, greeted by many. It was almost as if he had the run of the place.

Luke smiled when he mentioned it.

"Yes, I've been here a few times before."

"And a few other places too, I expect."

Luke smiled again. "One or two."

On the journey back, while Jack wrote up his notes, John settled himself into a corner of the Humber and, wrapped warmly in his greatcoat, watched as the dusk descended over the countryside.

It had been an interesting day. Running into Luke had been a considerable surprise, so too had been his knowledge of the place. John had confirmed that Luke was a member of the RNVR, but not in what capacity, only that it was technical and something to do with weapons.

It was the nature of the war and the blanket of secrecy that smothered everything – that unless it was a person you were working directly with, one had absolutely no idea what anyone else was doing. He thought of all the people at SHAEF. He knew practically nothing of what most of them did. And so, it was for the four of them. Luke now knew that he was attached to SHAEF, but nothing else. Matthew was up somewhere near Fort William with the Commandos instructing on explosives, while Mark was stationed down in Dartmouth, navigating with Coastal Forces. Beyond that, none of them knew anything else of the other. He thought of Celia. Yes, she was at the main female ATA base at Hamble and busy delivering aircraft, mostly Spitfires hither and thither, but beyond that he knew very little.

John wiped the condensation from the inside of the glass as he continued to stare out at the darkening sky. Sometime after the war was over, and assuming they all survived, there were going to be a lot of stories to tell.

Jack had finished his notes and with a few words of apology announced his intention to sleep. Within minutes, he was. John continued to stare out of the window at the moving scenery, his mind drifting.

That the British, and the English in particular, were a nation of eccentrics was a pretty well-worn cliché. Nevertheless, it was true. It was a trait celebrated, encouraged and, for the most part, admired. A form of individualism frowned on in most other societies and punished in some.

What was remarkable to John, that in time of war these eccentric individuals somehow rapidly gravitated to positions where their peculiar talents could be put to use to do the most good.

Having spent the day in the company of some of these gifted people, John could only feel pride for the country of his birth and the society it fostered.

Rather ludicrously, at least to John's mind, a special meeting had been convened to approve an insignia for SHAEF. Army tradition, never to be underestimated or worse, ignored, was intertwined with its love of badges and insignia. While every RAF squadron had its own crest, they were not required to be worn on uniforms. Not so the army; there was a plethora of them varying from the bland to the surprising.

After months of deliberation involving the College of Heralds the design of a badge for SHAEF had been approved and all were now required to wear it as a shoulder flash. With the badge came an official description to explain its lineage.

"Upon a field of heraldic sable (BLACK), representing the darkness of Nazi oppression, is shown the sword of liberation in the form of a crusader's sword, the flames arising from the hilt and leaping up the blade. This represents avenging justice by which the enemy power will be broken in Nazi-dominated Europe. Above the sword is a rainbow emblematic of hope containing all the colours of which the Nation Flags of the Allies are composed. The heraldic chief of azure (BLUE) above the rainbow is emblematic of a state of peace and tranquillity the restoration of which to the enslaved people is the objective of the United Nations."

John read the description twice, wondering who had written it, concluding it was the Heralds. Wordy and solemn, ponderous, though it did describe what they were about.

Meanwhile, a sewing bee had begun amongst their secretarial staff and gratefully John surrendered his tunic to have it returned minutes later suitably adorned. As Julia, his designated secretary remarked, the effect on an RAF officer's uniform was really rather rakish. And a rarity.

At school they'd been taught to study their own effluent, both solid and liquid. Perhaps not study exactly, more observe, something to do with Greek and Roman medicine. It was a habit that had stuck.

John stared into the lavatory bowl for some considerable time, his expression one of surprise and incredulity. His morning defecation was one of peculiar proportions, continuous, half the diameter of normal, but at least four times as long. Consistency, towards soft.

As he dressed, he thought about it. Taking a cylinder of fixed volume, halving its diameter would result in an increase of length by a factor of four. Simple arithmetic. It had to be the food. A lack of fibre perhaps.

He'd been on a US base for the last three days. A conference to finalise the air campaign in the weeks leading up to D-Day. Progress had been slow, positive, but painfully ponderous. Americans took so long to say anything of substance, and there were an awful lot of them to say very little. Had this meeting been with, say, the Canadians, or any other of the Commonwealth Allies, it would have been concluded in a day.

American bases in England were effectively US sovereign territory, and everything on them, apart from fresh water, had been shipped in from the US. There were obscene quantities of food of every description, including, it appeared, unlimited supplies of ice cream. John hadn't seen ice cream in years.

It had to be the food. Luke, he knew, had spent some time with the Americans – he must remember to mention the phenomenon to him in his next letter and ask if he'd had a similar experience.

Dressed, and with a final ritual tug at his tunic, he steeled himself for another day of tedium. It would be eggs, bacon and hash browns for breakfast. More eggs than the British ration for a month. And coffee by the gallon. Always coffee, as the Americans did not favour tea. It was odd that, considering that it was the taxes on tea that had supposedly precipitated their war of independence. He must remember to ask about that.

John laughed. Perhaps not.

Their three-day conference had produced a plethora of American reports and John had spent his morning ploughing through them. A multitude of pages, closely typed containing all the usual levels of verbiage he'd grown to expect, superfluous sentences that did not need to be written, and long tedious paragraphs, whilst written in English, conveying little or no meaning. Reports that were tiresome to read at best and rarely rewarding the effort.

He made a few notes, produced *précis* and despatched them back to where they had come. Lunch did not dispel the headache his labour had inflicted.

Though the weather was cold, it was dry, and he sat on a bench in the park opposite Norfolk House to clear his head.

His morning had confirmed something that John had noticed before. The inherent violence of the American language. As he sat smoking, watching the sparrows and the pigeons, he thought of examples of it. The disassembly of, say, an engine. The English would strip it down, the American, tear it down. Measures of spirits, in English referred to as shorts, American, shots. Golf, not a game he much favoured, in English measured in strokes, American shots. The English played a round, Americans, shot a round. The English used spanners, Americans wrenches.

Lighting another cigarette, John thought of other examples until he bored of it. America was a violent society, wedded to the gun, reflected in its everyday language.

Draped over the radiator, it had taken half an hour for his socks to dry out. Padding around his office in his bare feet, trying to keep off the lino had got beyond a joke.

John examined his shoes carefully and reluctantly concluded they were beyond redemption. While the soles might be repairable, the uppers, slit across the toe on either foot, were not. Superbly comfortable, he'd been fond of them; old friends. Sadly, he wrote out a requisition form for a new pair of uniform shoes.

An orderly delivered the replacements during the afternoon. Shiny, black and extremely stiff. Flexing them repeatedly before putting them on made little difference. Walking in the rain might help. Failing that he would resort to stuffing them with potato peelings overnight.

He lay the old pair in the box, as one might place a body in a coffin, ready to go to some salvage scheme or other. Had he been in Leningrad a few months before during the siege the shoes most like would have been eaten. Like Charlie Chaplin in *The Gold Rush*, but without the humour.

***

The smell was unmistakable. As Jane, one of her fellow pilots at Hamble, carried the bag into the room, everyone gathered around her. They watched as she emptied its contents onto a table. Oranges, dozens of them, a present from an American base.

They stared at them, picking them up, smelling them. No one had seen an orange in years. The next question was what to do with them.

Someone worked out there were enough for everyone on the base to get one segment each. Plates were brought out and with much excitement, the oranges were peeled and divided up for distribution. The peel was not wasted. Put back in the bag it would go to the cook house for marmalade and cakes.

With something resembling a religious sacrament, they each ate their single segment, slowly, savouring the taste.

It reminded Celia of Christmas past. An orange always to be found at the base of a Christmas stocking.

83

A late afternoon meeting with Henderson had found them in the pub by the early evening. Henderson's favourite, overlooking the river.

He was, Luke had noticed, in one of his more reflective moods. Their business had been concluded amicably and quicker than was usual; ready agreement reached, Luke's suggestions accepted without the normal advocative inquisition. Perhaps he was tired.

The weather was quiet, early April, and though the temperature was not yet spring like, they had chosen to sit in the open. Henderson was looking at the river, paying particular attention to an elm nodding towards the water.

"That tree's going to fall any time now," he said, finally. "It won't make leaf again. The first strong blow and it will be gone."

Luke had followed his gaze. The tree was indeed leaning. He estimated the angle at about twenty-five degrees from the vertical. Luke wondered at the mass of the tree, how far up the trunk the centre of gravity was. What would be the turning moment acting on the base; how did that compare to the combined resistance of the root ball and the surrounding soil. When the first exceeded the second, the tree would fall.

"I've been re-reading Gibbon," said Henderson, bringing Luke's thoughts to an end.

"Decline and Fall. Roman Empire."

"Very good."

"Not really. I saw it on the floor by your coffee table."

Henderson nodded.

"Any particular reason?"

"Refreshing my memory. Always good to do that occasionally."

Henderson took a long draw on his pint then poked away at his pipe.

"When any repressive regime collapses – monarchies, empires, dictatorships – anarchy and chaos invariably follows. All the factions within a society, political, religious, social, freed from the yoke of suppression come to the fore and rise to the surface from some hidden depth to then slaughter each other in biblical proportions. It can take years, centuries sometimes, before the situation settles into something resembling normality. Or, more correctly, a new normality."

Luke waited a moment before he replied. Though well used to Henderson's observations, few were as apocalyptic as this one.

"And then, I suppose, the whole process begins again."

Henderson sighed. "Eventually, inevitably. Geological, like the earth's crust. Never still."

***

The Overlord plan, in addition to landing tens of thousands of troops and umpteenth thousand tons of stores, also required the landing of over 20,000 vehicles on D-Day itself and continuing into the following day. The Mulberry artificial harbours, meanwhile, were not expected to come into commission until some days later.

Landing off the ramps of the various types of landing craft required transit through sea water and, depending on the particular circumstances, the depth of the surf would vary between a few inches or a few feet. All vehicles, irrespective of type, were required to be waterproof. Snorkelling systems for the air intakes and exhaust systems was relatively straightforward and could easily be manufactured in quantity. However, the waterproofing of vehicle electrics and the other sensitive pieces of equipment was more complicated.

The problem was further compounded by the sheer number of different types of vehicle in current use by the British Army. Unprepared, as usual, for the outbreak of war, motor transport and equipment had been added ad hoc as it became available. The luxury of standardised equipment for all the units had never been achieved. Thus, excluding all armour, well over a hundred different types of vehicle needed to be waterproofed, each with their own peculiarities. The US Army, having entered the conflict later and from a lower base, had managed to standardise its vehicle types to less than a dozen.

What was required was a substance, universally deployable by untrained troops in the field, that was plastic in nature, that was heat resistant, provided insulation and was impervious to water and salt. It was also required to be easily moulded by hand to suit each and every contingency and, most importantly, when applied would stay put.

After much study and experiment, a compound of heavy grease and lime mixed with shredded asbestos as a binder appeared to be the most promising solution. But there remained one problem. Once applied, it showed a marked reluctance to stay where it was put when subjected to vibration and gravity. With thousands of tons of this stuff about to be produced, a solution was required, and required quickly.

The US Army contained a small but highly competent scientific and experimental section who, with other efforts failing, were tasked with finding a solution. Returning to basics by examining each of the compounds' individual constituents, they discovered that the problem lay in the minute moisture fraction naturally contained in the asbestos. Baking it dry before mixing immediately solved the problem. And to everyone's immense relief. As the final report commented, by such simple things can hinge the success or failure of great campaigns. It was Luke's story of Napoleon's horseshoes in Russia all over again.

It was a lesson. John could only ponder what others were still to be learned. However great the planning for Overlord, irrespective of the thousands of people employed, something was bound to be missed.

Every branch of the Armed services had its own particular phraseology or jargon. It was the same in all the major professions, especially in financial circles and again particularly with lawyers. Like members of any exclusive club, it reinforced a sense of belonging, a delusional feeling of security.

While John was previously well acquainted with the conversational tropes of the RAF, he was now trilingual insofar as he could now speak navy or army as circumstances required. Of these, the army was the most prone to speak in acronyms. Whole sentences could be constructed which would have been utterly meaningless to an outsider. For his own amusement John had composed a couple that, while sounding mightily impressive were, in themselves, complete gobbledygook. He was saving them for the next time he had to deal with a particularly pompous army officer.

In this atmosphere of language reduction, some acronyms had more significance than others. D-Day, for example, meant nothing more than the start day of any given operation: likewise, H-Hour.

But some D-Days were bigger than others. D-Day for Overlord was destined to dwarf all others.

*

Since COSSAC's inception, Norfolk House had incorporated an Army photographic unit reporting directly to General Morgan. As the months progressed, and now absorbed by SHAEF, their numbers had gradually increased to the extent that by the spring of 1944 there were around fifty of them, about equally split between photographic interpreters and supporting draughtsmen. Display boards in the map room, updated daily, illustrated the current state of the defences on and around the Normandy beaches and in almost real time.

Aerial photographic reconnaissance by the Allies had grown to the point where the whole of western Europe was now under constant surveillance. Ever-increasing numbers of reconnaissance squadrons using the latest Spitfire XIs and Mosquito XVIs, based at RAF Benson in Oxfordshire, were flying up to eighty sorties a day producing over a million photographs a month. Such a prodigious output of raw material had spawned a huge organisation.

RAF Medmenham centred at Danesfield House on a picturesque bend on the Thames between Marlow and Henley had been requisitioned early in the war and had become the Allies prime location for photographic interpretation. Conveniently placed close to RAF Benson, its ample grounds had allowed for a rapid expansion. By the spring of 1944 over three thousand people were based there, including a very large number of WAAFs.

John had been looking for an excuse to visit Medmenham for some time, so when Jack Sheppard, who was a regular visitor, suggested they have another outing, John immediately accepted.

Danesfield House was an imposing, though not particularly attractive mock Tudor pile built of white chalk. It was peculiar looking with tall brick chimneys combined with a series of castellated towers imposed upon it. Neither house nor castle, it looked confused, if a building could be confused, not entirely comfortable in its surroundings. It was that type of construction erected in the home counties by nineteenth century industrial barons from the north to celebrate their success and to launch them, and their daughters, into society. Surrounding the house, the formal gardens had been subsumed by a succession on interlocking Nissen huts sprouting over a large area.

While Jack went off to do whatever it was, John accepted the offer of a tour. They were well used to accommodating visitors at Medmenham even retaining a pool of staff to act as guides and a large room was laid out for the purpose.

Using a series of similar photographs, the three stages of photographic interpretation were explained to him.

The first phase was exclusively tactical – immediate examination of the photographs often while they were still wet. Position of ships in harbour or whether at sea, bomb damage assessment, enemy airfield developments or, in the case of large engagements, enemy troop movements and dispositions. These assessments were made at whatever airfield the photo-reconnaissance aircraft had landed. Completed within an hour, any information gleaned would be then conveyed by teleprinter to whatever force or command that required the information.

Within the next twenty-four hours, the second phase of the interpretation would be undertaken. This was the co-ordinated analysis, where teams of interpreters combed through the day's output producing enemy activity reports every twelve hours, summarising the particular intelligence gathered from the past twenty-four hours.

The third phase of the process was the most extensive. Specialist operators would subject each of the images to detailed analysis. Shipping, railways, industry, aircraft and airfields, damage assessment, troop movements, road traffic and all the rest. From these assessments and all the previous assessments made use of for comparison, the activity of the enemy could be monitored continuously to the most extraordinary levels of detail. Under constant and relentless surveillance, there was precious little that happened in western Europe that escaped the scrutiny of the eyes of Medmenham.

Typically, a roll of film taken by the reconnaissance aircraft produced five hundred photographs. These were shot as stereo pairs, since each exposure was timed to give an overlap of sixty per cent with the previous shot. The forward movement of the aircraft between the two changed the relative angle between the pair of images. This alloyed the employment of stereoscopic viewing.

A stereoscopic viewer combined a pair of magnifying lenses mounted in a fixed frame resting on the pair of photographs. By moving the photographs relative to each other while under the viewer, there was a point where the images would fuse together to give a 3-D image similar to that produced by a magic lantern show. Suddenly, leaping into life, the level of detail would increase dramatically allowing not only easy identification, but facilitating accurate measurements to be made. It took a while for the technique to be learned, but once it was, the results were such that stereoscopic viewing had become the basis of the whole of photographic interpretation.

By way of demonstration, Medmenham had a viewer set up on a stereo image pair taken directly above the Eiffel Tower. Having been shown what to do, John sat down leaning over the viewer, an eye to each glass, while moving the pair of photographs beneath. Suddenly, and dramatically, the image came into relief. The Eiffel Tower seemed to leap upwards towards him and involuntarily John jerked his head back to avoid being stabbed in the eye. He joined in the laughter around him. This was the effect his guides were intending to achieve.

John spent half an hour looking at matched pairs of photographs. It was quite addictive. Airfields, town centres, a series of Normandy beaches. Viewed in stereo the level of detail was astonishing, making a deep impression on him.

The last part of his tour took him to the model making section. This was housed in one of the larger huts on the site and resembled one huge workshop. The models produced were of three basic types. Small scale models of the maps of northern France fully representative of the landscape; roads and buildings on a model about five feet square. The models of the Normandy landing beaches were the largest at about sixteen feet square, and stretched from the shoreline to twelve miles inland. They gave precise details of every building, defence installation and fixed gun emplacement of whatever calibre. Roads, rivers, footpaths and tracks between the patchwork of hedges and fields clearly delineated in three dimensions. The final type of model was being produced specifically for the airborne assault troops, particularly the glider pilots. These showed the landing and drop zones in minute detail, every tree and bush clearly modelled in their area of operation. Well over a hundred of these models were being produced in support of the landings and, by making plaster casts of the originals, copies were being made for distribution to the various commands. Every soldier once he landed would recognise immediately where he was and know what was around him.

Overall, Medmenham was a most impressive organisation, the product of its labours of inestimable value. While it was but one of the many tools the Allies were employing in support of the invasion, it was certainly one of the more impressive ones. The moment when the tip of the Eiffel Tower seemed to stab him in the eye would stay with John for a long time.

It was rare to see civilians at Norfolk House, but there had been a couple wandering around for the past few days. John had no idea who they were or why they were here, but one thing he was certain of: one was American while the other was English. It was the cut of their clothes that gave the clue.

Both were middle aged and wearing dark suits. The Englishman's, beautifully cut of expensive material, worn in the English style of being slightly oversized. The American suit, plainly cut and ill fitting, machine made. What really distinguished them from a distance was the trouser length.

Englishmen wore their trousers long at the back, down over the heel, the front creasing on the ankle. American trousers were cut shorter, front and back, an inch or two above the ankle; half mast, almost as if they had been grown out of.

John had enquired as to why several times and had garnered a variety of answers. The one he favoured was spurs. Americans wore their trousers above the ankle so as not to impede their spurs when mounted on horses. It was a western tradition. Also, higher trouser bottoms avoided them getting caked in mud on dirt roads. It had become the American fashion, however inelegant.

John had never really understood fashion. He remembered women before the war, eagerly awaiting news of the latest Paris fashions in the spring – had hemlines risen an inch, dropped, adjusting the skirt lengths thereafter so as not to be 'out of fashion', the ultimate disgrace. Somehow it all seemed so trivial.

But fashion was important, especially for women. Evenings spent with Celia and Elizabeth proved that. To John, fashion seemed just an endless series of departures leading to unknown destinations. Perhaps that was the point of it. Who knew?

And then there were the ties. While both were wearing a similar style of stripped tie, their nationality determined the direction of the stripes. British ties, diagonal from the right shoulder. American, the opposite, from the left. It was the question of a monarchy or a republic. Napoleon again.

The first act Napoleon made after invading any territory was to impose a new law of the road, henceforth, you drive on the right-hand side of the road. Since ninety per cent of the population was right-handed, it was the natural practise to drive on the left. The favoured arm towards a potential assailant when passing on the road.

Napoleon, by reversing the natural practice, immediately demonstrated the change in regime. For similar reasons, the Americans had switched to riding on the right after declaring independence from Britain.

Symbolism was power.

84

Luke had seen less and less of Henderson for the past couple of months. The professor's involvement in a project he dismissively referred to as 'tube alloys' was consuming more and more of his time. What this concerned Luke had no idea. He'd asked a couple of questions and received vague and meaningless replies. Though his curiosity was roused, Luke had chosen to enquire no further. Something in Henderson's tone indicated that nothing more would be forthcoming. A consequence of Henderson's preoccupation meant that more of what had previously been his exclusive domain now devolved to Luke.

One bright Tuesday morning in late April a college porter arrived at his rooms to present him with two large files accompanied with a covering note from Henderson. Under the generic heading of 'Operation Crossbow', the files contained everything that was currently known of the secret German vengeance weapon programmes.

Luke's instructions were short. Absorb the contents of the files and thereafter act as Henderson's representative at any future committee meetings held in London or elsewhere. His brief was to observe and report to keep Henderson abreast of progress and developments.

Though excited by a whole new project, this brief rather reminded Luke of how his work with Henderson had begun. This reversion to mere monitoring and reportage rather irked him. However, given the subject matter, he chose to swallow his pride, at least for the moment.

They were large files, each several inches thick, containing all the major reports of the investigations to date, together with Henderson's somewhat waspish commentary. Henderson's opinion of most people was fairly contemptuous at the best of times and utterly irreverent regardless of station or reputation. Light relief to leaven the otherwise sombre content.

Since the very beginning of the war, German propaganda had threatened the use of secret weapons which would revolutionise modern warfare. Starting with a speech by Hitler in September 1939, Goebbels had repeated the claims, and more regularly as the war progressed.

Though initially dismissed and belittled by the British press, the claims had been taken seriously by British scientific intelligence. Slowly, through a wide range of disparate sources and greatly augmented by the ever-increasing aerial photographic reconnaissance of Germany and the occupied countries, a gradual understanding of what these secret weapons might be, and the threat they posed, began to be realised.

The first real evidence came in December 1942 from Sweden; reports of gossip overheard in Berlin of a ballistic, long-range rocket being developed by the German army. Further reports in January indicated that the Germans had constructed a research facility, factories and a testing site, at Peenemünde on the Baltic coast due north of Berlin.

These later reports prompted the first dedicated photo-reconnaissance sortie of the Peenemünde area. Poor weather over the target mixed with heavy snow on the ground combined to make the results inconclusive. A second sortie in March confirmed large-scale construction works, but little else. Nothing resembling a rocket, or what might possibly be one, was to be seen on the prints.

At this stage, while rumours had suggested these rockets were over a hundred feet long with a range approaching two hundred miles, no one had any idea what they actually looked like. There was also a total ignorance of what sort of infrastructure would be required to support such a weapon. The photo-interpretation specialists at Medmenham were severely hampered without a knowledge of what they were looking for.

Whilst hard evidence was proving difficult to acquire, intelligence from a widening base of sources, not least eavesdropped conversations between German generals captured in North Africa and now held in an exclusive prisoner-of-war camp in north London, confirmed the existence of the rockets.

This rising tide of fragmentary information, reported to a wide number of organisations, resulted in a memo being sent to Churchill by the Chiefs of Staff Committee in mid-April 1943. The memo suggested that all these disparate activities be brought under the control of a single man tasked to direct and co-ordinate these efforts and establish the true reality of the threat. Duncan Sandys MP was the suggested man.

Duncan Sandys was an interesting choice. A man of proven ability who, rarely, had practical experience of rockets since, when in the TA, had commanded an experimental anti-aircraft rocket battery based at the testing ground in Aberporth in Cardigan Bay on the west Wales coast. Following a serious road accident he had been appointed as parliamentary secretary to the Ministry of Supply with responsibility for weapon research, development and production. In addition to this he was eminently well connected and he also happened to be Churchill's son-in-law. His immediate appointment by the Prime Minister ensured complete political and inter-service support while demonstrating an urgency of purpose.

Duncan Sandys did not tarry. Setting up an office in Shell Mex House, strategically placed mid-way between Westminster and the Air Ministry in Kingsway, he immediately began to establish direct communications with all the appropriate agencies and government departments. He also recruited other able people, both military and civilian, to be seconded to his office.

Recognising that his first task was to determine the credibility of all the intelligence so far acquired, copies of every file was sequestered to a central registry at Shell Mex House. Further, as an opening gambit to gain an understanding of the prevailing knowledge, a questionnaire was prepared and circulated to every interested party.

Two of the many people to whom this questionnaire was addressed were Dr R. V. Jones, assistant director of scientific intelligence at the Air Ministry, and Professor Lindemann, Lord Cherwell since 1941, scientific adviser to the Prime Minister.

While Jones thought the possibility of a German long-range rocket was entirely feasible, Cherwell's view was the complete opposite. Such was Cherwell's scorn of such a development, his spurious suggestions did nothing but hinder progress.

At this point in the file there was a page of Henderson's pointed observations. R. V. Jones, Luke read, was a man somewhat seduced by his own feelings of self-importance. But, undeniably brilliant and generally sound. Lindemann, a fellow professor at Oxford, had been loathed by Henderson for many years. He described him as a non-smoking, teetotal vegetarian with a pathological, wilful unsoundness of judgement who, given a choice between two opinions, would invariably support the wrong one. Jones and Cherwell's fractious relationship was not helped since Cherwell had been Jones's mentor when the later had been at Oxford.

Peenemünde featured in a great number of the reports that Duncan Sandys and his staff reviewed. Being on the coast of the Baltic Sea it bore an immediate resemblance to the position of Aberporth and the Irish Sea. It was a coincidence that drew an immediate suspicion.

Duncan Sandys issued his first interim report in mid-May 1943. It was at best vague and inconclusive reflecting the maze of conflicting information so far obtained. That said, on one point it was unequivocal: the Germans had been developing a heavy rocket capable of long-range bombardment for some considerable time. The collected evidence suggested that these development efforts were well advanced.

His report recommended a series of actions to be put in place immediately: a counter bombing programme on all the facilities suspected to be involved, while the full implications of such a long-range rocket attack on the UK should be considered.

The report was immediately approved by the Joint Chiefs and, in the English way, the Air Ministry formed a subcommittee to make recommendations on a series of topics. These included reconnaissance, pre-emptive bombing and the formulation of an outline deception programme.

Duncan Sandys's report had also suggested that the long-range weapon work was being conducted in parallel with other developments such as airborne rocket torpedoes and jet-propelled manned aircraft. It had proved to be a prescient comment.

Cherwell meanwhile castigated the report's conclusions, particularly the suggestion that the rocket used some form of liquid fuel. Since the British had failed to produce such a rocket, so therefore had the Germans. In his view the whole thing was a giant hoax designed to deflect the Allies bombing effort. While he viewed the possibility of some type of flying bomb more favourably, his view on the rocket did nothing but confirm his myopia and descent into the classic trap of 'if we can't do it, neither can they'. Cherwell's views, though he continued to snipe from the sidelines, were increasingly ignored from this point.

Henderson had put a star against Cherwell's name at this point and had scribbled 'utter prick'. It was a sentiment shared by many, particularly R. V. Jones.

In late June, Duncan Sandys produced another report including a review of all the intelligence reports received since his interim statement and a selection of the latest reconnaissance photographs.

Two days later a meeting of the War Cabinet Defence Committee was held chaired by the Prime Minister. The combined arguments and logic of

Sandys and Jones prevailed over Cherwell's intransigence. It was agreed that Peenemünde, now recognised as the centre of the German rocket activity, should be attacked by a heavy bomber force at the earliest opportunity.

Further instructions were issued. Duncan Sandys's remit was now extended to include pilotless aircraft and, or, jet-propelled aircraft developments in Germany, and a report on these additional investigations was to be issued in a month's time.

Luke was now about halfway through the first file. It was, he thought, somehow akin to reading a detective novel, albeit one with a haphazard plot. Feeling hungry, he went to lunch before beginning the next chapter.

As the search for the German secret weapons widened, so the committees and their associated subcommittees reporting to Duncan Sandys multiplied accordingly. Having previously been known as the German long-range rocket detection investigation, or GLRRD, it was decided that a new code name was required to reflect the now expanded remit.

There was a view, particularly prevalent in Whitehall, that long-range bombardment through the use of unmanned delivery systems was somehow unsporting, ungentlemanly. Thus, from late July 1943, the whole of Duncan Sandys activities came under the heading of Operation Bodyline.

This was a reference to the infamous England Ashes cricket tour of Australia in 1932–33 where England developed a theory of leg side bowling, or bodyline, to negate the superiority of the Australian batting. It was intimidatory, dangerous, and as a result many of the Australian batsman were hit by the ball and badly hurt. This had led to a serious diplomatic spat between the two governments. Judged by the cricket authorities to be not in the spirit of the game, bodyline bowling was subsequently banned and the laws of cricket changed.

Luke had shaken his head sadly at reading this. War had ceased to be gentlemanly, if it ever had been, in the eighteenth century. 1914–18 and the extensive use of poison gas bore witness. The use of the word bodyline said something about the British civil service that did not encourage.

Following the instruction from the War Cabinet in late June, Operation Hydra, the bombing attack on Peenemünde, had been in preparation for several weeks. It was to be a concentrated force attack aimed at a small area, the first such type of operation attempted by Bomber Command. Almost six hundred aircraft, the majority Lancasters, where to attack an area of roughly seven square miles. Bright moonlight, sufficient hours of darkness and suitable weather was required and the night of 16–17 August provided just such an opportunity. Eighteen hundred tons of bombs were dropped for the loss of forty aircraft.

Aerial reconnaissance after the raid confirmed considerable destruction, particularly to the buildings making up the Peenemünde complex. Whilst the threat posed by the German secret weapon programmes had not been eliminated, the operational deployment of the weapons had possibly been delayed by some months. Meanwhile, the intense intelligence effort continued unabated.

By early September, independent intelligence sources from France, Geneva and Denmark via Sweden had begun to confirm that there were two distinct secret weapons. A rocket projectile, under the direction of the German army and known as the A-4; and another, a pilotless aircraft designated PHI-7, under control of the Luftwaffe.

The realisation that there were two distinct weapon programmes prompted Duncan Sandys to restructure his department. While Bodyline would continue with the pursuit of the A-4 rocket, the search for the PHI-7 flying bomb would now devolve to the Air Ministry.

With these new arrangements agreed by the Joint Chiefs, Duncan Sandys issued a report reflecting these changed responsibilities. An attached annex reviewed what was known of the flying bomb.

It was launched from the ground by catapult and thereafter propelled by some form of rocket unit. It carried an explosive charge of perhaps several thousand kilograms. It was autonomously guided, without the intervention of ground-based aids, and was, therefore, not susceptible to jamming.

Assuming that it flew neither exceptionally high nor exceptionally fast, it would be vulnerable to standard interception methods in common with any other aircraft. In order that these defences should be sufficiently prepared for such a device, it was now imperative to ascertain the range, operational altitude, speed and accuracy of the weapon.

Putting a marker in the file, Luke closed it and made himself some tea. Lighting a cigarette, he stared out of the window looking at the sky.

While reading he'd been making a few notes. He now split these into two separate sections: one for the rocket, the other for the flying bomb. On a separate sheet he listed the governing criteria for the PHI-7: range, altitude, speed, warhead size, accuracy, propulsion method. It was the latter, the means of propulsion, which interested him the most.

Rockets were devices that carried both fuel and an oxygen supply to enable combustion. By nature, they were short duration devices: otherwise, their dimensions would become so disproportionate, and so heavy, that the rocket thrust would not support them.

A flying bomb, powered by a rocket, would not need a catapult to launch it. But, some form of air-breathing rocket propulsion system, which didn't carry its own oxygen supply, might.

Luke stopped speculating at this point. There was another six months' worth of the files to read yet. And now, he had the added incentive to see whether he was right.

Arguments around the feasibility, or otherwise, of a successful German rocket continued to bound around Whitehall throughout the autumn and winter of 1943. There were pages of it in the file, and while interesting in itself, Luke chose to read through it at speed since the debates contained little fact.

The intelligence investigation had shifted, more from the weapons themselves, to the ground facilities being built in France that were suspected to be in support of them. In late October Duncan Sandys had instituted a programme to re-photograph the whole of the French Atlantic coast from Cherbourg northwards. Around the same time, data from the French resistance via Berne in Switzerland, carried to England in diplomatic bags, had arrived at the Air Ministry. It was a major prize – a complete set of builder's construction drawings for a cluster of low buildings of a very peculiar nature. Two of these buildings had a very distinctive shape resembling skis laid on their sides. There was also a line of concrete plinths, gradually rising in height.

By early November, six of these sites had been recognised and photographed. Analysis and the use of compass bearings showed that a line through the axis of the plinths all pointed at central London. The conclusion drawn was that the plinths were footings for some kind of catapult ramp.

In addition to these distinctive structures, several huge bunkers appeared to be under construction, and well inland from the coast of France. The purpose of these was unknown.

The constant arguments in Whitehall had caused the Prime Minister some vexation. In an attempt to resolve the matter, he had formed a special committee of enquiry chaired by the Minister of Aircraft Production, Sir Stafford Cripps. This was to make recommendations as to the direction and purpose of future investigations.

Before Cripps could make his final report the rivalry between the various factions, particularly Duncan Sandys and the Air Ministry, had come to a head. Only one side could win, and that was the Air Ministry. Duncan Sandys would relinquish his responsibilities in the search for the German rocket and the Shell Mex House operation would be disbanded. Henceforth, the Air Ministry in general, and Dr R. V. Jones in particular, would assume full responsibility for both the rocket and the pilotless aircraft investigations.

Bodyline was no more. Now the official designation was Operation Crossbow.

Sir Stafford Cripps issued his report in mid-November. He concluded that there was no doubt the Germans had been experimenting with a series of long-range weapons for some considerable time. Amongst these were a glide bomb, a pilotless aircraft, and a rocket. Beyond this statement, the report was poor, muddled in its arguments and confusing in its conclusions.

Henderson's comments were caustic. He loathed lawyers almost as much as he loathed ascetics; it was Cripps misfortune to be both.

The Joint Intelligence Committee formulated its new Crossbow subcommittee in late November, the membership of which was somewhat substandard. The chairman, Claude Pelly, an air commodore, plucked from some relatively obscure job in Cairo, had no previous intelligence experience. It was a very doubtful choice.

The brief of this new subcommittee was to monitor and advise, request air reconnaissance as it saw fit and recommend targets for attack. Henderson thought them singularly ill-suited to the task.

The dynamism injected by Duncan Sandys had been dissipated, digested by the Whitehall bureaucratic machine. It did not bode well.

The new Joint Intelligence Committee, JIC, subcommittee had issued its first report in late November. It added little but further strata of confusion. The report had reviewed the threat to Britain from glide bombs, pilotless aircraft and long-range rockets by attempting to place the latest intelligence into the context of the previous reports by Duncan Sandys and Sir Stafford Cripps. Endeavouring to be consistent, what new evidence there was had been manipulated to suit the previous conclusions. It was not a particularly helpful approach. While there was some discussion of the construction sites in France and their current rate of progress, there were no additional details on the weapons themselves.

As Henderson had scribbled, the shiny new Crossbow was yet to fire a single bolt.

It was the photographic interpreters at Medmenham who were to make the definitive breakthrough. By careful, meticulous examination of all the relevant aerial photographs, of the launch sites at Peenemünde and the similar French installations taken over the last six months, and by making very careful measurements of the layouts of the buildings and the gaps between, Medmenham had concluded that the PHI-7, now known as the FZG76, resembled a very small aeroplane with a wingspan of around twenty feet. The trick now was to find it.

Knowing what they were looking for, the best available images were re-examined. The work took days but something resembling a tiny cruciform shape, hardly larger than the grain of the photographic emulsion, was discovered alongside one of the ski ramp buildings.

Another specific reconnaissance mission over Peenemünde was ordered and flown in late November. This provided the final proof. A tiny pilotless aeroplane, sitting on the base of an inclined launch ramp pointing out to sea. Further analysis of areas along the Baltic coast, eastwards from Peenemünde, revealed launch sites identical to the ski sites found in France. The flying bomb's form and the method of its launching were definitively proven.

The work at Medmenham had been a triumph of analysis and, in some ways, a reverse of the normal process. Typically, something observed would be analysed to determine what it was. While this had been done for the launch sites, what it was they had been designed to launch had first to be postulated, then tested by observation to be proved, and then confirmed by further observation.

Theory, experiment, repeat and confirm. It was the scientific method applied to aerial reconnaissance, and it had worked, spectacularly.

Armed with this conclusive evidence from Medmenham, Dr R. V. Jones combined it with all the data gleaned from his array of intelligence sources. Just before Christmas he issued a report, the most comprehensive yet on the flying bomb.

The report was wide ranging and covered not only the weapon itself but details of its manufacture and deployment, the German organisation formed to support it and a full summary of the results of the weapon's trials monitored from Peenemünde.

The FZG76 was an unmanned flying bomb of cruciform shape around twenty feet long with a wingspan similar to its length. It was catapult launched from an inclined ramp 125 feet long rising at ten degrees. The maximum range was 155 miles at a maximum flying speed of 400mph. Warhead size was around 2,000 pounds. Guidance was magnetic. The only vagueness in Jones's report was the means of propulsion, concluding it was some kind of rocket.

The report concluded with an estimate of the likely size of the forthcoming attack. Taking account of the number of launch sites, estimated to be around one hundred, and the maximum rate of fire of each site, Jones predicted a launch rate of up to 800 missiles each day.

The Germans intended this to be the greatest air assault mounted against southern England since 1940. Massed pilotless aircraft attacks, continuously launched day and night, might completely overwhelm the Allied air defences inflicting massed destruction while, at the same time, jeopardising the invasion of France due for the spring of 1944.

Luke finished writing up his notes and closed the completed file. Taking off his glasses he rubbed his eyes. He had been reading all day, and it had been a long day ending with a chilling finale. Tomorrow he would start on the second file, beginning in January 1944.

Luke had lingered over his breakfast. The prospect of another day of intense reading was less than enticing. Nevertheless, having exhausted his supply of excuses, he returned to his desk soon after nine and opened the file.

1944 had not begun well. Attempts to destroy the French ski sites by bombing from altitude were not proving successful. The Americans, now fully briefed and involved, were becoming fractious. Frustrated and irritated they had begun to construct a replica ski site, using the German plans, methods and specifications, on a range in Florida. This would then be subjected to a series of experimental attacks intended to determine the best approach to ensure their destruction.

The ever-festering relationship between R. V. Jones and the JIC Crossbow Committee had escalated between Christmas and the new year. Jones, who much preferred to work alone, considered the Crossbow Committee to be an irritating irrelevance and had consistently briefed Cherwell privately in an attempt to undermine it. It was a situation that could not be allowed to continue. In early January responsibility for both the rocket and the pilotless aircraft was handed to Air Vice Marshal Norman Bottomley and the JIC

Crossbow Committee was abolished. Jones had won: both weapons would remain his exclusive preserve.

Reading of these bureaucratic battles around Whitehall drove Luke close to despair. That so much effort was expended on internecine turf warfare appalled him. The politics of large organisations was something he knew little of and had minimal interest in. Whatever it was he might do in the future it was an area he resolved to avoid wherever possible.

There were some positives. The defensive component of Fighter Command, charged with the defence of the United Kingdom from air attack, had issued its first plan for the defence of London, Bristol and the Solent from a pilotless aircraft attack. Code names had been issued: 'Diver' for the flying bomb, 'Big Ben' for the rocket.

Whilst there were plenty of pages in the file to cover the next couple of months, very little new information was forthcoming. The bombing of the ski sites had continued unabated with some success and, while some were seen to be under repair, the majority appeared to have been abandoned. A suspicion had begun to grow that something else was afoot, though what it might be was unknown.

In March the air defence plan from the Air Ministry was finalised. There were to be three lines of defence. Fighters were to be the initial line, flying standing patrols over the Channel. Anti-aircraft guns spread across the North Downs in Sussex and Kent were to be the second. Finally, barrage balloons would form a physical barrier south of London.

Ninety-six ski sites had been identified in France by March 1944 and all of them had been subjected to bombing attack, some multiple times. Extrapolating forward, from the results obtained so far, suggested that every site would be destroyed by the end of April. Thus, the report added optimistically, the threat of the FZG76 would be considered neutralised by May.

While the new year had yielded little new information on the flying bomb, intelligence on the rocket was, if anything, even less. Some form of reorganisation was underway in Germany with indications of a power struggle between the Luftwaffe and the army, and all the various organisations they supported.

Bureaucracy was not the exclusive preserve of the British and Americans.

Luke had completed his reading of Henderson's files. He wrote up his notes and then rearranged his filing system, allocating a particular piece of floor space to the German secret weapons. The locks on the door to his rooms had been revised at the beginning of the year. He now lived in what was, effectively, a safe.

The Germans had made a substantial investment in these weapon programmes and Luke doubted if the destruction of all the ski launching sites would be the end of the threat. There was also the outstanding question of the rocket.

Something else worried him. Whilst there was considerable data on the capabilities of both the flying bomb and the rocket, there was still very little information on the actual vehicles themselves and, as far as he was aware, no physical evidence whatsoever. Without this it was impossible to gauge the true nature of the threats or devise effective countermeasures against them.

85

April now passed into May. As the date for the invasion approached, the mood within SHAEF had changed. Speculation and theoretical planning now became reality, and with it the nagging fear, the awful doubt and the low sickening feeling of dread at the consequences of failure.

While, on the surface, optimism had become not so much an attitude as an outright duty, John knew that all within their private selves harboured the same fears.

Should Overlord fail, Germany's grip on western Europe would be consolidated, and the Russian campaign would be thwarted by the release of German troops and resources from the west. Another invasion attempt would not be possible for at least two years, if at all. And worse. If America, bloodied and defeated by Germany, decided instead to concentrate on its war in the Pacific and Japan, Europe would be under German domination for years to come. Generations. Alternatively, the Russians might eventually prevail, stopping only when they reached the English Channel, the whole of western Europe under the Soviet yoke.

The consequences of the failure of Overlord were truly terrifying.

There were now three and a half million US service personnel in the UK, who between them had taken over about twenty per cent of the country. Vast swathes of southern England had been appropriated to house their camps, equipment parks and training areas, while the bulge of east Anglia was now affectively one huge US air base. Personally, John had benefited, he was drawing a huge rent from his own house courtesy of the American Army.

His daily commute to Norfolk House was now complicated by hordes of Americans swirling around on the roads and pavements taking in the sights. London's local economy was booming. The soldiers, in their tailored uniforms, had plenty of dollars and were eager to spend, while Londoners found ever-increasing ways to relieve them of their money, both legal and otherwise.

The Germans had never managed to invade, but now the Americans certainly had.

Operation Neptune, the seaborne component of the Overlord plan was, in Admiral Ramsay's words, destined to be the greatest amphibious operation in the history of mankind. In early June, seven thousand ships of every description, including over four thousand landing vessels, would cross the Channel and converge on a fifty-mile front ahead of the Normandy coastline. Their task was to safely deliver 133,000 men from the sea to the shore together with thousands upon thousands of tons of stores and equipment, and all within the first twenty-four hours of the invasion.

By early April, Ramsay had issued a provisional copy of his orders, followed by a full distribution of the final plan by the end of the month. For the co-ordinated movement of seven thousand ships the orders were, of necessity, extremely detailed and complex. Arranged chronologically, they ran over a thousand pages of closely typed foolscap text.

With the plans laid and the orders distributed, in early May SHAEF had arranged for a series of briefings for its staff not directly involved with the naval operation as an appreciation exercise. Similar, reciprocal briefings were to be given by the Air Forces and the British and American Armies.

Several hundred had gathered in the map room at Norfolk House that afternoon, John included, as two senior naval officers, one RN and a commander from the American Navy, gave an overview of the Neptune Plan.

A huge map at the end of the room was the focus of the presentation and, after a few preliminary remarks, this was unveiled with a suitable flourish. Concentrating on the middle of the English Channel, with the Isle of Wight at the top, the Bay of the Seine at the bottom, the logic of Neptune was immediately apparent.

While naval forces from as far as the Clyde estuary on the western Scottish coast and Felixstowe in the North Sea were to be involved, the vast majority of the armada would sail from an array of southern English ports.

These various fleets would converge and gather in an area of sea south of the Isle of Wight designated appropriately as Piccadilly Circus. Here they were to form up and proceed due south to Area Z, the formal assembly and departure point for the whole invasion armada.

The minesweepers would lead the way, themselves led by specially equipped harbour defence motor launches acting as navigation marker boats for the mine-sweeping flotillas. In all, over two hundred and fifty vessels would be employed for this task alone. The attrition rate for the minesweepers was anticipated to be high. Consequently, spare ships would tail close behind the active sweepers ready to act as immediate replacements.

To begin with, five channels would be swept, one for each of the task forces allocated to the individual beaches. They would steer south-south-east. Just ahead of the major minefield laid by the Germans to guard the French coast, each of these five channels would divide into two, one each for fast twelve-knot convoys and slow five-knot convoys. These ten channels, four for the American Western Task Force heading for the Utah and Omaha landing beaches, six for the Eastern British and Canadian Task Force heading for Gold, Juno and Sword, would terminate at a point close to the French coast.

With these ten channels successfully swept, the mine-sweeping flotillas would then conduct an offshore sweeping programme running parallel to the beaches where the landing ships and transports were to anchor, and where all the bombardment ships were to congregate.

With their primary sweeping operation completed, the ships would backtrack to widen the ten channels laterally until a completely swept area approximately fifty miles wide, thereafter to be known as The Spout, lay before the French coast. Given that the whole of this enormous mine-sweeping operation was to be conducted in the dark before dawn, it's successful completion would be a major achievement in itself.

This initial part of the presentation had been given by the American commander. Throughout he had continuously referred to Dan Boyies which caused a certain amount of incomprehension amongst the British in the audience since they had no idea what he was talking about. The RN officer, speaking next and commenting on the sea lanes, stressed the word buoy, lighted dan-buoys to mark the swept channels. So that was it, American pronunciation. It was hard to get boyies from buoys, but the American had managed it with ease.

There then followed a detailed description of the assault phase. Thousands of craft involved, each allocated its own specific destination and task, co-ordinated and timed.

John found this mass of detail impossible to digest in one gulp and allowed the whole spectacle to wash over him. He observed as one might watch a performance in the theatre. Abreast of the action but retaining little of the plot.

One impression though was obvious for all to see. The sequential nature of the invasion landings, with each phase timed almost to the second, left no room at all for error. None whatsoever. For an unopposed landing on an undefended shore, and in flat calm sea conditions, it was ambitious.

Against a hostile shore, in less than perfect conditions, Neptune was a gamble of immense proportions.

As the largest ever single military operation in the history of warfare, the figures associated with Overlord were astronomic. Whilst John had ceased to be surprised at their size, he remained never less than impressed. Eisenhower now had well over three million men under his direct command and, with it, effective control of huge swathes of southern England.

Since Overlord II had been formally adopted in January, more men, more ships and aircraft together with enormous quantities of equipment and materiel had poured into the country. In support of the landings and the subsequent ground invasion over one hundred and sixty new airfields had been built to supplement the several hundred already in existence. Over eleven thousand serviceable aircraft would be available for D-Day. But that was just the beginning.

Over fifty thousand military vehicles, tanks, half-tracks, armoured vehicles, lorries, jeeps and a huge quantity of ambulances were arrayed in sprawling equipment parks measured by the acre. Then there were the heavy guns, self-propelled and towed, together with thousands of specialist anti-aircraft guns of all calibres packed herring-bone fashion wherever there was a vacant field. The quantities of ammunition were truly staggering. Every road, every country lane, every hedgerow within fifty miles of the embarkation ports was being utilised, hundreds of miles of new railway line being laid to service the exit ports.

And it wasn't just military equipment that had been stockpiled. Huge quantities of earth-moving equipment and prefabricated buildings for continental airfield construction had been established. Never had the country seen such a collection of excavators and bulldozers, already put to use to build giant warehouses to store millions of ration packs, clothes and medical supplies. The US Army had fifty-four thousand support personnel alone for their invasion force.

John thought again of the explosives storage. Several times recently he had given specific thought to Marjorie and Richard on the farm south of Bath. Beneath the city were countless miles of tunnels and galleries left over from the numerous mining activities over hundreds of years. Now, beneath Bath, was the greatest concentration of munitions the world had ever seen. A single stray detonation would obliterate the whole of the city and a considerable amount of the countryside beyond. It was not a thought to linger with.

The most outstanding provision to John's mind was the equipment destined for the French railway network. Since 1941 the French railways had suffered considerably from the attentions of the RAF, and from 1942, the US Air forces as well. An attrition by interdiction that had accelerated since 1944. Everything possible was being done to disrupt the French railway network prior to the invasion to deny the German army rapid movement towards Normandy after the invasion. Now, hidden within valleys along the south coast were a thousand brand spanking new steam locomotives together with over twenty thousand associated pieces of rolling stock.

Not only were the Allies to invade France, but they were also to rebuild its transport infrastructure as well.

Whilst thousands upon thousands of Allied soldiers, sailors and airmen had laboured long and hard to ensure the success of Overlord, there remained the one great unknown: the weather. Unpredictable, uncontrollable and capricious.

For the landings to succeed, a string of criteria had to be satisfied, the first of which were the tides and the moon in the area of the Normandy beaches. The seaborne landings were to take place when the tide was at its lowest ebb, exposing the whole complex of beach obstacles, and since this initial landing was to be made at dawn, this low tide was required to coincide. Additionally, another low tide was required later in the day, and in daylight, to facilitate the unloading of all the follow-on troops and their equipment.

The airborne forces, dropping six hours before dawn, required complete darkness to achieve their initial objectives and thus required a late rising moon.

In any given month, a dawn low tide reduced the number of suitable days to six, and considerations of the relative positions of the earth and the moon halved this to three. These two factors alone determined the possible dates for the invasion to the fifth, sixth and seventh of June.

Furthermore, three further criteria were required. Good visibility to allow the naval and air bombardment good target acquisition, a calm sea state for the landing craft to operate effectively and, finally, a benign wind, blowing inshore to carry the smoke and dust from the assault towards the German defenders and not over the invasion fleets.

And, if that was not enough, several more days of calm conditions were desirable to allow for the rapid unloading of men, equipment and supplies into the lodgement areas before the Germans could strengthen their defences.

While tides and moon could be predicted with certainty, none of the other criterion could. Never before would the weather, and particularly the forecast of it, become of such crucial, and indeed vital importance.

***

As part of the preparations for the invasion, the Dart and its estuary was getting crowded; really crowded. Small craft of every conceivable description packed into every available berth, side by side. Apart from a narrow channel in the middle of the river, it would have been possible to cross, bank to bank, deck to deck, dry shod.

Bridget now had a team of over sixty Wrens reporting to her and all were immensely busy continually servicing the guns on the boats. Sea water played havoc with guns. After every sortie they required stripping and re-greasing. The exposed cartridge cases turned green from the salt. Her little teams worked from first light to dusk every day. No days off and no leave. Throughout late April and now May, Mark was lucky to see her for more than a few snatched hours every week; and while no one had any idea of when the invasion would be, all agreed it had to be soon.

To add to the boats, many more nationalities were now crowded in around the Dart. In April the American PT boats had appeared and were now based upriver. Their shore complement dwarfed that of the RN Coastal Forces. The Americans never travelled light.

The French 23rd Flotilla had been based at the mouth of the river for some time. They were controlled from HMS Cicala based in the Royal Dart Hotel as was Mark's 15th Flotilla, ensuring the minimum of friction with Coastal Forces operations. There was also a political dimension. General de Gaulle's son was an officer on one of their boats and he took a keen interest in their activities.

To further enhance harmony, the French boats carried regular RN telegraphists on a permanent secondment. Denied their daily tot of navy rum they received instead the French equivalent: half a litre of wine.

Quite illegally, Mark had an arrangement with one these telegraphists. Hoarding their allotments, they exchanged rum for wine. Mark was building up a handy little stock, saved until such time as he could enjoy it with Bridget.

**

It was a bright sunny day and John, needing air after lunch, took a walk around the park opposite Norfolk House. Spring growth, a gradual greening, bulbs now well-established showing through.

There was a group of boys, children no more than eight or nine, playing war games. English versus German. English winning. They were making a hell of a lot of noise: guns, aeroplanes, multiple explosions.

John remembered them playing on the farm in the early days. Cowboys and Indians, cap guns and bows and arrows made from old bean canes. The good guys versus the bad guys. As he remembered, he and Matthew had always been the Indians, more fun with a bow.

And so innocent then. Not so much now. The kids with their carefully collected shrapnel collections. So much real violence for children to grow up in.

It was a basic human trait that people always believed what they wanted to believe. There was even an old Latin phrase for it. The German's firm believe that the invasion assault would be launched at Calais was the basis for all the deception plans.

Psychologists called it confirmation bias, the tendency of human beings to strongly believe something they previously suspected. Evidence that supported the conviction was easily recognised, while other, conflicting evidence, was ignored. The rationale of Fortitude South, the deception plan to convince the Germans that the invasion would land in the Pas-de-Calais, depended in part on the German's active participation and compliance. They were being much encouraged.

Eisenhower had imposed a simple rule: for every bombing raid, air reconnaissance mission, or whatever it was that was flown over Normandy, two more had to be flown over western France, and particularly in the Calais area. Let the Germans draw their own conclusions.

John had read a discussion paper on the quality of the Allied troops preparing for Normandy. Less than half of the British Army had any combat experience at all. While the troops allocated to the invasion contained a core of battle-hardened, well-experienced soldiers, the majority, however well trained, were untried and untested. The Americans were in an even worse position since their supply of seasoned troops was even less.

Comparisons were drawn to Kitchener's army, freshly trained volunteers, whose first taste of battle had been on the Somme in 1916, slaughtered in their thousands on 1 July.

The paper had concluded that these shortcomings of troop quality would be compensated for by the quality of leadership, clear and decisive direction, real time communication and exhaustive forward planning.

John, in common with many others, could only hope and pray, like so much else, this supposition would prove to be correct. There was also the question of luck. No one spoke about that, but all thought it.

86

Preparations for the invasion were approaching their peak. As part of this another complete photographic survey of the whole of northern France, within 150 miles of London, had begun.

In late April a Spitfire PR sortie over the Cherbourg peninsular revealed something suspicious in a village called Belhamelin. Stereoscopic analysis revealed what might possibly be a ramp, twelve feet wide, two hundred and fifty feet long with a collection of small buildings close by. Tracing the axis of the ramp showed it was directed at Bristol.

Immediately the Crossbow team at Medmenham, working continuous shifts, began a search for similar launch sites and within days had found another dozen. And within another week, a possible further hundred had been identified. Abandoning the previous ski sites, the Germans were developing a parallel launching network. The fixed concrete ramps that had been so easy to identify were now replaced by prefabricated ones manufactured off-site in six metre sections, only erected immediately prior to launch.

More worrying still was the determination of the aiming points. Not only London and Bristol, but every major port on the English south coast from Plymouth in the west to Dover and beyond in the east. Every port that might be an assembly point for an anticipated invasion fleet. As the investigation went on further targets were identified in South Wales and the Thames estuary.

The discovery of this new network of parallel launch sites caused consternation in the Air Ministry and beyond. That it had been discovered so soon after the report suggesting the threat had been eliminated was an irony that Luke, amongst others, commented upon.

Around the same time as the prefabricated ramp sites were being discovered, Dr Jones produced his latest report on the German testing trials of the flying bomb over the Baltic. Analysing one hundred and fifty-four firings since January he had transcribed the results as an overlay onto a map of Greater

London. The resultant plots indicated that forty-two per cent of the missiles would have landed on heavily populated areas. Jones had concluded his report by stating that he considered the weapon close to a full deployment.

In early May another intense trial of multiple firings was undertaken. Several of the missiles had gone astray, one of which had landed on the southern coast of Sweden.

Alerted by the British air attaché in Stockholm, two Air Ministry intelligence officers were despatched forthwith by BOAC Mosquito and, after certain diplomatic niceties, were allowed to examine and, importantly, photograph and document the wreckage. Returning immediately to the UK, this data had allowed preliminary sketches of the vehicle to be prepared and these, together with the photographs, would be the subject of a special meeting of the Crossbow Review Committee within days.

As instructed by Henderson, Luke was to attend the Crossbow meeting in London.

"I suggest you wear civilian clothes," Henderson said when they met up the afternoon before. "Turning up in your RNVR uniform will only complicate matters."

Luke had been wondering about that. "Do you have any specific instructions for me?"

"No. Nothing particular. Just listen and then write me a brief report."

Henderson had then become uncharacteristically paternal. "Your first encounter with the, so-called, great and the good. No need to be nervous. You won't disgrace yourself." He suddenly laughed. "And, if all else fails, remember they have to sit on the bog just like everyone else!"

On Wednesday, 17 May, Luke presented himself at the Air Ministry in Kingsway. He was wearing his best suit.

Shown up to a conference room he found a large table with chairs for twelve, with another row of chairs stretched along a wall at the back of the room. There were no papers on the table and, for the moment, no other occupants. He stared out of the window for a while, but there was little to see.

As people began to file in, Luke stood by the row of chairs along the wall, his feelings a mixture of excitement and nervousness. He was there to observe, he reminded himself, not participate. A seat along the wall was perfectly adequate for that.

There were ten of them in all. Army, navy and air force all represented together with a scattering of civilians. Surprisingly, Duncan Sandys was there. Luke recognised him from his picture in the newspapers, still using a stick following the car accident in Wales months before. Another surprise, Lord Cherwell was not there. The last to arrive was Dr R. V. Jones, a briefcase under his arm. Luke watched him as he sat down and hitched up the sleeves of his jacket. Oddly, a watch on each wrist and, unusually, he appeared to be wearing a short-sleeved shirt. Luke thought he detected a slight look of contempt as he glanced around the table sharing pleasantries.

The meeting was chaired by Air Commodore Colin McKay Grierson; Claude Pelly, the previous incumbent, having moved on to other things.

Grierson seemed pleasant enough but, as he explained in his opening remarks, he was completely fresh to the Crossbow subject, but was eager to learn. Not an especially good start. Luke was introduced as Henderson's representative. A few faces turned to inspect him, and Luke wished them good morning. To his relief, his voice sounded steady, well-modulated.

Grierson began by reporting on the countermeasures campaign to bomb the recently discovered alternative flying bomb launch sites. Results had been disappointing with little destruction achieved. But preparations were in hand using revised tactics and he was confident of success very soon, notwithstanding the pressure on air resources caused by the imminence of future operations.

Luke took that as a reference to the forthcoming invasion. It suddenly struck him that he was probably the only person in the room who did not know when this was to be. No matter. He wasn't sure if he wanted to know.

Jones then gave a briefing of the flying bomb trials in the Baltic. He spoke with authority and in a tone that did not encourage interruption. He concluded his remarks by saying that unless the deployment was comprehensively interdicted in the meantime, he would expect the bombardment to begin within the month.

In the silence that followed, slender dossiers were distributed by the committee's secretary and minute taker. Luke took possession of Henderson's copy.

Prominent in the file was a three-quarter view cut-away sketch of the Swedish missile produced by an artist attached to the Enemy Aircraft Evaluation Unit. It was impressive. The flying bomb consisted of a long cylindrical body with an ogival pointed nose blending to a taper over two thirds of the body's length towards the rear. Its shape was not dissimilar to that of a heavy calibre artillery shell.

Mounted on two struts, detached from the main body, above and to the rear, was another smaller diameter cylinder. This too tapered towards the rear. This was the propulsion duct. It was hollow, apart from something resembling a motor car radiator mounted inside the inlet.

Short, straight, stubby wings extended from either side of the main body, a small horizontal tailplane with elevators, and a rudder incorporated into the rear propulsion support strut. There were no ailerons in the wings meaning the vehicle was roll restricted. The length of the missile had been measured at twenty-seven feet, the wingspan seventeen feet and it was a little under five feet high overall. All up weight had been estimated at around 5,000 pounds, forty per cent of which was the warhead, which in this case was a concrete dummy.

The vehicle was fitted with three gyroscopes, one of which was connected to a magnetic compass. As the sketch showed prominently, there were two large spherical containers made of wound lengths of impregnated cardboard many layers thick, then wrapped in multi-strand lengths of piano wire. These were found to be compressed air bottles used to activate the flying controls and drive the gyroscope platforms. A large fuel tank was mounted in the fuselage between the wings, positioned at the missile's centre of gravity; the fuel was found to be low grade aviation spirit, 75 octane petrol. Construction throughout was of low-quality steel pressings, welded together.

The Swedes had also made their own evaluation. They had estimated an air speed of 1000mph with a range of over 300 miles.

Jones had laughed at this, ridiculing their numbers and referring the meeting to his report before Christmas, quoting a maximum speed of 400mph and a range of up to 155 miles.

Luke was fascinated by the sketch. Though he was loathe to admit it, from an engineering perspective, he found the flying bomb's shape one of great elegance. There was an almost terrifying beauty to it. Simple in form, simple in function.

The meeting concluded with an agreement that a condensed version of the data obtained from Sweden, but including the sketch, should be distributed to the whole of the home defence forces as soon as possible.

Luke drafted his notes for Henderson on the train back to Oxford while his memory was still fresh. What had particularly intrigued him was the propulsion duct mounted above the rear fuselage and the peculiar looking device mounted in the inlet. It obviously wasn't a car radiator, but Luke was at a loss as to what it might be.

But one thing was for sure – he was determined to find out.

Luke delivered his notes to Henderson first thing the following morning. "How did you find the meeting?"

Luke paused before he answered. "Not as exciting as I'd expected. A bit bland frankly."

Henderson nodded. Exciting would not be the word to describe Whitehall meetings.

"Was Lindemann there?" Henderson still refused to call him Lord Cherwell.

"No."

"That must have been a relief to everyone. Jones?"

"Yes."

"Grumpy. Air of superiority?"

"More or less." Luke thought of the other attendees. "Duncan Sandys was there, though he didn't say anything that I remember."

"Was he now?"

Henderson glanced through Luke's notes and then together they examined the sketch from the evaluation unit.

"So that's what the bugger looks like."

There was a small propeller, only a few inches in diameter, mounted on a stub probe on the tip of the nose. Turned by the airflow, it was not dissimilar to the arming mechanism of a free fall bomb. Henderson was suspicious of it, wondering if it might serve some other purpose.

Luke drew his attention to the radiator-like device shown in the propulsion intake duct. Henderson didn't recognise it either.

"Have a word with Tom Hughes. He's a research fellow working on combustion. He might have an idea."

Tom Hughes was a tall, austere looking character in his mid-thirties. Taking care not to explain the context, Luke showed him the relevant portion of the sketch.

Hughes stared at it for some time without saying anything. Then, taking a piece of paper he translated the three-quarter view sketch into a side section of the propulsion duct. The strange mechanism in the inlet, a tapering tube, and then a long parallel section tailpipe.

"I think I know what this is," he said, finally. "We need to make a visit to the engineering reference library."

Taking down a volume marked 'Intermittent Combustion Devices', Hughes flicked through a few pages before opening the book out fully and laying it on a table.

"There you are," he said triumphantly. "The pulsejet. That's what this is. A pulse jet. That radiator looking thing are movable vanes."

Luke stared at the illustrations and the cross-sectional sketches.

"I don't know much about them myself, but it should all be in there. Let me know if you need any more help."

Luke sat at the table and began to read, making notes as he did so.

Invented around the turn of the century, a pulsejet engine was a resonant pipe combustion device producing a pulsed jet to produce a net thrust. Air entered through an inlet duct to be directed through a rectangular array of sprung slats, rather like a Venetian blind. These slats act as a one-way valve. Fuel, typically petrol, is introduced and detonated in an open chamber downstream of the slats. The resultant pressure wave closes the sprung slats shut, driving the hot exhaust gasses rearward and out of the tailpipe. The inertia of the expelling combustion products causes a partial vacuum in the combustion chamber allowing the slats to spring open again to admit another charge of the air–fuel mixture. The combustion cycle then repeats itself. Ignition is self-perpetuating from the residue of the preceding combustion.

Size ratios for pipe resonance vary with diameter. A typical ratio for a resonant pipe is a length 8.7 times the internal diameter, this in turn equates to a cyclic rate of forty-three combustion pulses per second.

Although the thrust to weight ratio of a pulsejet is excellent, the limited pressure ratio achieved by the resonance is poor, typically limited to around 1.2. Fuel consumption, consequently, is very high. Another disadvantage is, since the engine acts like a giant organ pipe, the noise level is disproportionately high, well over one hundred decibels, with a characteristic buzzing noise caused by the intermittent combustion process.

Luke began to walk back to his rooms slowly, calling into the refectory for a late breakfast. As a weapon, the great innovation of the flying bomb was not the vehicle itself, which was crude compared to contemporary aircraft practice, but rather with its concept. Numerous attempts had been made before to produce unmanned flying bombs, beginning with Napoleon's attack on Venice using balloons launched from ships. The Great War and beyond had seen several attempts at autonomous aircraft, but none had overcome the problems associated with accurate guidance and targeting.

The German flying bomb overcame both these problems by being directed at a large city on the one hand, and by being used in large numbers on the other. If thousands of the weapons could be launched, the limitations of the individual would be subsumed by the whole.

Being Henderson's deputy was all very well but, given no specific tasks, Luke was of a mind to devise his own. Having recognised the significance of these new types of weapons he resolved to gain a thorough understanding of them, both their capabilities and their shortcomings.

The A-4 rocket was already subject to extensive investigation by some of the best minds in the country and, as Luke recognised, was probably beyond his capabilities. There was little he could contribute. But the flying bomb was, he thought, something he could get top grips with.

Back in his rooms, Luke began to formulate a plan.

While Luke now understood the basic principles of the pulsejet and how it functioned, he lacked any detailed knowledge or the means to do any meaningful calculations. The Royal Aircraft establishment at Farnborough, specifically their jet propulsion department at Pyestock, was the obvious source to which to turn. A brief telephone call was sufficient to secure him an invitation for the following morning.

Pyestock, a couple of miles from Farnborough itself and sited next to the airfield, was, in conjunction with Rolls-Royce and de Havilland, the centre of the UK's gas turbine research activity on turbojet engines. These were being developed for the new Gloster meteor twin-engine jet fighter. First flown the year before and now in limited production, it was expected to come into service in the autumn. With a speed approaching six hundred miles an hour, it represented a quantum advance in performance over piston-engine, propeller-driven aeroplanes. Jet engines, self-evidently, were going to be the future.

The performance of a pulsejet was entirely dependent upon its proportions and dimensions. It took Luke a while to get the telephone number of 1426 Flight, the Enemy Aircraft Evaluation Unit, but once he got through and explained what it was he wanted, the information was immediately forthcoming. Speaking directly to the artist who had prepared the cut-away sketch, Luke listed the dimensions as they were relayed to him. He also discovered the size and capacity of the fuel tank and a promise that any further information they discovered would be passed on directly.

In preparation for his visit to Pyestock, Luke now prepared an accurate side section of the pulsejet propulsion duct. There wasn't a great deal to it. He could only hope it was enough.

Arriving in the early morning, Luke stayed at Pyestock until the evening. Pyestock's staff were particularly helpful, generous and patient as they transformed Luke's understanding from basic principles towards an analytical competence. It was an intense few hours of instruction but to Luke of great personal satisfaction. He now had an agreed methodology of how to calculate pulsejet performance.

As one engineer had taught him the calculation method, another had compiled a set of the basic data he would require. Luke was to come away with sheaths of compressible airflow tables and graphs, the properties of air against a range of Mach numbers. Standard atmosphere figures at various altitudes, fuel temperature rise charts against inlet temperature and a range of fuel–air ratios, calorific values together with a host of other information ranging from pressure losses in ducts to combustion efficiency estimates.

While he'd been at Pyestock, a request to Farnborough's aerodynamic department had delivered a set of drag coefficients for a range of cylindrical body shapes and implied variations from slender body theory.

The list went on. All this information and technical data, together with that he had already obtained, gave Luke everything he needed. Now he had the tools – the only question remaining was what to do with them.

He thought about this on the drive back to Oxford. What concerned him most was the capabilities of the weapon. The flying bomb's speed, which would have a direct bearing on the ease of interception, and its range, what it was likely to hit.

Jones had quoted four hundred miles an hour and one hundred and fifty miles. But, as far as Luke was aware, no one had made any detailed analysis of these figures or what the variations from them might be. That, Luke decided, would be the basis of his investigations.

Saturday morning found Luke well rested, but hungry. After getting back to Oxford, late the night before, he had gone straight to bed. Now, after ten hours sleep, he needed feeding. Breakfast in the rectory, adequate but uninspiring, a walk in the May sunshine, and a glance at the morning's papers. Soon after ten he was ready to start. It was going to be a long weekend.

Luke's first task was to assemble all his accumulated data and technical information into some kind of logic. His drawing board, tilted horizontal, became an open plan filing system piled by category. Clearing a large space on his desk he began a few trial performance calculations. They went well enough, but there was still a couple of pieces of technical information required.

Another trip to the library and the seeking out of a senior lecturer on fluid dynamics which, in turn, led to a further conversation with another. His questions raised a few eyebrows, but no embarrassing questions. It was well known that he and Henderson were engaged on some kind of 'war work', but what this involved no one within the college was aware. Even Allegra, while she might have some inkling, kept her suspicions to herself. The secrecy and security of war pervaded through civil society just as much as it did the military.

By six in the evening, Luke had succeeded in completing a set of net thrust and fuel consumption figures for the flying bomb's pulsejet for a series of flight conditions. Using standard atmospheric conditions, temperature and pressure levels, he'd calculated the performance at three Mach numbers; static, 0.25 and 0.5, roughly four hundred miles an hour, and at two altitudes; sea level and 3,000 feet.

According to Luke's calculations, the pulse jet produced 740 pounds of thrust at static conditions equating to around 700 pounds at the cruise speed of 400 miles per hour. Should the speed increase, so would the thrust as a benefit of the ram air pressure overcoming the inlet drag.

By way of comparison, the latest Rolls-Royce Griffon engine produced a maximum equivalent thrust of around 1,800 pounds, a 1940 vintage Merlin about a thousand. Pulsejets were powerful little beasts.

Luke now turned his attention to the airframe, calculating its drag over a narrow range of Mach numbers: 0.4, 0.5 and 0.6 at sea level and 3,000 feet. These he plotted on a couple of graphs. He then plotted the pulsejet's net thrust on top of the drag curves. Where the thrust and drag curves intersected, where the one equalled the other, gave the point of equivalence and hence the flying bomb's steady state or equilibrium air speed.

There were two other aspects to be taken into account. Typically, aero engines had individual performance variations, one or two per cent either side of their designated maximum performance. For the pulsejet, its tolerances and the quality of its production would be poor. Luke reproduced his curves for a net thrust reduction of six per cent.

The second consideration was the effect of fuel consumption. As the flying bomb travelled the fuel consumed would reduce its overall weight. With a fuel capacity of 625 litres, this equated to a mass of 1,100 pounds, or twenty-three per cent of the all-up launch weight. As the fuel was burnt off, this weight reduced which in turn would decrease the amount of lift required and hence the lift induced drag. This meant that for a given thrust the vehicle would slowly accelerate and, as the speed increased, so would the net thrust obtained from the pulse jet.

These were time spaced, interactive calculations, relatively simple in themselves but time-consuming and repetitive. Using five-minute time intervals, it took Luke almost two hours to compute a complete flight cycle for each of his chosen altitudes.

It was now well gone midnight and while he was pleased by the results of his day's labours, fuelled by a pile of sandwiches and endless cups of tea, he was now exhausted. But it was satisfying to know he'd broken the back of it. Tomorrow, he would review his results, make a few checks, and write up a brief report.

Luke awoke to bright sunlight streaming into his eyes. He'd forgotten to pull the curtains the night before. He more crept into the day than sprang into it, and it was mid-morning before he got back to work.

He spent the first hour reviewing his sums from the day before, checking then cross checking. Then he began to give some thought as to how to present the results.

With a heading of FZG76 Performance Calculations, he wrote an introductory paragraph summarising his sources, then sub-headings to present the results.

Vehicle Speed: from a minimum of 320mph to an ultimate maximum of 410mph, with typical cruise values between 340–360 at an altitude of 3,000 feet.

Vehicle Range: typically 120–140 miles, though in exceptional cases 160 miles was possible.

All of Luke's results were compatible with the observations made by R. V. Jones of the Baltic trials.

After lunch, Luke typed up his one-page report for presentation to Henderson the following morning.

That evening, it being Sunday and their usual practice, Luke and Allegra went to the cinema. Luke had only a little recollection of it since he slept through practically the whole programme.

87

The rehearsals for the landings were over. Apart from one notable and tragic exception, they had gone well.

The British had begun in mid-April with Operation Smash, a full-scale dress rehearsal off Studland Beach near Poole in Dorset. The beach, in composition and gradient was similar to those in Normandy, and with the added advantage that it was overlooked by a huge concrete bunker and observation post at Fort Henry. Before an audience including King George VI, Churchill and Eisenhower, the exercise had unfolded. To preserve equipment, the training Valentine swimming tanks had been used in preference to the Shermans, but in the event the sea state and the wave height had been too great for them. Several were swamped with the loss of a few of their crews. Beyond that, and while there remained some fine tuning to the sequence of the landing events, overall, the exercise had been declared a success.

The Americans had followed in late April with Operation Tiger on Slapton Sands in Lyme Bay. Tiger, the largest of the rehearsals, was a full-scale simulation of the landing on Utah beach. Through a combination of bad luck, procedural errors and plain incompetence, it had been a disaster. Through an earlier accidental collision insufficient navy escort had been provided, and what little there was, failed to protect the convoy with a defensive screen. Communications between the navy and the American troops was non-existent due to the wrong frequencies being specified. An unforgiveable error. Seven German E-boats, on a routine patrol, had intercepted the convoy while it was in transit and had attacked, sinking two of the eight landing ships, and severely damaging another. Although they were belatedly driven off, the damage was already done. Seven hundred and fifty of the Americans had died.

There was a rather gruesome conclusion to Tiger. Ten of the American officers drowned off Slapton Sands were Bigoted, the specific SHAEF security classification for those privy to the whole Overlord Plan. A vast search and recovery operation was instigated to recover all of those who had died and while a hundred bodies were never recovered, every one of the Bigoted officers' remains was.

Under the overall code name of Fabius, final landing exercises by the British, American and Canadian assault forces were conducted in early May. While there still remained some technical issues, all were adjudged a success.

With the training complete, now began the final briefings and, for all, the most difficult of all. The wait.

***

Monday morning brought more information arriving from Sweden, specifically the function of the small propeller mounted on the nose of the flying bomb. It was perfect timing.

With his performance assessments completed, Luke had begun to give some thought to the accuracy of the thing. The standard measure for projectile accuracy was referred to as a circular error probability, or CEP. This was defined as a circle, centred on a target point, where fifty per cent of the projectiles would impact. Based on standard deviation theory it had originally been devised for artillery munitions, though due to the particular dynamics of gun-fired shells, the area was defined as an ellipse, with the longitudinal axis aligned with the gun's barrel.

For a half-decent artillery piece, with modern ammunition, the CEP was about the size of a tennis court over a range of, say, seven miles; with over ninety per cent of the shells landing within the confines of a football pitch. For naval guns, produced to tighter tolerances and of heavier calibres, these deviations could be halved. For air dropped ordnance, the CEP reverted to a circle. CEP was not a measure of the competence of an individual gunner or bomb aimer, but that of the munition itself. Anything manufactured would have numerous small variations within its production tolerances. CEP was a measure of them.

Such precision could not be obtained by an autonomous flying vehicle – the number of independent variables was just too great.

The flying bomb's guidance system, though simple and, compared to that of a modern aircraft, crude, was entirely sufficient for an area attack weapon. It used an autopilot to control and regulate air speed and altitude combined with a simplified gyro-compass driven by compressed air to maintain a fixed heading.

With an aim point of central London and the launch point known, range was predetermined. According to the data from Sweden, flight duration and hence distance flown was measured by the little propeller on the nose. This was a vane-driven anemometer, or wind gauge, connected to a hodometer counter. Pre-set before launch with a figure corresponding to the required range, when the counter reached zero a firing circuit initiated a terminal dive manoeuvre. Fuel starvation stopped the pulsejet, and the warhead was detonated by an impact fuse.

Half a morning, or so, of relatively simple calculations, for a variety of assumptions, suggested a CEP of anything between ten and thirty miles. Luke split the difference and called it twenty.

The ramifications though were stark. The flying bomb could land anywhere within greater London and the natural scatter would be considerable.

Henderson had forwarded Luke's report on the flying bomb's performance and his accuracy predictions to the Crossbow Review Committee. Another meeting had been called for late May and Luke was to attend.

It was a miserable day in London, rain and low cloud. The meeting reflected the weather, subdued, procedural, the attendees seemingly preoccupied by other things.

Grierson reported on progress. It was limited. Recent reports from France were sparse, little activity had been observed. Likewise, intercepted signals traffic had yielded little in the way of new information. What discussion there was petered out fairly quickly. Conjecture without fact, leading nowhere.

Luke's reports had been distributed before the meeting. He was thanked for his contribution though someone, rather sourly, commented that they didn't tell them anything they didn't already know.

R. V. Jones's response was swift.

"I disagree. The identification of the propulsion unit as a pulse jet is significant, and while the numbers themselves may be familiar and similar to those we already have, I should remind you those were obtained from intelligence and observation. These are the first we have derived by calculation from first principles. I think the young man should be complemented for his efforts."

Several around the table turned to give Luke a nod. One or two even smiled. Luke felt himself blush.

Soon after the meeting broke up. The committee's secretary intercepted Luke on the way out and checked his contact details. In future, further information would come to him direct and not through Henderson.

On the train back, Luke pondered as to what he might do next. Wait was the only conclusion.

***

After a particularly hectic morning, an endless stream of telephone calls, two meetings and a string of reports to read and absorb, John grabbed a couple of sandwiches for his lunch and took himself out to the park opposite Norfolk House.

Spring seemed to be early. While it wasn't particularly warm, the sun was out. The growing season had definitely begun. The grass was badly in need of a cut. The May weather had been kind. It promised to be a good harvest come autumn.

The planning activity for Overlord was now in its final phase. Fine details, further honing, reams of paper describing every event with their timings calculated to the second. Even the simplest set of orders ran to several hundred pages. Absolutely nothing had been overlooked, worked to the nth degree.

But, as Eisenhower repeated at every available opportunity: before the battle plans are everything, once battle was joined, plans were worthless. It was, sadly, almost a foregone conclusion. Then, as one American Army colonel had memorably described to John, it would be a case of snafu. Situation normal, all fucked up.

While Bomber Command and the US Eighth Air Force bomber fleets were now under the firm control of Eisenhower to directly support the invasion, there were still the occasional long-range penetrations into Germany. One such raid had destroyed forty per cent of Germany's capacity for synthetic oil production. Since the Russians had overrun the Romanian oil fields, Germany was now almost entirely reliant on synthetics.

The raid was not accomplished without loss – forty-six B-17s were shot down while Luftwaffe fighter losses were thirty from the eighty aircraft they had managed to put up. Luftwaffe fighter losses since January had been over three thousand and while their production output from the underground factories and slave labour continued to be high, their shortage of pilots was becoming acute. Fuel shortages had cut their training programmes to the bone. What replacement pilots there were resembled the least able of those RAF pilots who were slaughtered during the worse days of the Battle of Britain.

But it was a different war now, fully professional, hardened. It was boys against men, with the boys decimated like so much cannon fodder. John read the reports with little sympathy. The Luftwaffe was no longer the force it once was and, extrapolating forward, by early 1945 it was unlikely to exist as an effective force at all. A lot of good men from the Allied forces had died to achieve this. John had no sympathy whatsoever.

A further effort was now underway to blind the Germans by systematically destroying all their radar sites in France before the invasion. The Allied Expeditionary Air Force, formed from Fighter Command and the US Army Air Force fighter wings, were decimating the sites. Rocket firing Typhoons were proving to be particularly effective. In addition to four 20mm cannons, the ground-attack Typhoon could carry eight unguided three inch rockets each with a warhead of 60 pounds. A full strike from these was the equivalent to a full broadside from a Royal Navy heavy cruiser.

By the eve of the invasion, the only ground-based radar the Germans would have left would be a couple of sites around Calais, chosen by SHAEF to be retained for the Fortitude South deception plan.

As part of the Allied 'Transportation Plan', or, more accurately, the plan to destroy the French railway infrastructure ahead of the invasion, Montgomery had been pressing for the destruction of all the remaining railway bridges across the Seine south of Paris. Over sixty of these bridges had been identified and their destruction, to deny the Germans the ability to rapidly strengthen their forces in Normandy, was seen by the army as critical.

Bridges are notoriously difficult to hit successfully from the air. Bomber Command had estimated that twelve hundred tons of bombs would be required for each bridge. Since every one could be expected to be heavily defended, Leigh-Mallory had rejected Montgomery's request on the grounds of cost effectiveness. It was a decision that had done him no favours, reinforcing Montgomery's conviction that Leigh-Mallory was gutless.

The Americans, in the form of Major General Quesada, who headed their IX Fighter Group, and no friend of Leigh-Mallory, had other ideas. He prevailed upon him for the opportunity to attack the bridges by using a different technique. Forget the heavy bombers, use his P-47 Thunderbolt fighter bombers in precision strikes, flying at low altitude and armed with two-thousand-pound bombs.

Leigh-Mallory, only too conscious that his standing at SHAEF had sunk even lower, authorised a trial. In early May, eight Thunderbolts each with a pair of bombs, flew down the Seine to attack the railway bridge at Vernon.

Flying low along the river at close to four hundred miles an hour, and below the level of the bridge deck, they released their bombs horizontally before zooming up. It was a technique referred to as 'skip bombing'. Their target was not the bridge itself, rather the abutments that supported it. The attack was a complete success. The bridge was dropped, cutting it in half, and the Thunderbolts returned without loss or damage.

A full-scale interdiction plan using P-47s was immediately instigated with devastating effect. By the end of May, only four of the bridges remained standing.

To John's mind, it was a brilliant demonstration of the targeted use of fighter bomber air power. The US Air Force richly deserved all the plaudits it had received. Much was now expected from the Thunderbolt wings, and their equivalent rocket-armed Typhoons of the RAF, once the invasion got underway.

Leigh-Mallory had become increasingly concerned about the airborne element of the D-Day landings. Sixteen thousand American airborne forces together with eight thousand British were due to land in the early hours of the morning to secure the right and left flanks of the invasion beaches. So great had become Leigh-Mallory's fear that he had become fixated by it. Quoting loss rates at anything up to ninety per cent, he had pleaded with Eisenhower to cancel the operations. Eisenhower, steadfastly, had rejected these requests, understanding, as Leigh-Mallory did not, the essential need to secure the flanks of the seaborne force before they attempted a landing. John had been tasked to produce conclusive evidence to support Leigh-Mallory's conviction.

What John knew of airborne landings, while considerably greater than your average RAF fighter pilot, could not be described as extensive. He therefore sought help by drawing on the experience of previous relevant operations. There were three: the airborne element of Operation Torch – the Allied invasion of the western shore of North Africa – the German invasion of Crete, and the airborne element of Operation Husky, the Allied invasion of Sicily. A series of telephone calls produced the operational reports and appraisals within an hour of his first request.

The airborne component of Torch was of the least interest. The overall operation had been small, mostly concerning the capture and securing of an airfield. The defending force had been the Vichy French, not known for their tenacity in battle. The airfield had been secured for relatively light casualties.

The German invasion of Crete had been spearheaded by a large number of parachutists landing on Crete's central airfield. Airfields are, by definition, flat and offer very little cover. While the defending British troops were something of a hopscotch, they managed to take a dreadful toll of the Germans whose losses approached ninety per cent for the initial waves. It was a fierce and bloody battle for the airfield but, eventually by sheer weight of numbers, the German parachute troops had prevailed. But at a price. Indeed, so great were their losses that Hitler had subsequently forbidden any more large-scale airborne operations. *Verboten.*

It was this experience on Crete that Leigh-Mallory had in mind. It was these German losses on Crete, combined with the subsequent surrender of Tobruk, that had spared the invasion of Malta while John was posted there. John paused for a while after reading that, remembering, casting his mind back. It now seemed so long ago. It was two years. A long time in wartime.

The Allied airdrops associated with Husky were designed for much the same purpose as those for Overlord. Alas, their prosecution had been at best farcical with tragic consequences. Made in daylight, and overflying the seaborne invasion force, the C-47 Dakota transports had come under severe fire from their own ships which in turn had alerted the Flak gun batteries, mostly German, on the island. Under fire from both sides, the C-47s had discharged their troops far too early and to a large extent while still over the open sea. A great many of the parachutists had drowned as a direct result. While the objectives of the airborne forces had mostly been achieved, this was only due to the tenacity of the surviving troops and the weakness of the Italian opposition.

Thoroughly depressed by what he had read and with the whole subject churning in his mind, John went to lunch. He then walked around the park a few times, smoking more or less continuously, before returning to his desk.

The best comparison with Overlord was the Husky operation, but there were major and very significant differences. Husky was in daylight; Overlord would be at night. The flight paths were designed not to overfly the invasion fleets, coming in as a right and left hook. Furthermore, the invasion fleets were to be strictly forbidden to fire on any overflying aircraft. Such was the weakness now of the Luftwaffe that all aircraft should be assumed to be friendly.

As regards the opposing ground forces and their anti-air capabilities, this should be severely degraded by the air interdiction attacks in the days leading up to the invasion. Also, the airborne operation would come as a complete surprise. The German ground forces would be subject to great initial confusion and this would be greatly enhanced by the simultaneous dropping of dummy parachutists in specious areas to further confuse and confound the defenders.

Affectionately known as 'Rupert', these three feet high rubber dummies in appropriate dress were designed to detonate on impact with the ground producing a series of explosions to replicate attacking parachutists. In the dark they would be impossible to distinguish from the real thing. Something approaching a thousand Ruperts were to be scattered in areas away from the actual drop zones.

Having written his comprehensive analysis, John now considered casualty figures, concluding rapidly that this was beyond his competence. Reaching for the telephone, he began to consult. By late afternoon, he had convened a meeting with half a dozen army officers, US and British, drawn from in and around Norfolk House. All had experience of either planning or participating in airborne operations.

Having explained his task and the reason for it, the results of his comprehensive analysis and its rationale, he then asked for their best estimates on casualty figures. Limiting their deliberations to ten minutes there were several rapid conversations, arguments and counter-arguments before a consensus was agreed. It was a range of best and worst scenarios.

At the very worst, landing in the midst of an enemy force concentration, losses would be up to forty-five per cent. At best, undetected and landing unopposed in open country, two to three per cent. Overall, ten to fifteen per cent. The figures were high, but considering the prize, acceptable.

John thanked them all for their attendance and expertise and then ushered them out. The meeting had been quick and efficient, helped in part by the fact that there had not been enough chairs to go around.

John dictated the remains of his report and, having overseen its typing and completion, despatched it. He'd given it a wide circulation, not restricting himself to the official list; he'd also ensured the blind copies would reach those who would find it of most use. Amongst these had been a copy specifically for General Morgan together with a note from John. If all else failed, Morgan could be trusted to ensure it reached the right circles.

The report, contradicting his view, would do John no favours with Leigh-Mallory, but that bridge had been burnt years before.

On 29 May, a massed painting exercise began at all the military camps and airfields in the United Kingdom. Special invasion recognition markings.

All Allied military vehicles, of whatever description, were to be painted with a five-pointed white star surrounded by a white circle. Likewise, every aeroplane was to have three broad white bands, separated by two bands of black, applied around each wing and around the rear fuselage ahead of the tailplane.

Supplies of black paint were not a problem, but supplies of white, not a colour much in use in wartime, were. It was estimated that the UK's entire stock of white paint would be exhausted by the time the job was completed. Two factories working twenty-four hour shifts just managed to meet the demand.

All sorts of weird and wondrous things were coming into SHAEF for inspection. John had first mistaken them for some new type of grenade, but no; self-heating rations, a choice between soup or a liquid chocolate. Resembling a normal tin of food, they had a fuse running up the middle. The operation was simple: punch a hole in the bottom with a bayonet, ignite the fuse and within seconds the contents were piping hot and ready to eat. Caution: failure to punch the hole would result in the tin exploding. John's first guess not so wide of the mark.

John read the instructions printed on the side of the tin. What could be simpler. Since they were being encouraged to try them, he pocketed one of the soups intending to try it in the evening with some of the bread that Marjorie had recently sent up.

Later, with bread prepared, he lit the fuse with the butt of a cigarette, waited, then poured the contents into a bowl. Though hard put to describe precisely what type of soup it actually was, there was no denying its worth. Combined with the bread, he rather enjoyed it. He'd look for more of these.

British rations were notoriously poor compared to the American and particularly the French, but self-heating food was one thing they did not have.

John imagined their use in the field. Stuck in some cold, wet foxhole, frightened and miserable, instant hot food would be a godsend.

88

The American Army's build up in the UK had reached its crescendo. For weeks thousands of men had been despatched across the Atlantic on the Queen Elizabeth and Queen Mary, running at full speed. And with the troops followed their logistical support. The figures were astonishing. Whilst the British and Canadian Armies were well and adequately supplied, it was as to nothing compared to the Americans. The American Army, reflecting its domestic economy and standard of living, was resource rich, almost obscenely so.

An army division, depending on its speciality, was typically somewhere between 15,000 and 20,000 strong. Each American armoured division required 386,000 tons of stores, around forty ships' worth, to support it. For an infantry division it was about 270,000 tons. These were staggering numbers.

The British habit of making do with limited resources was a concept unknown to the American psyche.

In modelling the German response to the invasion, SHAEF had calculated that the Germans would need at least 175 locomotives and associated rolling stock to supply and supplement their forces around Normandy. In late May the Transportation Plan was extended to deny them the asset. Operation Chattanooga Choo-Choo – for once an appropriate title.

Massed attacks by Spitfires, Typhoons, Thunderbolts and Mustangs, eight hundred aircraft at a time, began to attack every moving train in France they could find. A favourite method, developed by a group of Spitfire pilots and then adopted by all, was to make two passes over the length of the train. On the first, and attacking head on, they dropped their long-range auxiliary fuel tanks on the train; on the second pass, from behind, they lit it up with incendiaries. French railway workers and crews had begun to desert in droves.

By the end of May, 475 steam locomotives and a high proportion of the rolling stock had been destroyed. The French railway system was littered with destruction.

Only eight engines remained. It became a matter of pride amongst the pilots to get those too before the launch of the invasion.

Whilst the planning of the land-borne and seaborne aspects of Overlord had proceeded relatively smoothly and in good time, the air plan for D-Day had been fraught with difficulty since the beginning of the year. It had generated more heat, passion and bloody-minded obstinacy than any other aspect of the invasion.

Both RAF Bomber Command under Harris and the US Eighth Air Force under Spaatz considered the invasion an irrelevance and a distraction to their utter conviction that Germany could be crushed by bombing alone. Only a direct intervention by the President and the Prime Minister had brought these 'Bomber Barons' to heel, forcing them to place the direction and use of their bomber fleets under Eisenhower's direct control.

The appointment of Trafford Leigh-Mallory as Air Commander-in-Chief for Overlord had been greeted by John without enthusiasm, both professionally and personally. It could now be seen as a serious mistake. Rarely had a commander been so comprehensively loathed by those he supposedly commanded. A prerequisite for any commander was optimism, clear-headedness and an ability to lead. Leigh-Mallory had none of these attributes. Gloomy, hesitant, pessimistic and indecisive. Totally uninspiring and lacking in any vision. Harris and Spaatz flatly refused to accept any orders from him and would only take their directions from Air Marshall Tedder, Eisenhower's Deputy Supreme Commander. It effectively side-lined Leigh-Mallory and encouraged his natural tendency to concern himself with trivia.

It was the personality and faults of Leigh-Mallory which had led directly to so many delays to the air plan for D-Day, a plan only finally settled a mere thirty-six hours before the invasion was due to begin. And even then, it was incomplete.

Close air support for the ground forces as they advanced from the lodgement areas, and so successfully employed during the desert war in 1943, had hardly been addressed.

To practically all, and John in particular, Leigh-Mallory did not represent the RAF's finest hour: his appointment by Portal, chief of the Air Staff, represented a classic case of a man promoted beyond his competence.

With the final preparations for the invasion continuing apace, Eisenhower and Montgomery had decamped to Southwick House, a grand Regency pile five miles inland from Portsmouth. Here, where Admiral Ramsay had already established his headquarters for Neptune, would be SHAEF's advanced command post for Overlord. With all the commanders, including Leigh-Mallory, gathered physically in the one place, communication and collaboration would be at its peak – not that there was much they could do on the day itself. Plans had been laid, orders had been issued, intelligence distributed. D-Day would be fought by the troops and their officers on the ground.

John could only imagine the stress levels circulating around Southwick House and its surroundings. For himself he was jittery enough. God alone knew what it must be like for them.

For the more thoughtful commanders, this was the most difficult time. Some, typified by Montgomery, were just eager to go, full of confidence and swagger. But, for the vast majority, on this eve of the greatest amphibious invasion in history, their mood fell some way short of that.

To break the tension, Eisenhower and Montgomery had organised a farewell party for all their operational commanders on the night of 3 June. Southwick House lacked the facilities so it was to be held at Hursley Park outside Southampton.

Parties before battles were not unknown in the British Army, most famously the Brussels Ball before Waterloo, but the practice had rather faded in the intervening years. It was a brave idea to revive it. If nothing else, it would serve as a diversionary activity.

Earlier in the year, SHAEF had reviewed their security classifications for all the staff involved with Overlord and specifically for those who knew both the date and the location of the invasion. For these personnel a super security designation, above the normal Top Secret, had been introduced. Bigot. Those so chosen were said to be Bigoted. Why Bigot? John had no idea, but while he would never wish to be described as bigoted, now it conferred certain advantages. With the American's predilection for word inflation, 'cosmic' would not have surprised him. Cosmic: not only this world, but the galaxy beyond. But Bigot was a clever choice, impossible to reference its meaning. Asking anyone if they were Bigoted would not receive a positive response unless they understood the meaning of the question.

While the granting of the designation had made little or no difference to his work, he did now get to see the weekly intelligence summaries a little sooner, albeit one day late. Dated 3 June, the Joint Intelligence Sub-Committee had produced a 'German Appreciation of Allied Intentions Regarding Overlord'. It concluded that there had been no indication that the Germans had accurately assessed the area where the main assault is to be made. Rather, he expects several landings between the Pas-de-Calais and Cherbourg. The Germans also continued to overestimate the size of the Allied forces committed to Overlord and they still expected landings in Norway. The deception plans, Fortitude North at Norway and Fortitude South aimed at the Pas-de-Calais, were holding up.

John also read SHAEF's 'Weekly Intelligence Summary' number 11 assessing German strength in France. Whilst there was considerable movement of divisions within the country, there was nothing to indicate a net strengthening of their forces in and around Normandy. The redeployments were similar to those undertaken the year before in early June.

John read these reports, as others would have done, with enormous relief. The great secret had been kept. Today was 4 June. Tomorrow was the planned date of the invasion. But the weather was on the turn.

Whilst the weather for the first three days of June had been glorious, warm, clear skies, little wind; overnight on the fourth it had begun to deteriorate rapidly, worsening by the early evening. The high-pressure system was moving out and a deep depression was heading in. The forecast for the fifth was overcast and stormy, a cloud base maximum of five hundred feet, force 5 winds. Aircraft would not be able to see the ground, ship bombardment would be seriously impaired and a large proportion of the landing craft would be swamped before they ever reached the shore. Normandy would become a Somme by the sea.

Further, such was the state of the deteriorating weather, it was impossible to accurately predict more than twenty-four hours ahead.

Eisenhower had no choice. He ordered a one-day postponement.

John had stayed at Norfolk House and, if necessary, he would sleep at his desk. He wasn't alone – most of the other staff had stayed as well.

He thought of the poor bloody troops, stuck in the most miserable of conditions, locked down on their landing craft. The hundreds of ships in the Channel, steaming around in circles. Everybody waiting. Waiting. Someone had said that waiting for history to be made was the most difficult thing. John now knew exactly what he meant.

Every half an hour he went outside to stare, listen to the weather. It was a fairly fruitless occupation, but it gave him something to do. The rain continued with the wind behind it. Windows rattled in sympathy down the street. He saw the page of a newspaper tossed around on the wind and landing in a tree. The weather was truly dreadful.

If the invasion was postponed again the ships would have to return to port to refuel. The next available date when moon and tides coincided was the nineteenth of June. What to do with all the troops? They couldn't leave them loaded on the landing craft indefinitely. What about security? John thought of these and another host of problems. Had it not been for the fresh air he'd probably vomit. Chain smoking helped. Helped a lot.

At 2300 he went back through the door of Norfolk House and began to wearily climb the stairs to his office. Suddenly, a roar went up, echoing around the building. Eisenhower had decided. The invasion was on. Tuesday, 6 June 1944. D-Day.

John bounded up the rest of the stairs two at a time. They were on their way.

On 5 June Rome was liberated – the first capital city in Europe to be so. It was more a public relations exercise than a battle since Rome had been declared an open city by the retreating Germans some hours before.

The American General Mark Clark, vain, self-serving as ever, had led the way in to then perform for the cameras at a pre-arranged press conference.

The early editions of the morning papers the following day proclaimed in headlines. John had glanced at a couple, amused. Mark Clark's day in the Rome sun would be very short-lived – something John was profoundly grateful for since his opinion of the man was contemptuous. An inward shudder at the very thought. Patton and Montgomery, vainglorious and egotistical, were bad enough, but at least they were proven and exceptionally talented soldiers of significance. Clark was not, at best, moderately competent. Nevertheless, his vanity knew no bounds.

Referred to by his troops as Marcus Aurelius Clarkus he employed over fifty staff in his public relations section, insisted that his name and rank appeared three times on the first page of any press release and at least once on each of the subsequent pages. Further, photographs should only be taken from his, presumably best, left-hand side. It beggared belief.

89

Having returned to Kensington soon after midnight, John woke from a fitful sleep, then sat up in bed and lit a cigarette. He glanced at his watch: 0430. The invasion fleet had sailed and was now approaching the Normandy coast, the aircraft were airborne, the first of the paratroops already landed, engaging the enemy. As described by Eisenhower, the great crusade to free the people of Western Europe was underway.

John tried to picture it, thought for a while, and then tried equally hard not to. Nervous, apprehensive, frightened, fatalistic, deeply worried. And excited. It was an odd mix of emotions. And nothing now he could do, one way or the other. Only wait. At least he'd be flying again in a few hours. Strings pulled had secured him a reserve Spitfire for an overflight of the Normandy beaches. And he wasn't the only one. There'd be quite a few others doing much the same thing.

Lighting another cigarette, he thought of other times of similar emotions. His first solo, Tiger Moth, late 1938, seven hours dual beforehand. The instructor climbing out. Turning back.

"Bugger off then. One circuit and land. No showing off. Try not to break the aeroplane."

Turning into wind, taking off, flying the circuit, landing without bouncing. Taxiing back and switching off. Sitting in the cockpit, listening to the engine cooling. Smiling. Just the beginning.

He rolled over, attempting more sleep. This too was just the beginning. He wondered if he'd be smiling come the morning.

He thought of the Great War and the poetry: Sassoon, Owen, Housman and Kipling. How young men had died because the old men lied.

Young men would die again today, but not through ignorance and deceit.

*

At six in the morning, having abandoned any thoughts of sleep, John got up and shaved, and then took a long bath. Dressed in his flying kit he was sitting in the entrance lobby as his transport arrived promptly at seven. A drive to Northolt delivered him to dispersal and, using his normal call sign of Rover One, he was airborne soon after eight, the Spitfire IX climbing in wide circles before heading southwest to cross the Channel.

His left leg was starting to ache. At the altitude he was flying, around thirty-five thousand feet, the outside air temperature was something like minus fifty degrees centigrade and the cockpit of the Spitfire was unheated. He was wearing two of Celia's old stockings as well as a very long sock, but still it was reacting to the cold. Should he do this again, he would have to think of another solution.

John's original intention was to fly as high as possible to keep out of the way. But now he could see bugger all. Almost solid cloud cover beneath him, the brilliant sunshine above, mocking.

Tentatively, he dropped down to fifteen thousand and flew wide orbits over the beaches while taking care to avoid the constant streams of allied aircraft in both directions. Of the Luftwaffe, there was nothing to be seen; not one single aircraft.

Allied dominance of the air was total.

Through gaps in the cloud he could see it all, a full panoramic view of the Channel; something approaching 7,000 ships, a truly astonishing sight. He flew on, witnessing. He would remember this; it would be impossible not to. Wherever he looked there were ships, every possible size, the highest concentration the world had ever seen.

Below him, he knew, were the Polish Spitfire squadrons patrolling the beaches, an honour well deserved. He thought fondly of Dopey, lost in 1940, and how he would have relished this day.

John was thoughtful as he flew his circuits. There were upwards of eleven and a half thousand allied aircraft in the air today, close to four thousand of them fighters. The air power was astonishing, overwhelming.

As he turned for home a sudden thought occurred to him. It would be a pity to return without using his ammunition. It was not as if they were short. But where, and at what?

Flying east he headed for Le Havre and reaching the estuary dived down to sea level swinging north. Carrying his speed, he swept over the harbour installations at over four hundred miles an hour, strafing anything of interest in one long continuous burst. He was well clear before the Germans had time to react. Dopey would have approved of that.

John arrived back at Norfolk House soon after two o'clock. He'd caught the tube from Northolt on the central line, got off at Oxford Circus and walked the rest, limping all the way. The streets were practically deserted – empty taxis circulated without success for fares. Grabbing a sandwich and a coffee, he went straight to the map room.

Mounted at the far end of the room was a large-scale map of the Normandy beaches. Women NCOs, non-commissioned officers, on stepladders were continuously updating different coloured ribbons as information came in via a teleprinter line direct to Southwick House. Apart from his immediate interest in the size of the lodgement areas, John's greatest concern was the level of casualties for the airborne operations. Figures were, by necessity, sketchy. While the American's losses in certain areas were said to be around fifteen per cent, overall the aggregate suggested somewhere below ten. Eisenhower's decision to ignore Leigh-Mallory had been proved correct. And, to John's greatest relief, the losses had fallen to the lower end of his estimate.

During the afternoon it was the naval reports that came in first, encouraging. Whilst the Norwegian destroyer Svenner had been lost on the eastern flank of the armada and, by a strange symmetry, another destroyer had been sunk on the western flank. This was the USS Corry, hit by a mine while travelling at its full speed of twenty-eight knots. Cut almost in half and held together only by the deck plating, it had ploughed on for another thousand yards before sinking in shallow water.

As the last boats and rafts pulled away from the stricken ship, one sailor was seen to re-enter the water. Climbing the Corry's stern, he removed the ensign and then struggled forward through the wreckage in an attempt to reach the main mast. With the ship still under accurate fire from the shore, he tied on the flag and ran it up the mast. Once lofted, his job done, he dived back into the sea.

As the ship settled in the shallows, the mast remained above water, the flag flying proudly defiant from atop. It said a lot for the American Navy and that sailor. John smiled as he read the final sentence of the report. When last observed, the flag still flew.

Of the nearly one thousand capital warships deployed off the Normandy coast, these two destroyers were the only losses.

Miraculously, the fragile and vulnerable fleets of minesweepers had attained all of the allocated tasks without registering a single loss. And that against a predicted attrition rate of thirty per cent.

That was only one of the extraordinary reports that John read during the afternoon. Another concerned HMS Ajax, the light cruiser famous for its participation in the Battle of the River Plate that sank the Graf Spee in December 1939.

Standing seven miles offshore, the Ajax had become involved in a running dual with a gun battery on Sword Beach. So accurate was Ajax's firing that within minutes two of the emplacements were abandoned by their shattered gun crews. On the third emplacement, either by luck or judgement, or both, Ajax had inflicted devastating and mortal damage. It had put one of its 6-inch shells through the gun embrasure of a 155mm cannon while the breech was open and the magazine exposed.

The resultant explosion had been massive: chunks of reinforced concrete the size of cars had been blown over a hundred yards in all directions. The German gun crew had been vaporised.

Throughout the evening John was constantly on the move. Tasked with writing a briefing summary by midnight, he read the huge variety of reports as they came in, made frequent visits to the map room and had numerous conversations with all manner of fellow officers as he ran into them around Norfolk House. The place resembled a railway station – people unable to sit, keep still, constantly seeking fresh information.

Gradually, he began to build up a comprehensive and coherent picture of the day's operations, and, as important, their limitations. As with all military activity, reality always falls short of expectation.

The British had begun the landings soon after midnight. The eastern flank of the invasion beaches contained three crucial waterways. The Caen canal and the river Orne ran perpendicular into the sea at the edge of Sword Beach. About three miles inland at Bénouville and Ranville was a pair of bridges running over each and in close proximity to each other. Further to the east was the river Dives, which itself was spanned by another five small bridges. The fate of these seven bridges was crucial to the success of the British and Canadian landings.

With the main German armoured reserves to the east of Caen, it was imperative that the fives bridges over the Dives were destroyed ahead of the landings to thereby deny them access to the beaches. By contrast, the bridges over the Orne and the canal lay between the main British airborne drop zone and the invasion beaches. Consequently, these bridges needed to be taken intact and undamaged to allow for rapid reinforcement by seaborne troops.

The first action of the whole invasion was to be the capture of the canal and Orne bridges by men of the 6th Airborne Division flown in by Horsa gliders. Heavily laden military gliders do not so much land as have semi-controlled crashes. Six gliders, three for each bridge, with a total of one hundred and sixty men had been allocated to the operation.

The first target was the bridge over the canal. By a quite brilliant feat of airmanship and piloting, the first glider came to rest within twenty yards of the bridge with the other two very close behind. And this in pitch darkness. What's more, they landed without alerting the Germans guarding the bridge. A brief engagement of ten minutes saw the bridge secured. On the Orne bridge, though the landing had not been so accurate, surprise had been total and this too was taken without a shot being fired.

As for the five Dives bridges, despite the parachutists being badly scattered on the first drop, all of the bridges were blown by dawn and ahead of the landings.

A further landing by over seventy gliders, guided in by pathfinders from the first drop, had landed with the heavy equipment while at the same time over 370 Dakotas had dropped the whole of 6th Airborne. These troops were tasked to capture all the territory in the immediate vicinity of the canal and Orne bridges, while other groups destroyed several inland coastal large-calibre gun batteries that would otherwise threaten the invasion beaches.

The RAF Dakotas had crossed the Channel in two groups. Whereas one was well-trained, a proportion of their pilots having experienced bombing missions over France to acclimatise them to ground fire, the other group was not so prepared. The results were predictable. Whilst the first group had achieved their drop-in roughly the right place, the second, overreacting to the ground fire, had scattered their contingent all over the countryside. Some of the troops had landed over twenty miles from their designated drop zones.

Nevertheless, and despite the scattered drop, by dawn 6th Airborne had achieved every single one of its immediate objectives. Bridges had been taken or destroyed as required, gun batteries had been neutralised and to the south, facing Caen, an outer perimeter of defences with anti-tank weapons was in place.

The eastern flank was secured, as planned, before the landings began.

In a similar fashion to the British, fifty miles to the west the American Airborne, the 82nd and the 101st Divisions were to land on the right flank of the American beaches together with a large contingent directly behind Utah Beach. There were six designated drop zones, all close to the strategically important village of Sainte-Mère-Église from where all the local roads and communications radiated. Not only were the American Airborne required to secure the immediate area, but they were also required to clear the landing grounds for the glider trains carrying the heavy equipment the first of which, over a hundred gliders, were to land before dawn.

The Americans had assembled a huge force: a total of 13,400 men, uplifted by 882 C-47 Dakotas. It was to be the greatest airborne operation ever attempted.

Flying in very close formation, this vast air fleet had crossed the Channel and the Channel Islands without encountering any difficulties, but, as they approached the Cherbourg Peninsula, the situation changed dramatically. Sudden dense cloud totally obscured the aircraft from each other and any form of ground reference. This, combined with heavy German flak, caused the aircraft to separate violently from each other and their intended flight paths.

Any semblance to accurate navigation was immediately lost and with only a few minutes to make the drop, this immense fleet scattered its paratroopers far and wide over the Normandy countryside. The accuracy of the drop was even worse than that suffered by the British. Some troops had landed behind the British beaches, while a proportion had landed at the base of the Cotentin Peninsula, forty miles off track. A few overshot completely to land in the sea ahead of the beaches. Although a fair proportion of the troops had landed in roughly the right place, over ten thousand of them were liberally distributed over a hundred square miles of country.

This area of Normandy was more labyrinthine than that to the east. Bocage country, small patchwork fields surrounded by thick, high and dense hedgerows, separated by narrow winding sunken roads.

In the dark, before the moon rose, it was impossible to see more than fifty yards at best, sometimes no more than a few feet. One report John read described it as one giant and lethal game of hide-and-seek as groups of defending Germans searched, and were stalked in turn by, little bunches of Americans.

The scattered nature of the drop had yielded an unexpected bonus, however. The Germans, unable to determine the focus of the landings, were forced to direct their limited resources over a very wide area and were thus unable to achieve a sufficient force concentration at any one point. Considerable confusion was also caused by the British Ruperts, the dummy parachutists, coming down all over the place, suggesting that many of the landings were a bluff. Further, since the Americans immediately cut every communication cable they could lay their hands on, neither could the German command gain any firm understanding of the nature of the attack or the threat they faced.

As another despatch rather neatly put it, the Americans knew what was happening and why, but few of them knew where they were. Whereas the Germans knew where they were, but none of them had any idea what was happening.

By dawn, the village of Sainte-Mère-Église had been secured, as had the area behind Utah Beach. German and American paratroops were contesting large areas of ground to the west while German support troops were now denied access to the rear of the American beaches. The right flank had been made secure ahead of the seaborne landings.

Both the British and American airborne forces had achieved their primary objectives.

Between the US Utah and Omaha assault areas lay a narrow rock promontory one hundred and eighty feet high and jutting into the sea. Known as the Pointe du Hoc, it commanded a clear view of both invasion beaches.

As an ideal defensive position, the whole area had been heavily fortified with strong points connected by an extensive trench and tunnel system. Most significant was the belief that several large and heavily defended re-enforced concrete gun emplacements contained batteries of up to six 155mm long-range cannon. From their elevated position they could either fire directly onto Utah Beach or at the seaborne forces attacking Omaha. It was imperative that these guns were neutralised before the main attacks went in.

The small footprint of the point meant that attack by glider or parachute forces was not feasible. The assault would have to come from the sea. The American 2nd Ranger Battalion were given the task.

A cliff assault, with defenders firing from above, is hazardous in the extreme. Although the site had been heavily bombed beforehand and was subject to continuous naval shelling during the initial phases of the attack, the

Rangers suffered in the region of forty per cent casualties before they succeeded in overcoming the positions. It was, alas, a hollow victory.

The guns, and their mountings, had never been installed. Not even the black painted telegraph poles to act as simulations jutting from the embrasures, as had been used in several other places, were there either. To find their quarry missing, after so much effort and loss, had come as a heart-breaking blow. Angry Rangers had searched the site for evidence and had found deep track marks around the casements which suggested the guns might not be far away.

With the point secured, the Rangers immediately began patrol activity to find the guns. Following a dirt road leading south, marked by the same heavy tracks, they found six guns under dense camouflage about a quarter of a mile inland. Ranged on Utah Beach they were surrounded with stacks of ready use ammunition.

The German gun crews had left the guns unattended, preferring to take shelter from the offshore bombardment, and away from the exposed ammunition, a further one hundred yards inland.

Unobserved, the Rangers used thermite grenades placed in the recoil and traversing mechanisms of the guns, effectively welding the separate components together in a clump. The threat was now rendered useless.

With their primary mission successfully accomplished, though not in the manner expected, the Rangers had withdrawn back to the point to take up defensive positions and await relief coming up from the main landings.

When Overlord II had been adopted in January 1944, increasing the initial assault wave to five divisions, Utah Beach, to the right of Omaha, had been added to the invasion areas. The beach was practically straight and backed by a succession of moderate sand dunes running inland. Lacking sufficient natural cover, the beach defences had been constructed above the dunes to gain an adequate field of fire.

In common with the other beaches, there was to be a prolonged naval bombardment complemented by an air bombardment immediately prior to the landings.

However, unlike the air assault on the other areas where the aircraft, B-17 and Lancaster heavies, would approach from over the sea to make a high attack perpendicular to the beaches; the Utah attack was to be along the length of the beach instead of using a force of medium B-26 Marauders and A-20 Havocs. Another difference was they were to bomb from a very low altitude, a mere five hundred feet. Over two hundred and fifty aircraft were to drop six hundred tons of bombs along the length of the beach in under five minutes.

Concerned for navigational accuracy, the British had positioned a pair of midget submarines several days before. Lying submerged a couple of hundred yards offshore, they would surface as the assault began to mark the extremities of the British landing areas. The Americans, having rejected the idea on security grounds, had no such aids. Instead, they had chosen to employ marker craft: four small boats manned by men from the US Coastguard. In the run in to Utah Beach two of these boats had been lost to mines, while another became disabled, leaving just the one guide boat remaining.

A combination of poor visibility, a strong offshore wind blowing dust and debris from the bombardments seaward, and a fierce tidal stream running from the north across the beach, resulted in the initial landing going seriously off course, to make a landfall over a mile to the left of the intended position.

What could have been a disaster was, in the event, turned to an advantage. This particular stretch of beach was less heavily defended than the one selected. General Roosevelt, a distant cousin of the President and, at fifty-seven the oldest man participating in the landings, was in the lead landing craft. He took an immediate decision. Recognising that the follow-up waves would come after them wherever they were, he chose to start his war from where he found himself.

Though the DD tanks had landed late due to the initial mistake, most had made it to the beach. Soon, they were supplemented by more tanks landing directly from the landing craft ramps. Immediately they began to engage what was left of the beach defences.

The fight to gain a decisive foothold was brief. Soon troops were into the dunes and within an hour a substantial lodgement was being established. It wasn't a walkover, but it had been considerably easier than it might have been but for Roosevelt's decision. Losses had been very light; indeed, the American 4th Division casualty levels were considerably less than they had suffered during Operation Tiger in April. Having landed at 0630, by 0730 the first troops had begun to move inland to join up with the airborne forces.

The landing at Omaha Beach had begun with a tragedy and had ended up as an heroic triumph. It was the compete antithesis of Utah.

Timed to coincide with the Utah assault at 0630, Omaha was always going to be the toughest beach to assault. Shaped as a shallow crescent, it had bluffs around one hundred and fifty feet high in the centre and, at either side, similar rises which ran up to near vertical cliffs. These were impossible to climb and, extending for miles in each direction, were also impossible to flank. The only natural cover from seaward was a narrow shingle bank ahead of the central bluffs.

The problems of the beach itself were compounded by the lack of exits. There were only five along the whole length: narrow rising ravines, heavily defended by bunkers either side, dense barbed wire and minefields. Furthermore, the heavy guns at either end of the beach were trained to fire along the length of it, not out to sea. Set within massive concrete structures, the seaward side was built without apertures and consisted of re-enforced concrete walls up to twenty feet thick, impervious to even the heaviest naval gunfire. Each of these gun emplacements were connected by trenches and an extensive tunnel system containing underground magazines together with a living complex for the crews.

Apart from these active defences, Omaha also had the greatest concentration and density of passive defences. There were numerous beach obstacles, densely packed and constructed of steel girders and wooden poles all of which were mined. There were over sixty artillery pieces sited on Omaha Beach apart from a plethora of heavy and light mortars and heavy machine guns. Nowhere was there an area that had not been pre-sighted for grazing and plunging fire. From a defender's aspect, Omaha was the perfect killing ground.

But Omaha had to be taken. Lying between Utah to the west and the British and Canadian beaches to the east, without the occupation of this ground there was the very real danger that the Germans could counter attack, isolate the two bridgeheads, and then destroy them.

While SHAEF had recognised the formidable nature of the defences on Omaha, there were four factors which it had assumed would give the Americans the advantage.

Allied intelligence had reported that the quality of the defending troops was poor and their morale low. The vast majority were forced recruits from Poland and Russia – more likely to surrender than fight. Secondly, the B-17s assigned to the air bombardment would drop such a weight of bombs that the greater proportion of the beach defences would be destroyed or incapacitated, while the surface of the beach itself would be heavily cratered supplying the assaulting troops with ample cover.

Thirdly, the massive naval bombardment, culminating in the simultaneous launching of several thousand rocket projectiles, would comfortably destroy whatever was left of the beach defences. Finally, the DD tanks, timed to land with the first assault wave, would immediately engage any remaining pockets of resistance while providing mobile cover as they advanced up the beach. Such was the confidence in the planned assault that the troops were briefed that their only real problems might begin once they had surmounted the bluffs.

If only it had been so. Not one single aspect of the plan had been realised.

Recognising the weakness of the defending troops, Rommel had tripled their numbers several weeks before. These additions had been taken from the eastern front. Highly capable and well-trained, they were battle hardened soldiers, not reluctant forced recruits.

The B-17 aerial bombardment had been a fiasco. Heavy cloud, plus a natural reluctance and fear of hitting their own forces, had caused the bombardiers to delay their weapon release by crucial seconds. Bombs had fallen by as much as three miles inland. Not one single bomb fell on the beach or the bluffs.

The naval bombardment had been too short and, for the most part, inaccurate. Instead of firing into the bluffs where the gun emplacements were, they had concentrated on the top of the ridge with the result that most of the shells passed over to explode inland. And, if all of that was not bad enough, the much-vaulted rocket fusillade had fallen short of the beach to land in the surf. Thousands of fish had been killed, but alas no Germans.

As with Utah, the strong cross-current had confused the guide boats shifting the assault east directly ahead of the most heavily defended areas. Though the sea conditions were much rougher than anticipated, still the DD tanks had been launched from six thousand yards. With a freeboard of only nine inches most had immediately foundered and sunk. Of the thirty-two launched, only five had reached the shore and then behind the assault troops instead of ahead. Very soon they were incapacitated by the enfilading fire from either side of the beach, twenty thousand bullets and shells a minute.

The first hour of the assault had been carnage. As the ramps of the leading landing craft dropped, the Germans unleashed a fire of monstrous proportions. Within five minutes over two thousand men lay dead or wounded, stranded, caught between the rising tide and the shingle ridge. The second wave of landing craft merely disgorged more men to slaughter.

Gradually, painfully slowly, small packets of survivors began to reach the shelter of the shingle ridge and a few to the low sea wall behind it. As their numbers began to grow, the few surviving senior officers, particularly

General Norman Cota of the 29th Division, together with a few NCOs, began to reorganise the assault.

Around the same time, and on their own individual initiative, the destroyers laying offshore moved in until their hulls grounded and began to target the strong points built into the bluffs at point blank range. They fired continuously without pause. Ratings on the decks rigged hoses to pour salt water on the gun barrels to keep them from overheating.

Slowly, small unit initiatives and a considerable number of individual actions of great courage, spurred on by Cota, began to have an effect. First one ravine was breached, then another. In single file, picking their way through the minefields, the Americans advanced and reached the top of the bluffs. Here they could begin to attack the German positions from behind.

By 0830, two hours after the initial landings, there were enough troops above and behind the Germans to allow the Americans to make significant headway. Other exits were opened and by noon the immediate beach area was secured. It had been a close-run thing. Three thousand American casualties, the majority dead, remained on the beach.

But for the tenacity and shear guts of the 1st Infantry Division, The Big Red One, the Rangers, and the destroyers coming inshore, the assault would have failed. Utterly and completely. Mercifully, tough as the crust was, it was thin. Once above the beach the Americans had found little opposition.

Fifteen miles to the east of Omaha the three British–Canadian beaches began. Gold, the Canadians at Juno, and Sword. Determined by the tide, the landings were scheduled to begin at 0725, an hour later than the Americans.

The topography off all three beaches was similar to Utah, a gradual almost imperceptible rise from the shoreline, terminating at a sea wall about ten feet high. Unlike Omaha, there were none of the high cliffs and bluffs beyond any of the beaches in which to build defensive positions. This area of the Normandy coastline was a popular holiday destination for people from the interior of France. Various buildings typical of resort towns lay immediately beyond narrow promenades, mixed in with a fair number of holiday homes and private houses. All of these had been commandeered by the Germans and converted into defensive positions. In addition, there was the usual range of pillboxes and bunkers interspersed between them. Critically though, lacking elevation, none of the installations were in a position to dominate the full length of the beachfront. The frontage of Gold Beach ran from Arromanches in the west to Ver-sur-Mer in the east.

The later timing of the landing gave the British the advantage of better visibility and an additional hour for the seaborne and aerial bombardments. The fire from the capital ships was more accurate and better directed while the assault from the Lancasters, though suffering similar overshoots as had the Americans at Omaha, did at least put a proportion of their bombs on the beaches and the foreshore. Additional artillery fire from the army's twenty-five pounders on the LCTs, firing continuously during the run-in to the beaches, was particularly effective at destroying the majority of the beach defences. This destruction was also amplified by the rocket assault, again fired just as the landing craft were about to reach the shore, which, for once, did not fall short.

The sea conditions were rough: six-foot waves with a strong cross-current. The order to launch the DD tanks from five thousand yards out was rightly ignored by the local commanders. The first launch, at a thousand yards, resulted in eight of the tanks being broached. Consequently, the remainder were launched in shallow water, with several of the landing craft waiting until they reached the surf. Though the tanks' arrival was later than intended, following behind the infantry, enough were available to immediately engage the remaining hard points on the beach.

Most significant to all of the British–Canadian landings was that 'Hobart's Funnies' had come into their own, and just as intended. Landing in strength, they had performed in sequence precisely as designed, greatly enhancing the speed of the attacks. The intense rehearsals had borne handsome dividends.

Within half an hour the sea wall at Gold had been breached in several places with troops and armour beginning to move into the town beyond. Losses from the initial assault had been surprisingly light and the move inland faster than expected. Within a very short time the build-up on the beachhead was well advanced.

Juno, the Canadian beach in the centre of the British sector, lay between La Rivière to the west and Saint-Aubin-sur-Mer to the east. The Canadian troops were vengeful, the memories of their countrymen's slaughter at Dieppe in 1942 still raw. Little if any quarter would be shown to the German defenders.

The beach itself had a heavy concentration of static defences and other areas further complicated by a series of offshore rock formations only exposed at low tide. The shoreline too was heavily built up, more so than at Gold, and every building was fortified.

Obscured by dust and debris from the initial firings, the results of the bombardments had not been so effective as that achieved on Gold, a considerable number of the heavy shells passing over the beach to fall inland. Many strong points remained to confront the assault troops.

Delayed by the rough sea, the landings were anything up to half an hour late which gave the defences crucial time to prepare. Coming in on the ebb tide, the landing craft became mixed up with the beach defences, the mines of which accounted for roughly a quarter of the assault craft and drowning a large proportion of their men before they reached the water's edge. In places, the casualties from the initial assault resembled those on Omaha.

On one half of the beach, mostly untouched by the bombardments, the Canadians had to fight their way ashore through a succession of lines of pillboxes and trenched back by fortified houses. Once across the promenade, it became close quarter house to house street fighting before they began to approach the open ground beyond.

While the specialist fighting vehicles had performed their part well, the infantry fighting was vicious, savage and bitter. The Canadians had not concerned themselves unduly by taking prisoners.

Within two hours a workable bridgehead had been established as the follow-up troops began to land and move through to widen the perimeter. Resistance beyond the immediate landing zone had become decidedly intermittent allowing for rapid progress to be maintained. The Juno assault had been short, but particularly bloody. Dieppe had been avenged.

Sword, the most easterly of the assault beaches, contained the small port of Ouistreham on the mouths of the Orne River and the Caen Canal. The Germans had converted the port into a small naval base and added an array of strong defences. Elsewhere along the beachfront the installations were similar to those on Gold and Juno. For those with military memories, there happened to be located at Ouistreham a monument recalling the successful repulsion of a former British landing attempt in 1792.

As with the other beaches, the DD tanks were supposed to lead the assault, but again due to the heavy seas, they were late. Nowhere on the whole invasion front did the DD tanks land on time. Again, delaying their launch to less than a thousand yards, sinkings were minimised: only six of the forty sank and two of those by collision.

The offshore and aerial bombardments had been reasonably proficient while the DD tanks, arriving in numbers, had made an immediate impact, not least by their shock value. Again, Hobart's other specialist vehicles had played a major *rôle*. The beach was heavily mined but was no match whatsoever for the flail tanks. Teams of them flailed up the beach, through breaches in the low sea wall blown by the flying dustbin petards, and then began to clear the immediate ground inland. Having achieved that, they moved left and right to clear more routes for the advancing infantry. Once done, they reversed their direction back to the shore to begin the whole process again in another sector. Soon, the whole of the beach area had been cleared. The whole process had been carried through to the pattern established through the training exercises and had gone without a hitch.

Progress began to be rapid. French Commandos, fighting on their home soil for the first time in four years entered Ouistreham and, after some short but brutal engagements, overcame all of the defences including a major strong point built into the central casino. A couple of well-placed shells from a tank collapsed the building on the defenders.

Although intense in a few isolated places, the fighting along Sword beach was brief. Within minutes, the majority of the fire directed towards the British troops was restricted to sniper fire and that too was quickly suppressed by the troops moving inland.

Sword had been anticipated to be the most heavily defended of the beaches in the British sector, but, in the event, it succumbed with surprising ease. The losses were midway between those of Gold and Juno.

Well within half an hour of the first landing, large numbers of troops were moving off the beach and into the hinterland beyond. They included Lord Lovat's Special Service Brigade of commandos, led by his personal piper in full regalia. They were tasked with the relief of the British 6th Airborne still holding the Orne and Caen Canal bridges. By 1300 they had reached them and only a few minutes late.

The landings had come full circle.

Back again at his desk, John studied his map carefully, comparing the ground now held with that as predicted and planned by Montgomery for the close of day one. As far as John could judge, about forty per cent of the territory intended had been taken.

Montgomery's plan had always been overly ambitious. A continuous beachhead from the mouth of the river Dives in the east to the inlet immediately bordering Utah in the west, with another large area around Utah itself. It was never going to be.

Seen from above the invasion beaches, the areas taken inland resembled the short, stubby foreshortened fingers of some giant hand.

On average the British had moved in around five miles from Sword and Gold while the beachheads from Juno and Gold had linked up. The Canadians had made the greatest progress in the British sector, advancing almost eight miles in the direction of Caen. The American beaches around Omaha and Utah were in complete contrast to each other. The lodgement around Omaha was shallow, barely a mile, but it was continuous. Forces were on the move east of the beach to meet up with those coming west from Gold to close the gap between them. The area taken around Utah was the largest, up to ten miles inland over a large front, tripling the width of the original landings.

John turned his attention to the numbers. In addition to the twenty thousand American and British airborne landed before dawn, fifty-eight thousand American troops had landed together with another seventy-three thousand British and Canadian. There were now over a hundred and fifty thousand Allied troops ashore. In addition, twenty thousand vehicles of all description had been landed with about the same number of tons of stores. The navies had done a magnificent job.

Compared to the pre-invasion estimates, casualty figures were low; around three thousand American and a thousand each for the British and Canadian. Five thousand total, plus those of the airborne. In contrast to some of the more pessimistic predictions which had suggested figures around thirty thousand upwards, the initial stages of the invasion had been achieved for a human cost below the most optimistic predictions.

Perhaps the most important thing of all was that the Fortitude South deception plan appeared to be holding. Whilst the Germans recognised Normandy as a major landing, they did not consider it to be the major landing. They still awaited another, the major invasion effort, to come at the Pas-de-Calais.

His briefing summary completed, it was well gone midnight before John got back to the flat in Kensington. The night porter, excited, insisted for some reason on shaking his hand. Embarrassed, John had thanked him, but excused any further conversation.

A hot bath and a large whisky. He fell asleep in the bath, only waking when the water cooled, his skin white and wrinkled.

It had been a long day.

90

Once the invasion was underway, SHAEF's Public Relations Division had begun to issue a series of official communiqués. Experience from other campaigns, particularly the Italian, had shown that unless official and factual news was received promptly, rumour and speculation from the press would rapidly fill the void.

Communiqué Number 1 was released on the morning of the invasion. It was brief, a single sentence, merely stating the landings had begun. Communiqué Number 2, issued in the afternoon gave a few more details of the operation and listed the senior naval personal involved.

Further communiqués were to be issued daily, at 1100 and 2330, timed for inclusion in the evening and morning papers. Though it wouldn't stop the rumour mill, it was obviously a sound idea. If nothing else it would give everyone a common point of reference. Twice on the bus that morning John had been asked questions. Now, he could give an officially approved answer.

In addition to these official communiqués, the BBC had begun to broadcast a nightly 'War Report' direct from Normandy after the nine o'clock news. Very quickly it had become required listening for the nation.

John was impressed by the standard of the broadcasts. The pieces were mostly short, they were factual and informed and, unlike the newspaper reports, they did not indulge in undue speculation. The populace was more inclined to believe what they heard on the BBC than what they read in the papers.

The public could not complain it was not being kept informed and, since the BBC also broadcast in their own native language all over Europe, including Germany, occupied Europe would also know the truth whatever Goebbels might do to persuade them otherwise.

Around mid-morning, a secretary brought him a report culled from the business pages of one of the morning papers. By coincidence, 6 June had been the date for the annual general meeting of the Channel Tunnel Company. The chairman had solemnly reported that, at the current time, the future of the tunnel was impossible to foresee.

John had guffawed when he'd read that, spontaneously. Though perhaps more by way of relief than humour. He sent the report back to the secretary with thanks, adding the suggestion she put it on a general circulation. There were many around the building who could do with a good laugh.

As with any forms of human endeavour, the excitement, the hope and expectation, as well as the fear, reach their peak immediately prior to the event. Anticipation allows the mind to run free, unbounded by reality. Once begun, disappointment and disillusion are bound to follow. And, as it is with life, so it is with war.

The emotional release, the relief so common once the invasion had begun, drained rapidly. As assumption confronted reality, the inconvenience of truth began to erode the fiction.

The progress of the invasion was slowing, stalling as German resistance stiffened. The open, mobile battle planned for Normandy threatened to disintegrate, to become instead one of simple and bloody attrition.

Since the invasion, John's mornings at Norfolk House had slipped into a new routine. Arriving at his desk by eight, he concentrated on the reports that had arrived overnight. Then, at ten, by which time all the updates would be in place, he took himself down to the map room collecting more coffee on the way.

A word much used in the past few days was momentum, that most important aspect of any assault, and the need to sustain it. As the evidence on the maps clearly demonstrated, this momentum had rapidly dissipated from almost the moment the landings had been consolidated. The battle had become bitter, slow, brutal and all consuming. It was a disappointment around Norfolk House, keenly felt.

So much thought, energy and investment over many months had gone into the landings themselves, that planning for the actions immediately afterwards had been neglected. Not that there wasn't a plan – there was, but it failed to take account of the likely condition of the troops immediately after the landings. The ability of the Allied soldiers, both British and American, to take advantage of the German confusion and then to press on inland, had been considerably overestimated.

Psychologically, having trained for months for the invasion itself, and having achieved it, few of the forces were physically or mentally able to adjust immediately and respond adequately to what now lay before them.

Not that some progress hadn't been made. By 10 June, four days after D-Day, all the landing beaches had been linked up with moderate extensions to each flank. The Allies now held a front sixty miles wide and had penetrated to a depth varying between two and twelve miles.

The Mulberry artificial harbours, Mulberry A off Omaha Beach for the Americans at Saint-Laurent-sur-Mer and Mulberry B for the British off Sword beach at Arromanches, were both in the process of rapid construction. Each would be the size of Dover Harbour. In the meantime, men, equipment and stores continued to pour ashore. Over 335,000 soldiers had been landed in four days, delivered directly onto the beaches.

German counter attacks, including several armoured thrusts, had been beaten back relatively easily. Their armoured formations being decimated by a mixture of land-based artillery and, particularly, by bombardment from the American and RN capital ships offshore. Naval supporting gunfire to the various elements of the British and American armies, both its weight and its accuracy, was seen as a particular success. But still, progress remained slow.

One major shortfall had become immediately apparent. Neither the British nor the Americans possessed an armoured personnel carrier that would allow the infantry to accompany the tanks. The ability to move troops rapidly around the battlefield to exploit breaches made by the armour did not exist. Men walked, as the well-named 'poor bloody infantry' had done for centuries. It was a major Allied failing and was contributing greatly to the failure to advance.

The loss of momentum had provided the Germans with critical time in which to reorganise, bring forward reinforcements and begin to devise a coherent and comprehensive defence to confront and contain the Allies on their wide, but narrow, front.

The British faced the Germans on the outskirts of Caen. Montgomery, fancifully, had intended to take the majority of the city on D-Day itself. Caen was the gateway to the whole of central France beyond it, and the Germans were determined to hold it at whatever cost. The vast majority of their armour was now committed to the city's defence. With the initial impetus now gone, the British were now faced with a long, hard and bloody slog.

On the western side, the Americans had a whole different set of problems. Around the Cotentin area a great deal of the ground was reclaimed marshland, impassable to armour, much of which had been further flooded by the Germans. Additionally, this was the area of the Normandy Bocage, literally box country, small fields surrounded by high hedgerows.

Developed over centuries to protect Norman agriculture against the vagaries of the Channel weather, the bocage had become a system of small fields surrounded by massive hedgerows, three times as high as their English equivalents rising twelve feet and heavily banked. Wide and dense, thickly woven with tree and hedge roots, they made a formidable barrier against tanks and were practically impenetrable. Bordering these fields was an interlocking matrix of narrow sunken roads, sometimes ten feet lower than the fields they served and often completely camouflaged by the overhanging foliage. It would have been hard to devise a landscape and field system more suited to defence.

That the Allies had not recognised the bocage for the formidable barrier it was, and how dissimilar from the English countryside the Americans had trained in, was a significant intelligence failure prior to the invasion. This misunderstanding, and the lack of suitable tactics and equipment to overcome the bocage was costing the Americans dear. Every single little field was a formidable and frightening defensive position, taking time and losses to subdue.

While the Allied air forces over Normandy faced little airborne opposition and were doing well, and the navies were doing everything and more that was asked of them, the British and American armies had begun the cruel realities of fighting the Germans on mainland Europe.

There were to be no spectacular pyrotechnic displays of military brilliance. Instead, it was going to be a long-drawn-out process of gradual learning. This knowledge of how to fight, and how to win, was going to be earned in blood.

***

The weather over the Channel and northern France had made detailed reconnaissance of anything, apart from the invasion beaches themselves, impossible. It was not until 11 June, when the weather cleared sufficiently, that detailed aerial coverage of the inland belt of flying bomb launch sites could resume.

The results were startling. Taking advantage of the weather, the Germans had not been idle. Much activity around the sites in the Pas-de-Calais area was detected and launch rails were observed at four of them. Medmenham issued a flash alert that an attack was likely immediately.

Luke received this information on the afternoon of the twelfth. Now, another wait, likely to be soon over.

Shortly after 0400 on 13 June, a Royal Observer Corps post mounted appropriately on the top of a Napoleonic Martello Tower at Dymchurch on the Kent coast, reported the first sighting of a flying bomb over England. Memorably described as sounding like a Model T Ford going up a hill, it was plotted heading north-eastwards.

A few minutes later the missile came to earth near Swancombe to the west of Gravesend on the Thames Estuary in a field beside the A2 trunk road. The explosion caused no reported damage. Two more fell in quick succession: one on open farmland seven miles inland of Brighton, the other further inland in Kent. A fourth travelled further, exploding in Bethnal Green east London, demolishing a railway bridge and killing six people.

The Germans had launched ten flying bombs that night. Five had crashed as soon as they were launched, one had disappeared into the Channel, the remaining four had reached England. It was not the crushing initial assault the Germans had hoped for.

Since there had been no public statement from Berlin, the joint Chiefs meeting that morning chose not to inform the British public that they were now under a new form of attack. So small had the assault been, it was not considered necessary to put the Diver defence plan agreed in March into effect. For the moment, the anti-aircraft batteries, fighters and barrage balloon companies south of London would remain in ignorance.

The full War Cabinet met later in the day and saw no reason to change the Joint Chiefs decision. Understandably, the invasion of Normandy, only a week old, dominated all discussion.

***

As the days past and the flow of reports passing across John's desk threatened to become a flood, little scraps of information, not entirely of a military nature, also began to appear.

Unlike the Allied armies who made extensive use of canvas for ammunition pouches, webbing and the like, the German used leather exclusively. While it might look smart on parade, particularly when intimidating a captive civilian population, it was an impractical material in the field, prone to crack and rot. This German fashion combined with the Nazi predilection of long black leather coats had led directly to a shortage of leather throughout continental

Europe and a ban on its use by other than the Germans. Allied soldiers had been amazed at the sight of French civilians stripping the boots and other leather accessories from dead German soldiers. The explanation was simple: they had no shoes. All leather production had been shipped immediately back to Germany since the occupation in 1940.

One little report had caused John, and a good many others, a great deal of amusement. On the morning after D-Day the military police had arrested three French prostitutes who had set up a brothel in an abandoned tank landing craft on the evening of the invasion. One could only admire their enterprise. While the MPs had confiscated their takings, the number of men they'd managed to service in the meantime was not recorded. A lack of initiative there, unlike the French women. All they had to do was ask the going rate and then make a simple division. It would have answered the obvious question many in Norfolk House were now asking.

While the British and Canadian armies continued to fight their way through their own area of small fields and hedgerows to hammer at the German armour around Caen, the Americans were learning how to fight in bocage country.

In each of this patchwork of fields there was usually and entrance just wide enough for a farmer to get his cows in and out. The Germans standard tactic was to have MG42 machine guns set into each corner of the field to bring a cross-fire on anything attempting to cross. Furthermore, fighting in areas they had occupied for more than four years, they had precise co-ordinates for every one of the fields allowing them to pre-site each for mortar and artillery fire. Denied the mobility they had trained for, the cost to the Americans in casualties and time had become prohibitive.

Following a series of brainstorming sessions the Americans came up with the idea of using modified tanks as a type of bludgeon to cut through the earth banks of the bocage. Using the steel rails of the German defences recovered from Omaha Beach, these were cut and shaped into dragon's teeth and then welded low down on the front of the Shermans. Driven into the earthen banks at speed, the teeth would dig deep into the banks while the momentum of the tank would carry all before it. Thus, the Rhinoceros or Rhino tank was born. Another alternative method was to use TNT to blow a hole through the banks, but it required a huge quantity of explosive and time to position the charge.

While the infantry sheltered in a sunken road, the Rhino would punch its way through and then fire white phosphorous shells into the corners of the field. Following close behind the tank, a Quad 50 half-track would hose the sides of the hedgerow. The Quad 50 was a formidable weapon. Four Browning 0.5-inch heavy machine guns mounted on the back of a half-track arranged to fire simultaneously. Intended primarily as an anti-aircraft weapon, and with the Luftwaffe only recognisable by its absence, there were plenty spare available. Firing at a rate of 2,200 rounds a minute, the Quad 50 would shred the foliage of the bocage to matchwood. It was not without reason the Americans called it the meat chopper.

Slowly, aided by the Rhino tank and revised tactics, the Americans began to progress. While it was only to the extent of a mile a day, their lodgement area was gradually increasing.

Since the invasion, some of the American contingent at Norfolk House, including some of the more senior officers, had taken to wearing helmets and carrying side arms. This sudden change in dress code had caused a degree of wry amusement within the British staff, and particularly amongst the few Canadians, who saw it as little short of posturing.

On asking why a couple of times, John had received a vaguely plausible answer. Showing solidarity with their buddies on the other side. A laudable intent, though hardly an appropriate gesture. Quite soon a directive followed. Helmets and side arms were not to be worn at SHAEF unless specifically directed.

The fashion had lasted only a few days, but it said something about the Americans. Quite what, John wasn't sure.

***

Another flying bomb assault was ordered for the night of 15 June. Stung by their failure two nights before and under severe threat to improve, a maximum effort had been demanded.

Beginning before midnight, and in heavy rain, by the early hours of the sixteenth the Observer Corps had tracked 155 missiles crossing the coast. Of these, 144 reached the inland defence belt who shot down fourteen. Fighters accounted for another seven. Of the remaining 109, seventy-three reached Greater London, the others coming down in Kent, Sussex and Surrey.

The attack dominated the Chiefs of Staff meeting the following morning and Herbert Morrison, Home Secretary and Minister for Home Security made a statement to the House of Commons in the afternoon. It was nothing more than a confirmation that London was now under attack by a new German secret weapon taking the form of a pilotless aircraft. He further stated that defensive measures, long ago determined, were now being put into place.

As indeed they were. The balloon barrage to the south of London was being raised by the evening while anti-aircraft guns were being erected on pre-prepared sites across the North Downs. In the meantime, the War Cabinet issued a request to Eisenhower to take all possible measures to neutralise the supply and launching sites from the air.

Churchill followed this request with a personal visit to Eisenhower's headquarters to emphasise that, beyond the immediate requirements of the battle in Normandy, the Crossbow targets had the first priority.

The *Daily Mail* published an account of Morrison's speech the following morning including an official sketch of the flying bomb. Rather incongruously, the same page featured an advertisement, showing the silhouette of a naked woman, for Ballito stockings.

Luke had never heard of these. He would ask Allegra.

91

As the mood ebbed, as progress failed to achieve what had been anticipated, relations between the Allies began to deteriorate while that between the ground commanders and the air commanders had begun to sour rapidly.

The capture of Caen, planned to be achieved on the night of the first day, was essential for the rapid development of tactical airfields to the south of the city. Caen had not been taken and, furthermore, showed no sign of being so. What advances Montgomery had achieved were small and piecemeal while the lodgement area became increasingly congested as the build-up of men and equipment continued.

COSSAC, and subsequently SHAEF, had always assumed that once the Allies had successfully landed, the Germans would sensibly do what the Allies would have done had the *rôles* been reversed; namely, conduct an orderly withdrawal to a line on the river Seine in order to fight a grand battle for France on ground of their own choosing. The plans for the Allied breakout from the beachheads was predicated on this.

Instead, the Germans had refused to comply with this expectation and had fought, with some skill, for every yard of ground. This is precisely what they had been doing in Italy for months and continued to do so. John and others, reviewing the Italian campaign a few weeks before, had suggested that the Germans would repeat the same process in Normandy. Driven by Hitler's constant rants, the German generals would sooner sacrifice their soldiers rather than stand up to Hitler. The same behaviour could be seen on the Russian fronts. John's view, however, was very much in the minority and found no favour. It did now. With Hitler demanding death for every yard yielded, it was being realised that the Germans would fight, and fight savagely, all the way back to Berlin.

As part of the Overlord plan, so-called phase lines, the predicted extent of the Allied advance each day after the invasion had been prepared. From

Montgomery's and Eisenhower's standpoint, the phase lines were estimates and as such were recognised for what they were and likely to be subject to much revision once the invasion had begun.

However, the air commanders, with their limited appreciation of army operations, had viewed these phase lines as holy writ, written in stone. The failure to take Caen and the area south-east of it earmarked for immediate airfield construction had caused a widening rift between the army and the air commanders.

It was a question of personality and the clashes between them. Under benign circumstances relationships would be continued, emollients regularly dispensed; but once the real action and the real difficulties emerged, the simmering tensions had broken out alarmingly.

Whilst Montgomery had many strengths as a commander and was trusted to the point of unreason by the men he led, his abrasive, egocentric personality was a real hindrance when dealing with any of the other services within SHAEF. None more so than with the air commanders.

While Leigh-Mallory, as Commander-in-Chief of the Allied Expeditionary Air Forces, had learnt to work alongside Montgomery in the months leading up to D-Day, his subordinates had not.

Coningham, a New Zealander and commander of the British Second Tactical Air Force, had developed a bitter personal hatred for Montgomery believing him to have usurped the Desert Air Forces' achievements for his own ends. He also had a very low opinion of his character convinced that he was dominated by feelings of self-interest, a view incidentally shared by John. Tedder, now Eisenhower's deputy commander, had also developed a disdain for Montgomery after Sicily, but had developed a close working relationship with Coningham. Between them, they contrived to ignore Leigh-Mallory in formulating operations, only reporting them after the event. Meanwhile, Leigh-Mallory remained the only commander to whom Montgomery would communicate with.

The upshot of all of these personality clashes was that air operations, since the invasion, were now hampered in two ways. The failure to secure tactical airfields in Normandy meant all missions had to be flown from England, vastly complicating battlefield effectiveness, and the outright contempt of each other shown by the senior commanders. It was a situation unlikely to improve until Eisenhower chose to move his command base to France.

It was indeed fortunate, thought John, that the Luftwaffe's response to the invasion had been at best feeble to non-existent. Had it been otherwise the Allied position on the ground would have been even worse than it was.

By 17 June the Allies had landed 557,000 troops, 81,000 vehicles and 183,000 tons of stores ashore in Normandy. The numbers landed, both men and equipment, comfortably exceeded the losses and expenditure of munitions for all the armies.

Whilst the Allies got stronger, the Germans were getting weaker. The decision to hold the ground in every sector, dictated by Hitler, was costing them heavy losses, and replacements, such as they were, had become few and far between. With complete dominance of the air, the tactical Air forces savaged any attempt by the Germans to bring up reinforcements by day. Intelligence reports suggested a gradual degradation and, in some cases, annihilation of German divisions.

But still they held on. The Americans had not been able to take Saint-Lô on the western flank, the main road junction and hence the key to the Cotentin Peninsula, while the British and Canadians had not taken Caen. It was not a complete stalemate, but it was close to becoming one.

Despite this, there were a couple of positive developments. An opportunistic thrust by the Americans had cut across the base of the Cotentin and reached the far coast at Barneville. The German forces were now divided north and south, with those in the north centred on Cherbourg denied any further supply.

Meanwhile, on the Russian front to the east, and of immense strategic importance, the Russian's had launched Operation Bagration. This, the Soviet summer offensive, was to be the largest of the war so far. Almost two million men, 6,000 tanks, 30,000 thousand guns and 7,500 aircraft. Extending over a two thousand mile front it would dwarf the battles in Normandy. And it would benefit the western allies directly. No longer would the Germans be able to transfer any more forces from the east to the west.

Sitting at his desk, John received the latest weather forecast now issued every four hours. Since the invasion, though it had been unseasonably wet, the weather had generally been benign.

That, it appeared, was about to change. There were early indications of a storm in the Channel, possibly of greater intensity than the one that had delayed the invasion.

This was not good news.

On 18 June a flying bomb had struck the Guards Chapel in Wellington Barracks. It was a Sunday, midway through the morning service to commemorate Wellington Day – the building was full. One hundred and twenty-one people had perished. While news of the incident was immediately suppressed, rumours with inflated casualty figures had rapidly spread.

That it had been so close to the seat of government produced an immediate galvanising effect. On 20 June Churchill reformulated the Crossbow Committee as part of the War Cabinet. Representation included the Commanders-in-Chief of all the appropriate commands and various other senior officers and technical specialists. R. V. Jones was included. Most importantly, Duncan Sandys was appointed as chairman, with sweeping powers. The Shell Mex office suite was immediately reoccupied.

Early Tuesday morning brought Luke copies of the latest assessment reports. 674 flying bombs had now made landfall of which fighters had shot down 76, anti-aircraft guns 101, and barrage balloons three. Casualties in London were 499 killed, 2,051 seriously injured. One hundred and thirty-seven thousand buildings had been damaged. Over twenty thousand men had been drafted in from all over the country to work on repairs.

The public mood was one of concern, but there had been no reports of panic or demands for evacuation. London Underground stations were being utilised as night shelters as they had been during the Blitz.

Luke studied the map of Greater London marked up with where the flying bombs had come down. Taking Trafalgar Square as the central point, he scribed a twenty-mile diameter circle. At least fifty per cent of the strikes fell within it. It was as his calculations and R. V. Jones had predicted. It was of little comfort.

From a crashed example in Sussex, details of the warhead had been determined: 850 kilograms, 1,870 pounds, of high explosive. Amatol with aluminium metal loading. Exploding at ground level, the effect was blast damage over a diameter of up to 600 yards as a huge pressure wave propagated from the epicentre. This produced a partial vacuum which then produced another wave in the opposite direction as the air rushed back to fill the void. The classic push–pull effect.

Luke recalled how, as boys, they'd used the same technique of aluminium dust loading to increase the power of Matthew's gunpowder charges while constructing the lake on the farm. It came as a shock when he realised how long ago that had been; almost ten years. It had been a different time.

German propaganda, in the shape of Joseph Goebbels, had proudly announced that London was now under continuous attack from the new Vergeltung vengeance or revenge weapon, the V-1. All London was burning and the population was panicking and demanding an immediate peace.

It wasn't and they weren't.

The newspapers and the politicians were calling it the flying bomb, to the air defence forces it was the Diver. But, to Londoners, never ones to be told, it was either the Buzz Bomb or the Doodlebug, a reference to a particularly pernicious and irritating insect.

**

Sunday morning found John at his desk a little after nine thirty, later than usual, a combination of the buses' Sunday service and disruption from the V-1s overnight. As usual, a pile of reports awaited him together with one slender file containing a single sheet of paper. A communication somehow appropriate for a Sunday. It was the first authorised account of casualty figures since the D-Day landing listing the losses 6–20 June inclusive.

Pausing to light a cigarette, John ran his eyes down the tabulations; dead, wounded and missing, split between the Americans, British and Canadians. In total, for the first fifteen days, there were forty thousand casualties including over five thousand dead of which sixty per cent were American. Twenty-three thousand wounded, twelve thousand missing.

Casualty figures were invariably described by the black humour of the army as the 'butcher's bill'. John, more used to the lower cumulative figures of his own service, was never less than disheartened by the losses from a land campaign. Even the knowledge that the German losses were very much greater brought little relief. War was a time of waste: lives, material and treasure. But it could have been so much worse.

The best estimates before the invasion had predicted ten thousand British and Canadian casualties for the first day alone, three thousand of which were expected to drown. The actual figure had been five thousand two hundred for the American, British and Canadians combined.

John initialled his name against the circulation list stapled to the front of the docket and put it in the out tray. Lighting another cigarette, he shuffled through the rest of the files.

With the slow progress in Normandy continuing, again the question of the quality of the Allied troops compared to their German adversaries became another subject of quiet discussion. A report commissioned from the experiences in Italy during 1943 had suggested disturbing disparities.

In the British Army, a typical platoon of say twenty men divided into three distinct categories. A quarter were self-motivated, willing to fight and were good-quality soldiers. Half of the platoon were akin to sheep; they would follow but not lead, either going forward or back according to circumstances. The final quarter would either hide, or run, only reappearing when the immediate danger was over.

Montgomery had been appalled when presented with this report which he immediately suppressed, while the officer who had produced it was immediately returned to England.

Analysis of battle actions conducted by the Americans on their own units suggested much the same division of ratios. Even reports from the Red Army indicated that sixty per cent of their soldiers never fired their guns in anger.

Amongst the British and Americans, it was rare to find a soldier who did not have a reluctance to kill – immediately, and without hesitation.

The British, Canadian and American armies were fundamentally civilians in uniform. They were not professional soldiers; they were combatants only for the duration.

The German Army was a professional force. Since childhood they had been indoctrinated and conditioned to be so, and the majority of them had been fighting non-stop for almost five years. They were well-trained, well-practiced, and had few expectations of anything else.

Democracies versus dictatorship; this quality gulf between the opposing individual soldiers was inevitable and, in a moral sense, was admirable. But, in the context of war, it ill-served the Allied cause.

It was only the overwhelming superiority of the Allied resource that would determine the eventual outcome. But it was going to take a considerable time.

John liked London. The people, the energy, the humour and the wit. The smell of it. He also understood its rules, those unwritten conventions that all abided to. One was talking to complete strangers on public transport. No one ever did – bus and tube journeys were conducted in complete silence. Any approach otherwise was invariably shunned.

But, since the invasion, people shared newspapers, spoke to each other without embarrassment. A shared excitement, a shared relief. John was very struck by it, while wondering how long it would last.

Too soon he received an answer. The optimistic mood evaporated immediately the V-1 campaign began. The convention re-established as people returned to a grim silence.

The V-1 was a new type of weapon, it was a new type of war. For Londoners, a time to hide again. A cruel irony so soon after the excitement of D-Day.

Had there been any doubt before, the D-Day landings had demonstrated more clearly than ever before the philosophical differences between the British and American armies, particularly as to how to conduct a battle. The British approach was to fight with the aid of every conceivable technique, special weapon and subterfuge available, to outthink rather than outfight the Germans. The American approach lacked that subtlety; it was head-to-head supported by overwhelming firepower and troops numbers.

The arguments, previously only muttered, had now become more vocal as John had witnessed. The British contention that the Americans took needless casualties by their gung-ho approach was matched by the American contention that the British risked avoidable long-term casualties by adopting caution ahead of a more rapid conclusion by pressing home an engagement regardless of short-term loss.

John doubted that the dichotomy would ever be resolved. The two armies did nothing more than reflect their nations' characteristics. Younger countries took more risks because they had more to prove. And there was another British characteristic that drove the Americans to distraction. Tea.

While the British officer class might run on gin, the British Army as a whole ran on tea. Gallons of it at every available opportunity. And, as with the Army, so did the rest of the country. As many industrial strikes attested, tea breaks were sacrosanct, almost a religious observation.

To the American's consternation, the British Army would contrive to stop at infuriating intervals throughout a battle for a brew, irrespective of circumstances or real need. So ingrained was it in the national psyche, nothing, not even the risk of imminent death could curtail it.

***

RAE Farnborough had been collecting V-1 wreckage since the bombardment had begun and more was arriving every day. Several of the flying bombs had landed almost intact and these were now subject to the most intense scrutiny. Luke drove down from Oxford to look at them.

Farnborough had devoted a whole hangar to the collection – there were pieces everywhere. Some enterprising soul had ordered the cross sectioning of the pulsejet unit. A small band of apprentices, armed with hacksaws, had spent a whole day on it and now the results were impressively displayed on a couple of wooded trestles.

Luke compared their tabulated dimensions with the figures he'd used a few weeks before and was gratified to discover they varied by only a couple of inches.

RAE had also made a production cost audit of the whole vehicle. Using typical material costs and the British hourly labour rates, their unit cost estimate was £114 of which £62 was labour. Since it was suspected that the Germans were using forced labour for the production, their cost would be a mere £52. It was an astonishingly low figure. For comparison, a standard Royal Navy torpedo cost £2,000. An RAF 1,000-pound bomb around £200. It was little wonder the Germans could produce the V-1 in such quantities.

Luke left Farnborough in the afternoon, in his packet what had become the most prized trophy of schoolboys all over London. A Bosch spark plug, model W.14, used for starting the pulsejet engine.

With his position firmly re-established as head of the reconstituted Crossbow Committee, by the end of the month Duncan Sandys was making it crystal clear how he was going to interpret his mandate.

It was not the task of the committee to simply report on the flying bomb attack and the effect, or otherwise, of the counter-measures; it was his job as chairman to personally direct all the elements of the campaign. Not content to be merely at the helm of the bureaucratic machine, he intended to plot its future course as well.

That the success of the counter-measures was poor strengthened his hand. Although the V-1 was a compliant target, insofar as it did not take evasive action when attacked as would a manned aircraft, the anti-aircraft batteries were achieving only limited success. As regards air interception, only the Hawker Tempest V and the Griffon-powered Spitfire Mk XIV had a sufficient speed advantage to make meaningful contact. There were further complications.

Machine gun ammunition lacked the penetrating power against the V-1's steel construction and while cannon fire was effective, the resultant explosion of the V-1's 1,700-pound amatol warhead was considerable and could destroy the attacker if within three hundred yards.

Some of the more enterprising pilots had succeeded in toppling the V-1's gyros by flying parallel to it and placing a wing tip below that of the V-1 wing. The turbulence thus created would cause the V-1 to roll out of control. While undoubtedly daring, it still resulted in an explosion on the ground.

The fighter pilots were also suffering from the overzealous attention of the AA gunners. Clear demarcation between gun zones and fighter areas had not been achieved. Being shot at by one's own side had created great hostility between the two services. Off duty brawls had been reported.

Neither were the barrage balloons proving as successful as hoped. A thousand were now strung for twenty miles across the southern outskirts of London but had only achieved an impact probability of around fifteen per cent. A cable cutting device was fitted to the V-1 wing leading edges which was proving very effective.

By July, the Ministry of Home Security, in conjunction with London County Council, had begun to organise a massed evacuation of mothers and children from the capital. Some seaside towns to the north, their hotels, boarding houses and vacant rental accommodation were requisitioned wholesale. Unlike the 1940 experience, the evacuation lacked the drama and heart-wrenching pathos. The children were wise to it now and knew what to expect. And it was July – the school summer terms were cut short. An extra-long holiday by the sea. It was some compensation for the upheaval.

What was now obvious to everyone, and Duncan Sandys in particular, was that the defence plan was not working. Radical changes were necessary, and quickly.

92

As someone had remarked at the bus stop, it was like the end of the world. Continuous, unrelenting, louring skies, sudden thunderstorms, violent, hailstones the size of cherries crunching underfoot. And the constant chorus of the V-1s stuttering overhead. Londoners had learnt to listen, waiting nervously, pleading for the engine not to stop. And then, if it did, and close, falling flat to the ground. Around fifty V-1s were getting through and falling on London every day; the papers had Christened it 'the doodlebug summer'. And now, no bus.

The smell of the city had changed: catching in the throat, sticking in the nose, smarting in the eyes. It was the plaster dust hanging in the air like some malevolent fog. It covered everything: trees, buildings, streets, people, a fine grey dust. Red roofs turned to shades of monochrome. Rivulets of grey sludge running in the gutters. And faces, become as ashen, like death masks. People aged before the eye.

John heard three distinct explosions during the hour it took him to reach Norfolk House, his left leg not taking kindly to the enforced exercise. He brushed his uniform and washed his face, the grey scum on the surface of the water in the wash basin.

London was patient, London was stoic; but London was getting distinctly pissed off with this. It had been understandable in 1940, 1941. The country was weak and we were losing. But now, mid-1944, the country was strong and we were supposed to be winning. And now, suddenly, it didn't feel like it. Not at all. Doubt had crept back in to wag its crooked finger.

Immediately dubbed by the British as 'The Great Storm', the worst gales in living memory had savaged the English Channel from the nineteenth to the twenty-third of June. Four days and four nights of unrelenting carnage.

Temperatures plummeted close to freezing while the wind blew at over sixty miles an hour with heavy gusts at unrecorded speeds. The sea state was colossal, thirty-foot waves not uncommon. By the end, the destruction and resulting wreckage and debris on the Normandy beaches was of biblical proportions.

Over seven hundred ships and landing craft were thrown ashore, some of the smaller craft piled upon one another. Even the giant tank landing ships now lay way above the high-water mark, like so many stranded whales. Of the seven hundred, less than half were capable of repair. It was as if some giant hand had reached down and swatted the surface of the sea.

The Storm had also made a mockery of the Mulberry Harbours. Mulberry A, the American off Omaha, more exposed and less well protected, had been completely destroyed. A half-submerged tangled mess, a folly to man's invention in the face of nature's intervention. Mulberry B, the British counterpart off Arromanches, though damaged, had survived, benefiting from the partial protection of large rocks and a reef offshore. What could be salvaged from the American Mulberry was now used to repair and rebuild the British one.

The loss of ships and landing craft, together with all the stores and equipment they'd been carrying, had been greater than that lost on the day of the invasion itself. It was only fortunate that the loss of life due to The Storm had been minimised.

The effects and consequences of the weather were to last for many days. The unloading schedule, already two days behind, was delayed another week. The transit of six divisions, over a hundred thousand men and all their associated equipment, was held up while, in the immediate aftermath, Allied deliveries to the beaches dropped by two-thirds. It was not until the end of the month, with the British Mulberry returned to full capacity, that offloading recovered to its planned rate.

The Americans were less disturbed by the loss of their Mulberry than they might otherwise have been. Never entirely convinced of their need, their preference had always been to land their men, equipment and materiel directly onto the beaches using landing craft. They were well-practiced at this, having developed the technique on the Pacific islands. To this they immediately reverted, and with considerable success. Soon, their offloading figures exceeded those achieved using the Mulberry.

Not only was the Allied supply train disrupted, offensive air activity had been brought to an abrupt halt as the aircraft were grounded. As a consequence, action on the ground was limited to small scale advances of little headway, the tactical situation for the most part unchanged.

While the Allies were stymied by the weather, the Germans were industrious over the four days. Unhindered by Allied air activity, impediment or observation, they used the time well to reorganise their defences around Caen, shifting in further armoured support. Against the Americans they strengthened their defensive positions in the south of the Cotentin.

The weather had worked to the Germans distinct advantage and they had made every possible use of it. What advantage the Allies had gained was once again lost as a consequence of The Storm.

As John finished reading the reports, he pondered. Had Eisenhower not ordered the invasion for the sixth, the next date for the assault would have fallen right in the middle of The Storm. The effects would have been catastrophic. Thousands of lives lost, ships and equipment sunk, the assault a complete and utter failure. The invasion of Western Europe delayed until 1945 at the earliest. The consequences of that, incalculable.

Whilst The Storm itself had been unfortunate in its timing to say the least, there was another scenario that was too painful even to contemplate.

Even before the storm had struck, an action at Villers-Bocage, a village south of Bayeux on the road to Caen, had demonstrated like nothing else could, how hard the battle for the city was going to be. A handful of German Tiger tanks, brilliantly led, had destroyed a whole squadron of British Cromwells and Shermans without either missing a shot or damage to themselves. An initial British advantage had been squandered by a combination of poor tactics and insufficient leadership. Time and again with almost monotonous regularity, the British tanks outran their infantry support, exposing themselves to German anti-tank weapons, while in tank versus tank engagements, such was the inferiority of the Allied tanks that they required at least a four to one advantage to succeed.

Instead of the mobile battlefield beyond the landing beaches as fancifully envisaged by the planners at SHAEF, the fight for Caen was starting to resemble something more typical of the attritional battles of the Great War. Bitter, bloody and relentless.

The British advance through Normandy, slow as it was, had become one of brute force with lesser or greater ignorance by using massed bomber attacks.

Such had been the fate of Villers-Bocage. Only by completely destroying it could the British occupy the remains. It was a pattern constantly repeated, and to the despair amongst the higher echelons of SHAEF.

Montgomery's leadership and tactics were beginning to be questioned, not helped by his constant insistence that progress was going according to plan, while the evidence on the ground showed it patently wasn't.

From John's viewpoint, distant, observing from afar, there was something very wrong with Montgomery. The inability to admit to mistakes combined with his apparent need for constant praise. To John's mind, somewhere within Montgomery was a deeply ingrained inferiority complex. It drove his every action.

Despite the weather, the Americans had continued their advance on Cherbourg. The outskirts were defended by a series of strong pillboxes and multiple machine gun positions and the closer they got, the greater became the density of the defences. Each had to be attacked and destroyed individually and the Americans took an increasing level of casualties.

To break the stalemate, they launched a massive bombing raid directed at the port on 22 June followed by continuous artillery assaults. Most of the area surrendered three days later. The Americans too were resorting to brute force.

Of the port's facilities, what the German's had not previously destroyed, the bombing raid had finished off. It would be weeks before Cherbourg would be brought back into commission as a functioning facility.

But Cherbourg had fallen and by July, the whole of the Cotentin Peninsula with it. It was the first major Allied success since the invasion.

***

Luke hadn't seen Henderson for a while and they were overdue a meeting. Luke to explain what he'd been up to and Henderson to listen, make suggestions and, occasionally, to issue a few instructions. Luke had grown very accustomed to these progress meetings. The traffic, invariably one way. It was rare for Henderson to mention or discuss any of his own activities. Unless volunteered, Luke had learnt not to ask.

It was a pleasant afternoon, the first they'd had for a while. The weather that had accompanied D-Day and the storms thereafter had blown themselves out and the English summer had begun to exert itself.

At Henderson's suggestion they were to meet in his favourite pub by the river. Luke, delayed by a couple of telephone calls, was late. He found Henderson sitting where he expected to find him.

Apologising for the delay, Henderson suggested he get a round in by way of recompense.

Returning to their seat, Luke noticed Henderson had been reading the day's paper. There had been an article describing the work of the War Graves Commission and their care in identifying the British and Commonwealth dead and the locations of their battlefield burials.

"It wasn't always so," remarked Henderson, casually. "It was the anniversary of the Battle of Waterloo a few days ago."

He frowned at Luke. "June the eighteenth, eighteen fifteen."

Luke nodded.

"There were about forty-five thousand dead by the end of that day, ours, the Prussians and, of course, the French. They were the majority. After the battle was over, they buried the bodies in communal graves. Just like slaughtered cattle."

Henderson paused to draw on his pint while Luke pondered on the size the grave must have been.

"During the construction of the Lion's Mound, an artificial hill a hundred and fifty feet high that now overlooks the battlefield as a convenience for visitors, they disinterred the bones of the dead from the battle. These bones were then shipped across the North Sea to Hull to be used as fertiliser."

Henderson gave a brief laugh. "To enhance England's green and pleasant land no doubt. The teeth, however, were reclaimed to be used for the manufacture of dentures for the living."

Henderson smiled at Luke's expression.

"Different times, different attitudes. Tears for the departed but no sentiment for the dead."

He paused, thinking. "For all I know the teeth are still being used."

Opening his mouth wide, Henderson snapped his teeth together several times.

"Waterloo teeth!"

***

Operation Epsom, a British assault south to the west of Caen, had come and gone. Sixty thousand men had faced the greatest concentration of SS Panzer divisions since the Battle of Kursk in Russia the year before. There had been four thousand British casualties.

Whilst the German losses were judged to have been higher, both in men and materiel, suffering particularly from successive salvos of the heavy naval guns from the warships offshore, little additional ground had been taken.

The attritional war around Caen continued. The Germans were certainly weakening, but there was yet no sign of an Allied breakthrough in sight.

John's update on Epsom was followed by the latest report on the casualty figures since the beginning of the invasion. They were very precise.

The British and Canadians had suffered 24,698 since 6 June while the Americans had lost 34,034. While the losses on D-Day itself had been much less than anticipated, the casualty rate subsequently had risen more rapidly than expected. The daily figures greater than at Passchendaele in 1917.

Though the German losses over the same period at over 80,000 comfortably exceeded those of the Allies, a worrying trend had begun to emerge. British and American infantry losses were around eighty per cent more than those predicted. Extrapolations indicated that, should the current level of casualty rates continue, the Allies, and particularly the British, would begin to suffer a serious manpower shortage by mid-August.

That said, by the end of June the Allies had landed 875,000 men, 150,000 vehicles of all descriptions and 570,000 tons of equipment and stores, The Great Storm notwithstanding. Congestion at the beachheads and beyond was becoming a serious problem. It was fortunate that the Luftwaffe were mostly inactive for the area was rich with target opportunities.

93

Three weeks into the V-1 bombardment, Churchill decided it was time to make a public statement to the Commons. It took the form of a review of the history of the German secret weapon programmes going back to mid-1943 and related the attack on Peenemünde and the Allies' subsequent actions. His statement included the observation that without the Allied interventions, the bombing of London might well have begun six months earlier and could have been of far greater intensity.

Churchill concluded his statement by recording that up to 0600 that morning 2,754 flying bombs had been launched from the French coast, resulting in 2,754 fatalities and 8,000 other casualties. Whilst the death rate amongst the injured would rise, the fact that each V-1 had killed exactly one person should be seen as a British success. It was but a fraction of what the Germans were suffering as a result of the Allied bombing raids on Germany.

While Luke understood that this part of the statement was an attempt to reassure the population, it was an invalid comparison. And, as several of the daily newspapers had commented, however heroic were the island's defences, far too many of the V-1s were getting through. There seemed no end to it.

Around the same time as Churchill's statement, Luke received a report on the Allied bombing offensive against the V-1. Not only were the new launch sites proving extremely difficult to find, but they were also proving to be equally difficult to destroy. Some positive results had been obtained, but they were not yet enough to materially affect the number of launches.

Airborne surveillance had begun to concentrate on finding the supply depots for the V-1. One such had been identified as a series of caves in Saint-Leu-d'Esserent in the Oise valley thirty miles north of Paris. Attacked by a force of Lancasters carrying 12,000-pound Tallboy bombs, followed up by another larger force dropping thousand pounders, the whole of the cave complex and its surrounding rail and road network had been destroyed, as were the 2,000 V-1s thought to be stored there.

It was certainly a welcome success, but many more of the storage and distribution sites were yet to be discovered and until such time as they were, and in their turn destroyed, the bombardment would continue.

While intelligence intensified to uncover further V-1 storage facilities, the raid on the Saint-Leu-d'Esserent cave complex had in days halved the number of V-1 launches against England. With fewer missiles coming over, the anti-aircraft guns were better able to concentrate their fire resulting in a greater proportion of the V-1s being destroyed. But it was still not enough.

Soon after, and prompted by Duncan Sandys, Air Chief Marshall Sir Roderic Hill, commander-in-chief of Fighter Command, flew a series of sorties over southern England to assess the defensive situation.

The current disposition of the anti-aircraft guns and the RAF's standing patrols overlapped resulting in complicated, and, sometimes, contradictory rules of engagement. It was neither an effective nor efficient use of either resource.

Hill concluded that the guns were sited in the wrong place. What he proposed was that they should all be moved from their inland positions forty miles to the south coast. Not only would they then have an uninterrupted field of fire out to sea, but by moving them it would allow two unambiguous fighter patrol areas. One along the Channel, the other inland, between the guns on the coast and the barrage balloon barrier south of London.

Duncan Sandys enthusiastically adopted the idea and orders were issued immediately.

It was a massive undertaking requiring the most tremendous feat of organisation. 800 guns, 60,000 tons of stores and ammunition, together with 23,000 service personnel moved south to the coast within forty-eight hours. It was estimated that the vehicles of the Anti-Aircraft Command travelled nearly three million miles during the course of the deployment.

There were two further innovations. Supplies of the American SCR-584 gun-laying and predictor radar sets had become available for use with the British guns; and, even more significantly, vast quantities of the new proximity fuses for the ammunition.

The move was complete by the morning of 17 July – remarkable in itself, and great were the hopes that hung upon it.

Luke awaited the returns for the days following the move with a degree of excitement. It was, he thought, a sensible plan that should increase the rate of interception.

It was not to be. In the first week fewer V-1s had been destroyed than in the week preceding the move. Of the 473 flying bombs that had come within range, 204 had reached Greater London. The guns were destroying more, as were the ever-increasing number of barrage balloons. But the fighter interception rate had dropped dramatically.

The report concluded with the usual weasel words: new arrangements, revised communications, unfamiliarity, time to bed the new systems in, the results did not auger well.

With progress in Normandy apparently stalled, and the bombardment of London continuing unabated, there was a growing sense of unease at the progress of the war. A feeling not experienced since the dark days of 1942.

Luke was writing a summary report for Henderson. Downhearted as he began it, he was depressed by the time he'd finished.

The tremendous effort to reorganise the defences had achieved nothing. The various Whitehall departments charged with defending London were at each other's throats. Massed evacuation was continuing with barely a child under five remaining. The, so-called, deep tube shelters, on interlocking chain of bunkers running parallel to the Northern and Central underground lines had been opened for the first time.

The counter-bombing of the Crossbow targets was in disarray with both the American and British bomber chiefs in almost open revolt at the way their resources were being squandered.

The only real definitive solution was for the Allied armies to overrun and capture the territory from where the V-1s were being launched in such numbers. But, with the armies still grinding it out in Normandy, there was little realistic prospect of that in the immediate future.

And it got worse. The Luftwaffe had begun to air-launch the V-1 from modified Heinkel 111s based on airfields in Holland. This had resulted in a further deployment of Fighter Command in an attempt to intercept. And, all the while, the spectre of the forthcoming long-range rocket assault hung over everything like an enveloping shroud.

Luke could find nothing even remotely optimistic with which to conclude his summary. Instead he wrote: mood grim, outlook bleak.

236

***

The original COSSAC strategic plan for the Normandy campaign and adopted by SHAEF and Montgomery had assumed the battle would be a conventional one; a series of what was referred to as linear objectives. This was a succession of engagements between lines of naturally occurring obstacles and German defensive positions. Furthermore, a steady if not spectacular rate of advance had been assumed, and this had formed the basis of the much-celebrated phase lines which calibrated the Allied advance. It was to conform to these phase lines that all subsequent transport requirements – men, equipment and materiel – had been formulated. It was the management of modern battle.

As one report John had read, a typically insouciant British comment stated, "The German resistance to our invasion of France had failed to comply with the accepted norm". Hitler's insistence and demand that not a single foot of ground be yielded unless by death, that forces from the interior be continuously moved up to the front, had meant that the phase lines now lagged weeks behind schedule and the battle for Normandy had become, not the mobile one the Allies had trained for, but one of simple bloody attrition more akin to those fought in Flanders twenty-five years before.

Eventually, the sheer weight of arms in the Allies' favour and their complete mastery of the air would prevail. It was only a question of when. Alas, at what point, it was impossible to predict.

A particularly vicious engagement by the Canadians against an SS Panzer division to take the Carpiquet airfield to the west of Caen had been the prelude to the next major attack on the city itself. Operation Charnwood had begun on 7 July.

Caen was now seen as the crux, the crucible of Montgomery's offensive against the German armour in the east and, as befits any crucible, fire was now poured into it. On the night of 7 July, a combined force of around five hundred Halifax and Lancasters dropped 2,300 tons of bombs on the northern side of Caen in the most concentrated air bombardment in direct support of ground troops ever attempted. As someone had rather charmlessly put it, after nine hundred years the Anglo-Saxons had finally taken their revenge on William the Conqueror's hometown. A witty, though humourless joke.

Through fear of hitting the British and Canadian troops, Bomber Command had shifted the bomb line south, and thus missed the main German troop concentrations. It was D-Day all over again. Over half of Caen had been utterly destroyed without positive results that merely created a rubble strewn landscape resembling Stalingrad and all that much easier to defend. The bombardments only real achievement was to raise the morale of the British and Canadian troops who were to attack the city.

It was just as well they began in good heart for over the next three days casualties averaged twenty-five per cent. Having taken the northern half of the city, the French tricolor was raised in the remains of the city centre while the Allies regrouped and resupplied for the next attempt.

Patience at SHAEF for Montgomery's progress was wearing painfully thin. John had heard mutterings to the effect that by August he might be replaced. What the effect on the army's morale and especially the British people who had been fed a diet of admiration for him for the past two years, could only be guessed at.

But there was at least one small glimpse of hope. Relieved of his command of the fictitious US FUSAG army in the south-east of England as part of Operation Fortitude, General George Patton had arrived in Normandy. Directly Eisenhower activated it, Patton would take command of the Third US Army under Bradley. Though he didn't entirely share it, John recognised the excitement of every American he spoke to.

Amongst the Allies the accepted wisdom for an attack to be successful, the attacker should outnumber the defender by three to one. While this number might be sufficient in benign terrain, it was often woefully short where local conditions suited the defender. As the Russians had repeatedly learned through bitter experience, for an attack to succeed, and then achieve a rapid breakthrough, force ratios more than ten to one were often required. Even given the Allied force build-up since D-Day, the force ratios typically employed by the Russians were nowhere near being achieved by the Allies. And the bocage area of Normandy – small fields, high thick hedgerows, sunken narrow roads – suited the German defenders perfectly. The capture of Caen, Montgomery's prime objective of day one of the invasion, had still not been achieved. It was a major failure.

Whilst not directly involved, John was monitoring the preparations for Operation Dragoon, the Allied invasion of southern France. Once the landings had been established, all subsequent activity would come under the direct command of Eisenhower and SHAEF.

To release French, and particularly American airborne assault troops for the landing, thirty thousand Brazilian troops, their country having now declared for the Allies, were being landed in Italy. It was a peculiar development, one of the many concerning the Dragoon operation.

As originally conceived, and under the code name Operation Anvil, the Mediterranean landings were supposed to coincide with Overlord in Normandy. A shortage of manpower and, particularly, a critical shortage of landing craft and crews had made this an impossibility. The landings had thus been delayed until mid-August.

To the British they were a distraction. By weakening the forces available to pursue the Italian campaign, it would not be possible to conclude it in time to break into Austria and move east to stem the Russian advances into eastern Europe; territory the Soviets were unlikely to relinquish once the war was over. The British, acutely aware they had declared war on Germany in 1939 in an attempt to rescue Poland, were bitter in their realisation that, post-war, the whole of Eastern Europe would come under the hegemony of the Soviet Union. What this would do for the post war geopolitical situation was anybody's guess. One thing that all agreed, however, was that it was unlikely to be positive, especially for the Poles.

The Americans though were adamant in their desire for the French Mediterranean landings and the need for what would effectively become a fourth land front after Russia, Normandy and Italy. Since they and the French were supplying all the necessary resource, there was little the British could do to counter their arguments. It was a reflection of how the balance of power within the alliance had shifted to the Americans.

Dragoon called for the simultaneous landing on six beaches centred on Toulon with Cannes to the east and the prize port of Marseille to the west. A considerable airborne contingent, parachute and glider troops, would be dropped inland to initiate the assault. Once a successful lodgement and force build-up had been established, the Allies would break out and drive north towards southern Germany. Two hundred thousand troops in total had been allocated to the operation.

With the British now, however reluctantly, supporting the operation and the French strongly advocating anything that would speed up the liberation of their country, Operation Dragoon had been authorised by the Combined Chiefs of Staff in mid-July. The assault was planned to begin on 15 August.

***

The situation in London was getting worse. In Lewisham, south London, a V-1 had exploded early on a Friday morning outside Marks and Spencer. Sainsbury's and Woolworths and the nearby street market, packed with shoppers for the weekend, were all badly hit. Fifty-nine dead outright, one hundred and twenty-four serious casualties.

Two hundred and fifty thousand people had already left the capital. And with the threat of the rocket ever approaching, the War Cabinet were drawing up contingency plans to evacuate another two million.

Around Whitehall there was talk of a general panic. As yet there was no sign, but careless comment only stoked the possibility.

And there was more. Fear prompts irrationality, and irrationality blinds to consequence. Mustard gas and phosgene were now being stockpiled for retaliation attacks, almost 20,000 tons of it. Within six months American production of anthrax would be sufficient to launch a blanketing attack. The whole of Germany would be drenched, poisoned for years to come. Maybe decades. Meanwhile, the Reich's Foreign Ministry had declared that, if need be, Germany would reduce southern England to ruins.

The British had tested the effect of anthrax on a small uninhabited Scottish island in the inner Hebrides in 1942. Eighty sheep were taken to the island and tethered in small groups. Thin cased bombs containing anthrax spores were then detonated. The sheep all died within days. Unlike poison gas, anthrax does not dissipate naturally – the spores lie active in soil for hundreds of years. Extrapolations from the island experiment suggested that 100 kilograms of anthrax had the capability of killing three million people. The widespread use of anthrax would turn Germany and the whole of central Europe to a void, uninhabitable for a century.

The war had reached another phase. Pitiless, bitter unto death.

94

After Charnwood, Montgomery, however conscious he was, or not, of the rising tide of criticism amongst his superiors, now turned his attention to the next phase; in his words, the decisive phases of the Normandy battles.

He planned it as a double phased, double pronged attack. While Patton's Third Army would swing west into Brittany, the US First Army were to drive towards Le Mans and Alençon in the east. To coincide with the American offensives, the Second British Army Group were to launch a major armoured operation through the open country now laying before them to the east of Caen. These double pronged attacks were to be Operation Cobra for the Americans and Operation Goodwood for the British.

There remained the outstanding occupation of Saint-Lô by the Americans, now a month overdue. As Caen had been for the British, Saint-Lô had been for the Americans. Mounting another attempt in early July they had run directly into a pre-planned German Panzer counter-attack. It was a massive clash of arms with the battle lasting over two weeks. Using huge reserves of firepower, the Americans had prevailed, pushing the Germans back over four miles and beyond the little that now remained of Saint-Lô. The Saint-Lô offensive had been the most sustained engagement the Americans had conducted since the invasion and the victory had cost them 40,000 casualties. This loss, and the need to reorganise and regroup, combined with the consistent and continual rain, delayed the start of Cobra. But, by now, the Germans were weakened to such an extent that few if any substantial formations remained to oppose them.

Anticipating another attack in the east, the Germans pulled the remainder of their troops and equipment from the south of Caen to strengthen their defences further back. It was their first significant strategic withdrawal. Goodwood had begun on 18 July; another massed artillery assault combined with heavy and medium bomber raids on an even greater scale than those used on Caen. The British shortage of infantry was to be compensated for by a massive use of firepower.

Goodwood went badly. Though the Canadians easily took the south of Caen, much to everyone's relief, a massed armour attack by over a thousand tanks failed to make any meaningful penetration beyond a couple of miles. The operation proved, yet again, that tank assaults, unsupported by infantry moving together in concert, were unlikely to succeed when faced by prepared German defences including a significant number of strong points. With the offensive grinding to a halt, not helped by torrential rain turning every track into a swamp of mud, Montgomery abandoned Goodwood after only two days.

While Goodwood was lauded for keeping the majority of the German armour in the east, rather than transferring to the west to face the Americans, the impression given beforehand, and much talked up in the press that this was going to be the big break out, did nothing but further the weakness of Montgomery's position. John heard reports that many senior officers, including significantly General Morgan, had formally called for his replacement.

However loud the cries from the chorus, only Eisenhower could remove Montgomery and that only with the agreement of the Combined Chiefs of Staff. The one man who could act unilaterally was Churchill, and while he was angry with Montgomery, he showed no signs yet of such a decision. Montgomery seemed secure for the moment, but complacency was not to be recommended.

Soon after Goodwood, news reached SHAEF of an assassination attempt on Hitler. It had failed. The reaction within Norfolk House was mostly one of relief. While everyone wanted Hitler dead, his insistence on running the German war almost single handed, overruling his commanders at every turn, was seen as a greater benefit to the Allies than his death. Unconditional surrender would be demanded irrespective of the prevailing political situation within Germany.

As the British and Canadians continued to chip away at the German Panzers south of Caen – again much aided by long range naval salvos, impressively accurate from fifteen miles away, and artillery supplemented by continuous air strikes from the Typhoons prowling overhead – the Americans launched Operation Cobra on 25 July.

It too got off to a bad start. Delayed twenty-four hours by weather, some of the bomber formations detailed for the preliminary bombardment failed to hear the recall signal and bombed some of their own troops waiting on the start line.

With the weather improving, the full onslaught of over 1,500 bombers, mostly B-17s of the USAAF, was unleashed. Again, they bombed short. Over a hundred US infantrymen were killed with a further five hundred wounded. The lack of a direct radio link from the ground to the air, which would have avoided this, was a serious shortcoming. Amongst those killed was General McNair who was in the process of relinquishing his command of US ground forces in Normandy to replace Patton as head of the fictitious FUSAG in the home counties. Own goals hardly came any greater.

Nevertheless, this opening bombardment decimated the German defences. One of their highest quality divisions lost every one of its tanks and the vast majority of its men. The other divisions fared almost as badly. As important, their internal communications were severely disrupted hampering any attempts to reorganise and regroup.

The Americans, unlike the British, were not hampered by a shortage of infantry. On the first day they advanced over two miles and on the second another four. General Bradley, in overall charge, was quick to exploit the penetration. With armour and infantry working closely together, by the end of the third day Coutances was taken, a total advance of over twelve miles. Another two days saw the fall of Avranches, the dominant confluence of road junctions at the base of the Cotentin Peninsula.

The US Third Army under Patton became operational on 1 August. With Patton desperate to further his reputation by succeeding in Normandy and with a combination of continuous air attacks and ground armour to hold the flanks, Patton drove four divisions through Avranches within twenty-four hours. Over sixty thousand men, the vast majority of whom were motorised, had now escaped the constrictions of the bocage.

Unlike the heavy bombers of the USAAF, the tactical air support was directed by dedicated air liaison officers and ground controllers travelling with the lead tanks. Consequently, tactical air power had begun to work in perfect unison with the ground forces. It was not new. The system had been previously perfected by the Germans and was the basis of Blitzkrieg tactics used so effectively in Poland and France. While imitation might be the most sincere form of flattery, in this case it was also the most effective at winning the battle. Should a position of strong German resistance be identified, be it even a single tank or an 88mm gun, a simple radio call directly to a squadron of

P-47 Thunderbolts wheeling above the battlefield would ensure its immediate destruction.

By a combination of ample resource, good planning and quick reaction to changing circumstances on the ground, plus a not inconsiderable amount of luck, by early August the Americans had made a decisive and lasting breakthrough on the western side of Normandy. The open roads of France now lay before them. Now was the time for the breakout.

While the Americans were making their great leap forward, Montgomery, urged on by Eisenhower, had planned his next offensive. Operation Spring, timed to coincide with Cobra and designed to convince the Germans that the main Allied thrust would again come from the east, was launched. In strength the Canadians began to advance along the axis of the Caen–Falaise road. Two Panzer formations concealed in strong pre-prepared positions, though heavily degraded during the action, still managed to stop the Canadians breaking through. The operation was halted after twenty-four hours. Spring had been unfortunately named. Not so much a spring as a shuffle.

Spring had been part of the larger Operation Bluecoat. Its progress had been slow and in response Montgomery began a series of sackings, replacing field commanders whom he considered lacked the necessary drive. Most significantly Lieutenant General Brian Horrocks, now returned from wounds sustained in the Western Desert, took over command of XXX Corps. Horrocks was a very fine field commander and the effect of his appointment was immediately apparent.

The vast majority of the Allied Tactical Air Force, Typhoons and Thunderbolts, Spitfires and Mustangs, were now operating from airstrips in Normandy. Spared the need to commute across the Channel, sortie rates had increased dramatically. Constant groups of aircraft landing in relays to refuel and rearm to then re-join those already above the battlefield, all of them ready to be called to immediate action.

The British called it the 'cab rank' system, and it was aptly named, for that was exactly how it worked. They could be whistled up at a moment's notice to attack whatever was required. The record so far from request to attack was fifty-three seconds.

As fighter pilots, their claims were always inflated, multiples of actual kills. But, as John knew, without independent verification, real numbers were difficult to judge. Nevertheless, so fearful were the German tank crews of the Typhoons, that on first sight of them they would bail out from their tanks. It was a foolish action. If the rockets didn't catch them in the open, the subsequent strafing would. Tanks needed train crews. Killing them was just as effective as destroying the tanks.

It had taken a while for the British to harmonise their air–ground co-ordination. Too long. But now it was working to maximum effort.

The British and Canadians continued to press. By 7 August Bluecoat had become Operation Totalize. This time the German defences were minimised by co-ordinated infantry attacks at night to be followed immediately by armoured thrusts through the breaches they'd created. As was now the established pattern, carpet bombing by Lancasters and Halifax's would support the attack, much supplemented by the army's own artillery regiments which had grown considerably since the earlier attempts to break through the German lines.

There was also one further tactical innovation which was to prove decisive during the coming days. Since Goodwood, problems of mixed infantry and armour operations in open country had exercised many minds. A solution had finally been found and, in common with many good ideas, it was relatively simple.

By now there were a considerable number of Priest self-propelled guns available to the battlefield. By stripping out the main gun and its associated equipment and welding steel sheets across the now open apertures, an effective armoured personnel carrier was improvised. Although there was a shortage of armour plate available in Normandy, an ingenious solution had been found for that too. Sheets of mild steel were assembled as a sandwich construction the filling of which was a layer of dry sand, densely packed. This composite armour proved surprisingly effective. These new vehicles were immediately Christened 'holly rollers', or more wittily, 'defrocked priests'.

A combined force of Canadian, British and the 1st Polish Armoured Division advanced steadily for four consecutive days until their momentum began to flag.

Following a short pause to regroup and resupply, Operation Tractable, following the same pattern, began. In another three days the Canadians had taken control of Falaise. Many German prisoners, both captured and surrendered, were taken with much of their equipment destroyed. As important was that German attempts to organise themselves against the Americans advancing from the south were totally disrupted, and completely disorganised.

Following the breakthrough achieved by the early stages of Cobra, the Americans made a rapid reorganisation of their forces. One group under Patton swung west into Brittany to seal it off and protect the right flank, while the greater majority of the American formations continued to press south-east.

Patton's advance into Brittany was extraordinary. With the armour formations forbidden to stop, they were provisioned with fuel and munitions while still on the move. Everything was stowed on the outer hull of the tanks: 150 rounds of 75mm and 12,000 rounds of 0.30 calibre, twice the normal compliment of ammunition. Neither did the crews stop to eat – instead they existed on a diet of boiled eggs and instant coffee. A lot of coffee, a lot of cigarettes. Defecation and urination were by use of their helmets, emptied overboard and washed out. Steel helmets, with their liners removed, had many a use including cooking and washing. Being American, they were invariably fastidious in cleaning their teeth.

John had climbed into a Sherman during the demonstration at Whitchurch in March. As he remembered, there was not a great deal of room and the smell was raw; metal, petrol and oil mixed with stale sweat. It would be fetid to say the least after days of constant movement.

The formations spread out over many hundreds of square miles. They ran clear off their maps and had to rely on members of the French resistance, now surfacing in profusion, to tell them where they were and guide them further. And all the while, the Germans, or what remained of them, retreated as fast as possible.

Soon, the great majority of the Brittany Peninsula was in American hands. Only the ports of Brest, St Nazaire and Lorient were held by the Germans. All contained formidable defences in depth and had been ordered by Hitler to be defended until death. Sensibly, SHAEF decided to leave them there to stew. Isolated and unable to impede future Allied operations in any way, they could be left besieged until they either starved or surrendered.

With Brittany now secured, the Americans could concentrate all their attention onto a swing to the east. Le Mans, Orléans and onward towards the Seine and Paris.

While Patton's newly formed XV Corps encompassing the freshly landed French Armoured Division under Leclerc headed for Le Mans, taking it by 8 August, XXX Corps raced south to take Nantes thus securing the right flank of Patton's main thrust. As in Brittany, the much-heralded American battlefield mobility, questioned during the stalemates of June and July, was coming into its own.

Although the Germans mounted a spirited counter-attack at Mortain they made practically no progress and then were beaten back while their armour was pounded to wreckage by American artillery and the ever-increasing hordes of fighter bombers swirling above them. It took several days, but nothing now was going to seriously impede the American advance.

So rapidly were the assault lines moving forward, particularly the Americans, that John was drawn again to the map room on the ground floor of Norfolk House. It was like D-Day all over again.

So used had he become to the steady attritional warfare of the past few weeks, he was amazed at the speeds of the advance. All the more so for he knew the details of the logistical train that lay behind it.

For every American soldier fighting at the sharp end, there were twenty-six others behind him in supporting *rôles*. The British equivalent, at best, was around twelve. The American armies were run to a business model, more Harvard than West Point; a logistical production line, industrial, continuously rolling.

A single Sherman tank consumed 8,000 gallons of petrol a week which equated to a whole division requiring a minimum of 60,000 gallons a day. And that was on paved roads. Should the advance have to cross rough country, one American quartermaster had calculated that to move a whole division a mere one hundred yards, he would require 125,000 gallons. While this was US gallons rather than the British imperial of twenty per cent greater volume, these were still staggering numbers. And that was just the fuel. For a typical armoured division of 21,000 men, including those associated with it, thirty-five tons of rations a day were needed. And, as John reminded himself, that still left the enormous tonnages of ammunition and other munitions to be provided.

It was no wonder that the American Military Police, the so-called snowballs on account of their white helmets, were ruthlessly efficient at keeping the supply trains running.

While the British armies were adequately provided for, they had nothing like the wealth of riches available to the Americans. The relative speed of their advances was evidence enough.

John had a map of north-west Europe spread out on his desk. He'd been staring at it, re-educating himself on the towns and villages of Normandy, the major population centres beyond and the distances between them. The surface of the paper was marked with little pin pricks from the dividers he'd been using.

Standing up, he put his left hand on the map to lever himself up. He glanced at it. His thumb was on Cherbourg, while his little finger had reached up to Brussels.

Under his palm they were all there, the famous battles of English history. Crecy, Agincourt, the Somme, Passchendaele, Waterloo. The English-speaking peoples had been dying on the European continent for nine hundred years. Normandy, just the latest example, while those on the mainland had been regularly slaughtering each other since before recorded history.

With Dragoon now landed almost unopposed on the French Mediterranean coast and with the German forces in the south now streaming back towards Germany, further possibilities began to present themselves in Normandy. An encirclement of all their remaining forces.

Even before Dragoon had launched, Bradley, with the active support of Eisenhower, had begun to consider a plan to trap the Germans between Argentan in the south and Falaise in the north.

With the British now moving rapidly eastwards from Flers, the Germans were being progressively squeezed into a salient or pocket. To seal this pocket on the western edge the Allies had two options: a short hook to close the pocket near to Falaise, or a long hook to the Seine to achieve an even greater encirclement.

Bradley ordered Patton, now returned from Brittany, to clear the southern flank along the Loire Valley taking Angers, and when that was done, immediately to turn ninety degrees north towards Argentan. The lead formations of the US XV Corps, accompanied by Leclerc's French Armoured Division, reached the city by 12 August. But their rapid advance had thinned the American line considerably, leaving it vulnerable to counter-attack, and the logistics train now trailed far behind as did the follow-up forces.

It was the question of logistics that finally determined the short hook option. There were simply not enough supplies available to support a run to the Seine. It was a pity but, as John was reminded by an army officer in Norfolk House, amateurs talk tactics, professionals talk logistics. But there were other reasons as well. Bradley and Eisenhower were by now only too aware that the Germans had much experience of being surrounded by the Red Army in Russia and were adept at engineering an escape. That the Allies had no previous experience of co-ordinating such a manoeuvre, combined with a healthy respect for the well-demonstrated German army's tactical superiority, the ordering of a halt at Argentan was a prudent decision. Better to go for the smaller option and succeed, than go for the larger prize and fail.

In the meantime, Allied air power supplemented by massed artillery would continue to pound the Germans in the Falaise pocket. While the Americans strengthened their forces in the south, the British and Canadians, with Polish support, continued to push from the north and the east.

With a relentless inevitability, the pocket continued to be squeezed until the remaining area was packed with desperate and fleeing Germans trying to escape to the west.

Within a very few days every road, major and minor, was choked with destroyed and abandoned vehicles. Discipline within the German forces completely collapsed. The Waffen SS in their desperation to escape mercilessly shot anyone who got in their way, including members of the regular German army. Short vicious engagements between the *Wehrmacht* and the SS were regularly reported by prisoners. The barbarous were feeding upon themselves. This, and the carnage and destruction, found little sympathy from either the Allied forces in the field or from SHAEF and Norfolk House.

The Typhoons and Thunderbolts continued their orgy of destruction of the Germans on the ground, the only complaint from the pilots being that the stench of decomposing flesh was distinctly unpleasant, even at fifteen hundred feet and four hundred miles an hour.

After some vicious and close quarter fighting the gap was closed around Chambois on 19 August by the Polish Armoured Division from the north and Patton's XV Corps from the south in the vanguard. By the twenty-first the gap was sealed. Shut.

Now, the Allies could advance west on a continuous front of over a hundred miles against virtually no organised opposition. The race for Paris and the Seine was on.

The battle for Normandy was over.

SHAEF's original plan was to bypass Paris entirely since, from a strictly military standpoint, the city held no strategic objectives. This, however, was to ignore the politics of the situation and particularly the pressing need to keep de Gaulle and the French on side. Politics overrode all the military considerations: Paris would have to be liberated, and Eisenhower and SHAEF would just have to accept the delay and disruption to the general advance that would inevitably follow.

On the evening of Paris's liberation John lingered in the map room before catching the bus back to Kensington. That map of Normandy and beyond, so familiar now in the weeks since the invasion, the once obscure names of towns and villages now became household names.

The map still showed the invasion phase lines, those notional measurements of advance projected before the invasion had been launched. The last of these lines, D+90, followed the course of the River Seine, from its mouth at Le Havre inland towards Paris and beyond.

Now, at D+80, the four Allied armies were astride its whole length and, what's more, ten days early. Overlord and the Battle for Normandy had gone according to plan though not according to its original incremental timetable. For all its faults and mistakes, no one could deny that it was a magnificent achievement.

Led by General Leclerc's French armoured division, with de Gaulle in close attendance, Paris was liberated on 26 August. The sky was a cloudless blue, the women wore red and the men fresh white shirts. Blue, red and white; the colours of the French tricolor.

Thereafter, fuelled by copious quantities of alcohol, the evening and particularly the night had become one huge street fuck-fest. Anywhere and everywhere. Inevitable somehow.

There was something about the French, de Gaulle in particular, typifying it. The arrogance, the bloody mindedness, the self-serving attitude, the wilful unwillingness to consider anyone or anything beyond themselves.

Every country has a natural enemy. For the English, it was the French. But it was not exclusively an English choice. It was shared by all of France's neighbours. German, Spanish, Italians, Belgians – even the Swiss who particularly loathed them. There was something about the French that made it inevitable.

And de Gaulle: the very name, a man who had written a comprehensive history of the French Army, while contriving to never once mention the Battle of Waterloo.

After the liberation of Paris, John had devoted a day to update himself on the situation on the Eastern Front. His information was drawn from a series of despatches from British and American military observers together with reports from the various Allied journalists based in Moscow.

Operation Bagration, begun on 22 June, the third anniversary of the German's Barbarossa in 1941, and timed to coincide with the Normandy invasion, had now concluded.

The results had been staggering. In sixty-eight days the Russians had advanced four hundred and fifty miles on a broad front and had regained all the territory, and more besides, lost to the Germans since they had invaded. Pausing to re-equip and resupply, they were now poised to begin the advance into East Prussia.

Whilst the Russian losses had been substantial, the German losses were enormous. The Soviets claimed 381,000 dead, 384,000 other casualties and 158,000 captured. In addition, the German equipment losses were equally large: 20,000 tanks, 10,000 guns and 57,000 vehicles of all kinds.

As John noted in his summary, these figures were an order of magnitude greater than the British and Americans had achieved at Falaise.

While the British and American press naturally concentrated on their war in the north-west of Europe, as did their readerships, the real and decisive war, ten times larger than that in the west, was being fought on the Eastern Front. It was here where the war against Germany would be won.

Two days after the Falaise gap had been closed, Eisenhower, accompanied by a US Army film crew, had made a tour of inspection.

A twenty-minute extract of the silent footage shot was screened at Norfolk House at the end of August. Beyond a few involuntary gasps, it was viewed in complete silence. This was not something to be enjoyed by the public in the cinema newsreels.

Eisenhower, not a man given to any form of exaggeration, had been conducted through the area on foot. When interviewed, he said he had encountered scenes that could only be described by Dante. It was literally possible to walk for hundreds of yards at a time, stepping on nothing but dead and decaying flesh.

As John and the others in the audience at Norfolk House could attest, Eisenhower's description was bleakly accurate. That the footage was in black and white somehow lent it an air of unreality, but not the essential truth of it.

Whilst the Allied soldiers who had passed through the gap were unconcerned with the numbers of German dead, they had been impressed and somewhat amazed at the quantity of destroyed tanks and vehicles, the abandoned and burning guns and equipment. They had reserved their compassion and distress for the thousands of dead and dying horses.

Even after a thorough survey, the Allies were finding it practically impossible to determine the levels of destruction within the gap. Perhaps contained in that small area, 10,000 enemy troops had been killed. Another 50,000 had surrendered, very many of them wounded. Less than 20,000 had escaped, many of them wounded also.

By the simple expedient of counting, 570 tanks and self-propelled guns, 950 artillery pieces and 7,000 other vehicles had either been destroyed or abandoned within the pocket. Of the thirty-eight German divisions committed during the battle, twenty-five had been annihilated. What the Germans had managed to withdraw beyond the Seine amounted to a mere seventy tanks, thirty-six artillery pieces and fourteen weak and under-equipped infantry battalions.

The Allied armies' various statistical departments had drawn up a tally to the end of August. From the time of the invasion on 6 June, over a million German soldiers had fought in Normandy. Of these 240,000 were either dead or wounded with another 200,000 missing or captured. Ships were now leaving the English Channel daily transporting German prisoners direct to either Canada or the US for internment. In addition to the troops, the Germans had lost 1,500 tanks, 3,500 artillery pieces, 20,000 vehicles and around 3,600 aircraft. Perhaps half a million horses had been killed.

On the Allied side, since the invasion thirty-nine divisions had been landed, over two million men, nearly four hundred and fifty thousand vehicles and over three million tons of stores. The cost of the victory had been 210,000 casualties of which 37,000 were dead. Allied aircraft losses, the majority to ground fire and accident, stood at 4,100 with 17,000 aircrew killed. In addition to this, it was estimated that 60,000 French civilians had died, the majority in Normandy of which only sixty per cent remained standing.

The battle for Normandy had lasted ten weeks. By any measure, the cost had been fearful.

John was reminded of Wellington's words after Waterloo. "Next to a battle lost, there is nothing so sad as a battle won."

95

A month in the preparation, Dr Jones had produced a thirty-thousand-word report on the rocket. There were forty copies, all numbered. Luke had not received one – not that he would expect to. What he did receive was a *précis* of a couple of thousand words containing all the salient points.

Jones had reviewed the intelligence investigations since 1939 onwards. All the various leads, confusions, inaccuracies and misinterpretations were categorically explored and explained.

He had identified the principal site of the production as being within an old gypsum mine burrowed into the Kohnstein mountain north of Nordhausen in central Germany. A concentration camp called Dora, contained both within and outside the mountain, supplied the slave labour. Thousands were involved.

Jones had included a definitive description of the rocket, using its German technical name of Aggregat 4 or A4. Length forty-five feet, diameter five and a half feet with four fins at the base. Weight twenty-seven thousand pounds of which twenty thousand was fuel; an ethanol alcohol and water mixture distilled from potatoes, with liquid oxygen as the oxidant. The warhead was similar in size to the V-1: one ton of amatol. Reaching an atmospheric height of fifty-five miles, range from the launch point was two hundred miles, where it hit the ground at eighteen hundred miles an hour. Flying supersonically, no warning would precede the impact. Assuming earth penetration, the detonation would create a crater sixty feet wide and twenty-five feet deep.

Jones had concluded his report in an almost philosophical style. The A4 rocket contained almost 20,000 components and was immensely expensive both in terms of materiel and manpower. While as a technical achievement it was enormous, as a strategic weapon – one ton of explosive delivered two hundred miles – it was completely useless, making no sense whatsoever. Jones could only surmise that the Nazis had been consumed by the almost romantic notion of such a weapon and its successful deployment.

Luke could only agree with Jones' conclusion but, romantic or not, the Allies had no effective defence against it.

In the meantime, the Allied armies' breakout from Normandy, begun in late July, was having a dramatic effect on the V-1 campaign. So too, after a disappointing start, was the redeployment of the southern English defences.

While in the first week of the new positioning only 17% of the V-1s had been brought down by the guns, they recorded 24% in the second week and, by the end of August, 74%. This improved rate of gun success combined with a doubling of the balloon barrage to almost two thousand south of London, and improved procedures for the RAF's standing fighter patrols, now being directed from the Royal Observer Corps HQ in Horsham, West Sussex. Fighter response times had shrunk dramatically and had, finally, reduced the threat to a minimum. On 28 August, ninety-seven V-1s had left the French coast. The combined and now fully integrated defences brought down ninety – only four reached the outskirts of London.

The last V-1 launched from France was on 1 September. It was shot down.

There remained the threat of both ground- and air-launched attacks from Holland, but these would never reach the intensity, or threat to London, of the French-launched campaign.

It was over.

Luke closed the file. The great threat to London from the V-1 might be over, but there was still the A4 rocket, no doubt to be called the V-2. With a range of two hundred miles, it would easily reach London from Holland. It was not a question of if – it was only a question of when and how many. Celebrations were premature. And, as he'd read in a separate report, the preparations for a massed poison gas attack on Germany continued to be made. Production of anthrax was being accelerated.

It was not over.

***

On 3 September the war became five years old. As someone commented to John, carefree infancy was over, school was about to begin. It was not a remark he considered of much relevance, though the allusion to infantile behaviour was to become apposite.

As was his declared intention, on 1 September Eisenhower had assumed formal command of the whole of SHAEF's ground forces in Europe replacing Montgomery. Bradley commanding all the American forces and Montgomery commanding the British and Commonwealth armies would now report directly to Eisenhower as supreme commander.

Montgomery accepted these new arrangements with extremely poor grace, barely alleviated by being appointed by Churchill to the rank of field marshall, at five stars, one rank higher than Eisenhower. Washington immediately responded by creating the rank of general of the army, an equal five stars, for Eisenhower to restore parity. These shenanigans did little to lessen the feelings of mutual antagonism between the British and American factions at the higher echelons of SHAEF. While Montgomery's position was now safe, there lingered persistent reservations, particularly from the Americans.

There still remained the unresolved question of strategy for the future advance. With Paris liberated and the Allies spread along a broad one-hundred-mile front beyond, decisions were required immediately for the next phase of the advance. The original Overlord plan for a broad front had been formulated to counteract any German attempt at counter-attack concentrated into a narrow thrust. A broad front would negate any attempts at flanking attacks and encirclements practised so successfully by the Germans against the Red Army in the east.

It was an approach still favoured by Eisenhower. At a large press conference given in London at the end of August he had declared that Montgomery's forces were to defeat the Germans in the north, Bradley to defeat them in the centre, while the Mediterranean forces from Dragoon would continue to advance from the south.

Montgomery however, had other ideas. Still smarting from what he saw as an effective demotion, he wished above all else to retain the lead *rôle* for the British Army, and hence, for himself. That this defied the logic of the Allied force numbers now onshore in continental Europe seemed to have alluded him.

Eisenhower now controlled three army groups. Twenty-eight American divisions, eighteen British and Canadian, one Polish together with eight sub-standard French formations which were included in the Allies order of battle more for political considerations than military might. Thus, the American contingent now outnumbered all the other Allies combined. Moreover, further fully-equipped American divisions were yet to be shipped across the Atlantic.

Montgomery, after sending streams of detailed notes to Eisenhower, now formally submitted his plan for what was now known as the 'Northern Thrust'. It was to be a very large operation involving the whole of the British 21st Army Group and probably two of the US 12th Army Group's armies besides. Meanwhile, Patton's Third US Army would effectively be relegated to a secondary *rôle*. While it would continue to threaten Germany from the area of north-east France it now occupied, it would be denied the means to mount any major offensives.

With this plan Montgomery demonstrated, with typical myopia, his lack of sensitivity and his failure to understand how the dynamics of the Allied campaign had developed since the invasion. Montgomery's proposals would reduce the Americans to playing second fiddle to the now junior partner while Montgomery continued to conduct the orchestra. It would be as if Eisenhower's assumption of supreme command of the whole of SHAEF's forces had never taken place.

Unsurprisingly, on the very same day Montgomery formally submitted his plan, Patton countered with another of his own. This, equally unsurprising, was the complete opposite to Montgomery's. The Third US Army, suitably supplied and re-enforced, would drive straight at the heart of Germany towards Berlin.

Irrespective of the merits of either of these blatantly egotistical plans, both were bedevilled by the same problem. As always, logistics. There were simply not enough stores, particularly fuel and ammunition, in the immediate theatre to support either Montgomery's or Patton's proposals.

At the end of August all the Allied armies' supplies, of whatever description, were still coming across Mulberry B or the open beaches of Normandy. Moving them northwards to where they were needed still required an enormous resource and consumed a third of all the fuel shipped across the Channel. The obvious solution would be the use of the French ports further up the coast.

Fittingly, Dieppe was taken by the Canadians on 1 September, and while it could be brought into commission within days, its capacity was small. Boulogne and Calais, also taken by the Canadians, had been systematically destroyed by the besieged Germans much like Cherbourg had been. Dunkirk, very heavily defended, was judged not to be worth the effort and was merely isolated to deny all forms of external support. Left besieged, it was a reversion to medieval warfare. Meanwhile, Le Havre was being comprehensively reduced to rubble by the defending Germans to make it unusable.

To be successful, the conduct of any war depends upon the integration and coherent application of three separate strata of activity. The strategic, which sets out clear, unambiguous intentions; the tactical, the means by which the strategy is to be achieved; and the logistical, the supply of all the necessary forces. The men, the equipment and the support: the means. Without the means, nothing was achievable. Nothing whatsoever.

In his early months of the war, John had given little or no thought to logistics. Now, years in, he seemed to think of little else.

While all these arguments, and counter-arguments went on, conditions on the ground continued to evolve. On 3 September the vanguard of the Canadians liberated Brussels and on the following day Antwerp. Such was the speed of their advance, Antwerp was taken before the Germans had time to destroy the port. It had been a major achievement. Antwerp's huge port facilities could solve the Allies logistical chain at a stroke. Alas, the port itself was not enough. Antwerp, like London, was an inland port, sited some fifty miles from the North Sea. The estuary and the banks of the river Scheldt dominated its access and it was to here where the retreating German forces had congregated. Denied an open route to the sea, the capture of Antwerp would remain a hollow prize.

Eisenhower, with the demands of his competing generals on the one side and the crippling logistic problems on the other, chose to compromise and refused to adopt either of the British or American plans. Instead, he continued to advocate his 'Broad Front' approach, arguing that this would bring all the available Allied strength to bear on the enemy, irrespective of where he was to be found.

To achieve this end there was to be a reorganisation. The American 12th Army Group was to be split. Most of the First Army was to move north to support Montgomery while Patton's drive to the Saar would be supported by the American 6th Army Group coming up from the south. Thus, the whole of the Allied armies would advance side by side on a front that now extended from the Channel on the left to Switzerland to the right.

But Eisenhower's plan contained a bias, and it was towards Montgomery. The V-1 flying bomb offensive against London was continuing, with the V-2 rocket attacks expected imminently. The British 21st Army Group was for the moment to be given the priority for the bulk of the supplies to allow them to continue their advance and overrun the remaining V-1 fixed launch sites.

Eisenhower's plan was sensible if not dramatic. It offered the least risk, recognised the situation on the ground for what it was, and satisfied the political imperatives and realities.

However, in according 21st Army Group the priority, he encouraged Montgomery to formulate another plan that was completely uncharacteristic of him and lacked any semblance of his usual cautious and meticulous planning.

John had been astonished to receive a few days earlier an official memorandum from the Air Ministry concerning precautionary measures to be taken regarding celebrations of the end of the war in Europe. It was detailed and specific and, worse, pompous. No extravagant displays or destruction. No access to firearms or pyrotechnics, and, especially, no access to explosives of any kind.

It was an extraordinary document, not couched in any way with the usual precautionary phrases, such as, in the event of. It presumed the end of the war was but a few days away.

John wondered which idiot in the Air Ministry had sanctioned it, with timing so spectacularly premature. There were a good many to choose from. The signature was a name he did not recognise. John immediately dictated a reply, acerbic, sarcastic and laced with contempt, copying it as appropriate.

True, the Germans might be in retreat, but that was all. Savage resistance to the Allies advance would continue.

John feared the war would not be over until the last German aircraft was destroyed, their last ship sunk, and their last soldier shot dead on the steps of the Reichstag.

***

On the evening of Thursday, 7 September, Duncan Sandys called a press conference. Chaired by Brendan Bracken, the information minister, it was held in his HQ at Senate House. The attendance was suitably extensive with every major newspaper and broadcasting organisation represented. Likewise, the official attendance was equally impressive. Air Marshalls Hill of Fighter Command and Gell of Balloon Command and the Army's Chief of Anti-Aircraft Defences, General Pile. There was also USAAF representation. All wished to share in the glow of what was meant to be a celebratory occasion.

Sandys began by declaring that, beyond a few last shots, the Battle of London was over. The German's secret flying bomb weapon, the V-1, had been defeated. Much applause and a little cheering greeted this remark.

He then gave an extensive review of the whole campaign: from the earliest suspicions and intelligence, the Peenemünde story, the extensive Allied counter-measures and bombing programme and then a full explanation of the three UK defence bands and their individual success rates together with the dramatic improvements achieved through the campaign.

His presentation took over an hour and handsomely achieved its desired effect. The press coverage was extensive the following morning, considerable column inches of text and reproductions of official diagrams.

Herbert Morrison, not wishing to be outdone, issued his own statement immediately afterwards. He praised the London authorities and the people of London for their response in the weeks of the attack and their fortitude in withstanding it, declaring, should anyone doubt it, that London is invincible.

Luke smiled as he read the report of Morrison's statement. Not that he disputed its content – more its existence. Herbert Morrison had only demonstrated the predilection of politicians that, spotting a passing bandwagon, they were ever eager to clamber aboard.

***

The day after Duncan Sandys's press conference and with Celia joining him for the weekend, John had stayed late at Norfolk House on the Friday night, attempting to get ahead before taking a couple of days off. She was due to arrive at Paddington soon after nine o'clock where he planned to meet her with a taxi.

A little before seven he heard a very loud double crack and soon after the sound of something travelling very fast through the atmosphere. Distantly, there was the sound of a large explosion. John knew immediately what it was. The first of the V-2 Vengeance Rockets had landed. Within minutes telephones began to ring.

Another hour and he had the story. The rocket had come down in Chiswick – the government cover story being that it was a gas main explosion.

John's immediate thought was of Celia's parents. Getting on the phone it was her father who answered.

"Thank God for that," said John on hearing his voice. "Are you all right?"

George Ashby sounded his usual unruffled self.

"Yes, we're fine. The explosion was on the other side of the cemetery, about half a mile above Dukes Meadows."

John knew the area, a little upstream from her parent's house, alongside the river.

"Close enough."

"Indeed so. Irene is over there now with the WVS."

"It was a gas main explosion as I understand it," said John, repeating the cover story."

259

"Is that what it was? One hell of a bang though, considering."

His tone did not sound entirely convinced and John was not surprised. He wondered how long the cover story would hold once the firings became more frequent.

"Celia's travelling up to London this evening, is she not?"

"Yes, I'm meeting her at Paddington soon after nine."

"Please give her our love and stress that we are both unharmed."

"I will, of course. I expect she will call you herself later on."

"Tell her we look forward to it."

John rang off then called for a taxi. It would be a difficult first couple of minutes when he met her.

They were due at her parents' for lunch on the Sunday.

After lunch a gentle afternoon stroll along the river had taken them as far as Hammersmith. A pause for a drink overlooking the bridge, itself not without charm, reminiscent of a model version of Tower Bridge and then, the long walk back upstream to Chiswick. Celia had talked the whole time, keeping him amused by pointing out places of interest and historical significance, recalling anecdotes. John had mostly listened, just happy to be with her. A short space together, 48-hour passes, two whole days: pathetic but precious.

The sun was still shinning, a reflected gloaming from the surface of the river. Standing outside the house she suggested they walk on a little, to the end of Chiswick Mall and St Nicholas Church and the graveyard beyond.

The tide had retreated and the slipway out into the centre of the river was now fully exposed. John walked down the length of it.

"I remember. This is where we stood during that air raid."

Remembering more, he kissed her, though not in the way they had that night.

"I used to play a lot around here when I was a little girl. That's Eyot Island," Celia said, pointing a little downstream. "I was forbidden to go on there. Didn't stop me, of course, but I always got caught. It's the white mud, gives you away." She laughed. "A few slapped legs for that.

"Over there," continued Celia, pointing now across the river, "is the Chiswick Steps."

John looked at what resembled a narrow flight of stairs leading up the bank.

"There used to be a ferry here until a few years ago, cost one penny. The ferrymen once rescued a boat race crew when they sank. Some of them couldn't swim," she added, surprise in her voice.

"Mark tells me a fair number of the navy can't swim. It's almost a tradition."

They walked back up the slipway, Celia continuing in her *rôle* as tour guide. She waved a hand vaguely upstream.

"That's the Chiswick Products' loading wharf, Cherry Blossom shoe polish and things, and beyond that, Crew's Hole."

John commented on the oddness of the name.

"It's Dutch. This is where the sailors used to lodge. Crew's Hole was mostly a collection of dives and brothels." Celia laughed. "I was totally forbidden to go anywhere near it, and I didn't."

Back on the road, she led him past the side of St Nicholas Church and into the graveyard. They stopped almost immediately by a large tomb still surrounded by iron railings, surprisingly not cut down for scrap.

"Hogarth's tomb. His house is still there up on the Great West Road, that little narrow one."

The writing was faded but John could still make out a few words – not any dates though.

"There's a few of the Rossettis around here as well."

She walked on, leading him into the main body of the cemetery.

"Another of my playgrounds," explained Celia. "There wasn't a lot of other children around my age, so I spent a lot of time in here by myself. I used to collect the names and the dates, you know, like you do."

John didn't, but he thought he knew what she meant.

"It's very peaceful."

"Isn't it? Always is. After all the noise from the river, instant peace."

John looked across the rows of headstones, the carefully tended graves.

"Not a bad place to be buried."

"We've got a plot," said Celia, brightly. "It's over there, under those trees."

John didn't comment. "What's that down there?" he asked, pointing to a large memorial.

"That's where I'm taking you."

On an intersection of some footpaths was a large block of granite around six feet wide, a couple deep and about five feet high. An oversized sola topee,

261

a pith helmet, carved in stone mounted on top. Frederick Hitch VC, Rorke's Drift, 22 January 1879.

"The Zulu Wars," explained Celia. "You see the date? It's on your birthday."

John was about to comment on how he also shared it with Lord Byron when they heard a distinctive sound coming from across the river. A V-1, the intermittent buzzing of the pulsejet engine, unmistakable. It was very low, only about three hundred feet. They stood and watched it, both commenting on how small it was.

"As long as the engine doesn't cut out, we'll be OK."

"I know," replied Celia.

They continued watching it as it approached, got nearer, moving fast, the orange jet plume trailing behind. Then the engine stopped.

"Shit."

John pulled Celia close against him, his eyes still on the bomb. The nose pitched downwards almost immediately. He hauled her down with him, lying flat behind the granite of Hitch's memorial.

"Cover your ears! Open your mouth!"

The explosion made a massive sound, obscene in the peace of the cemetery. The hot blast skittled ornaments on the graves as it passed through and then dust and grass rose into the air on the suction wave. Dense smoke began to rise less than a couple of hundred yards away. The distant sound of sirens.

"Some poor sod's caught it."

John stood up and helped Celia to her feet. Holding her very close, he kissed her.

"That was too close for comfort. I could almost take that personally."

Celia was shaken, but otherwise intact.

"If that engine had cut just a few seconds earlier, we'd be needing the plot."

John nodded; he'd had much the same thought. "Not just yet though."

"You bastards," shouted Celia to no one in particular as she retrieved a shoe.

John gave the memorial a gentle pat. "Thank you, Frederick."

As they walked back towards the church and Celia's home beyond for much needed tea, they passed a freshly dug grave awaiting a funeral. Something caught John's eye and he paused to pick it up. A triangular piece of flint, partially worked, the tip broken off. A discarded arrowhead.

How man had progressed through five thousand years. From flint tipped arrows to unmanned flying bombs. Same intent, different tools.

***

Late night train journeys; never pleasant, often fraught, best avoided. It was their fourth stop since leaving Paddington and Luke began to wonder a quite what time they might eventually reach Oxford.

It was his own fault. Starting from early morning he'd had three meetings in London, all of which had overrun, and lingering to grab something to eat had further complicated his day. The last train, constantly redirected into sidings to clear the track for munitions traffic headed to the south coast.

With his notes from the day long since written up, Luke settled himself as best he could, intent on getting as much sleep as possible.

As he dozed his mind drifted, thinking of the day's events, shuffling his priorities for the next few days ahead. He had two outstanding reports waiting to be written and there were several visits he needed to make that were now overdue. He was also behind with his reading and some letters were outstanding. They would have to wait for a few more days.

Five years of war had stripped everything to the bare essentials and the country showed it. Brutalised and desensitised it was now simply a case of live or die. Nothing else mattered. Not anymore.

96

However much Montgomery was lauded by his own troops, to an outsider observing from a distance, he suffered from several significant weaknesses.

John had read an appraisal of Montgomery's character produced by someone in the psychological warfare department of the US Army. Its circulation had been suppressed, but not before John had squirrelled away a copy in his filing system.

It was not a flattering document, concluding that Montgomery suffered from an inherent insecurity complex and was prone to irrational jealousies. This made him particularly intolerant of any criticism of his conduct and approach to the war and the questioning of the rightfulness of his orders. Though his talent for the set-piece battle was recognised, his absolute insistence that whatever the outcome things were going to plan did him few favours. His insensitivity to, in particular, the political implications of his actions highlighted by his press statements concerning the Americans, required great tolerance and forbearance from both his staff and his superiors.

There was one final weakness. Montgomery's approach was gradual. Great imagination and what was called tactical flair were not descriptions readily applied. They might be to Patton, but certainly not to Montgomery.

It was a reflection of the speed the whole operation was being put together that it was not until the Friday afternoon, only two days before it was due to commence, that John received the first briefing document.

Operation Market Garden, as conceived by Montgomery, was a bold and audacious combined forces plan to exploit the perceived German weakness in Holland. One single deep northern thrust of sixty miles, culminating in a crossing of the lower Rhine to form a platform for further rapid advances into northern Germany and the Ruhr.

His plan was composed of two interlocking and mutually supportive elements. A series of airborne operations, 'Market', and a rapid 21st Army advance, 'Garden'. The airborne element would be the largest insertion of paratroopers and glider borne infantry ever attempted. The freshly created First Allied Airborne Army, the FAAA, a combination of all British and American airborne would lead the way. With 21st Army massed and waiting to break out from the Dutch–German border at Neerpelt on the Meuse-Escaut Canal, three separate airborne landings were to be made ahead of them.

The US 101st were to land at Eindhoven on the south of the route, the US 82nd in the middle at Nijmegen, while the 1st British Airborne and the 1st Polish Independent Brigade were to land at the northernmost point outside Arnhem.

The route to Arnhem and the lower Rhine from the Dutch border was strewn with rivers and canals through the Dutch polder, an area similar to that of the Somerset Levels before it was fully drained. The minor road network was impassable for armour, the only major highway being on a causeway constructed mostly above the surrounding countryside. Thus, the 20,000 vehicles of XXX Corps and 21st Army would be forced into a convoy, constrained to this one single road, until it reached Arnhem.

The airborne's task was to create a sanitised corridor to allow XXX Corps' armour to pass through unhindered and at maximum speed.

Their tasks were multiple and various. The 101st were to seize nine road and rail crossings in the region of Eindhoven together with the securing of fifteen miles of roadway. In the middle centred around Nijmegen, the 82nd had a similar list of objectives. Secure a number of bridges and water crossings, take control of a ten mile stretch of roadway, together with the occupation of an area of high ground overlooking Nijmegen and the adjoining Reichswald forest which ran along the border with Germany and was where any German counter-attacks were likely to originate.

The British 1st Airborne and the Polish Brigade were the most northerly of the drops. Their task was to seize the Arnhem road and rail bridges and establish a bridgehead of sufficient size to accommodate the arrival of XXX Corps and 21st Army.

Due to the nature of the local terrain the British 1st Airborne would have to set up a perimeter around the whole of the city of Arnhem as well as their drop zones external to it. Arnhem was a large city with over 100,000 inhabitants in peacetime. The British paratroopers would be very thinly spread.

The total distance from the Meuse-Escaut Canal to Arnhem was sixty-four miles. The timetable was extremely tight and allowed for no delays.

Eindhoven was expected to be reached in two to three hours, while the British at Arnhem were to be relieved in two to three days.

John read this briefing paper twice before going downstairs to the map room. A large-scale map of the Market Garden area had been erected at one end of the room. Meanwhile, small scale reproductions were being printed off at speed. After a careful study of the map on the wall, he collected one of these and, pausing only to secure more tea, returned to his office. He then began to consider the second half of the briefing document. The logistics of the airborne lift.

The delivery of the paratroopers and the glider borne infantry, plus all their equipment and stores, was the responsibility of the IX US Carrier Command. To ensure the required accuracy, unlike D-Day in Normandy, all the drops were to be made in daylight. Such was the sheer size of the forces involved, it was impossible to achieve this with a single lift. The number of aircraft required to achieve it on a single operation did not exist. Instead, it would be spread over three separate airlifts.

Bearing in mind the whole *raison d'être* of airborne operations was to get the maximum force on the ground in the minimum time to achieve the force multiplier of surprise, John read this need for three separate lifts with dismay. That, for the supposed reason of crew fatigue and aircraft maintenance, the US Carrier Command were to spread these airdrops over a whole three days, concerned John even more. Not only were the initial attacking forces to be diluted unnecessarily, but there was also the very real likelihood that the mid-September weather, in either southern England or Holland, would delay the drops further. The mounting concern John was feeling began to turn to serious doubts as to the efficacy of the whole plan.

These doubts were further exacerbated as he read on. He discovered that the initial advance of the ground troops of XXX Corps was to be made without the benefit of close air support. No Typhoons or Tempests, no US Thunderbolts or Mustangs were to be allowed to operate in the immediate airspace of the transport fleets. US Carrier Command were much exercised by concerns of interference, confusion and possible collision in a congested area. While the transport streams would have fighter protection from Luftwaffe aerial interdiction, there would be no suppression of ground fire. None whatsoever.

John read this with a mounting sense of disbelief. The Luftwaffe might not be up to much these days, but German flak was fearful. It was the one thing they were really good at, plus they were well-practiced as he knew to his cost.

Dispensing with flak suppression was counter to every established doctrine. Making several telephone calls, and with increasing anger, confirmed it. The whole operation had been placed in serious jeopardy by the selfish attitude of the US Carrier Command and their evident concern for their own welfare above all else. And even in that they had misunderstood the threat.

And it got worse. The airlifts, his briefing described, was to be a 'bottom to top' operation. Those closest to the ground advance were to receive the greatest concentration of troops and supplies. The British northern contingent, who would have to fight the longest, were to get the least of the resources.

This John considered to be lunacy. It flew in the face of even the simplest logic.

The whole plan was predicated on the assumption that the Germans, when faced with such a concentration of force, would simply give up and gratefully surrender to the Allies. Three times he had read the phrase, 'if all goes well', or variations of it.

It wouldn't. It never did. Not ever.

Just ask the Russians about the recuperative ability of the German Army and the SS after a retreat. This they had learned at enormous cost.

John felt sick. He foresaw a disaster about to unfold and there was absolutely nothing he could do about it. Nothing whatsoever. He felt impotent and powerless.

He began to write a short, fierce and vicious critique of the whole operation to be typed and registered overnight. It would achieve nothing beyond a salve to his conscience. And nothing at all for the poor bastards on the ground whom he feared were about to die.

The plan had an addendum giving an indication of events once Market Garden was successfully concluded. Once across the bridge at Arnhem, Horrocks' XXX Corps would take the Luftwaffe base at Deelen, reinforcements would then be flown in, and XXX Corps would advance to the shores of the IJsselmeer, a hundred miles from their start line. The whole of western Holland would be cut off, the Siegfried Line outflanked and the Rhine crossed.

It was a utopic plan, the sweep of a hand across a map. And, like all utopias, impossible and impractical, bearing no resemblance to true reality.

Notwithstanding John's misgivings and a few other dissenting voices, he recognised that Market Garden had gained such a momentum that whatever the increasing evidence to squash it, it had become impossible to cancel. The cohort of supporters was growing by the day, all wishing to be associated with this future bold success.

US General Brereton, in command of the US Airborne and his British counterpoint General 'Boy' Browning, known for his immaculate uniforms and social connections, though lacking any operational experience whatsoever, were the leading proponents. In this they were supported by a host of senior figures, some of whom were energised for not always strict military reasons. From the US, Marshall and Arnold were eager to see what the newly constituted FAAA could do. Churchill, increasingly concerned by the effects of the V-1 assault, and the soon to be expected onslaught of the V-2, was urging an advance to destroy the Dutch launch sites. Eisenhower, keen to justify his strategy of the Northern Thrust and a Rhine crossing; and finally Montgomery, who saw the opportunity to re-establish his primacy on the battlefield and wrestle the overall field command back from Eisenhower.

Below this exulted level there were the immediate airborne commanders. Since their actions and subsequent withdrawal from Normandy, they had been stuck back in England. Every single future operation had been cancelled, mostly due to the speed of the Allied advance after Falaise. The count of these aborted operations now approached a dozen. There was a limit to the amount of time these specialist airborne divisions could be kept at peak battle readiness. Boredom and the subsequent decline in morale and discipline had already begun. The attitude of their commanders had become whatever the operation, whatever the difficulty or the opposition, they no longer cared. All they wanted was that it should not be cancelled yet again.

There was but one dissenting voice. Major General Stanislaw Sosabowski in command of 1st Independent Polish Parachute Brigade, who's forces were scheduled to land at Arnhem on the third day. His contention was that the British had seriously underestimated the German's ability to regenerate effective and co-ordinated defensive forces. Furthermore, since the fall of Brussels and the taking of Antwerp, there had been a three-day halt and then another week for the Market Garden preparations. Ample time for the Germans to prepare a comprehensive defence.

Accused of being unnecessarily pessimistic, his solitary voice lacked a chorus of support.

97

Starting as a low distant rumble, the sound increased rapidly to become a thunderous roar. Windows rattled around Norfolk House and normal speech became impossible. Operation Market, the airborne lift to Holland, had begun.

Abandoning any thought of work, John walked down the stairs and out of the main entrance of the building to the park opposite to watch. Half of the people inside Norfolk House seemed to be out there too.

Nearly five thousand aircraft in total, over two thousand Dakotas, gliders and their Halifax and Stirling bomber tugs were crossing the Channel and the North Sea. London lay on the path of the lower corridor and around half of the aircraft would pass overhead.

The size of the formations was simply staggering. On each of the routes, three triple columns over ten miles wide and a hundred miles long, taking almost an hour to pass. And the escorts were almost as numerous. Massed formations of fighters and fighter bombers stacked on the flanks of the transport streams while several dozen squadrons ranged ahead. Spitfires, Typhoons, Tempests and Mosquitoes from the RAF; Thunderbolts, Mustangs and Lightnings from the US Air Force. An unparalleled display of offensive air power. Beyond defending the airlift from any Luftwaffe interference, their main task was to attack and strafe what remained of any German defences that had survived the bombing assaults on the drop zones and along the length of the attack corridor.

John smoked a final cigarette before returning to his office. He had begun to hear rumours of serious German opposition on the ground, and particularly around Arnhem, rumours that only fuelled his misgivings around the whole operation.

It would be several hours yet before the first reports began to filter back. He needed something to occupy his mind in the meantime.

*

Conceived in haste, Operation Market Garden had taken a mere seven days from approval to execution. Montgomery, the master of the set-piece battle always preceded by slow and deliberate preparation, had completely contradicted all his normal rules for engagement.

The Germans had long considered Montgomery as over cautious, systematic by habit, and plodding, and were far more afraid of Patton, who since North Africa had been identified as their main adversary. Consequently, they had anticipated a major attack by the American Third Army, led by Patton, towards Saar. The best of their available troops had been positioned north of Third Army to oppose him.

Gleaned from intercepts, the first intelligence report received at SHAEF, suggested that the German high command was totally stunned by Market Garden.

Whilst John found that encouraging, it mattered little what state the German high command was in. What did matter was the German reaction on the ground and how fast they could respond and organise their forces into an effective defence.

It was a race. Restricted by airlift capacity, the airborne drops were to be spread over three days; the ground advance by XXX Corps to Arnhem was a total of sixty-four miles concentrated down a single road. Any successful delay achieved by German counter-attacks would be crucial, threatening the isolation of the forward elements of the airborne, no more so than at Arnhem.

Employed on other tasks, it was Monday afternoon before John got a chance to review the reports from Market Garden. The first twenty-four hours appeared to have gone well. The initial German response had been characterised by confusion, and total surprise appeared to have been achieved. All the American airdrops had gone to plan, on time and, unlike Normandy, in the right place. The ground advance too had gone well, though not as rapidly as planned.

By contrast, the news, or lack of it from the Arnhem area was of increasing concern. There appeared to have been a total communication failure from the airborne forces on the ground. No reports had been received at either Montgomery's tactical headquarters or by Eisenhower at SHAEF. The only information had come through the Dutch underground who had a network of covert telephone lines spread across the whole of Holland.

These reports, forwarded by Dutch liaison officers, indicated that the British at Arnhem had run straight into several German Panzer divisions who, withdrawn from the front line to regroup and re-equip, were resting in the area. There was only the one report, but it was detailed and lucid, describing how the airborne were being gradually overwhelmed. Should it be accurate, the whole rationale of Market Garden was already in jeopardy.

Arnhem had been compromised from the beginning. Poor intelligence compounded by the denial of anything that contradicted the prevailing view, insufficient troops and equipment on the first drop, and the position of the drop zones. These were up to eight miles from the bridges and were placed on the north side of the Rhine. This position had been determined not by the airborne and the needs of their assault, rather by the caution of the RAF. It was another case of the tail-wagging the dog.

John thought back to the airborne assault of the Caen Canal bridges in the early hours of D-Day. There, and in the dark, the gliders had landed within fifty feet of the objectives. Granted the topography at Arnhem was different, but eight miles?

The quantity and frequency of the reports on Market Garden arriving at Norfolk House was spasmodic at best. None were particularly encouraging. After the initial success on the first day, on this, the second, progress appeared to be limited.

The Son bridge, a main target for the first landing zone had been blown before the American 101st had reached it. A Bailey bridge, of which the American's had no experience of building, had been brought forward to replace it. It would take time. At the second landing zone, the 82nd had run into serious opposition and their advance towards the bridge at Nijmegen was being seriously delayed. Of the British at Arnhem little was known for certain. The radios carried by the troops appeared to have crippling deficiencies. A small group were holding the approach to the north bank of the road bridge but could advance no further. In other areas of the town, small pockets had been occupied but all were coming under heavy counter-attack. In the meantime, the advance of XXX Corps had fallen behind schedule immediately. The thirteen miles to Eindhoven was intended to take two to three hours. Only seven miles had been achieved.

Due to the unexpected level of German resistance in all the drop zones, expenditure of men, equipment, ammunition and stores had been far greater than anticipated. Resupply was badly needed. Fog over the whole of southern England had delayed the second drop by three hours and then, poor visibility and low cloud over Holland had complicated it further. It was suspected that much had been dropped in the wrong place. In Belgium, the fog was even worse than in England. Dense, with no sign of lifting. All the close air support fighters, so desperately required, sat useless, stranded on their Belgium airfields.

Scout units from XXX Corps had linked up with elements of the 101st sometime on Monday afternoon. While this was to be welcomed, the link had been made eighteen hours behind schedule.

John waited until the Monday evening but no further reports came through. Dejected, he extrapolated the delays so far to the rest of the operation. At best, XXX Corps would not reach Arnhem until the Friday. Three days late. Whether any British airborne would be left to greet them was a moot point.

John, monitoring Market and particularly the Garden airborne operations from the map room at Norfolk House, had become increasingly troubled. It was the third day and the third and final drop.

He thought of the poor bloody Dakota pilots, forced to fly straight and level whatever the intensity of the ground fire. It was the same for the bomber crews now streaming day and night into the heart of Germany. Conditioned to never flying straight and level for more than fifteen seconds at a time, it was a task he would find utterly impossible. As a fighter pilot, manoeuvre was all.

To fly straight and level and not deviate whatever the circumstances required a type of courage he simply did not possess. It was not an original thought, but it was a reminder. A fighter pilot's fate rested more in his own hands than his colleagues in Bomber or Transport Command.

It was an old adage: whilst success had many fathers, failure has but one. As the days went by, the support for Market Garden amongst the staff at Norfolk House began to evaporate at an accelerating rate. By Friday, it had all but disappeared. The daily communiqués issued from Allied HQ had become even blander than ever, lacking any sense of optimism and deflecting attention from Holland by concentrating on the other fronts.

That said, there had been some progress. What had begun as a corridor had grown into a salient as ground on either side was taken and held. But the thrust forward to Arnhem had faltered badly. German resistance continued to stiffen. They were not strong enough to drive the Allies back, but strong enough to stop them going forward.

To John, reading the reports as they came through, some several days old, one thing was blindingly obvious. Market Garden was a failure and its fate had been sealed within the first few hours.

The 101st's failure to secure the Son bridge before it was demolished by the German's. The 82nd's three-day delay before taking the bridge at Nijmegen. The failure of the British Airborne to take the road bridge at Arnhem, being restricted to a small pocket on the northern approaches and a few fiercely contested areas in the town beyond. And finally, the ground advance by XXX Corps. Slow from the outset, beset by the difficulties of the solitary road, where small German interdictions brought progress to an immediate halt, together with all the delays ahead of them.

True, the Americans had fought well – the 101st and especially elements of the 82nd. A truly terrifying assault across the four hundred yards of the river Waal under fire, in nothing more than collapsible canvas assault boats where they succeeded in taking the northern end of the Nijmegen bridge. But it was all too late. The cause was by then effectively lost.

Anyone who compared the timescale of the original plan and what had actually been achieved, now two days behind the original date of completion, could come to only one logical conclusion. The operation was a complete and utter failure. Abject. It was time to call a halt and recover as many men as possible who otherwise faced annihilation. Particularly, the British Airborne at Arnhem.

Except, no one did.

Days before John had written a short report recommending cessation and was accused of being defeatist. He'd included a couple of predictions. When these had been realised, he'd written another. This time he was greeted by complete silence.

There was another old adage. Whilst it was hard enough to be forgiven for being wrong, to be forgiven for being right was practically impossible.

Monday night saw Operation Berlin, the withdrawal of the remnants of the 1st Airborne Division from north of the Rhine. Based, in part, on the evacuation from the Dardanelles during the Great War, it was perhaps, ironically, the most successful of all the Market Garden operations. Two thousand four hundred men were successfully extracted from the ten thousand five hundred who had landed. Fifteen hundred dead, six and a half thousand taken prisoner of which a high proportion were wounded.

Originally tasked to hold for a maximum of two to three days, they had held to the ninth day. It was heroism of the highest order, paid in blood. A clutch of Victoria Crosses, only one of which was not posthumous.

As September turned to October and autumn turned to European winter, there would be no more talk of great offensives, a war over by Christmas. Just the continuous hard slog, incremental gains and consolidations along the broad front, while the Scheldt estuary continued to be fought and cleared by the Canadians to allow the port facilities of Antwerp to become operational.

Montgomery, never one to admit to failure, continued to insist that Market Garden had been a success, saying at a press conference that it had been ninety per cent successful. He was wrong. Without the taking of Arnhem to then outflank the northern edge of the extensive German defences of the Siegfried Line, opening up into the Ruhr beyond…the whole operation was pointless. All Market Garden had achieved was to produce a salient, leading nowhere. Another hundred and fifty miles of front to be defended. And, with Holland split in two, it would be the Dutch civilians now trapped between the Allies and the sea, and still under German occupation, now guaranteed to be ever more oppressive, who would pay the price.

Bernhard, the Prince of the Netherlands, had given a swift riposte to Montgomery's claim. "My country can never again afford the luxury of another Montgomery success."

98

John had done himself few favours by his string of reports over Market Garden. Not that he cared. War is not a popularity contest. Taken aside one morning by a very senior officer, it was sympathetically suggested that for reasons of tact it might be best if he took himself away on leave for a little while. What finally decided him was the award of a knighthood to Browning: the final bloody insult. As John observed, had he been a German general, he would have been rightfully shot.

October is not the obvious time for a seaside holiday, but the Cornish cottage where they'd been in 1941 was available and easy to arrange. Celia had been flying almost continuously all summer and was overdue a long leave. Several telephone calls were all it took to arrange.

Collecting Celia from Bath railway station, they spent their first night at the farm being spoiled by Marjorie. A warm familiarity. After a breakfast of industrial proportions and with the car loaded with provisions, they made an early start for Cornwall. The journey took over seven hours, including a prolonged stop for a late lunch.

The cottage may have been used in the past three years but, judging by the number of cobwebs, it would not have been recent. At least there were dust sheets over most of the furniture, if not the beds.

Switching on the power and checking whether the lights worked, John gathered firewood and began to light a series of fires in every room with a grate. Celia meanwhile stripped the bed they were to use and arranged the blankets and the sheets for airing. The mechanics of the kitchen range had not improved. Through a mixture of patience and cussedness it was coaxed into life and soon they had a copious supply of hot water.

Neither had the energy to cook. Their evening meal was bread, butter and cheese all fresh from the farm. Half a bottle of American Bourbon topped it off. Tired, but happy, and a little drunk, they slept well into the following morning.

John had picked up some of his pre-war clothes from the farm: woollen pullovers with interesting holes, old trousers, a touch short in the leg. After dressing one morning, he presented himself downstairs to be met with a large burst of laughter from Celia.

"You look like a tramp," she said, laughing.

"Thank you, how kind."

He laughed in return. "Not that I care much. Most of the country looks the same."

Thinking further, he realised that apart from uniforms, he'd not had any new clothes since 1939.

After an exchange of news on the drive down, they had made a conscious decision to ignore the war completely. No discussion of it either generally or specifically. Denied newspapers or radio, it was to be a time of total isolation. Simple pleasures, minor occupations, something easily achieved in Cornwall. And a lot of sex.

There was a fair amount of land attached to the cottage, somewhere between three and five acres. What was once a considerable garden surrounded by a screen of trees and backed by a large area of woodland and dense scrub. Now massively overgrown it took John the best part of a morning to explore it. And that was incomplete; he found no fences, no walls, no indications of where the property ended. Just more and more trees. There was an energetic stream to one side from where the cottage drew its water, and what might once have been a large pond or miniature lake set towards the remains of extensive lawns. The cottage and its grounds, set at the base of the cove with cliffs on either side extending forward like arms, was in an idyllic position. There was something strangely restful, timeless about this place.

John wondered how much it was all worth and whether it might be possible to purchase it. Presuming they both survived, it would be good to have something of a permanence, an unsullied space of their own, after the war. A physical refuge, a place of solace.

It was dangerous territory this and John recognised it. Although he accepted that now he was more likely to live than die, thoughts as to the end of the war and what might follow it were, for the most part, an indulgence. Far too many unknowns to contemplate. Best left unthought.

In wartime, with questions reduced to a mere life or death, life was very simple. Come the peace, life would be much more complicated.

For a small consideration, Celia had arranged for them to borrow a couple of horses for the following day.

Soon after ten found them back at the local pub to collect them. While Celia had plenty of riding practice in her youth through her local pony club, John's experience was limited to occasional excursions around the farm on Dobbin. Consequently, John opted for the mare, leaving the larger stallion to Celia. She did not complain.

Unsurprisingly, the horses knew the area better than they did. They set off northwards, letting the horses find their own way. Climbing up a long winding lane on the side of a hill, the horses stopped by a gate. Celia dismounted and opened it, shepherding them through. Gate carefully closed, they ambled on; another gentle rise up an aged track, more gates, more paths. After about two hours they came to a grass and gorse covered plateau which stretched to the horizon.

Obvious from their behaviour, this was where the horses were used to having their run. And they did. They galloped for what seemed miles until the horses began to tire.

With their progress reduced to a slow dawdle, they tethered the horses to a stunted tree, and stretched out on the grass for a cigarette. It was very quiet – the odd bird singing, insects, the horses grazing.

"Have you any idea where we are?"

"Cornwall," replied Celia, laughing. "Inland."

John took off his watch and, by using the hour hand and the position of the sun, guessed they had travelled roughly north by west. How far was another matter.

Sharing this deduction with Celia received a conformation. Her navigation skills were far in excess of his.

"It doesn't really matter though," she added. "The horses will find their own way back."

"I'll take your word for that."

Celia smiled at him indulgently.

"You'll see."

Unhurriedly, and without much prompting, the horses with them astride began the long traipse back. It was two hours before John recognised anything and another hour before they were back at the pub.

He had remembered something about riding horses. Walking and galloping were relatively straightforward as long as one held on. Anything in between, cantering, required far more skill.

There was soup and homemade bread available in the pub and they spent a pleasant early evening there. With dusk, they headed back to the cottage.

As they drove off, John was reminded of something else. Driving a car was so much easier than riding a horse. There was no negotiation required. The car went exactly where one wanted it to go, and immediately.

High winds and rain – neither encouraged optimism or feelings of wellbeing. From one of the top windows, John watched the weather rolling over the sea and into the cove. The tide was up and waves were breaking over the sea wall and flooding the lane in front of the cottage. His car was parked a distance up the hill that led down to the cove. Should they wish to go anywhere, it would be a wet walk before they reached it.

The evening before he'd trailed some fishing lines off the rocks hoping to catch a few mackerel overnight. It would be late afternoon before he could reach them again.

Faced with an inactive day, he wondered what they might do. He was unused to leisure and he found it unsettling – too much time to think.

He could hear Celia in the kitchen preparing breakfast. It would be eggs and bread. Marjorie had supplied them with so much food they'd be taking half of it back with them.

As he wandered down the stairs to join her, he wondered if she had any plans for their day.

Celia sat on an outcrop of rock as she watched John checking his overnight lines for mackerel. Three so far, triumphantly held up for her to admire.

It must be something primeval, she thought, how men seek praise and approval from some tasks successfully completed. She thought of little boys rushing to show their mothers some new trick accomplished. Not that she resented it; it was how things were. Women's *rôle*, domestic. Cook, clean, bearing and raising children while expected to support and admire their men folk. At least, that had been the accepted norm before the war. Now, with women fulfilling every occupation imaginable, including herself, supplanting the exclusivity of men; she wondered how things might change once the war was over. More equality would be demanded. Whether it would succeed was another matter.

She lit a cigarette and gazed out over the waves. The rain and wind of the morning had passed through and there was the promise of a fine afternoon. Their time together had been restful, uncomplicated and unhurried. Unlike their usual, intermittent brief liaisons, always marked by impending endings.

John too had relaxed, though not entirely. Life at Norfolk House was becoming a tide of rising frustration, and while their leave together gave some relief, there appeared to be no long-term solution. She too felt the discontent. Flying most days, delivering Spitfires for consumption by the war in Europe. There seemed no end to it.

The whole of the country was getting tired, weary. Five years of war had seen to that. And another winter soon to come. And now, the onslaught from the V-Weapons.

Celia threw the end of her cigarette into the sea and stood up. John was on his way back, five mackerel hanging from a length of line in his left hand. Five was enough for their evening meal. She would fry a few potatoes to go with them.

It was a reluctant journey back from Cornwall. Though the day had begun brightly, with few clouds and a pale blue sky, a weather front had rolled in from behind them and by early afternoon it had started to rain.

With the first one hundred miles accomplished, they stopped in Devon for lunch in a pub. Then later, a teashop in a market town in Somerset. Both now dressed again in uniform, they'd generated a little curiosity but little more.

Arriving early for Celia's train from Bath, they sat on the platform. Railway stations were sad places in wartime; the joys of arrivals far outweighed by the pain of departures.

A return to their solitary beds, their working lives and uncertain futures. John held Celia very tight as the train began to load. A final kiss, brave smiles, promises to keep safe, a final wave amidst the clouds of steam and noise. Hateful.

John had spent a couple of days on the farm with Marjorie and Richard after Celia had gone back to Hamble. Courtesy of the mess in Norfolk House, he had secured a case of Kentucky Bourbon, the remains of which he would leave at the farm.

On his last evening the three of them sat before the fire, John and Richard talking into the night. Marjorie was not particularly enamoured of Bourbon.

"Don't the Americans drink sherry?"

They'd laughed at that.

"Very occasionally, and not by choice," had been John's reply.

After Marjorie had gone to bed, Richard had asked about Arnhem as Market Garden was now being referred to in the press. The coverage had been extensive and, despite Montgomery's attempts to deflect the criticism, the reporting had generally been hostile when the truth had eventually been told.

John told him what he knew. It was nothing that a close reading of the reportage would not have yielded, though better sourced and better told, with reason rather than rumour.

John took another drink, lighting a cigarette.

"Hastily conceived, poorly planned and begun at least two weeks too late. And then, everything that could go wrong, did."

He listed the failings, from the plan of the drops, the impossibility of the single road, the delays, the weather, the speed of the German reaction.

"Everything," he said, finally. "Every fucking thing you could imagine."

Richard was taken aback. Not so much by what John said, but by the way he said it. He'd heard John swear before, but never with such vehemence.

99

Friends amongst Henderson's contemporaries at Oxford were rare. He had colleagues certainly, but not friends. Such was the nature of Oxford. In a university city, a community of academic excellence and fierce competition where weakness was always exposed, friendship was seen as a luxury, not a necessity.

But he had one friend: a classics don at one of the other colleges. Much the same age, similar background, similar sceptical attitude. And now his friend was dead. Killed by a V-2 on a visit to London.

The only thing they had ever really disagreed about was clothes. Henderson, mostly indifferent; his friend, punctilious, always immaculate. It had been a high price to pay for a visit to one's tailor.

Henderson finished shaving. Luke was due for one of their regular review meetings. They were not as necessary as once they had been, nor had they been for some time. Now they served more to keep Henderson abreast of developments. Luke had become perfectly capable of working without supervision, prioritising his time and effort for the maximum return. He had grown into their job as Henderson had anticipated he would. At least that was a success. He foresaw a rewarding career ahead for Luke should he chose to pursue it.

He swilled some water around the basin to wash away the soap. If only his friend hadn't felt such a dire need for some new clothes. If only: the saddest phrase in the English language.

War was no different to life – people still died for totally meaningless reasons.

***

As he sat on the bus during the journey to Norfolk House, John pondered as to what his reception might be. Would it be neutral, hostile, welcoming; even if he still had a job? The day was cold and dank, fog, not a promising start.

Climbing the stairs to his office three or four people stopped him for a quick chat, glad to have him back. Similar greetings from the staff in the outer office. Even smiles from those not normally given to outward demonstration.

A large pile of reports awaited him and, after ordering tea, he immediately piled in. Again, the war had continued in his absence.

Group Captain Baker appeared in his office soon after eleven.

"Welcome back," he said, pulling up a chair. "How are you?"

"Well, I think. Rested. Cornwall retains its charms," replied John, smiling.

"Glad to hear it."

They talked generally for a while, mostly about what had happened in his absence and, what was likely to come in the immediate future. Finally, Baker stood up to leave.

He glanced back at John from the doorway.

"It's good to have you back, John. You've been sorely missed."

John thanked him. "I had wondered if I'd still have a job."

Baker gave him a broad smile.

"No fears on that score. Carry on as normal."

Later, in the mess for lunch, John encountered only the old familiarity. No hostility, no animosity, though someone did comment on his lack of a tan.

All forgiven then.

During early September, Eisenhower had been based at Granville on the Brittany coast. Originally selected before the Allied breakout from Normandy, it had proved to be a disastrous choice. Hampered by extremely poor communication links, even when they worked, and now almost four hundred miles behind the front lines, it had become an irrelevance during Market Garden.

Now Eisenhower and SHAEF headquarters had moved again, this time, significantly to the splendour of the Palace of Versailles close to Paris. It was an unequivocal statement. Eisenhower was now exerting his authority from the former seat of Louis XIV, the Sun King. There could be no doubt any more as to who had the ultimate authority. Supreme commander meant exactly what it said.

The American method of battle was to maximise the use of firepower and equipment in an effort to minimise their casualty figures. Invariably, massive fire concentrations preceded any forward assault. The British, while not so well provided as the Americans, had adopted a similar approach.

The main reason was necessity, not altruism. Both the British and the Americans had been dismayed at the level of infantry attrition since landing in Normandy. While replacements were coming through, particularly for the Americans, both armies remained depleted, with many infantry units severely under strength. While infantry accounted for only 14% of the US Army, they sustained 70% of the casualties. Front-line troop rotation was no longer possible. Once moved forward, they stayed on the front line. A recent American report on the psychiatric effects of combat suggested that American soldiers could withstand two hundred days of continuous combat. British soldiers, who were routinely rested for a few days after twelve days of combat, could last unaffected for four hundred days.

It was these critical manpower shortages, as much as any other consideration, that impacted upon the Allied strategy for the western front as the harshness of a continental winter began to bite.

With the unanticipated speed of the Allied advance after the breakout from Normandy, it was inevitable that all impetus and momentum would be lost as the well-prepared German defences west of their heartland were reached. A heavily defended and well-integrated band of fortifications perhaps twenty miles deep stretching from the North Sea to the Swiss border west of the Ruhr.

It was destined to be a campaign of small-scale attritional actions involving at most a few hundred men, a couple of dozen armoured vehicles, fighting through the scattered villages, fields and hills for yard upon bitter yard.

After the failure of Arnhem and the slow realisation that sudden and spectacular success was not to be realised, the mood at SHAEF, reflected in Norfolk House, was characterised by a certain grim resolution.

It was going to be a long, and hard, and bloody winter.

***

It was strange to cross the Channel in daylight. With Brittany now liberated and the Germans now cleared from the sea, there was no longer any need for subterfuge. Navigation too was considerably simplified, allowing Mark plenty of time topside instead of none.

While the nature of the Brittany coast held no surprises, it was a revelation in daylight. All the rock outcrops, little islands and coastal features, so well recognised in the darkness, were now fully revealed. So too was the dangerous nature of the immediate coast. They were not places a boat would frequent from choice which, of course, had made them ideal for pinpoints while also explaining the difficulties and frustrations they had suffered for so many months.

The Admiralty, in its wisdom, now required a detailed photographic survey of the whole of the Breton coastline shot from the sea. As someone had remarked, the MGB had become something like a seaside day tripper. Roll up, roll up, five bob for a trip around the bay. But it was still a hundred miles in each direction and the weather, daylight or not, was as capricious as ever.

***

Tirpitz, the enormous German battleship named by Churchill as The Beast, had finally been sunk. After over thirty previously failed attempts, the RAF had succeeded. The Dambusters' squadron had bombed it from fifteen thousand feet with twelve-thousand-pound Tallboy supersonic bombs.

It was a magnificent feat and all the newspapers were rightly full of it. That it had been achieved without any Lancaster losses was even more remarkable.

Matthew thought back to the carnage and sacrifice that was St Nazaire. It was only a pity that it hadn't been possible two and a half years before.

***

The Americans and SHAEF had now effectively monopolised Paris as their own. All other nation's troops, including the British, were now restricted to Brussels. John had read several reports expressing strong resentment.

In the summer of 1936, as boys, they'd been taken on a brief school cultural exchange tour of the continent; three days in Brussels and four in Paris. While Brussels had been impressive, particularly the Grand Place, Paris had been the highlight.

Unlike London, Paris is a small city. So much to excite in such a small area. Everything of interest easily visible from the top of the Eiffel Tower from which, incidentally, and to their guide's chagrin, they had launched paper aeroplanes with RAF roundels drawn on, to then see one of them floating in the Seine hours later.

It had been August and the city had emptied of Parisians, the hotels had been practically empty, likewise the bars and restaurants. It was as if they had the city to themselves.

One particular hot night, having slipped their escorts, they had walked the width of the city, a four-hour hike, which proved to be far more educational to impressionable sixteen-year-old boys than anything remotely included on the official itinerary.

John had fond memories of Paris, it being their first experience of 'abroad' – the adventures had been especially vivid. Though, whatever else, his one abiding memory of Paris had been the smell. All cities have a distinctive smell, but Paris was unique. A mixture of raw sewage and strong perfume. John had never smelt anything like it, before or since.

***

Engrossed at his desk, the sudden crash at the window made Luke jump. A flurry of feathers, a wing flapping.

Luke stood to find a sparrow hawk standing on top of a pigeon, one clawed foot on its belly, the other clamped around the throat. The beak, viciously hooked, tearing into the feathers and the flesh of the pigeon's neck. Not bothering to kill the bird first, the sparrow hawk fed at a ferocious pace, a bright-yellow eye, wide, evil, focussed on the prey. Nature's pitiless savagery displayed in all its furry.

The pigeon was dead, its back half stripped, blood running, feathers scattering to the wind. The hawk adjusted its grip on the carcass and flew upwards towards the roof to devour the remains.

With nothing left to see, Luke returned to his desk. Nature knew no compassion.

He had begun to write a summary report for Henderson on the V-2 campaign. Following sporadic attacks during September and October, the number of missiles falling on London had risen considerably; six a day was not uncommon. Though not as intense as had been the V-1 onslaught, it was enough to generate considerable concern.

To begin with, the government, for some reason best known to itself, had made no official comment on the rockets until it was forced to do so. Following a German communiqué on 8 November announcing the existence and use of the V-2 against London, and reported in the British newspapers, Churchill had made a statement in the House two days later. He confirmed that Britain had been under attack from this new weapon for some time. That it had taken so long for an official response had fuelled some disquieting conspiracies and suspicions. The British public were by now used to the truth about the war, however unpalatable. They did not appreciate being kept in the dark. Furthermore, since there had been so many anecdotal reports, Londoners referring to the V-2s as flying gas mains, recalling the earlier cover story, all they ever needed was a simple confirmation.

Some days later, Duncan Sandys had issued one of his regular reports. Unlike the V-1 that predominantly used fixed and recognisable ground facilities for launching, the V-2 was a fully mobile system utilising only a small convoy of vehicles. The missile could be launched from practically anywhere, with small crossroads hidden within forests appearing to be the favoured locations. Erection and firing could be achieved within a very short time, and once completed, the convoy would immediately move on to another, equally obscure location. To date, no launches had been observed and, as far as the Allies were aware, none of the ground launch convoys had been destroyed.

The V-2, once launched, was invulnerable since the Allies lacked any means to intercept a ballistic missile.

Whilst intelligence efforts and aerial surveillance continued, few positive results had been obtained. The best hope remained that the Allied armies continuing their advance into northern Europe would drive the V-2s out of range of England. But, with the failure of Market Garden, large areas of Holland still remained under German control and available as launch sites.

Luke concluded his summary with a report of a V-2 strike, the 251st, on 25 November. It had hit a Woolworth's store in New Cross in Deptford. It was a Saturday and the rumour had spread that the shop had just received a rare consignment of saucepans. Striking at lunchtime had found the area packed. One hundred and sixty-eight died, one hundred and twenty-three seriously wounded. Amongst the casualties were the passengers on a passing bus, found still in their seats staring straight ahead, killed instantaneously by the force of the blast.

This image had stayed with Luke for a while, as it had with Londoners as the news went around. Since there was no warning of a V-2 strike, and nothing that could be done to avert it, London's population had, instead of fear and panic, adopted an air of compete indifference. Since there was nothing they could do, they did their best to ignore it. Defiance by denial.

Some reports suggested expressions of nostalgia for the good old doodlebugs – they, at least, gave some courteous indication of their arrival.

***

The weather had been foul for the past two days, but now it had begun to clear. Celia left the operations room at Hamble and walked over to dispersal, a list of her day's deliveries stuffed into a pocket of her flying suit. Four Spitfire delivery flights to the central pool at Middle Wallop.

Settling herself into the cockpit, she went through the pre-flight checks and started up the Merlin. The usual coughs and bolts of flame from the exhausts before it began to run smoothly. With oil and radiator temperatures stabilised, she opened the throttle and began to taxi onto the runway.

The aircraft seemed to be pulling to the right a little more than was usual and the slew increased dramatically as her speed rose. Celia was about to abort the take-off when there was a tremendous crack from below the starboard wing. At once the wing dipped as the right undercarriage collapsed and the wing tip ploughed into the grass.

Slamming the throttle closed she kicked on maximum port rudder while hauling the control column left. The propeller blades started churning at the grass ahead as following another crack the port undercarriage broke off. Her quick reactions had saved the Spitfire from cartwheeling or worse, flipping over onto its back. Now it merely slewed to a halt on its belly, the radiators under each wing carving wide furrows into the grass.

Celia switched everything off, slid back the canopy, opened the little cockpit door and stepping onto the port wing root, ran down it and onto the ground. She kept going until she was fifty yards clear in case the aircraft caught fire.

Turning around she watched as the crash tender pulled alongside the now stricken aeroplane and began to envelope it in foam. Then a car and an ambulance arrived. She opted for the car and was driven back to dispersal.

A cup of tea, a couple of cigarettes and a chat. No one had been close enough to confirm it, but the suspicion was there must have been a slow puncture on the starboard wheel which caused an immediate deflation once she had started to move. The increased resistance on the wet grass would have done the rest.

Forty minutes later she was airborne in another Spitfire. The take-off had been entirely normal, though she had taken the precaution of giving the tyres a bloody good kicking beforehand.

100

The main Commando training camp at Achnacarry had grown extensively since Matthew had first seen it, extending almost beyond recognition in the months before D-Day. There was no shortage of facilities now. They even had a full-sized cinema; feature films on occasion but mostly used for training films of which there were now many. They ranged from basic training and individual skills, operational tactics and formations to suit various scenarios, and what was referred to as the Commando's greatest hits. Lofoten, Vaagso and St Nazaire: Operations Claymore, Archery and Chariot got the top billing.

What they saw were the full versions of the War Office films, not the abbreviated and edited versions that had done the rounds of the cinemas on general public release. They even included German footage of the aftermaths captured since the invasion and spliced on at the end.

Matthew had watched them a few times but had more or less given up now. He knew them frame by frame. His stabbing of the German officer in the doorway at Vaagso always drew a reaction. It had ceased to make him feel sick any longer when he saw it. Too much had happened since. Now, it was just like watching any other character on the screen. Not himself.

Though the attitude of the recruits towards him always changed after they'd seen it. Amongst the less disciplined a not totally unwelcome outcome.

But there was another reason he tended not to watch them now. He recognised too many of the faces. So many now dead. It made him sad, too reflective. The training of the recruits demanded a totally positive and upbeat approach. Enthusiasm and commitment, self-belief, not an overdose of reality. The irony that the whole of his active service had been preserved on celluloid for posterity did not escape him.

No doubt they'd still be shown in the years to come. Perhaps, long after his own death. Matthew wasn't sure what he thought about that.

***

John had received a letter from his bank, a periodic review of the state of his finances. An enclosed statement listed all his transactions for the past six months together with the return of all his used cheques, now processed and franked, over the period. Why banks always returned the cheques with the statements had always mystified John, but no doubt there was a reason.

Apart from his monthly salary from the RAF, including his flight pay, there was also credited the monthly rent receipts for his house from the US Army. This rental income was considerable and easily outstripped his other earnings, including the dividends from a small portfolio of company shares inherited from his parents. With his outgoings being minimal there was almost an embarrassment of riches lying idle in his account.

He'd been living in Marjorie and Richard's Kensington flat for almost two years and was likely to continue to do so for the foreseeable future. What had started as a temporary arrangement had become a permanency. Reminded by the rent he was receiving from the US Army induced a feeling of guilt.

While he'd been paying the gas and electricity charges on the flat for some time, he'd never paid any rent. The service charge and all the other expenses associated with the flat continued to be paid direct from the farm account. He wasn't even sure if they had a mortgage on it. It didn't seem fair.

During one of his evening conversations with the building's commissionaire, he learned the current going rate for the flat rentals. That gave him some guidance.

A couple of evenings later he sat and wrote a short letter to Marjorie and Richard explaining his reasoning and enclosing a cheque for a thousand pounds. It was a generous amount but, nevertheless, well within his means.

They would, no doubt, protest, but that was hardly the point. Money in wartime, just like any other time, was always of use.

Leigh-Mallory was dead, killed on 14 November. Appointed air commander in South-East Asia he was en route to Burma when the Avro York, the civilian version of the Lancaster, he was travelling in crashed in the Alps. All on board were killed including his wife.

The Board of Inquiry determined that the accident was the consequence of bad weather and could have been avoided if Leigh-Mallory had not overridden the advice of the aircrew by insisting the flight went ahead.

John found it typical that he had been killed by his own arrogance. And there was a further irony. His replacement for the South East Asia Command was Air Marshall Sir Keith Park.

***

Luke received a note to say the plans for using poison gas attacks or anthrax on Germany had, for the moment, been quietly dropped. The reason had not been moral repugnance but practical reality.

With the V-1 and V-2 launches now coming exclusively from Holland, it was considered inappropriate to use such agents on the country of an ally. Also, the use against Germany would contaminate the very ground the Allied armies were expected to cross.

While the gas bombs had been withdrawn and returned to their secure depots in Wales, anthrax production continued uninterrupted in the US.

There was always Japan. No one gave a shit about the Japs.

***

Whilst the dock complex at Antwerp had been seized in early September, it had taken another eighty-five days for the Scheldt estuary leading to it to be cleared. The first Allied ship to unload was on 28 November. Montgomery's failure to seize the estuary immediately before it was reinforced could now be seen as a monumental blunder. At least now the Allied logistical train that had stretched back to the Normandy beaches since D-Day could reflect the advances since.

That it had taken so long to clear the Scheldt was also down to the Canadian Army. In common with its British and American contemporaries, it too suffered from a severe shortage of men. But in the case of the Canadians it was due directly to a lack of political will.

From the very beginning of the war there had been great hostility amongst French Canadians to participate in what they saw as 'England's War'. Mackenzie King, Canada's prime minister, chose not to confront this, instead decreeing that only volunteers would be sent overseas, and then, only to Europe. As a direct result, seventy thousand fit, well-trained troops remained in Canada doing precious little while their depleted countrymen fought and died in Europe.

Mackenzie King's expedient political decision was to cost Canada dear. While as individuals, some Canadians were very proficient soldiers, the Canadian Army taken as a whole was a poor excuse for what it might otherwise have been. It was a price paid in blood.

290

Not that the British Army were doing that much better. Records indicated that it was the wettest winter in Holland since 1864. The terrain flat, the ground flooded, the mud drew comparisons with the Somme and Passchendaele. Mobility on the battlefield had become a forgotten dream. Between late October to the middle of December, the British Second Army had advanced a mere ten miles.

It had become obvious to all, especially the Americans, that Montgomery's grand plans had become literally stuck in the mud. The great advance into Germany was unlikely until the ground began to drain in the early spring of 1945.

It was a depressing reality. Yet another.

The opening up of Antwerp had other substantial benefits. Once France had been liberated, the population had turned its attention from the continuing defeat of Germany preferring instead to profit from the presence of the Allied armies. Pilferage and theft had begun to reach epic proportions.

Between September and October, it was estimated that a third of all the Allied army's stores, other than armoured vehicles and ammunition, landed in Normandy had been lost en route to the indigenous population. The black market in France was now the mainstay of its economy and was supported, in part, by thousands of American servicemen employed in the supply train only too willing to profit by supplying any immediate demand.

It was doing France, as a nation, no favours.

The French, cynical before defeat in 1940, were now sullen after liberation in 1944. Paris, where ten thousand American troops arrived daily on seventy-two-hour passes, had become one enormous twenty-four-hour brothel.

John read another logistics report that stated that half of all the jerry cans used to transport petrol across France had gone missing: eleven million of them. Likewise, sixty-six million packs of cigarettes a month were being stolen. Not for nothing was Paris now referred to as Chicago-sur-Seine.

France was now a country bereft of pride.

It wasn't just the British Army that had achieved little during the autumn. The Americans had done no better. And while their forces had reached the German border, areas like the Hürtgen Forest had taken a terrible toll. Almost sixty thousand combat casualties, with another seventy thousand non-combat related. Trench foot was rife: morale was low and fatigue levels high. Disenchantment and dissolution ran through the Americans like a word through a stick of seaside rock. Enthusiasm was not an emotion much found around Norfolk House. Winter always seemed to come as a surprise to the American Armies. Tunisia in '42, Italy in '43. Now again in '44. December had found a woeful shortage of winter clothing and associated kit to counteract the full misery of a continental winter.

'Digging holes in water.' As a description of a fruitless activity, it was an appropriate metaphor. The classical example was of Sisyphus, condemned by the gods for eternity to pushing a boulder uphill with his nose. Whichever one chose, neither offered any hope of redemption. It was not a comforting thought.

John was attempting to compile a report on the remaining strength of the German Air Force in the west, the once lauded Luftwaffe. It was no longer the formidable force it once was, in truth never having fully recovered from the mauling it received during the Battle of Britain. That said, it still presented a considerable threat.

There was some evidence of a resurgence during November; several co-ordinated massed daylight attacks on the American bomber streams. The P-51 Mustangs, now escorting the bombers in overwhelming numbers, had responded vigorously. Intelligence estimates suggested the Germans had lost over six hundred fighters with up to three hundred and fifty pilots killed. It was a loss rate of over twenty-five per cent, impossible to sustain. The American attrition was below four per cent to all causes including accidents, easily accommodated by an ever-growing strength.

But the threat from the Luftwaffe still remained. Quite what level this threat represented was, however, proving extremely difficult to determine.

The traditional approach to assess the strength of any enemy was to draw up an order of battle: in effect a tabulation of the assets held by the opposition. An order of battle though was only indicative insofar as it described potential, but not the true capacity. Having the assets was not the same as being able to deploy them, and then use them effectively.

The sheer quantity of intelligence now emanating from the continent was enormous, and much of it, contradictory. Thousands of man hours in numerous departments were devoted to sifting through it. John was subject to a constant stream of briefing documents and reports, the majority of which reflected the bias and attitudes of their sources.

After several days of accumulating data, he was no further forward than he had been before he started. A different approach was needed, something more fundamental.

What concerned John was not what the intelligence contained, but what it did not. He also had another worry, something that had been nagging away in the back of his mind ever since he had returned form Cornwall.

The Allied line on the Western Front was long, around seven hundred miles, stretching from the Netherlands to the Swiss border. With the general shortage of American and British front-line troops it was inevitable that some sections of the line were poorly manned. While the defending German troop's crust was considered thin, the Allies too had chosen to deplete their forces in some areas in order to supplement their strength in other, more promising positions. In some quiet sectors of the line, the American dispositions were little more than rest camps.

If – as had been suggested in some quarters, though not generally accepted – the German overall strategy was to contain the Russians in the east while concentrating the best of their remaining forces in the west, the intent being to inflict such a level of casualties on the Americans and the British for their populations to force their governments to seek a separate peace, the vulnerability of the Western Allies became even more acute.

The more John thought on this, the more worried he became. That few others around Norfolk House contemplated this with any seriousness worried him the more. The Germans were not going to simply capitulate. Fighting German troops on German soil was going to be, as the American phrase had it, a whole different ball game. Fighting upon one's own homeland is no longer a foreign war. It is a fight for survival.

If the Germans could launch a counter strike at one of these thinly manned sectors on the Western Front, they might just achieve a decisive breakthrough. Both the British and American armies' dispositions were arrayed in attack formations, not defence. In the days it would take to re-adjust, the Germans would be able to advance considerable distances. It would be May 1940 all over again. And what capability the Luftwaffe retained would be crucial to this.

In simple terms, to be effective, an air force requires four things. A sufficient supply of operational aeroplanes; enough pilots, together with a cadre of trained pilots with sufficient leadership skills, to use them effectively; an ample supply of fuel and munitions; and finally a network of facilities, airfields and maintenance bases from which to operate them from.

John began to formulate a series of requests in an attempt to gather specific information. Once obtained he would be better able to estimate the true capability, and hence the threat posed, by what remained of the Luftwaffe.

John issued his report on the remaining strength of the Luftwaffe on the afternoon of 14 December, a Thursday. It was short, a single page, designed to be read.

He estimated that the Luftwaffe had around 2,500 operational aircraft in the west of which 1,800 were fighters, Fw 190s and Me 109s, operating from ten separate fully functional airfields. There was a more than sufficient number of pilots, and while some were poorly trained, there remained a significant cadre of experienced personnel to make them an effective force. Comparisons of estimated German aviation fuel production and recent consumption rates suggested that stocks were at a three-month high. The same could be assumed for munitions. In short, the Luftwaffe's strength was currently greater than at any time since the autumn.

The following day his conclusions were met with a considerable level of scepticism and, in some areas, downright scorn. The preoccupations within Norfolk House seemed to be more about the arrangements for the various Christmas parties than the threat from the enemy.

To say that John felt discouraged that Friday evening would have been the very least of it. Later, travelling back to Kensington on the bus, he stared at the thick fog swirling in the air around them.

This winter was the cruellest he could remember.

101

Saturday morning. The luxury of a whole weekend off.

John rose around ten. There was no coffee left so he made tea and idly listened to the radio while glancing occasionally from the window. There was little to see – the weather, bitterly cold, dense unremitting fog. It did not inspire. More tea, a long hot bath and then write a few letters perhaps.

John fell asleep in the bath, waking momentarily confused by the sound of the telephone ringing. It rang for a long time, but not long enough for him to reach it. Ten minutes later, it rang again. His office at Norfolk House.

There was a flap on. The Germans had launched an attack, details vague. John began to dress. So much for his weekend off. He called down to the commissionaire to have a taxi waiting.

John found Norfolk House in a state of total confusion and disarray. No clarity, no direction: the normal tone of a well-oiled bureaucratic machine completely out of kilter, fractured.

Overnight there had been distressing news from Antwerp. The city and its port facilities were now subject to continuous bombardment from the V-Weapons much as London. A V-2 had hit the Rex cinema, the largest in the city, killing nearly six hundred people outright with several hundred more casualties. Most had been Allied servicemen on leave. Another shock, particularly for the Americans, had been the loss of the band leader Glenn Miller over the Channel. And now there was this news of a massive new German offensive, launched through the Ardennes, towards the weakest sector of the American line.

A mood, sombre, hung within the building as thick as the fog outside. What most concerned John was the state of the Americans. Ashen faced: for the first time he saw fear writ large in their expressions. They were completely unused to reversals. The American Army had no experience or mechanisms, training routines, to handle a retreat. And fear was a contagion that killed.

Shock, numbed to inactivity; the mind, paralysed, groped for reason and found none. Despair and disintegration followed. A state of catatonia. The solution was firm and above all – decisive leadership. But the state of catatonia did not promote its leaders. It sat staring into dark places. SHAEF Headquarters at Versailles was ominously quiet.

John returned to his office and cleared his desk. Spreading out a map of north-west Europe he tried to make some sense of what was going on. Reports were many and various, fragmentary and confusing: clarity, none.

After six or seven hours John had managed to come to some very tentative conclusions. There appeared to be several considerable thrusts over a front of roughly sixty miles from the Ardennes forest north-westwards towards Belgium and Luxembourg. Plotting the lines of the advance, John extrapolated them in an attempt to determine their eventual destination. John's lines passed directly through Brussels, and then, Antwerp.

John stared at the map. That part was plain, so too would be the consequences. Should the Germans succeed in taking Antwerp they would split the British and American forces in two. The British isolated in the north and denied Antwerp as their logistical base, and the Americans restricted to the south. It was very similar to what he'd been fearing.

Some weeks before someone had commented that the Germans tended to be creatures of habit. This attack through the Ardennes was something of a confirmation. The offensive was very reminiscent of 1940, 1914 and even 1870. The massive, armoured thrust through the Ardennes in 1940 had been Hitler's one masterstroke of the whole war.

Though the one major difference to 1940 was the lack of Luftwaffe activity. No airfields had reported any significant attacks. That the whole of inland north-west Europe was blanketed by dense fog was probably the reason. Even so, the lack of activity surprised him. Air and ground co-ordinated movement had been the hallmark of all major German offensives. They had, as he had reported only the day before, the resources to mount a strike on the Allied airfields. It must be coming.

John pondered his preliminary conclusions late into the evening. Only two things really mattered to decide the eventual outcome. Did the Germans have the necessary troop levels, particularly infantry, armour and materiel and, most important of all, fuel to sustain the momentum and speed of their advance on the one hand? And could the Americans reorganise and regroup rapidly enough to mount a defence sufficient to blunt and then repel the advance?

Should they not, the results would be catastrophic.

By midnight, John had produced a single one-page report summarising his assessment. It would be typed up and distributed overnight. He left his final comment unsaid. It should be obvious to all.

Sunday morning. More of the staff at Norfolk House had attended church than was normal. In times of crisis people turned to God. Especially armies.

The situation had deteriorated overnight, that much was clear, but by how much and to what extent, was impossible to judge. The German bombardment, that had preceded the attack, had cut many of the fixed communication lines. Artillery to the rear relied on direct communication links to the infantry occupying the forward positions so as to provide them with effective support. They could not fire unless they knew were the enemy was. The terrain did not suit radio communication which, now, was subject to intense German jamming. Human runners were too slow. As a result, the German Panzers continued their advance practically without hindrance, impeded only by small, isolated groups of US infantry.

John reviewed the reports that had come in overnight. Fragmentary, partial, confused. Some, too many, were registering panic.

SHAEF's communiqués during the night and another that morning had been an exercise in blandness. None had made any mention of the German attack in the Ardennes. Not so the Sunday morning's newspapers. Their reportage was excellent, precise and detailed. Across a sector of sixty miles, twenty German divisions, 250,000 men, with up to a thousand tanks had launched a dawn attack in the Ardennes, an area occupied by just six American divisions totalling 83,000 men. The Germans were reported to have made considerable gains and deep armoured penetrations. Persistent fog and freezing conditions had grounded the majority of Allied air power hampering attempts to repulse the German advance.

From what little John knew, there was nothing to contradict the coverage, though it would do little to improve the nation's morale.

The US First Army, upon whom the brunt of the German attack had fallen, had performed badly. So too had its commander, General Courtney Hodges. Although known to be considerate of his men's welfare, he was considered to be lacking in his ability to exert assertive leadership. So it had proved. Fearing his headquarters was about to be overrun, he and his staff had decamped rapidly towards the west. This had only served to further confuse a confusing situation. Communications had completely broken down as First Army ceased to function as a co-ordinated whole.

Eisenhower, although confined to his headquarters at Versailles by repeated assassination rumours, had at least recognised the threat. By nature a cautious man, his first instinct towards a threat was to contain it. Without any hesitation he ordered an armoured division from the Ninth Army in the north and another armoured division from Patton's Third Army in the south to close upon the flanks of the German advance.

And advance it was. The lead panzer formations had advanced over twenty miles behind the US front line. They had moved further in two days than most of the Allied armies had achieved in the previous three months.

It began to remind John, uncomfortably, of the great German offensive in the spring of 1918. That had eventually faltered as the Germans ran out of fresh forces and supplies, but not before some desperate and costly fighting culminating in Haig's now famous backs to the wall order; "this far and no further". The pattern was set to repeat.

Further reports in the afternoon indicated some Luftwaffe activity. Sporadic but unco-ordinated ground attack sorties aimed at interdicting Allied units moving eastwards towards the German advance. In the poor visibility their achievements had been almost negligible but at the cost of over a hundred of their own aircraft. Some to air combat but most to Allied ground fire. John suspected that the great airborne assault they were capable of had been stymied by the weather. That, at least, was something.

During the evening Eisenhower activated his strategic reserve. From their rest camps in Rheims, 82nd Airborne was rushed forward to the north of the German thrust, while 101st Airborne was sent south to occupy Bastogne, a little town in itself, but the central junction of all the roads in the Ardennes area. Meanwhile, the British 6th Airborne began to be transported from their bases in England to join Montgomery's 21st Army Group to the north.

Again, John stayed at his desk until late in the evening. The German advance had not been stopped, but, and it was an important, actions had been taken to contain it as the Allied armies had begun to respond. The rout of the day before had ceased.

There had been a change of mood in Norfolk House, evident to John from the moment he stepped through the door on Monday morning. Anger, verging on blind fury from the Americans, hanging on the air like fire. During the night reports had arrived of German atrocities.

Near Malmédy, and witnessed by a horrified US military policemen a short distance away, SS Panzergrenadiers had herded a hundred and thirty US prisoners into a field alongside a road. Here the SS had stripped them of anything valuable or of use: jewellery, watches, cigarettes, winter clothing. Then, preceded by an officer with a pistol, they had shot them with automatic weapons and tank-mounted machine guns. Eighty-four Americans had died together with a number of Belgian civilians. A few of the soldiers had managed to make a run for it through the trees and had regained the American lines by the evening.

This was not the only incident of SS massacres. Other similar executions occurred at Büllingen where fifty US prisoners had been shot, and Honsfeld, another twenty.

The Malmédy massacre was, by now, fully documented. After the panzers had moved on, a US combat engineer battalion had reached the area and the evidence; still fresh, still warm.

The news of the massacre had spread like wildfire. Back through the chains of command to SHAEF Headquarters. Maximum publicity was ordered, newspaper correspondents briefed, photographic evidence displayed. By the end of the night, there was not an Allied soldier who had not heard of it.

The outrage throughout the American ranks was universal. And it generated a rage against the Germans, all Germans, that the US armies in particular had rarely shown. Their resistance to the German advance immediately stiffened. Now, it was personal. Vengeance was the order of the day.

The reaction of the Americans did not surprise John whatsoever. He knew them well by now. They prided themselves as God-fearing, righteous, decent people. Näive in some ways to Europeans, but fundamentally good. They took time to rouse, but now they had. And they would react in kind.

Hatred, once kindled, burned long. The SS in their black uniforms would now either die on the battlefield, or at the hands of their captors.

After several days of frightening confusion and rumour, the mood at Norfolk House had calmed. Resolution had replaced panic, and there was a gathering sense that while fortunes were yet to turn, the tide had been stemmed.

Information, spasmodic, continued to be confused. Some days old, some only hours. Gradually, the full extent of the German offensive and its achievements began to be revealed. In the first five days of the battle twenty-five thousand American troops had been taken prisoner while three hundred of their tanks had been destroyed. Some of the lead panzer elements had advanced nearly fifty miles.

The Ardennes offensive now had a name: taken from the shape of the German advance, it had become 'The Battle of the Bulge'.

Eisenhower continued to exert his authority. Against some fierce American opposition, he had given temporary command of the US First and Ninth Armies to Montgomery to ensure clarity of action to the north of the Bulge. To the south, Patton's Third Army, 250,000 men with 130,000 vehicles, had begun a ninety-degree turn from the Saar northwards towards the Ardennes. Their task was to secure the southern shoulder of the Bulge and the city of Luxembourg, then advance northwards to Bastogne. Patton had promised this in days. It would be a staggering achievement if realised.

In the meantime, American forces in the Ardennes area had more than doubled to around 190,000. The Bulge was becoming a battle of epic proportions.

Midweek, SHAEF Headquarters had imposed a complete news blackout on all activity in the Ardennes sector. The Germans were adept at monitoring the American and British press and their radio reports. This denial of information was reflected in the state of the weather; zero visibility from the ground up. There would be no air activity, from either side, until it lifted.

Bastogne, on the southern side of the Bulge, was now held by the 12,000 men of the 101st Airborne augmented by an assortment of other units including elements of 9th Armoured. The Germans, intent on the forward rush towards the river Meuse, had chosen to bypass it leaving the town and the 101st surrounded.

As one senior American army officer commented to John, being surrounded wouldn't bother the 101st one little bit. They were paratroopers. They were used to it. It was their job.

Bastogne was seen as key to the whole battle. By choosing to bypass it, the Germans had made a serious mistake. As the centre of the local road network, a confluence of junctions, Bastogne controlled all movement in the German's rear, hampering their further advance. In simple terms it had become a race: Bastogne had to be held until Patton's relief column could reach it.

On Friday, 22 December, unusually Eisenhower had issued an 'Order of the Day' addressed to every member of the Allied Expeditionary Force. While the language lacked Churchillian rhetoric, the message was clear.

The enemy was making his supreme effort to break out of the plight it was now in due to previous Allied victories. He was fighting savagely and gambling everything but already he was being foiled. But mere repulse was not enough. The Allies had the opportunity to turn the enemy's great gamble into his worst defeat. Eisenhower then called upon every man to rise to new heights of courage, resolution and effort to destroy the enemy wherever he was to be found and, with God's help, go forward to the Allies' greatest victory.

Eisenhower's order was not quite as Haig's in 1918, or even Nelson's of 1805 before Trafalgar, or any others that John could think of, but it was close.

John again worked long into that Friday evening and it was late into the night before he prepared to leave Norfolk House. On his way out he called into the map room and the weather section. Zero visibility coupled with freezing temperatures had lasted throughout the day and again air activity had been minimal. These conditions had now lasted for a week.

The duty meteorologist was smiling as he handed him the forecast for north-west Europe for the following day. A high-pressure system was moving in from Russia. It would lower the temperatures even further, but it promised crystal clear skies.

At last, the Allied air power could be brought to bear on the battle.

102

As forecast the night before, the weather over the Ardennes was transformed. Brilliantly clear skies with unlimited visibility.

From first light, USAAF and RAF fighter bombers began to rip into the German formations wherever they found them. And, where there did, it was a slaughter. The Allied dominance of the air that morning was total. What few aircraft the Luftwaffe managed to put up over the Ardennes were immediately destroyed in air-to-air combat, mostly by the P-47 Thunderbolts queuing up to chop them down.

Resupply could also begin in earnest. Trains of C-47 Dakotas with Mustang escorts began to drop hundreds of tons of supplies over Bastogne. They were still surrounded, still fighting all around the periphery, but now no longer isolated without support.

The German panzers were beginning to reach their furthest point; sixty miles from their start lines, a few miles short of the river Meuse. Now, the Americans began to take complete control of the battle.

As implied by Eisenhower's 'Order of the Day', the Bulge presented the Allies with a great opportunity. Should the German forces committed to the attack be destroyed, the less there would be available to them to defend the fatherland as the Allies advanced.

After the despair of the past few days, the Americans had grasped this opportunity for optimism with eager hands. John had long thought that Americans, as a whole, were more susceptible to mood swings than their British contemporaries. This was another example of it. The weather continued to offer encouragement.

Not only were the fighter bombers and the transports up in force, so were the heavy bombers. Several dense, concentrated raids were made on the German supply and assembly points behind the front line. The clear air had also allowed for the resumption of photo-reconnaissance flights. Gradually an unambiguous pattern of the positions occupied by the German advance, and the Allied response, began to emerge, and importantly, be better understood.

The battle was not over, not by a long way, but the means by which the Allies would win were strengthening by the hour.

The mood around Norfolk House moved from optimistic to almost cheerful. And it wasn't just the imminence of Christmas.

Christmas Eve was freezing. Overnight in Belgium the temperature had dropped to zero degrees Fahrenheit; thirty-two degrees of frost. In London too, a thick rime smothered every external surface. Pavements and roads were lethal. John's bus skidded into the kerb as two cars collided ahead of it. Christmas shoppers, out in droves, fought to keep their feet.

John couldn't remember it ever having been so cold. Every window in Norfolk House had ice sliding down the inside of the glass, melting, dripping puddles on the windowsills.

One report overnight had caused a great deal of amusement. The previous Friday, a German delegation had approached Bastogne under a white flag. They had announced, pompously, that according to the Hague and Geneva War Conventions they were offering the American defenders of Bastogne an ultimatum in the form of a letter. It was a choice: either surrender or be annihilated by artillery fire. Received by Brigadier General McAuliffe, officer commanding, and woken from an exhausted sleep, his response had been but a single word. "Nuts." It was perhaps fortunate that the German forces surrounding Bastogne were insufficient to carry out their threat. Nevertheless, his response was now famous, destined to enter American folklore.

Patton's 4th Armoured advance had been much slower than he anticipated. German resistance was far greater than predicted and the previous demolitions by American engineers as they had withdrawn to Bastogne had been comprehensive. Not a single bridge remained, slowing the advance further. Patton, by all accounts, was deeply embarrassed and frustrated, but hiding his feelings with a display of boisterous good humour.

For the second day the skies were crystal clear. The rampaging swarms of Allied fighter bombers continued to roam above the battlefield. Guided by American forward air controllers, now positioned in Bastogne, they would fall on any German concentrations within minutes of being alerted. It was a repeat of the 'cab rank' system of ground–air control developed so successfully during the Normandy campaign. What few fighters the Luftwaffe deployed were again rapidly despatched.

So nervous were the Germans of the fighter bombers that they had curtailed the use of their artillery during the daylight hours for fear of giving away their positions. Bastogne, in particular, was benefiting from the respite.

While they were now unlikely to be overrun, the US troops in Bastogne were still totally surrounded. Conditions within the town continued to deteriorate. Food and medical supplies were short, while casualties continued to mount. More airdrops were urgently needed.

Bastogne, though pivotal, was only one part of the battle. Other close-fought actions were taking place throughout the area of the Bulge simultaneously. Reports trickled in all day. The Americans to the south and centre of the Bulge were making progress, as were the British in the north. But everywhere it was slow going. Hard fought, bitter fighting, no quarter given as the Americans, after Malmédy, were disinclined to take any prisoners. There had become a distinct shortage to interrogate.

John, in the map room at Norfolk House, compared the morning and evening dispositions. Ground had been retaken, but it was by no means as much as everyone had hoped for. And there remained the lingering fear that the Germans might yet launch another big push on Christmas Day. Again, there were precedents.

During the day, large-scale heavy-bomber missions had been launched against eleven of the more important Luftwaffe airfields in the proximity of the Ardennes. The bomber's escort, principally P-51 Mustangs in the usual overwhelming numbers, had mauled the defending Luftwaffe fighters severely. Over a hundred Me 109s and Fw 190s had been destroyed with the vast majority of their pilots killed. By contrast the Americans had suffered very few losses.

Such were the numbers of Allied fighters now based in north-west Europe that continuous combat air patrols throughout the hours of daylight were now being flown, irrespective of the demands of bomber escort missions and the fighter bomber operations. Several thousand sorties a day was not uncommon.

Late in the evening, John read an assessment written by a USAAF intelligence officer which used recent combat reports as its source. The report concluded that, while the Luftwaffe appeared to retain sufficient fighters to maintain a defence, and the pilots to man them, the quality of these pilots was poor. Airborne cannon fodder was the phrase used. It was a view borne out by the loss ratios.

In air-to-air combat the Luftwaffe was regularly losing ten times as many aircraft and pilots as the Allies. In several instances, it had been fifteen to one.

John totted up the Luftwaffe's losses since his report in mid-December. It was over a thousand. Subtracting that from the whole, increasing the unserviceability rate, while also taking account of recent production, he estimated that they might still have around twelve hundred Fw 190s and Me 109s remaining. Though reduced in quantity and quality, the threat from the Luftwaffe remained.

Christmas Day: peace on earth, none; little if any goodwill to all men.

Before dawn, waves of Junkers 88s had attacked Bastogne. Damage was extensive, starting many fires and, caught by surprise, devastating to the defenders. With their bombs dropped, the Ju 88s had returned to machine gun the streets causing further casualties and havoc.

Anti-aircraft defences inside the town were poor. Most of the guns had been redeployed to the perimeter to defend against a ground assault. Few of the 88s had been brought down. Emboldened by their success, another raid followed several hours later.

These raids were but a prelude for two separate but co-ordinated assaults towards the centre of Bastogne. One from the north-west, the other from the south-east. Again, the Germans were conforming to pattern.

It was to be another day of desperate, close-order fighting. High winds blew the frozen snow off the top of the drifts freezing men and their weapons alike. Machine gun breaches froze requiring constant streams of urine to keep them operating. Ground was lost, retaken, lost and recovered again. The individual battles savage in which only the brave would live.

The paratroops of the US 101st had developed a new tactic. While machine gun fire kept the advancing German infantry flat to the ground, small bazooka teams stalked the accompanying tanks, getting within fifty yards before firing at their flanks. It required guile and considerable courage, but it worked.

Every last reserve the Germans possessed was thrown into the battle, and every American soldier who could still carry or operate a weapon was called to repel them.

As the morning wore on, American artillery began to tell as the attacks began to be broken up. P-47 Thunderbolts, dropping napalm firebombs, jellied petroleum, spread brazing swathes of fire and smoke across the snow, incinerating the enemy formations. The Germans got within a mile of the centre of Bastogne, but got no further.

Across the North Sea, dense fog had settled over the whole of southern England. The high-pressure system from the east that had kept the skies clear over the Ardennes had met a low-pressure depression coming in off the Atlantic. Hundreds of C-47 Dakotas from the US Transport Command sat fully loaded but unable to take off. There would be no Christmas airdrops for Bastogne. Eisenhower's exaltation was wearing thin.

During the afternoon John received a summary of the previous day's air operations. A two thousand heavy bomber raid, together with nine hundred fighter escorts, had been launched at eleven airfields around Frankfurt. Seventy enemy fighters had been shot down by the escorts, a further eighteen by the bombers themselves. Six US fighters and thirty-nine bombers had been lost, though some of the bombers were believed to have landed away from their bases. It was a bomber loss rate of less than two per cent. Anything less than four was adjudged a success.

Post raid analysis indicated the complete destruction of several of the airfields. There had been other heavy raids during the day. More airfields, this time in the Ruhr and transportation hubs around Cologne and Bonn.

In his mind, John compared the size of these raids with those in the summer of 1940 during the Battle of Britain. They were over five times the size of the largest he could remember. It took no imagination to picture the effects.

The heavy bomber raids on Germany continued to increase in both frequency and size. There were now well over a hundred RAF and USAAF air bases in Norfolk alone. Thousands of aircraft and tens of thousands of personnel. It had taken years to build but now this force was being deployed with ever greater destructive power. Germany was gradually being reduced to rubble.

Towards the end of a calendar year, it was customary for a series of reports to be produced summarising the Allied progress and achievements during the past twelve months. A draft of one such report arrived at John's desk in the late afternoon. It contained a tabulation of comparative bomb tonnages: the quantity dropped by the Allies on Germany and German held territory compared with that dropped by the Germans on the UK. Few figures demonstrated the complete dominance of the Allies in the air more than these.

In 1944 almost one point two million tons of bombs had been dropped on Germany. The comparable figure dropped on Britain, including all the V-Weapons, was nine thousand tons. At the height of the Blitz in 1940–41, only thirty-six thousand tons had been dropped. The tonnage dropped by the Allies in '44 was over five times that dropped in 1943.

One point two million tons compared to nine thousand. A ratio of one hundred and thirty-three. John, aware of the damage done to London, found it impossible to envisage the level of destruction now being wrought on Germany. Not that he felt any sympathy.

Early evening brought a further series of reports from the Ardennes. Patton's forces continued to advance on Bastogne from the south. They were now four miles from the centre of the town.

In the village of Lutrebois an infantry regiment with mobile field artillery and tank destroyers in support had attacked a group of Panther tanks taking up position on the edge of a wood. The artillery, together with some Shermans in the vicinity, brought down a barrage of concentrated fire. Twenty-four of a total of twenty-seven Panthers and their crews had been destroyed.

These losses suffered by the German armour were not untypical. In several other engagements, starved of fuel and with declining ammunition stocks, the Germans were being forced to fight where they stood. Denied the ability to manoeuvre, destruction followed rapidly.

To the north and centre of the Bulge, British and American counter-attacks were increasing in intensity as the German positions were identified. Massed artillery assaults were reducing the remaining German strength by the hour.

Behind the German front, and in order to deny them the ability to resupply, hundreds of B-26 medium bombers systematically destroyed villages in order to block the roads. Advance they may have done, but now the majority of the German formations were marooned and beyond future redemption.

The back of the German assault in the Ardennes was comprehensively broken. Hitler's gamble, Eisenhower had referred to, was lost. The end result was not in any doubt; not if, only a question of when.

John left Norfolk House late in the evening. Under his arm he had a bag of turkey sandwiches to serve as his supper.

*

There was a Christmas tree in the entrance to Norfolk House. Stuck in a large pot, it was a rather baleful looking thing, about twelve feet high and, frankly, poorly decorated. It had gone up, mockingly, on the day the Germans had launched their offensive.

Gradually, almost imperceptibly, it had started to lean to one side. And it had started to shed, a carpet of pine needles beneath it, widening and deepening by the day. Given a few more days it would be completely bald and leaning over like a stunted shrub against the wind.

The usual plethora of reports had come in overnight. Fighting, intense all over the area of the Bulge. Significantly, there were an increasing number of instances of groups of abandoned German armour. In one particular case, thirty Tiger tanks had been discovered, undamaged but with their fuel tanks empty. A suggestion to reuse them rapidly rejected on logistical grounds. Fighter bomber, medium and heavy raids had continued.

As their villages were destroyed around them, there had been little mention of the indigenous civilian population in the combat reports. It was fortunate that the Ardennes area, mostly agricultural in nature, was not heavily populated. Those who could not readily evacuate had gone to ground.

Unlike England, where the height of the water table tended to preclude their construction, most of continental Europe's houses were built with substantial cellars. In the Ardennes every single village had its own church and these too had been built with vaults. As the battles raged above and around them, it was to here the people had taken shelter.

Large areas of Bastogne were still burning from the raids of the day before. Using explosive charges, engineers had created a series of firebreaks to contain the damage. Clear skies had allowed resupply and the insertion of badly needed medical personnel by glider. More gliders followed loaded with fuel and then, waves of C-47 Dakotas dropping ration packs, ammunition, general stores including winter clothing, boots and blankets, and finally, the all-important cigarettes.

The medical aid and particularly the surgical teams were badly needed and not only in Bastogne. Some of the soldiers had waited over a week without surgical intervention.

In one area the Americans had set up an aid station in the local church to serve both combatants and civilians. Amongst the medical assistants were an American Army catholic chaplain and the church's parish priest. The

American spoke no French, the Belgian no English. Working together, they communicated in Latin.

Where the American artillery engaged the faltering German formations the slaughter was fearsome. Firing high-explosive large-calibre shells, fitted with the new proximity fuses now released for army use, produced a consistent pattern of air burst close to the ground, lethal to infantry unless well dug in. Though even that shelter was of limited value since the Americans mixed the high explosive with white phosphorous shells igniting anything combustible. There was much to stoke the fires.

Generously, or more likely by accident, some units of American troops had taken a few prisoners. The Germans had been perplexed at the hostility shown towards them. It wasn't just Malmédy. Stories had emerged of German tanks overrunning American foxholes and trenches then reversing to snake their tracks side to side to crush and bury to occupants before they could surrender.

Even in the midst of mayhem, there was a recognised code of conduct for slaughter. Killing was not to be confused with murder.

In the early evening cheering began to break out in Norfolk House. It was brief, but significant. Patton's 4th Armoured Division had broken through to the centre of Bastogne. It had been an action typical of his reputation, brave and courageous.

Five Shermans and a half track of supporting infantry had attacked Assenois, the last village before Bastogne to the south-west. Following a brief artillery bombardment and fighter bombers dropping napalm, the Shermans had moved quickly forward before the defending Germans could regroup.

Charging at full speed, the lead Sherman firing forward, the other four firing to the side with every gun they possessed, they blasted the woods to either side to obliterate any remaining resistance. They travelled the mile and a half in three minutes breaking through to the American perimeter. The follow-up was immediate as the rest of 4th Armoured poured tanks and infantry into the narrow corridor, increasing its width and securing it for the massive convoy of supply trucks following up behind.

The siege of Bastogne was broken, but the battle for the remains of the Bulge was by no means over.

Later, as he was leaving, John glanced at the Christmas tree in the entrance. He stopped. It had been straightened up, the carpet of pine needles swept. Now it looked used, battered, though no longer sad and, in some curious way, defiant.

John scoffed at his own imagination, but there was an allegory there.

The Americans, having now proved it to themselves, were definitely in the ascendant. The humiliations of the days before, the mass surrenders and inability to fight, forgotten.

John had thought about it on the bus the night before. It was an odd thing, the psychology of battle. The perception of forward momentum, whether real or imagined, was vital. Now, to the Americans, it was real.

Patton and his 4th Armoured Division, together with 101st Airborne, were being lauded in the press. Headlines splashed across all the front pages, nothing but fulsome praise. For Patton, how different to a year before, when he had been publicly disgraced for slapping wounded men in Sicily accusing them of cowardice, leading to his dismissal as commander of Seventh Army. Such was the fickleness of fame.

A corridor to Bastogne might be open but the flow of supplies on the ground fell well short of the need. Another airdrop was urgently required. Foolishly, the air trains followed the same route as the earlier drops and consequently were met by heavy flak and machine gun fire. Of the nine hundred odd C-47s, gliders and escort fighters, twenty-three were lost with many more badly damaged. The Americans were fortunate that the loss rate had not been considerably more.

Irrespective of the airdrop, supply convoys of trucks escorted by light tanks had begun a shuttle through the corridor to Bastogne. Supplies in, casualties and the few German prisoners transported to the south. Meanwhile, the Americans were fighting hard to increase the width of the corridor while the Germans, with increasing desperation, attempted to reseal it.

In many other areas of the Bulge and in contrast to Bastogne, SHAEF Intelligence reported that the tempo of the German attacks had slowed to almost nothing. Denied resupply and with their fuel almost exhausted, their troops had begun to withdraw eastwards. It was going to be a long walk back to Germany.

Apart from occasional single incursions from the German jets, Me 262s and Ar 234s, more irritant than effective against the American positions, the Luftwaffe had been more noticeable by its absence for some days.

Again, John was suspicious. With their penchant for mounting attacks on what they saw as significant dates, he feared something major for New Year's Day.

Using his estimates of Luftwaffe strength from Christmas Eve as a basis, and adjusting the numbers to account for their losses since, he calculated they still had close to a thousand serviceable Fw 190s and Me 109s in the western theatre. It was still a substantial number and a remaining threat. John issued another short one-page report alerting to the threat.

Notwithstanding the accuracy of his previous warning, this new prediction was met with a similar level of scepticism, achieving little other than furthering his recent reputation as a doom-sayer. John bore that with grace – he could only hope they were right.

As December began to draw to its inevitable close, thoughts began to turn towards an Allied counter-offensive, and to what form it should take. Equally inevitable was the friction, disagreements and political manoeuvring that accompanied the deliberations.

John spent a while in the map room looking at the latest positions in and around the Bulge, making a few notes, debating the options with himself. Returning to his office, he sketched out what he had seen onto the map on his desk.

The situation was not dissimilar to that of the Falaise gap the previous August. Then, the German Army had been squeezed into a salient, or bulge, by the pincer of the Allied armies advance. In the Ardennes, the Germans had created their own salient by their offensive and subsequent advance.

At Falaise, the neck of the salient, only a few miles wide, had been eventually closed after a lot of hard fighting, and while a substantial quantity of German equipment had been destroyed, a good many of their troops had escaped across the Seine.

By contrast, in the Ardennes, the neck or base of the Bulge was, as far as John could see, still around fifty miles wide, almost as wide as it was deep. The situations were not comparable.

Little filtered back to Norfolk House of what was being discussed in the higher echelons of SHAEF. What did, did not encourage. Montgomery was being his usual obnoxious self.

Vainglorious as ever, he had returned to his demand of Eisenhower to appoint him as overall ground force commander, to then have total charge of both the British and American armies. Eisenhower had absolutely no intention of doing so and his reasons, both political and militarily, were obvious to all. All, that is, other than Montgomery. His attitude had soured Anglo–American relations almost to the point of fracture. Montgomery's behaviour was as foolish as it was destructive.

It was only the timely intervention of Major General Freddie de Guingand, Montgomery's long-time chief of staff, who saved him from being dismissed. De Guingand drafted a suitable letter of apology to Eisenhower which Montgomery signed 'Your very devoted subordinate'.

Eisenhower graciously accepted the apology. But it was an episode neither he nor the Americans would forget or forgive.

An obvious plan of attack would be to cut the salient off at its base. But this was not Falaise and, particularly, it was not the high point of summer. It was midwinter at its cruellest. The Allies lacked the men, the armour and transport modified with spiked tracks to operate in conditions more common in Russia, and most specifically, the will.

There was no appetite whatsoever for the type of fighting that massed Allied counter-attacks would entail. The consensus was to opt for a slow and cautious approach. A gradual squeeze, maximising the overwhelming superiority of the Allied firepower on the ground and in the air to destroy the enemy piecemeal while preserving the Allied soldiers. Attritional rather than spectacular.

To John, observing from the distant side-lines, there was simply no other choice, however some might prefer otherwise.

'Festive Season' had proved something of a misnomer. Christmas had been a write-off, the week leading towards New Year likewise. Celia's plans to come up to London scuppered by the increased tempo of delivery flights, while John was unable to travel down to Southampton. It was now over a month since they had seen each other; letters, augmented by the occasional telephone call, a poor substitute.

With Elizabeth somehow contriving to be in Scotland, New Year's Eve found John sitting on the sofa in the Kensington flat, feet up, glass of whisky to hand, waiting for 1945 to announce itself. There were people on the streets gathering in all the traditional places, but their mood, John thought, observing them earlier from the top deck of the bus, seemed subdued.

Turning on the radio, he listened to the Watch service being broadcast live from St Paul's. Shortly before midnight there was the distinct sound of a double explosion. A V-2 had fallen close to the cathedral. A reminder, where none was needed, of the war.

Wearily, and without enthusiasm, as the bell tolled, John toasted the arrival of 1945.

1945

103

Denied their Christmas, the Americans were determined to have their New Year. At the stroke of midnight practically every artillery piece in the Ardennes opened up to mark the turn of the year. Not to be outdone, the Royal Artillery joined in. It wasn't only celebratory. It was also intended to demonstrate to the Germans, had they not already noticed, the overwhelming firepower available to the Allies.

Away from the immediate front lines, and the further away they were, the greater the celebrations became. In the rearward areas, formal regimental dinners, and large party gatherings at practically all of the Allied airfields. Late nights for many with hangovers to follow.

John had not slept well. A restless night punctuated by worrying that his prediction would prove right and, in some ways, worried that it might not.

He arrived at Norfolk House early, well before eight, watching the beginning of the dawn through his office window. The weather had not improved; still bitterly cold, snow flurries threatening further falls, savage, raw. Within an hour he began to receive the first of the reports.

At first light the Luftwaffe had launched a full-scale assault on all the Allied forward airfields they could find, and with every available aircraft they could muster. Nearly a thousand fighters and fighter bombers in all. Worse still, being entirely unexpected, the attack had caught the RAF and USAAF at their most relaxed and unprepared. Thirteen British and three American bases.

Every one of the Allied airfields were by now overcrowded and, because of the weather, the aircraft were not dispersed in the usual way but lined up on the concrete taxiways which were easier to clear of snow. These neat rows of stationary aircraft had made perfect targets. That most of the airfields had previously been Luftwaffe bases of long standing, their layouts needed no prior reconnaissance.

The RAF and USAAF had lost over two hundred aircraft on the ground, the majority completely destroyed. British Typhoons and Spitfires, American Mustangs and Thunderbolts. Pilot losses were mercifully few, but over a hundred ground crew had been killed.

Numerous as the Allied losses had been, they were trivial compared to the number of aircraft now based on the continent and, once the wreckage had been bulldozed to make room, the losses would be made up in days by replacements from the UK. More importantly, the Germans had made major mistakes; two of them.

Exalted by the surprise and success of their initial attack, and the lack of any immediate response, instead of making just the one or two passes, they lingered. It gave time for the ground defences to start bringing them down in numbers and, when they did eventually turn for home, Allied fighters from the rearward bases caught up with them. Short of fuel and with their ammunition expended, the Me 109s and Fw 190s suffered a mauling.

And it got worse. Such was the secrecy of the attack, the German flak crews had not been briefed. Faced with the sight of numerous aircraft heading towards them from the west, they opened fire and brought down over twenty of their own aircraft.

The Luftwaffe then compounded their errors with another. Later in the morning their remaining aircraft launched another attack. They found the air thick with vengeful Allied fighters who proceeded to chop them to pieces. Those who managed to return were again fired upon by their own ground defences.

By the afternoon, John began to receive the tallies. The Luftwaffe attacks had been a disastrous failure. They had lost over three hundred aircraft, nearly forty per cent of their total force. Worse still, their pilot losses were grievous. Over two hundred and fifty dead, wounded or captured. And the most telling, forty of those lost were senior group and squadron commanders. The quality pilots they could least afford to lose and could not replace. It had been a slaughter.

In its way, this loss of experienced personnel mirrored the fate of the U-boat commanders in 1942–43 which had led to their loss of the Battle of the Atlantic. Now, the German fighter pilots, inexperienced and without effective leadership, would be cannon fodder for the Allied fighters. Literally.

In the evening, John made a few notes, more for himself than publication. Notwithstanding his efforts, this attack had been another significant Allied

Intelligence failure. It was fortunate that its execution had been so poor and the Luftwaffe's losses so great. So great it was unlikely to be repeated, at least, not on such a scale. John estimated they had less than five hundred fighters left in the west.

The Luftwaffe had reached its twilight.

The bleak midwinter continued. Weather foul, moods subdued, punishment of the innocent, more good men lost. And now, the news of the death of Admiral Sir Bertram Ramsay, killed in an accident while taking off from Paris to attend a conference with Montgomery.

Ramsay had been a quite outstanding naval commander, possessed of an extraordinary calm and skill. The driving force behind Operation Dynamo which brought the British Army off the beaches at Dunkirk in 1940, then the Mediterranean and the invasion of Sicily and latterly, the naval commander of Operation Neptune, the seaborne component of Overlord.

Based at Norfolk House for some months, John had occasionally attended meetings chaired by Ramsay. Never less than impressive, he was a man of extreme ability and competence with that special skill of bringing out the best in his men. SHAEF felt his loss keenly and John, remembering several short and witty conversations with him, was deeply saddened, both to the event and its means. Accidents in wartime killed as readily as enemy action.

***

Allegra was due to attend a two-day conference in London. The prospect of three uninterrupted nights together was an opportunity not to be missed. Luke would accompany her.

A hotel room was an impossibility. With people streaming back to the capital with the end of the V-1 campaign, the housing shortage had reached critical levels. Rents and prices were rising rapidly, likewise the cost of lodgings and hotel rooms. But there was the Kensington flat.

Travelling up the afternoon before, they pitched up at the flat around six. Elizabeth was away, as usual, and John was yet to return. Taking Elizabeth's room they unpacked, made tea and awaited John's arrival. It was gone seven before he did.

John had not had a particularly good day and his mood was grumpy. Alerted by the commissionaire as to their arrival, he forced a smile as he let himself into the flat.

Cheerful greetings, much conversation, amiable company. Feigning tiredness, John declined their invitation to join them for the evening and had retired to his room by the time of their return. Their excitement at this unexpected time together had been obvious and John took genuine pleasure from it. No doubt they had some form of arrangement in Oxford, but this, as he knew from his own experience with Celia, offered much greater freedom.

The layout of the flat was such that the bathroom lay between the two main bedrooms. Remembering Elizabeth's overnight guests, it would be an advantage; his sleep would not be disturbed.

Allegra, intending to catch the same bus, left with John early the following morning. Luke made himself more tea and wondered what to do with his day. He couldn't remember the last occasion when he'd had free time in London and he found the prospect a touch peculiar. It was cold, but at least it wasn't raining. After mulling his options, he decided to take a few buses, walk a little, and wander around as the mood took him.

He travelled east, then south until he reached St Paul's. The cathedral was an arresting sight, stood almost in glorious isolation surrounded by rubble and blasted, burnt-out buildings on every side. There had been numerous photographs published, some now famous, but none had truly conveyed the true magnificence. St Paul's Cathedral, London's parish church, utterly defiant.

Crossing the river, Luke took another couple of buses around south London. In common with many who knew the north of the city, south London was a bit of a mystery. The pattern of the streets unfamiliar, the housing in many places quite different. One could be forgiven for thinking it was an entirely different city altogether. In some ways, it was.

The V-2 bombardment continued. Luke heard four during the day. That sound, so distinctive, could be nothing else. First, the impact explosion, then the sonic booms from the supersonic entry to the upper atmosphere. None of the strikes had been close, as far as he could judge, further south and east.

He walked for a while without any real knowledge of where he was and coming across a municipal park strolled across it towards the streets beyond. As he approached the end of a row of terraced houses, quite suddenly the surface of the pavement turned black.

One of the consequences of a V-2 explosion was that, being so large, the suction wave following the percussive wave sucked all the soot out from the remaining chimneys. Such had been the effect here.

Tuning the corner, he found what remained from a V-2 strike from perhaps the day before. Three of the mean little houses had been destroyed with extensive damage to others along the street and more across the road. Roofing gone, windows shattered, curtains flapping, debris spilled in casual confusion along the roadway. The smell of soot and dust still hung in the air.

Beside one of the larger piles of rubble a whole family was standing with what remained of their possessions. They were piled on the edge of the pavement, waiting for a removal van. The most precious of what they'd managed to salvage was wrapped up in a curtain tied with an old piece of string. An old man, three women and two children, all their faces stained and dirty.

Luke thought it one of the most truly pathetic sights he had ever seen.

There was nothing he could do to help, nothing at all. He moved on feeling humbled, guilty. Worse, he knew why they'd stayed out in the open to wait. Should they leave the site of their shattered home, there was every likelihood the looters would move in to steal anything of value.

Luke took a final glance back before heading for the high street and another bus. Random death: there but for the grace of God.

For Luke it was a chastening few hours. The visceral reality of the V-Weapons compared to his detached analysis. A reminder, if one were needed, of the continuing destruction and death this bitter war inflicted on everyone. It was no wonder that public morale had reached its lowest ebb since the beginning of the war.

104

The weather had again closed in over the Ardennes. Snow, fog, freezing rain, temperatures never above freezing. The freshly dead, lying in the open, quickly froze, their faces a reddish purple as the blood capillaries beneath the skin began to burst.

The battles continued. The Allies had begun the counter-offensive on 3 January. US First Army and the British XXX Corps. Progress was slow, painful, but continuous as they squeezed in from three sides: the Americans from the centre and the south, the British from the north. Small incremental advances each day, some more significant than others, but always in a forward direction as the Germans, mile by mile, were driven back.

Meanwhile, the mutual loathing and animosity between Montgomery and Patton had plunged to new depths. Patton had referred to Montgomery as a cocky little limey fart, while Montgomery thought Patton a foul-mouthed lover of war. The time when niceties were exchanged, however begrudgingly, was long since over. Eisenhower, stuck in the middle, kept his two generals many miles apart.

By the middle of the month around sixty per cent of the ground occupied by the Germans had been recovered and, with the crisis now considered over and US communications re-established, command of all US forces in the field had reverted to US command, much to Montgomery's chagrin. Though his ambitions to be made overall ground commander still remained, by now Churchill had spoken to thwart. Montgomery had been instructed to direct his energies towards the planning of the battles to come against the common enemy, not his personal battle, now totally lost, against his allies.

Soon, it became obvious that the Germans had started to withdraw, sowing every road and track with a profusion of mines and booby traps. German propaganda broadcast, continually monitored by Allied Intelligence, reflected the change. What once had been called the Winter Battle had become the Defensive Battle.

Whatever it was called the actions in the Ardennes were about to be eclipsed by events in the east. The Russians had begun their winter offensive.

* * *

Luke, wearied from a day of meetings, began his trek to the station, his mind drifting. It was a thought that never lingered, but sometimes, just sometimes, he wondered whether it was worth it? So much loss, so much grief, so much destruction, waste. So much death.

London was tired, worn-out, exhausted. England was tired, Britain weary and grey. Like the faces. And, from the projections he'd seen, perhaps another two to three years. Germany would be beaten in '45, Japan in '47.

As he turned another corner heading for Paddington in the twilight, an old woman on the street looked at him. Luke smiled at her and she smiled back. It was a great big open smile and he found it curiously uplifting. Only another few years.

He more sensed it than saw it. Almost in silence ahead of him, no more than a hundred yards, a four-storey apartment block seemed to lift momentarily before starting to disintegrate. The blast wave threw him into a wall and then hard into the pavement. Then the sound reached him, an explosion, fierce like he'd never heard before. Then another sound, an express train bearing down on him, and debris, falling from above, rushing down the road like a tidal wave carrying everything before it. A car, spinning around, slowly toppling on its side, still spinning. A bicycle cartwheeling. Something tore across his back, numbing. More debris landing, rolling, hitting him. And then the dust, spreading out, enveloping everything. A malevolent grey blanket, choking, blocking out the light.

Stunned, unable to move, Luke lay in the gutter, trying to make some sense of it. He could hear voices but they seemed far away, a distant echo.

Then he realised he wasn't breathing. He forced himself to take a breath, gasping, coughing, tears in his eyes. His throat, suddenly raw, a sweet acrid smell. Pear drops.

He heard more voices, closer this time. The sound of wood and metal being moved, more dust, instructions shouted. There was something pressing down on his back. He tried to move, his arms, his legs. There was something holding them too. Waves of tiredness swept over him. He could sleep here. No, he couldn't sleep. There was a train. He had a train to catch.

320

More shouting, more calling. He felt the weight coming off his back, his legs. Pain. Arms were lifting him, moving him, sitting him up. A rag on his face clearing his mouth, his eyes, his nose.

Luke opened his eyes. A man in a steel helmet was crouched beside him.

"Can you hear me? Look at me."

Luke nodded, stupidly, stupefied.

The man leant him forward.

"Deep breaths. Take deep breathes. Keep breathing. That's it."

Luke did as he was told. More coughing. A handkerchief to blow his nose. Someone draped a blanket around him. Then a mug of tea was thrust into his hand. Another voice, instructions to drink. A woman. He did. The tea burnt his lips. More coughing, spitting. More tea, sweet, milky, gritty. He drank it, felt its warmth in his chest.

The air was clearing. He could see himself, his legs stretched out. The dark blue of his uniform had gone a kind of yellowish brown, patches of red. Dust. His left hand still clutching the handle of his briefcase. But no briefcase, just the leather handle. Must find it. Looking at the debris, he was surrounded with debris, it could be anywhere. No, leave it. It had his name and address inside the flap. Someone would find it, send it on. It had his slide rule in it. Hate to lose that.

Two men lifted him to his feet, held him up.

"It's alright, I can stand."

"Good for you, mate. Now just you lean on me."

They walked, not far. Luke was helped up a step and sat on a bench. Soon it moved – he could hear a bell. It was an ambulance.

He went to put his briefcase handle in his pocket but it was torn, hanging down, limp. He put it inside his jacket instead with his glasses. Thank God he hadn't been wearing them. His back was starting to hurt. He tried to reach around but couldn't reach it. Somewhere between his shoulder blades, burning, a rhythmic throb.

Soon they stopped moving. Being led out, stumbling. An orderly, strong arms, catching him, carrying him to a cot, lying him on his side. Told not to worry. More tea. Leaning up to try to drink it. Spilling it, then tasting. Stronger this time, still sweet.

Lights, a torch shone into his eyes, told to follow it. His coat being taken off, then his jacket, trousers. Scissors, cutting off his shirt, his vest. Something wet on his back, warm. More voices, more light. Bright light, another room. Different smells. An injection. And then a warm darkness.

Luke woke up, the sun streaming into his eyes. It hurt. He coughed and tried to move, roll over. The sudden pain from his back made him gasp and he rolled back. He was in a bed, white sheets, sun coming through a window.

A nurse appeared and sat beside him. Dark hair, brown eyes, long lashes. For some reason he thought of the Jerseys on the farm.

"Good morning. How do you feel?"

Luke thought. "Bloody awful." He thought again. "What's wrong with my back?"

"You've got a long gash in it, a deep cut. Don't worry, it's all been stitched up. It will be alright."

"Good."

He began to rub his hands on his face but the nurse pulled them away.

"Careful, you've got some cuts there too. And your legs." She smiled at him. "Don't worry, the cuts on your face are not that bad. You won't lose your looks."

Luke laughed and coughed again.

"That's the least of my worries."

He leant up on an elbow and looked around. He wondered where he was and asked.

"Paddington Hospital. You were brought in yesterday evening. After the V-2 dropped."

Luke remembered. So that's what it was. He remembered the sounds. Yes, it was consistent.

"Were there many killed?"

"I don't know. I think so. You're one of the lucky ones."

Luke nodded. Yes, he was.

"Are you hungry? I'll get you some breakfast."

After he'd done his best to eat a doctor came to examine him. Luke answered a lot of questions, walked up and down the ward without falling over, and managed to get some aspirins for his headache.

"How do you feel?"

"Sore."

"You will. Apart from the cuts and the gash on your back, you're quite badly bruised and swollen. It'll take a few days for the swellings to go down and the bruising to come out."

The doctor glanced around the ward. It was crowded and they were expecting more.

"If you feel up to it you can go home this afternoon. Where do you live?"

"Oxford."

The doctor frowned. "I don't know that you're up to travelling. Is there anywhere in London you can stay?"

"My sister, flat in Kensington."

"Good. Stay there for a few days before you go back to Oxford."

Luke listened while he was given some instructions. When the stitches should come out. Not to shave until they had done. He didn't know his face was stitched as well.

"Now, get some rest and you can leave after lunch."

In the evening, they got him a taxi. He was wearing a smock in lieu of a shirt, his uniform jacket and coat, large rents in the back, held together with safety pins. There were tears in his trousers. He looked like a tramp.

Luke thought it best not to let himself in but rang the bell first.

John answered.

"Christ. What happened to you?"

"V-2. Yesterday. Paddington."

John nodded. "We heard. That one."

Led through to the sitting room, Luke sat heavily on the sofa. Celia appeared, and after a brief look, immediately took charge.

"John, go and make some coffee."

She kissed Luke on the top of his head and then started to undress him. He did not resist.

"Mind my back," he said weakly.

Sat in a dressing gown and draped in a blanket, Luke related what he remembered of what had happened. As he talked, John started to make calls.

He rang Elizabeth first, then Henderson at Oxford and finally the farm. Marjorie answered.

John explained what had happened, that Luke was recovering and would be staying in the flat for a few days. He then handed the phone to Luke.

"Hello mum."

Neither of them cried, but Luke came close.

Then he rang Allegra. It took them some time to find her. John and Celia discretely retired to the kitchen.

Luke looked brighter when they returned.

"She's coming up on Thursday night. Won't be put off."

Elizabeth arrived and immediately slipped into her *rôle* as big sister. After they'd all eaten, she and Celia washed Luke's hair. Sitting him on a chair in the bathroom, his head supported on a towel on the basin, washing out the matted grit and dust. They washed his face too, dabbing it gently with a warm flannel. He felt a lot better after that.

Elizabeth then put him into her own bed, announcing she would spend the night on the sofa so she could hear if there was anything he needed in the night. Luke didn't protest. Years of being bossed about as a child had taught him that. Neither would she let him look in a mirror.

"You know what you look like. You haven't changed."

Once Luke was asleep, the three of them sat talking. The death toll on the Paddington V-2 was still coming in. Over fifty deaths reported so far and scores injured. And there would be more, there always was.

By the following Tuesday Luke was feeling relatively normal, bruised, battered but no longer bewildered. Continuous attention firstly from Celia and Elizabeth and a weekend's care from Allegra had speeded his recovery. Days where he mostly slept and when awake was waited on hand and foot. Despite Elizabeth's protestations he announced at breakfast his attention to get back to Oxford.

"I've got work to do and so have you. And besides, we do have hospitals in Oxford. I can get the stitches out there."

She couldn't disagree with that. It helped that John agreed with him.

After they'd left, he dressed carefully in his own clothes, or at least what was left of them. A borrowed shirt and a sweater from John, his own trousers, jacket and coat, the dust sponged off, the holes and tears stitched up by the girls. An early job would be the ordering of a new uniform and cap.

He took a final look at himself in the hall mirror. Unshaven, his face a mixture of hues. The bruises were lightening now, the cuts not so vivid and angry. He'd still get a few stares on the train, but at least no one would ask. That was something.

Luke recalled an airman he'd shared a compartment with some months before. He was recovering from facial burns, his face now an odd mixture of hues from pink to purple, brown. Lips rebuilt and recovered from skin taken from the inner forearm then tattooed red to get the correct tint. Luke had been lucky and he knew it.

The scout's concern had been touching. News of his incident had obviously got around. After shaking Luke's hand and wishing him a speedy recovery, he'd insisted on accompanying him up to his rooms and lighting the gas fire. Luke waited for him to close the door and then slumped gratefully into his armchair. He stared at the fire, listened to its hiss. The relief was immeasurable.

He rang Allegra to tell her he was back. She wasn't there so he left a message. Then he rang Henderson. Neither was he. Then he rang his mother.

It was a short call. He'd rung her most days – there wasn't a lot new to say. Having promised to look after himself and visit as soon as he could, he rang off. He'd ring her again once the stitches were out. As for visiting, he would wait until the bruising had faded.

There was a knock on his door and he answered it.

Allegra nearly knocked him over. She held his face in her hands and kissed him.

"Why didn't you tell me you were coming. I would have met you at the station."

Allegra made tea and they sat and talked. She told him a couple of stories about things that had happened in Oxford in their absence that she knew would make him laugh. She then suggested he have a bath and change into fresh clothes, offering to go and run it. Luke handed her a packet of salt.

She nodded. Salty water, saline solution, good for the wounds.

Luke was sitting in the bath, Allegra gently bathing his back when the bathroom door abruptly opened. Professor Henderson stepped in, closing the door behind him. He was holding a bottle of aged brandy, liberated from the college stock.

Luke, as calmly as he could manage, introduced Allegra.

"Good afternoon, young lady. How is the patient?"

"Recovering, thank you sir," replied Luke before Allegra had time to answer.

"And being well attended to, I see."

Henderson leaned forward and peered at his back. Luke could hear him counting.

"Thirty-eight stitches, very neat."

"They come out on Thursday."

"Good. Good."

Henderson eased his way past Allegra and sat on the lavatory seat. He looked at Luke closely examining his face. The bruises were much the same colour as the ones on his back. So were the stitches.

"Well, I won't keep you. Mustn't let the water get cold. Come and see me when you can. Good to have you back in one piece as it were."

He was still holding the brandy.

"I'll leave this in your rooms. There's a couple of other things too that will interest you."

He bid them farewell. "Good to meet you, Miss Walker."

The bathroom door closed.

"Is he always like that?" asked Allegra.

"More or less."

On the side table Luke found the brandy, his briefcase, battered but intact, and a note. There was a table booked for them at the Royal for eight, pro bono.

Luke was astounded, and said so. Henderson was not known for his generosity.

"He must be fond of you," commented Allegra.

"I suppose he must be."

The thought of the meal and their evening together buoyed Luke up. But the real joy was getting his briefcase back.

His briefcase, now thoroughly cleaned, lay on the desk. There were scuff marks and deep scores across the leather; battered did not begin to describe it. Heavy rivets had re-attached the handle. It wasn't pretty, but it was functional.

Luke carefully repacked it for the morning and put it on the floor leaning on the side of his desk. Irrationally, he'd become very fond of his briefcase – they'd been to a lot of places together. Similarly battered, they were, he thought, an appropriate pair.

105

From the middle of January, the weather in the Ardennes had deteriorated even further. Temperatures dropped to minus ten Fahrenheit, fields of snow three feet deep, drifts commonly over ten. The worst weather any of the locals could remember.

To John, it seemed inconceivable that anyone could continue to fight in such conditions, but they did. The Allies continued to attack, the Germans continued to defend.

Everything froze solid. Clothing, once wet, became like medieval armour, resisting movement then cracking open. Guns, ammunition, so chilled it burnt the hands, stripping skin. The Allies fought the elements as much as they did the enemy as the sick rate rose faster than did the casualties from battle. And, as ever, there was the question of boots.

Since time immemorial armies have complained about their boots. The Roman sandal in a British winter. The standard issue British Army ammunition boot was ill-suited to the extremes of low temperature. They froze, rock hard, inflexible; soldiers walked with their ankles stiff.

One little story was doing the rounds. The German jackboot was known to be more weather resistant. An officer from one of the British Highland Divisions had stumbled across one of his sergeants sitting before a campfire in a wood. Strung above from a convenient branch was the corpse of a German trooper. When asked, he explained reasonably, that he was trying to thaw him out so he could retrieve his boots.

By 29 January the Bulge had been squashed and the front lines restored to where they had been in mid-December. It had taken seven weeks. The failure of Allied Intelligence to provide any prior warning of the German intentions had been almost catastrophic. It was with some relief that Eisenhower declared the Battle of the Bulge over.

Well over a million men had been involved, the largest single engagement of the Western Front so far and the overall casualty figures reflected it. The Germans had lost 80,000 dead another 100,000 wounded. The Americans, 8,500 dead, another 75,000 wounded. The British figures reflected their peripheral *rôle*. 200 dead, 12,000 other casualties. There were no figures for the civilian casualties other than they were substantial.

While the Americans and British dead were afforded the dignity of individual graves, efficiently marked and carefully recorded by the grave registration teams, the German dead were dumped by the truck full in bulldozed pits then liberally covered with quicklime, then covered.

The fate of defeated armies for a thousand years.

***

At the turn of the year Matthew had been promoted to Captain, a very welcome development. He now had a team of over a dozen dedicated demolition instructors reporting to him, plus supporting staff, teaching each new intake as they passed through Achnacarry. There were rumours that come February, the course numbers would begin to decline, but so far there had been no sign of it.

Germany was losing, with every prospect of the European war ending in the summer. But that still left Japan and no one was placing bets on when that would end.

***

Much to everyone's surprise, a ship from Palestine had docked in the Pool of London carrying over twenty-two million oranges. Much public excitement, enough for a pound a head for everyone in London, the Evening Standard reported. Soon, Norfolk House was awash with them.

By carrying home a small bagful every evening, the Kensington flat had accumulated quite a hoard. The refrigerator was full and John had resorted to keeping a few on the window sills at night where they froze.

Included in the shipment had been a fair number of bitter marmalade oranges. John had secured a stock of these as well. The question was now what to do with them?

Using one of the farm's wooden boxes that Marjorie used to send provisions up to London, John packed it with the marmalade oranges. There remained only one problem: the smell. Oranges were quite distinctive and the chances of them surviving the railway journey without being 'lost' were slim. He wrapped the box in two stout layers of greaseproof paper and then smeared the outer layer with the contents of a tin of sardines. There was no shortage of these. Then he added an outer layer of brown paper tying it all up with string.

Grease patches immediately began to appear on the brown paper, smelling quite pungent. Pleased with the result, John repeated the process for a package of the eating variety for Celia at Hamble.

A few days later, telephone calls from both her and Marjorie confirmed the success of his subterfuge.

***

Sometime during the V-2 testing programme at Peenemünde, a rocket fitted with concrete ballast in lieu of a warhead had gone off course and landed in Sweden. After a considerable delay and diplomatic niceties, the remains had been spirited out of Sweden to the UK for analysis, the results of which were now being circulated. Luke had read these reports with close attention, his interest in the rocket now particularly personal.

That the V-2 contained components of Swedish manufacture came as no surprise. Disappointment, but not surprise. Sweden had supplied Germany with the bulk of its iron ore imports until very recently and a fair quantity of their ball bearing requirements. While they had supplied Britain too, the quantities had not become meaningful until their recognition that the Allies were going to win. It took a certain political cynicism to cease supplying Germany to then favour Britain instead. All the more so since their neighbouring Scandinavian countries, Norway and Denmark, had been invaded by Germany in 1940.

Breaking from his normal routine, Luke went for lunch in a pub, a pint and a spam roll, maybe with onion if they had any. Somewhere in his rooms he had a list of the countries who had joined the Allied cause by formally declaring war on Germany, having waited for years to judge the likely outcome. The list had grown quite dramatically in the last few months.

Whilst another twenty-four nations had signed up to Churchill and Roosevelt's original Atlantic Charter declaration of August 1941 by the beginning of 1942, by September 1944 over sixty nations had declared war on Germany.

International politics was for ever self-serving at the best of times. At times of war, it came with ever greater levels of cynicism. To Luke, it did not seem that altruism featured much in human behaviour.

The following day it being 1 February, Luke had his first formal meeting with Henderson since his injuries. Their conversation had drifted, through the state of the war, likely conclusions, or not, and had now settled on the situation in southern Europe. Luke had read an article in the Times comparing the condition of Yugoslavia and Greece.

329

Henderson had been standing, staring out of a window. "The law of unintended consequences," he said, slowly.

Sitting at his desk he began to refill his pipe. It was his habit before an exposition and Luke, recognising the ritual, waited.

"To overcome their increasing shortage of indigenous manpower during the last war, the French began to import workers from their colonies in Indochina. There were over a million of them by 1918. Initially there was great resistance from the French trade unions, for all the usual reasons, a resistance that was only overcome by allowing the unions themselves to organise the labour."

Henderson laughed. "The French unions were led incidentally by someone called Thomas, a Frenchman of Welsh extraction. The Chinese were instructed to nominate their own spokesmen who thereafter, spending all their time with their hosts, were politically radicalised by them. You won't know, but before the Great War there was a huge rise in communist sentiment in France. Had it not been for the war, France may well have become the first communist state ahead of Russia.

"After the war, the Chinese workers returned to Indochina zealous with their new education and beliefs. In due course the first eastern communist party was formed in Laos in 1922. Since then, of course, it has spread widely, particularly China."

Henderson gave a brief humourless laugh.

"As the French have found to their increasing cost in Indochina. Wars have unforeseen consequences. All wars," he added. "This one will be no different."

***

The war in the east was not to be confused with the war in the west. The enemy, the Germans, may have been the same, but nothing else was.

The Allies, British and American, in the west were democracies answerable to their voting populations. Soviet Russia was a communist state, in many ways more repressive than Nazi Germany. Under the pervasive hand of Joseph Stalin, failure equalled death. So did insubordination. Had Montgomery been Russian, he would have been shot. Immediately. As one senior British Army officer wryly commented to John, the fear of certain execution was a most effective incentive to succeed. Faced with such a stark and ever-present reality, senior Russian commanders were equally brutal with the soldiers under their command. Victory or death.

For some months SHAEF had taken only a passing interest in events in the east, preoccupied as they were with their own campaigns. Whereas SHAEF had Russian liaison officers permanently attached to Eisenhower's headquarters staff, no such reciprocal arrangement existed with the Red Army. Stalin had decreed that all contact must be conducted through Moscow and thus, under his direct control.

Any day-to-day understanding of events in the east was impossible, as John had discovered some months before. There were briefing documents to which he was now privy, but details were mostly scant and carefully controlled by the Soviets.

Perversely, one source of information was German propaganda. It told little of the fighting, but much on the behaviour of the Red Army. Late in the previous October in East Prussia, the Red Army had captured some outlying villages, some of their earliest successes on German soil. A few days later, the villages were retaken by the Germans.

What they found were atrocities shocking even by the standards of the east. Every civilian, all of them, had been simply massacred. Beaten to death. Women, of every age, raped then stripped naked to be crucified; nailed through the hands to barn doors. Others, raped, then crushed by tanks after use. Children, not worth a bullet, clubbed to death. Babies spitted on bayonets. Should anyone doubt, the Germans had documented the evidence with photographs. It was barbarism as national policy: atavistic vengeance.

The Red Army was now a pitiless killing machine. Ten million troops, six million of whom were in the front-line units. 14,000 tanks, triple that of the Germans and 15,000 combat aircraft, a ratio of ten to one. Added to this were another 30,000 armoured fighting vehicles and over 60,000 field artillery pieces and heavy guns. The Red Army now bore no resemblance to the one brushed aside by the *Wehrmacht* in 1941.

At the turn of the year the Russians faced the Germans on a front of 750 miles, from the Baltic in the north to Hungary in the south. They began their winter offensive on 12 January in the north with an assault across the Vistula river at a point some 120 miles to the south of Warsaw. Preceded by a concentrated artillery bombardment from a mass of five hundred heavy guns per mile, the initial assault was made by the penal battalions, the equivalent of the British forlorn hope formations of the nineteenth century. Cannon fodder.

With the initial ground taken, a second, longer bombardment began to a depth of six miles. After two hours the main assault went in and by the late afternoon had penetrated to a depth of twelve miles. By the end of the second day, the spearheads had advanced an average of twenty miles across a forty-mile front.

The second phase of the Vistula offensive had begun on 14 January, as the main body of the attack crossed the river fifty miles further south crushing the German defences. Within three days of the initial assault the bridgeheads had merged into a front of around three hundred miles and had penetrated over sixty.

It was a rate of advance the western Allies could only dream of.

It went on. By the beginning of February, lead elements of the Red Army had crossed the frozen river Oder to create substantial lodgements on the western bank; an advance of two hundred and eighty miles. But now it had begun to rain, and with the rain had begun the thaw. The Oder, from being a flat expanse of ice easily traversed, became a barrier, a German moat, while the eastern European roads reverted to their normal mud.

The Russian Winter Offensive, having now created a huge salient four hundred miles wide at its base and around three hundred miles deep, ceased abruptly. The Red Army's rampage in two short weeks had them positioned eighty miles from Vienna, a little over a hundred miles from Prague and around fifty miles east of Berlin.

Whilst he had always belittled Eisenhower's broad front strategy as lacking imagination, Stalin now adopted a similar approach. The Red Army's attention now turned to the northern and southern flanks of their advance to the Oder. Whatever the military reasons may have been, the real motivation was political. Stalin considered the war against the Germans already won. His focus now was on occupying as much territory in eastern Europe as possible before the end of hostilities to bring it under the Soviet yoke.

Berlin could wait.

February, the shortest month. The strategies for the ground campaigns to advance to the Rhine, now the Bulge was over, were being argued out between the British and Americans. These arguments over the various options had been, as usual, fierce and needed resolution.

A summit meeting between the 'Big Three', Stalin, Roosevelt and Churchill, was taking place at Yalta, a Soviet Black Sea resort, beginning on 4 February. Its purpose was to formalise the political arrangements for a conquered Germany at the conclusion of the war and to ensure the co-ordination of future military operations to bring it about.

In preparation for the Yalta Conference, the British and American Combined Chiefs of Staff had gathered in Malta in late January. It was at this meeting an agreed strategy for the advance on the Rhine would be determined.

Reports were landing on John's desk in shoals. One such was the latest Order of Battle for the Allied armies in the west, combined with the latest intelligence estimates of the remaining German forces.

In the north-west European theatre, Eisenhower now had a total of eighty divisions under his command, fifty-six of which were American. The British contribution was twelve, equal to the combined divisions of the French, Polish and Canadian.

Facing the Allied forces, SHAEF Intelligence were estimating the Germans retained seventy-six divisions which, at first glance, suggested something like parity. It was not. German divisions were much reduced; typically, an armoured division had only around ten per cent of the guns and tanks possessed by its Allied equivalent and significantly less than half the number of men.

Allied army divisions contained anything between ten and twenty thousand men depending on their *rôle* and speciality. A British infantry division at full strength numbered 18,400, with another 24,000 troops in support. An armoured division was around 15,000 with roughly the same number in support. John made a quick headcount, noting that for every British soldier now in north-west Europe there were at least three from the US.

It had now become an American war, with the British subordinate in practically every respect, obvious to anyone who chose to see. That some, typified by Montgomery, chose not to, was their failing. The reality was indisputable.

British influence was on the wane, diminishing by the day. The Americans, nothing if not courteous, would continue to be polite, but it would be them, and they alone, who would decide the future strategy for the advance on Germany.

What had filtered back from the Malta meetings, and subsequently Yalta, was indicative. What had once been the 'Big Three', was now the 'Big Two', plus Britain.

It was inevitable, and John recognised it as such, though the recognition did little to make it more palatable. Britain had laid the foundations, and it was the Russians and the Americans who would complete the construction, or more accurately, the destruction, the utter devastation of Nazi Germany.

106

One of the great rivers of Europe, the Rhine stretches roughly north-westwards for 550 miles, from the Swiss border at Basel to the North Sea through Holland. The Rhine is Germany's most significant river and is deeply embedded in the country's psyche by myth and legend. Typically, 450 yards wide and fast flowing, it was viewed by the Germans in much the same vein as was the English Channel by the British; their last great natural barrier to invasion.

Eisenhower's strategy for the advance to the Rhine, consistent with his broad front approach, was to occupy the whole length of the west bank before beginning any assaults to cross it. This would ensure there were no German forces west of the river to disrupt the Allied forward operations. The plan had a simple logic and had been endorsed by the Joint Chiefs of Staff and confirmed by the Malta Conference.

With the French holding their positions on the upper Rhine, from Basel north to Strasbourg, the Allies were to advance on a front of 250 miles. The Americans to the south and a mixed British, Canadian and American force to the north. The Americans in the south had the greatest distance to travel, in the case of Patton's Third Army something in the region of eighty miles. For the remainder, it was closer to thirty.

Between the Allies and the Rhine lay the much-vaulted defences of the German West Wall or Siegfried Line, originally constructed in response to the French Maginot Line. Both had been built between the wars and were directly opposed to each other.

The Siegfried Line, though neglected since 1940, stretched for 390 miles, contained 18,000 bunkers and pillboxes linked by tunnels, together with mile upon mile of dragon-teeth-shaped concrete blocks positioned in stepped rows many feet high designed to strand tanks. There were also numerous anti-tank ditches and extensive deep minefields.

The central weakness of any fixed fortification in a mobile war is that once a small section is breached, the remainder of the barrier becomes redundant, as had been so amply demonstrated by the Maginot Line in 1940 and the Atlantic Wall in 1944.

There was also the not insignificant problem of the troop numbers required to man such a construction. Allied intercepts indicated that the Germans were short of around half a million men in the west after the failure of the Ardennes offensive. The Luftwaffe and the German Navy, the *Kriegsmarine*, had been stripped of all available manpower to plug the gaps while the remaining shortfall was being made up by forced recruitment of old men and boys to the *Volkssturm*, the German equivalent of the British Home Guard, dismissed by the regular *Wehrmacht* as casserole: a mix of old meat and green vegetables.

Beginning in early February, four separate but nevertheless linked operations began towards the Rhine. Even to the tutored eye, the overall plan was impressive though again, John wondered at the choice of names. It was a trivial thing, but they never ceased to irritate him.

In the northern sector, as planned by Montgomery, there was to be a pincer movement. The upper claw, Operation Veritable, with forces from his 21st Army Group and led by the Canadian First Army with the British XXX Corps armour in support, were to attack east from the Nijmegen salient. With the Rhine on the left flank and the river Maas to their right, they were to advance through the Reichswald forest area towards the towns of Kleve and Goch and around the northern tip of the Siegfried Line.

The lower claw of the pincer, Operation Grenade, led by the US Ninth Army seconded to Montgomery for the operation, was to cross the river Roer and then head north-east to close on the Rhine towards Düsseldorf, then move further north to link up with the British and Canadians near Wesel, thus effectively encircling the Germans remaining on the west bank.

In the southern sector there were to be two other operations. Operation Lumberjack with forces from the US Twelfth Army Group, including First Army, would attack towards Cologne; while further south, Operation Undertone led by the US Sixth Army Group were to advance through the Saarland towards the Rhine at Mannheim. The US Third Army, under Patton, was to attack between the flanks of Lumberjack and Undertone protecting both while driving east towards Coblenz where the Rhine and the Moselle meet. Patton was then to swing north to meet the US First Army coming south and thus achieve another entrapment of any remaining German forces still west of the Rhine.

John had read his briefing documents several times, pouring over a map drawing arrows, trying not to get confused, failing, then trying again. It was certainly a most comprehensive plan whose only weakness was the start dates which, for reasons of logistics, were not coincident.

Veritable was to begin on the following day, 8 February, Grenade two days later. Lumberjack on 1 March and finally Undertone two weeks beyond that.

Having dutifully read the reports of the major air operations of the past few days, John scanned the map which highlighted their current airfield dispositions. It was a crowded map – the number of squadrons and the numbers of aircraft available were enormous. A few days before someone had told him that it was estimated that over half a million aeroplanes had fought over Europe since 1939. It was an astonishing number, terrifying to contemplate.

The Luftwaffe was now reduced to about three hundred operational fighters, all short of fuel, compared to the Allies count of seven to eight thousand. The German situation was calamitous, utterly hopeless. Not for the first time, John wondered why they fought on. There was no doubt as to the eventual conclusion. It just seemed so pointless to continue.

After the abject failure of Market Garden – hastily planned, hastily executed – Montgomery had reverted to his normal mode of operation. The master of the set-piece battle, but only after weeks of painstaking preparation. The staff work had been meticulous to a fault; every commander had been fully briefed and understood their individual objectives and how those contributed to the operation as a whole. Montgomery could ill afford another failure and, particularly, neither could the troops under his command.

Veritable had begun as scheduled on 8 February. Saturation bombing overnight from several hundred Lancasters softened up the German defences by way of an overture before the assault began before dawn with a five-hour bombardment from over a thousand guns, the heaviest in the west so far, beginning at 0500.

Advancing on a relatively narrow eight-mile front, with the flail tanks leading to clear the minefields, the attack had initially gone well. It was not to last. The Germans had flooded much of the area and the armour soon began to bog down. Where the ground remained dry there were formidable fortifications, in places five lines deep, and very speedily the Germans rushed forward whatever remained of their reserves to meet the attack.

It became a bloody slog through difficult terrain. The Reichswald forest, planned to be cleared in less than two days, took a week to occupy.

Operation Grenade, intended to begin forty-eight hours after the start of Veritable, failed to materialise. The US First Army, after many months, had finally managed to capture the Roer dams in preparation for Grenade. Unable to demolish the dams, the Germans had resorted to opening all the sluice gates and discharge valves to flood the whole of the valley downstream. The very ground Ninth Army were to advance over. Grenade was delayed until the water levels subsided.

Faced with just the one attack front, instead of the intended two, allowed the Germans to move further forces north to confront Veritable, slowing the advance further. Amongst those defenders were contingents of well-equipped parachute troops who, under direct orders from Hitler, were forbidden to withdraw. They fought until they died and they took a lot of killing.

Once clear of the Reichswald, Buffalo amphibious troops carriers were used extensively to move through the flooded areas. The depth of water neutralised the minefields and the underground interconnections of the various strong points leaving them scattered like an archipelago in a shallow sea. One by one they were eliminated.

At the tip of the Siegfried Line lay the city of Kleve, one of XXX Corps first objectives. Finding it more heavily defended than expected, General Horrocks, one of Britain's better field commanders, had requested an air strike. It had proved to be something of a pyrrhic victory. Bombed with high explosive rather than the intended incendiaries, the attack removed the Germans but replaced one obstacle with another by blocking the streets with rubble. So disappeared the childhood home of Anne of Cleves, sometime wife of Henry VIII.

Reading some of the combat reports from the fighting in the Reichswald forest, John could easily appreciate quite what a nightmare it had been. The five lines of defence, the German paratroops who fought until they ran out of ammunition and then refused to surrender requiring themselves to be shot. One sentence encapsulated it. Bloody mud, bloody trees, bloody cold, bloody incessant rain, bloody slaughter.

The Canadians and British had not been lucky with Veritable; the delay of Operation Grenade and the dreadful weather impeding most air operations.

When John enquired as to when the weather might improve, he received the answer, soon. As to how soon, there was no commitment. It was not the answer anyone wanted.

Once clear of the Reichswald and with the cites of Kleve and Goch to the south now occupied, the British and Canadians had paused to regroup and refresh. The fighting for the past two weeks had been much harder than anticipated and troops were desperately tired.

On 22 February the skies cleared. At last, the Allied air forces could be deployed with all their might. Operation Clarion, postponed for days and now fuelled by anger and frustration, was a massive undertaking. 3,500 heavy bombers and almost 5,000 fighters and fighter bombers operating continuously for twenty-four hours. The aim was to disrupt and destroy German transportation links across the whole of Germany from the Rhine eastwards. While the heavies went after the railway stations, marshalling yards, bridges and centres of population between; the fighters and fighter bombers went for targets of opportunity, which effectively meant everything else.

As he reviewed the target sets and the results obtained, John could only wonder what the effect on the ground must have been. Not only the physical damage, but the psychological shock of so many attacks, and so wide ranging, in such a short time. There were no restraints now – anything and everything was a legitimate target. Whatever were the scruples that may have existed in the early days of the war had long since evaporated.

John vaguely recalled the so-called bombing raids in early 1940 when toilet paper was dropped on Germany in the form of propaganda leaflets while someone in parliament worried about damaging German private property.

The attitudes had changed and so had the men flying the aeroplanes. There were few pilots left from those who had begun the war. As the Royal Air Force had expanded, those still alive had moved into non-operational *rôles*, as he had himself. The pilots, particularly the Americans, were nineteen-, twenty-year-olds who had been children in 1939. They'd grown up with the war, probably remembered little else. Benefitting from extensive training programmes they had been well schooled. Now, they were doing what the whole of their training had taught them to do and, as young men, enjoying it. Airmen were fortunate in that they were insulated from the results of their actions. Vision was selective at four hundred miles an hour. The mind was on other things.

As Clarion ended and Montgomery renewed Veritable as Operation Blockbuster, US Ninth Army's Operation Grenade finally began.

The right hook of Montgomery's planned pincer started with another massive artillery bombardment. The two-week delay had enabled a greater concentration of guns. Spread along a fifteen-mile front, with barely twenty yards between them, 1,500 artillery pieces opened fire simultaneously.

As the Americans began to move the guns switched from high explosive to smoke rounds to cover the advance. Whilst most of the standing water leading to the river Roer had drained, there remained many areas of thick, glutinous mud which slowed the advance of men and machines alike. It was only the dense smoke, constantly refreshed, that allowed the American troops to make headway without significant losses.

The Roer itself was still in full flood and running at some speed. The crossings were successful but many of the assault boats were swept downstream. Fighting on the east bank was fierce in places but it was patchy. Many of the German defenders previously there had been moved north to counter Veritable. The Siegfried Line's fixed defences remained but with insufficient men to man them effectively, and once the Americans had punched their way through, they found only isolated areas of resistance but little in between to hinder them.

Similar conditions were reported along the whole length of the front as multiple penetrations were achieved. Within four days Ninth Army was through, spreading out and advancing rapidly north-eastwards, towards the Rhine and Montgomery's 21st Army Group by now heading south-east.

The pincer had begun to hinge and, as the two arms closed, the German forces caught between them had a stark choice. Surrender, or be annihilated. Increasingly, they chose to surrender.

Prior to their advance into Germany, American jeeps were being fitted with a length of angled steel welded vertically to their front fenders. During the 'Bulge' strands of piano wire tied to trees either side of roadways had been discovered. Positioned at neck height for anyone mounted in a jeep, they were designed to decapitate the occupants. Once in Germany, bands of Werewolf Hitler Youth were anticipated to adopt such tactics. While few such incidents had been reported, the reassurance offered by the forward-mounted wire cutters was substantial, and since jeeps invariably rode ahead of the columns, it allowed them all to charge ahead regardless.

*

A former prime minister, Arthur Balfour, had once famously remarked that in life very little really matters, and what little that did mattered very little.

John thought it a tired view of life, however true, and his sympathy towards the sentiment varied as to how tired he was. And lately, he'd been tired. This war had gone on far too long.

107

With March came the opening of Operation Lumberjack, Bradley's big push to the Rhine. The plan, approved by Eisenhower, was commendably simple. US First Army were to attack and drive south-eastwards to head for the junction of the Rhine and Ahr rivers. Once there, they were then to turn south to join up with Patton's Third Army whose own attack was to be made through the hills and woods of the Eifel district. Third Army were then to head north-westwards. Bradley's plan was not dissimilar to Montgomery's – another pincer movement except that this encirclement would close on the west bank of the Rhine.

Lumberjack followed the pattern of the previous assaults by beginning with a prolonged artillery bombardment. Bridgeheads were quickly established on the east bank of the Erft river and rapidly exploited by the combat engineers laying pontoon bridges. Cologne was reached after five days and thereafter First Army moved towards the Ahr valley to block the anticipated path of retreat of the remaining German forces.

Patton's Third Army had hit pockets of determined resistance on the Siegfried Line and the associated Kyll and Prüm river complexes. It had taken several days of hard and sustained fighting to achieve a breakthrough but, once they'd made it, the advance then became another Patton charge.

Smashing through the Eifel woodland the lead column covered fifty miles in three days to reach Coblenz and the junction of the Rhine with the Moselle. Patton never allowed the columns to stop. They refuelled on the move, they ate on the move; above all, they kept going. Speed and surprise – it was all about momentum.

Heading north up the west bank of the Rhine, they very nearly took the bridge at Urmitz intact, destroyed by the Germans at the last moment in sight of an advancing Sherman column moving at full speed.

The resistance to the American advance swung between extremes. While the Waffen SS fought to the death, the regular German troops performance depended upon their weapon supply and their local leadership. The *Volkssturm* was almost totally ineffective, lacking weapons, conviction or leadership. They immediately deserted in droves on sighting the Americans, preferring to go to ground until the advance passed over them, re-emerging as civilians.

Patton's army in particular brushed aside any German resistance with contempt, suffering a mere one hundred casualties on their fifty-mile drive while inflicting over six thousand on the Germans. The only real threat had been from a few poorly executed Luftwaffe attacks. Patton's columns were well-equipped with anti-aircraft battalions whose gunners, recently under-employed, relished the opportunity the Luftwaffe targets presented. Few of the attacking aircraft survived.

As Third Army was making its charge, in the north British armour from the Dragoons met up with the US Ninth Army at Geldern closing their encirclement. The Canadian, British and American armies then struck east together towards the Rhine.

***

"Did you hear any of that? You didn't hear it. You didn't hear any of it."

The man's voice was stern, agitated and not a little frightened.

Luke nodded and turned to wash his hands. The man stood around watching him, fiddling with his hat, wondering, Luke suspected, what to do, or say, next.

"Good," he said, finally, and left Luke to finish drying his hands. As usual there was a shortage of clean towels.

As Luke began his trek back to Paddington and his train to Oxford, he pondered what he'd overheard and the circumstances. Why, he wondered, do men have conversations, dealing with the most sensitive information, in lavatories. The things he'd picked up around Whitehall, overheard lavatorial conversations, were now legion. And the subsequent warnings.

Procuring in lavatories normally meant homosexual advances. Not to Luke, though he'd had his share of those too. His speciality appeared to be eavesdropping.

It was second nature to him now, not hearing. It had become so common he could almost consider himself deaf.

As best he could remember, he went through what he had overheard, trying to pick out key words or phrases. Manhattan Project, Los Alamos, Special Weapon. None of it meant anything to him. But then, neither had Enigma or Ultra when first he'd heard them.

Henderson might know. He'd ask him at the next opportunity.

Henderson listened to Luke with a growing sense of alarm. The Manhattan Project, the American and British attempt to build a nuclear bomb in the New Mexico desert, was one of the greatest secrets of the war. For Luke to overhear discussion of it in a London lavatory was a serious security breach. A telephone call was urgently required.

In the meantime, what, if anything, to tell Luke. His curiosity was aroused and something was needed to quench it. Proscribed from telling him anything of substance he thought of the UK's cover story, something to do with tube alloys, a ridiculous, preposterous concoction. Forty thousand people, plonked in a desert miles from anywhere. Tube alloys, really!

No, it would have to be something close to the truth, but not it, and a stern reminder of secrecy. A very stern reminder.

***

It was Mothering Sunday, three weeks before Easter. John's memories of his mother had faded over the years. Having died when he was so young, his recollections became less as time and years of other memories separated. He still thought of her occasionally, though perhaps more somehow as a concept than a personality. But today was different.

The special church service. The going up to the altar rail, collecting a poesy of wet violets, presenting them proudly to her. A smile and a kiss. Going home and watching as she carefully put them into a little vase for display, and then, as they began to fade, pressing them inside a heavy book until they dried. Then kept within a wooden box wrapped in tissue paper.

John sat in the Kensington flat looking out of the window, a steady passing stream of young children and their mothers going to the local church. He could feel the steady grip of his mother's hand. Her oh-so-distinctive smell. Only his mother.

So long ago, he thought, gulping air, unexpectedly weeping.

The most recent Order of Battle statistics had landed on John's desk, detailing the total Allied forces in the field. The predominance of the US was remarkable. The total Allied divisions on the continent now totalled ninety-one of which sixty-one were American with thirteen British, eleven French, five Canadian and one Polish.

On the ground at least, it was now an American war. The erosion of equity between the British and American forces, which had begun so many months before, was now complete. Victory was impossible otherwise.

For John it was an obvious observation, one he made without rancour. Others, he knew, found it more difficult to reconcile.

The Americans were now rampant to the west of the Rhine occupying great swathes of new territory every day. John, attending the morning and evening briefings at Norfolk House, was astonished at the success and speed of it. He was not alone. The Allies had not enjoyed this level of success since the breakout from Normandy and the advance across France the previous summer.

As the Germans systematically demolished the bridges over the Rhine, the resistance of their forces now stranded to the west began to crumble. While some chose to fight to the end, increasingly they either deserted or surrendered at the first opportunity.

The US First Army's 9th Armoured Division was now moving at great speed down the west bank of the Rhine, heading south to meet up with Patton's lead elements heading north.

Breasting a rise on the outskirts of Remagen they came in sight of the Ludendorff railway bridge. It was battered, it was damaged, but to their great surprise and delight, it was still intact.

Riding their luck, three infantry platoons, backed with tank support behind them, approached the bridge under machine gun fire from the towers at the far end. Demolition charges on the bridge approach were blown, but without any noticeable effect. Covered by smoke charges and machine gun fire from the tanks firing down one side of the bridge, the infantry worked their way across down the other side moving girder to girder. Behind them were the combat engineers, swinging under the bridge, removing the main demolition charges, cutting every wire they could find, working at a feverish speed. One could only wonder at the courage of the men advancing across a bridge primed for destruction knowing it might detonate beneath them at any moment.

When they were about two thirds of the way across, a secondary charge detonated at the far end of the bridge. The bridge lifted, large pieces of the superstructure fell into the river, but the bridge remained substantially intact. The charge had been of inferior industrial-grade explosive rather than military high explosive.

In the confusion and with further covering fire, the infantry charged across the final span to reach the railway tunnel entrance on the east bank. As the infantry spread out either side to cover the bridge approaches, the lead tanks began to cross.

Trapped inside the tunnel were a couple of hundred civilians, mostly women and children, a few battered German soldiers and what remained of the *Volkssturm* commanded by the local school master. Sensibly, they offered an immediate surrender.

Coincidentally, the officer leading the infantry assault was of German descent. His father, part of the US occupation force in 1919, had married a local girl from Remagen and taken her back to America.

John had paused after he'd read that. It said something, though quite what he wasn't entirely sure.

***

In addition to the air-launched V-1s, the Germans had attempted to increase the range of the missile. Reducing the size of the warhead to allow for more fuel and replacing the steel nose cone and wings with ones constructed of wood to reduce the all-up weight, and hence drag, of the vehicle.

Luke had reworked his sums, concluding that a range increase of around fifty miles was possible, giving a total just in excess of two hundred. It wasn't much and it would achieve little.

The British air defences, guns and fighter patrols, were now aligned as a barrier between London and Holland, concentrated on the Suffolk coast. Several hundred guns and ten squadrons of RAF fighters including, for the first time, Meteor jets. Their kill rate, in combination with the guns, was averaging over ninety per cent. Very few of the V-1s reached Greater London.

The V-Weapons' campaigns were petering out.

***

The loss of the Remagen bridge intact had come as a profound shock to the German high command. As the Americans strove to exploit the crossing, pouring troops and equipment across as fast as possible and building five further pontoon bridges alongside, the Germans tried desperately to destroy them. Repeated attacks from Fw 190 and Me 262 jet fighter bombers, Arado jet bombers and even V-2s – eight of them, one falling forty miles away – failed to hit the bridges.

With massed anti-aircraft fire from either end of the bridge and several hundred Allied fighters flying standing patrols above and beyond Remagen stacked at three different altitudes, the Luftwaffe had lost over half of their attacking aircraft. The Germans even resorted to river attacks and single frogmen carrying explosive charges. Nothing they attempted was successful and while a couple of 190s came very close, the American build-up continued

345

uninterrupted. Within ten days there were six American divisions and well over 25,000 men on the eastern bank.

Weakened from all the previous assaults, the failed demolition and its recent heavy use, the Remagen bridge now collapsed of its own accord. It was too late to make any difference. During those last ten days of its existence the Americans had established a bridgehead on the eastern bank of the Rhine twenty-five miles wide and up to ten miles deep; from Bonn to the north to the outskirts of Coblenz in the south.

And it did not end there. While they exploited the Remagen breakthrough, the Americans had launched Operation Undertone, as scheduled, on 15 March.

Undertone was the fourth and the last of the large-scale Allied assaults towards the Rhine. Assigned to the US Sixth Army Group, the attack commenced on a forty-mile front led by the US Seventh Army aimed at Saarbrücken in the north of the sector, while the French 1st Army from the Alsace region in the south headed towards Hagenau.

It had taken ten days. The Germans, with some skill, fought a series of holding actions as the bulk of their forces, recognising the inevitable, began to pull back towards the Rhine. Belatedly, when orders were received allowing them to cross, a proportion had managed to do so via ferries and the one remaining bridge at Germersheim. But soon, as the Americans closed in, the bridge was blown, isolating the bulk of the German army, previously forbidden to evacuate and now at the mercy of the Americans sweeping down on them.

On 22nd March Eisenhower was informed that there were now no active German troops remaining west of the Rhine.

John read the reports from Undertone on the evening of 23rd March. Eisenhower had achieved his primary objective of occupying the whole of the ground west of the Rhine before launching the pre-planned assaults to cross it.

In all, the German losses had been prodigious: something in the region of 200,000 men of which seventy-five per cent were now prisoners of war. To this could be added uncountable quantities of materiel, particularly heavy armour. The corresponding Allied casualty figures were 36,000 including 6,000 killed. It could have been a great deal worse. SHAEF had declared the four operations an unqualified success.

John could only hope that Operation Plunder, Montgomery's crossing of the Rhine due to begin in a few hours time, would meet with similar good fortune.

108

Whilst the capture of the bridge at Remagen had been an unexpected and welcome bonus, Eisenhower's strategy for the invasion of Germany remained unchanged. The major assault across the Rhine was to remain with Montgomery's 21st Army Group in the north.

One reason was topography. The ground in the north-east, beyond the Rhine, was flat. That beyond Remagen was not. That Patton had slipped a few men across the river at Oppenheim, further south of Remagen, made no material difference. Patton's action was more to spite Montgomery than any real military significance, and while this and the Remagen bridgehead would be exploited, that would come after the northern operations.

Now, with over four million Allied troops in Western Europe, Eisenhower's strategy was governed more by practical considerations than any recent military developments. Montgomery's crossing of the Rhine, the planning and preparation for which had begun months before, was now physically impossible to change.

Named Operation Plunder, it was intended to be the last great set-piece assault of the war in the west and, as orchestrated by Montgomery, the largest amphibious operation since Normandy. It practically matched Overlord in scope – indeed, the one point two million troops devoted to it dwarfed those initially committed in June 1944.

While Plunder was the ground-borne element of the Rhine crossing, Operation Varsity was to be the airborne component. It was of an equally grand scale, set to be the largest airborne operation ever conducted on a single location in one day.

As set out in the preamble to the operational orders, the tactical intent of Plunder–Varsity was to seize the city of Wesel and create a lodgement of a depth sufficient for the rapid build-up of forces to allow for a drive to the east and north-east. The strategic objective was to secure a bridgehead east of the

Rhine from which operations to isolate the Ruhr and thrust into the heart of Germany would be developed. It was, stated the preamble, to be an attack of such drive and strength that the enemy would be swiftly overwhelmed leading to a final victory in the campaign.

They were, as John noted, bold words requiring bold deeds.

After the *débâcle* of Market Garden and Arnhem, John was granted a watching brief for Varsity, encouraged to make comments and criticisms wherever he saw fit. He saw this as something of a poisoned chalice. Norfolk House was far too remote to have any real operational bearing and there was no reason to believe that anyone would listen. Equally, should something go seriously wrong and, should that be something that John had not flagged up as a risk, he would be compromised. It was, to use the American phrase, a no-win situation.

He reviewed the plans with great care. Two airborne divisions, the British 6th and the American 17th, were to land on the ground immediately behind Wesel. They were to isolate the city, disrupt its defence by seizing key terrain, capture the bridges over the Issel river and its associated canal and by doing so rapidly expand the size of the lodgement being created by the ground forces crossing the river.

The drop zones, for both the parachute and glider borne troops, were only 2,000 yards east of the riverbank and within artillery range of the Allied guns on the west bank. Furthermore, the massed drop was to be made in daylight in one great lift with all the drop zones close to their tactical objectives. As planned, it was the complete opposite to Market Garden.

John's real concern was the level of ground fire that the airborne, particularly the glider force, would encounter. His report emphasised the need for the greatest interdiction possible of the German flak defences, commenting rather obviously that gliders were compliant targets.

What his report did not contain was the obvious question: whether the airborne element, Varsity itself, was a necessity to the operation considering all of its inevitable losses. No one, it seemed, had asked this question, so ingrained in Allied operations were the airborne in major assaults. Even against a weakened enemy they still formed an integral part.

Enormous effort and expense had gone into the creation of the Allied airborne forces. It was a weapon primed. Thus, it was a weapon that demanded use. Denying its existence was simply not an option and overrode any other consideration.

John knew, as did anyone who cared to look at previous operations, that the casualties suffered by airborne assault were always the highest in any attack, and this was particularly true of the glider-borne forces.

It was a cruel equation: the advantage gained set against the casualties and death incurred.

Operation Varsity at worst was an indulgence, the consequences of which would be the frittering of too many good men for a set of limited objectives.

John wrote an additional short note, questioning the need for Varsity and stating the reasons. A single page with a wide distribution. He felt like Pontius Pilate washing his hands before the Crucifixion. His note would make no bloody difference whatsoever. And he knew it.

The Rhine, as a river, dwarfs the Thames; over 500 yards wide at Wesel, to a small child it would appear as an inland sea.

To cross this great divide, Montgomery had assembled a force of men and materiel of a magnitude not seen since D-Day. 1,250,000 troops; British, Canadian and American including 60,000 combat engineers to construct the river crossing. 260,000 tons of supplies pre-positioned in the forward areas, 32,000 vehicles including 700 tanks, and numerous landing craft crewed by Royal Navy and US Navy personnel. In addition, there were hundreds of assault craft, storm boats, ferries, and particularly Buffalo amphibious vehicles, all assigned their own particular stretches of water to run shuttle services across the river as the bridges were under construction. The aim was simple: to get as many fighting men, their armour and equipment, across the river in the shortest possible time.

To disguise this massive build-up, artificial fog generators stretching for miles along the river bank, the miasma had been running continuously for ten days. The smoke was toxic and while it achieved the desired effect of masking all the activity from the German observers, it did nothing for the comfort of the Allied troops.

No one could ever accuse Montgomery of not being thorough in his preparations for battle. As the materiel resources were amassed, briefings, rehearsals and practice runs were being conducted down to squad level by the assault troops. Photo-reconnaissance, models, sand tables with every house, road and railway track represented to scale were being used to brief the assault teams. The level of preparation was similar in scope to that used for the D-Day landings. Every single man knew his place, his objectives and how that fitted into the overall plan.

Whatever his faults, Montgomery's attitude to casualties was an utter antithesis to that of the Americans. It determined his caution. While casualties in war are inevitable, he considered unnecessary casualties to be unforgivable. It was the battlefield creed he operated by; husbandry his watchword.

Intelligence estimates of German forces on the east bank around Wesel suggested around 25,000 regular troops including substantial elements from the remaining parachute divisions, various armoured units and artillery concentrations all complemented by around 30,000 men from the *Volkssturm* units. The German forces were not great, and concentrated attacks by Bomber Command and the USAAF destroying every transportation link eastwards of the Ruhr ensured they could not be reinforced; but even so, their numbers remained large enough to produce a not insubstantial defence.

Impatient now, Operation Plunder began on Friday, 23 March. At 2100 hours precisely, with dusk turned to darkness, the entire artillery strength of the British Second Army and the US Ninth Army opened fire simultaneously. 5,500 guns began to drop shells on 1,000 carefully identified and calibrated targets. This initial bombardment lasted four hours as the guns gradually reduced their range until the last hour when they concentrated on targets on the immediate foreshore of the eastern bank.

As the bombardment had begun, elements of the 51st Highland Division led by the Black Watch crossed the Rhine near Rees, ten miles to the left downstream of Wesel. Their Buffalo assault vehicles made short work of the swiftly moving current and they reached the far bank in around seven minutes, and undetected. The first British troops were across the Rhine. They immediately moved inland to protect the flank of the main assault.

Also at 2100 hours, 1 Commando Brigade, again in Buffaloes, began to cross to the immediate left of Wesel. Guided by the fire of a pair of Bofors guns firing continuous streams of red tracer across the river above them, the lead battalions landed within three minutes. There followed some short and sharp exchanges with the defenders but they were swiftly overwhelmed. Another hour or so saw the rest of the Commando Brigade complete the crossing, join up with their lead elements and advance to a pre-determined line inland.

Here they waited. Right on cue at 2330, 200 Lancasters flying at low altitude dropped over a thousand tons of high explosive on Wesel, barely 1,500 yards ahead of the Commandos. It was a bold decision to bomb so close, and in the dark, requiring complete trust from the men waiting on the ground. Their trust was rewarded – none of the bombs fell short.

The Commandos referred to Bomber Command as 'Arthur Harris & Company, House Removers'. It was an apt description. Wesel, not a large city, was totally destroyed. The Commandos, advancing after the strike passed, found their maps rendered useless by the devastation. They resorted to compass bearings to maintain direction. Most of the defenders had been buried in the debris and by 0100 hours the town had fallen and the Commandos began to consolidate their positions and dig in.

With the flanks secured, the main assault led by the 15th Scottish Division began to cross at 0200. Resistance was minimal and they soon achieved a considerable lodgement. At much the same time, the American Ninth Army began their assault to the right, south of Wesel. Using the same guidance technique as the British Commandos, first the 30th Division then the 79th completed the crossing. Again, resistance was minimal, the two divisions suffering only thirty casualties during the crossings. In addition to the preliminary bombardment, the Americans were greatly helped by an earlier withdrawal of a large number of the German defenders who had been relocated south to the north of Remagen to oppose an anticipated American breakout to link up with Montgomery's armies.

By first light, four separate secure bridgeheads had been established and were in the process of linking up. On the western bank of the river, the thousands of British and American combat engineers had begun the construction of the Rhine bridge crossings.

John had spent most of the night at Norfolk House and it was gone 3am before he returned to Kensington. A quick sleep, a shave and a change of clothes saw him back soon after nine. A hurried breakfast while checking the latest reports, a few short telephone calls and then to the operations centre next to the map room to await the beginning of Operation Varsity due to begin at 1000. He was not the only one waiting.

Winston Churchill, denied the opportunity to witness the Normandy landings first hand, was not to be frustrated a second time. From an observation post near Xanten overlooking the Rhine, and flanked either side by his Field Marshalls Alan Brooke and Montgomery, he listened for the approach of the airborne armada.

They were nine minutes early. 1,700 troops transports, 1,350 gliders and 2,200 Allied fighters in a sky train that stretched back over two hundred miles and took two and a half hours to pass.

First out were the paras: the British to the left, the Americans to the right. Crucially, the first of these landed right on their designated drop zones though, with increasing ground haze and smoke, some of the further landings were not so accurate.

Within forty minutes the whole of the British 6th Airborne had landed, over 7,000 men. The American 17th Airborne were not far behind – a little under 10,000 men landed within the hour.

The fighting, when significant numbers of Germans were landed upon, was vicious. As one subsequent report commented: nasty, brutal but, thankfully, short. The sheer force of numbers told and relatively soon practically all of the initial objectives were taken. The speed of the drop, and in such profusion, had a shattering effect on the German defenders making a co-ordinated defence impossible.

6th Airborne took the bridges over the Issel river while the 17th had taken their designated bridges over the Issel Canal and the wooded ground to the east. By nightfall, 1st Commando Brigade had linked up with the 17th in Wesel while 6th Airborne had made contact with the 15th Scottish Division. As the night began to close in, the Allies had established a secure bridgehead nearly thirty miles wide and up to eight miles deep. Three miles south of Wesel had seen the first of the floating pontoon bridges across the Rhine, all 1,100 feet of it, the first truck crossing at 1600 hours.

Operation Varsity was adjudged a complete success, the classic use of airborne troops to secure ground immediately ahead of a ground assault. But it had come at a considerable cost. Late in the evening John began to receive the casualty figures.

British 6th Airborne had a casualty rate of twenty per cent, 1,400 men, while the Americas had suffered a similar proportion. Over fifty per cent of the gliders had taken flak damage with many destroyed while nearly fifty of the troop-carrying aircraft had been shot down.

In addition to the C-47 Dakota, the Americans had used the Curtiss C-46 Commando, a larger, faster version of the Dakota, for the first time. It had been found seriously wanting. The main fuel tanks, inboard of the engines in the wing roots, were not self-sealing. When hit by shrapnel they leaked immediately into the fuselage which then exploded in a pressurised fireball when further punctured. Of the seventy-two C-46s employed, twenty-two had exploded: thirty per cent. To John's mind, to employ such an aircraft without self-sealing tanks in such a hostile environment was criminal negligence.

That an order was immediately issued that henceforth C-46s were never again to be used to transport paratroops into battle was scant consolation.

By 26 March, seven 40-ton capacity bridges had been built across the Rhine together with others of a smaller weight capacity. To the immediate left of Wesel cross-river traffic was intense. Over a thousand yard stretch the British alone were running three continuous ferry services alongside their five bridges. With typical British wit the ferries were named Tilbury, Gravesend and Polar, while the bridges were Blackfriars, Lambeth, Westminster, Waterloo and London. It was said to make the troops feel more at home. Not to be outdone, the Americans had built their own series of crossings though John lacked any information as to names.

By the twenty-seventh the bridgehead was thirty-five miles wide and twenty miles deep. By the twenty-eighth, seventeen Divisions had crossed, over a quarter of a million men readying themselves for the breakout.

Churchill had stayed for two days, meeting Eisenhower, crossing the Rhine and taking the opportunity to avail himself of the water by relieving himself into it. It was a gesture much copied. Pissing in the Rhine soon became a rite of passage.

Notwithstanding Churchill's urination, to the south Bradley had begun his breakout from Remagen.

***

Through March there had been two serious V-2 strikes. On the eight Smithfield meat market was hit, replete with a fresh supply of rabbit and eager customers. The result: 110 dead, 133 seriously injured. In late March a five-storey block of council flats in Stepney was hit. It stood between two others all of equally poor construction. The centre one totally demolished, the neighbouring ones seriously damaged. Many dead, many more injured.

But it was the end. On the twenty-seventh, the last V-2 landed on Orpington in Kent. The following day, the last V-1s were launched, the last being shot down into the sea off Orfordness.

The V-Weapon campaigns were over.

109

It was almost three weeks since the Americans had seized the bridge at Remagen. Since then, the bridgehead had been enlarged considerably and by late March practically the whole of the US First Army was encamped on the eastern bank. Further south, Patton's Third Army, rested and resupplied, was ready to break out from its own bridgehead at Oppenheim south of Mainz.

Operation Voyage, the breakout from Remagen, was initiated by Bradley in the early hours of 25 March. For once, it was well named.

Anticipating the forthcoming attack, the Germans had concentrated their forces to the north of Remagen expecting the Americans to move up the Rhine Valley to unite the First and Ninth Armies before turning east to attack the Ruhr, Germany's industrial heartland.

On the face of it, the German assumption was a reasonable one. Most Allied attacks to this point had been cautious affairs, typified by Eisenhower's broad front approach. What the Germans now failed to appreciate was the Western Allies, both the Americans and the British, had a renewed sense of confidence and purpose. Confidence breeds optimism and optimism encourages imagination.

Instead of heading north, the US First Army broke south. Within hours they had moved forward five miles; three army corps, infantry and armoured divisions in overwhelming numbers. The German defences, thinly spread, disintegrated. By nightfall First Army consolidated, brought forward supplies and readied for a major advance.

As First Army had struck, so too had Patton's Third Army. Breaking out of their Oppenheim bridgehead they had cleared the Main River and were now rapidly heading north.

On the morning of the twenty-sixth, First Army reached the autobahn that ran north-eastwards from Coblenz. Part of Hitler's great building programme of the 1930s, it gave the Americans twin dual carriageways to advance along, uninterrupted and leading straight into the heart of Germany, ideal for the armour and the wheeled vehicles of a fully mechanised army. The armoured columns raced along it, covering forty-five miles in two days.

Third Army, with Patton driving them on, was also moving at pace travelling north to the right flank of First Army.

As the various spearheads of the Allied armies, the British and Canadians in the north, the Americans in the centre and the south, advanced through the German countryside, they began to use a common tactic. On coming across a small town or village, they would pause, standing off to observe. The first signs of movement would result in a few artillery or tank shells aimed at the most prominent buildings.

The town either surrendered immediately, in which case a detachment was left to garrison the town, or, if it resisted, the buildings were systematically demolished by artillery and supporting air strikes.

Pause, observe, surrender or destroy. It was not subtle, but it was effective.

Eisenhower, based at SHAEF Headquarters in Reims, was in constant touch with each of his battlefronts and, as befits any Commander-in-Chief, had an overview denied any of his individual battlefield commanders.

With the successful conclusion of Operation Plunder and 21st Army Group now beginning to move in strength into northern Germany, Montgomery's subservience had begun to evaporate. Without consultation he sent a signal to Eisenhower declaring his intention to drive directly east towards Berlin. To make his point he had listed his route and itinerary. As was usual with Montgomery, it was a myopic view which took no account of events to the south of him and, foolishly, it assumed his retention of the command of the US Ninth Army, a presumption not in his control.

In addition, Eisenhower was also receiving a constant barrage of communications from Washington. The latest contained an explicit warning as to the very real dangers of conflict between the Western Allies and the Red Army when the two eventually met. An incident in March when US Mustangs had mistakenly shot down a number of Soviet aircraft near Berlin had caused consternation in Moscow. A similar clash between the armies on the ground had to be avoided at all cost.

After a considerable amount of thought, and a decent night's sleep, Eisenhower now reacted by making a number of strategic decisions, momentous in nature, that were destined to have profound implications for the persecution of the remainder of the war.

He first addressed himself to Montgomery. With the Rhine crossing now successfully achieved, the US Ninth Army would revert to the command of the US 12th Army Group under Bradley. Montgomery's 21st Army Group would now head north-east and north, towards Denmark and Hamburg on the Baltic while covering the left flank of 12th Army Group. Montgomery was not to advance towards Berlin.

To the south, Hodges and Patton were ordered to merge First Army and Third Army assaults until they reached beyond the Ruhr. At this point, First Army were to swing left to begin the encirclement of the Ruhr while Third Army would continue eastwards. Further south, 6th Army Group under Devers would cover 12th Army Group's right flank then head north to Bavaria and northern Austria.

Ninth Army, freed of Montgomery's yoke, having advanced east were then to swing right, around the Ruhr, completing the encirclement by joining up with First Army coming around from the left. Once achieved, they were to head towards Leipzig and beyond that, Dresden.

Eisenhower had before him a map which showed the designated occupation zones of a conquered Germany by the British, American, French and Russian armies as agreed at Yalta in early February. Berlin lay well within the Soviet zone. With Washington's warnings of conflict with the Red Army foremost in his mind, Eisenhower decided, without recourse to his superiors in either Washington or London, to communicate personally with Stalin in Moscow. His message was that the western armies had no intention whatsoever of advancing to Berlin. Instead, they would stop on a line roughly conforming to the path of the River Elbe some fifty odd miles west of Germany's capital.

Once sent, he copied the cable to the Combined Joint Chiefs of Staff. Whilst Eisenhower's unilateral action caused consternation in London, Washington immediately endorsed it, effectively quelling British opposition. It was a most effective coup.

As this was being played out, Ninth Army from the north and First Army from the south raced towards each other. On the afternoon of 1st April, they met up at Lippstadt. The Ruhr pocket, an area thirty miles wide with its base on the Rhine, seventy-five miles deep, was now sealed. Within its confines lay the remains of the German Army Group B, the last of the substantial German forces in the west.

It was Easter Sunday.

*

April found John promoted to wing commander. As to why, he had very little idea. True he'd been at the rank of squadron leader since Malta in 1942, so an advancement was overdue, but why especially now. His job hadn't changed, his responsibilities had not altered. Enquiry yielded little. Group Captain Baker merely smiled and congratulated him. Perhaps it was recognition for all the work done. Or maybe, it was simply time related. Also to his surprise he'd been awarded the AFC, the Air Force Cross, presumably for his work at SHAEF.

Unable to get a satisfactory explanation for either, he chose to stop pursuing it. The new uniform issue would be welcome though. His current sets were getting very tired.

Sitting at his desk, the well-used map of Germany and Western Europe spread out before him, with a red pencil John traced the path of the River Elbe, Eisenhower's declared stop line. Rising in Czechoslovakia it crosses the German frontier to reach Dresden, Wittenberg to Hamburg finally discharging into the North Sea at Cuxhaven, its route consistently north-eastwards. Though not as formidable as the Rhine, the Elbe was another of Germany's natural defences west of Berlin.

Using a river as a stop line was eminently sensible and had much to commend it. Rivers were easily recognisable and their existence could not be denied, unlike an arbitrary line drawn on a map. At its nearest it was forty miles west of Berlin.

Between the Rhine and the Elbe, John marked Eisenhower's intended routes of the British and American armies in blue. From the Rhine to the Elbe, both rivers running roughly parallel, was about 230 miles.

That the British and Americans would advance in triumph to take Berlin to end the war had never been questioned. Since Normandy it had become so ingrained as to become holy writ. That now, to some, to be denied the ultimate prize was met with stupefaction. Before coming to any conclusion, John chose to weigh the evidence in an attempt to understand Eisenhower's decision. There was much to consider.

Though conveniently overlooked by some, Eisenhower's political and military masters resided in Washington, not London. Distant from Europe, their priorities were turning towards Japan. Operation Downfall, the invasion and occupation of the Japanese home islands, was currently being planned. Intended to begin later in 1945, the anticipated casualty figures were truly awful. With the Japanese war unlikely to conclude until 1946–47 the estimates of American casualties alone ranged between one and two million. Even to a country with the resources of America, these would be hard to bear. As a consequence, a large proportion of the American troops now in Europe would need to be transferred to the Pacific theatre once Germany was defeated.

An advance from the Elbe to Berlin would incur perhaps another 100,000 Allied casualties, ground, that once taken, would be relinquished to the Soviet Union under the Yalta agreement once hostilities had ceased. It was a high price to pay for prestige.

Eisenhower had been appointed as supreme commander – a military appointment. His task was to conclude the war in Europe as quickly and efficiently as possible with the least number of Allied casualties. His job had no political responsibility. Western democracies do not work like that. To stop at the Elbe made perfect military sense. Politically, it was less obvious, but that consideration did not rest within Eisenhower's remit. While Berlin was by now almost an irrelevance to the Western Allies, to Russia and Stalin it was an absolute necessity. That said, better then Russian blood be sacrificed than British and American to take it.

As he came to this conclusion, something nagged away at the back of John's mind. It was not until the following day before he resolved it. It was a quote from Karl Marx. "Whoever possesses Berlin possesses Germany. And, whoever controls Germany, controls Europe."

And still Germany fought on. Continuous reports passed through SHAEF of the desperate defence being mounted by the remains of the *Wehrmacht*, the Waffen SS and the *Volkssturm* home guard, old men and children. Conditions now in Germany almost defied description. The bombing onslaught had reached its crescendo: thousands of RAF and US Air Force aircraft, thousands of tons of bombs were being dropped around the clock. Resistance was minimal; the Allies losses slight. Cities were being levelled systematically one after another, German society was broken, massed shortages of food and water. No fuel, no power.

Small voices of compassion began to be heard in Britain, mostly church-led, but those were soon stilled as the utterly inhuman conditions of the industrial murder factories that were the concentration camps were exposed to the world as they were overrun by the advancing Allied forces.

It was a compassion John did not share. He had no sympathy for the Germans whatsoever. None. His concern was the continuing level of casualties the Allies continued to suffer on the ground.

One question was constantly asked. Why did the Germans continue to fight on? They had already lost; the result not in any doubt. Not if, only a question of when. Easy question – complicated answer.

One was they had no choice, knew no better. The Gestapo would immediately execute anyone who refused to fight, so few did. Hitler, declaring Germany was unworthy of him, almost encouraged the total destruction of the whole country as some form of divine retribution.

Whatever the reason, it had become all too painfully obvious that the war would not end until the Western Allies and the Russians had occupied the whole country, including Berlin, and Hitler was dead.

There were other reasons too why the Germans fought on. Beyond the Allies demand for an unconditional surrender were the American proposals formulated by Henry Morgenthau, the US Treasury Secretary. Known as the Morgenthau Plan, this envisaged the de-industrialization of post-war Germany converting it to a country primarily agricultural and pastoral and thereby reversing over two hundred years of industrial development. It was the modern equivalent to the Roman's punishment of Carthage by poisoning their soil with salt.

Goebbels had seized upon this saying the Allies would turn Germany into one giant potato patch. The Germans characterised it as enslavement. It was a proposal guaranteed to ensure they would fight to a bitter end.

That Morgenthau's recommendations had rapidly lost favour, once the full implications had been understood, made little difference. The damage had been done.

110

Whether it was the weather, a long hard winter, his work, or just a general gloom, John had been feeling jaded, stale and weary since about February. A creeping malaise. That it was the state of the whole nation, though reassuring, didn't immediately help. What he needed was a diversion, something else to occupy his mind, however briefly.

It had been Celia's suggestion – go fly an aeroplane. A telephone call to Northolt had arranged it.

Waking early, he pulled back the curtains and looked at the sky. Clear, high cloud, plenty of blue. It should be a good day for it.

He dressed carefully. A couple of Celia's old stockings on his left leg, a full set of thermal underwear, courtesy of the US Army Air Force, from neck to foot, long socks and a full Sidcot flying suit over his uniform. His usual fur-lined flying boots and inner and outer gloves topped him off. He was determined to enjoy this and not get as cold as the last time he flew. Finally, he tucked the Colt automatic down his right boot as normal; more for familiarity than any practical use.

Being driven out of London on the Great West Road John noticed how the flowers had started to come through in a few suburban gardens. Another spring to come. He also realised that he was slightly nervous. He'd not flown since D-Day the previous June and his skills were bound to be a bit rusty to begin with. It was a warning: be careful, this little jaunt could be lethal. Dying now would be particularly irritating and downright inconvenient. He glanced through the 'Pilot's Notes' booklet again. All was familiar and, telling himself to relax, he lit another cigarette. It was his fourth since leaving Kensington.

Delivered to dispersal at Northolt, John introduced himself to the flight lieutenant in charge and signed for the aircraft he was to borrow, a Spitfire Mk XIV.

Sat on the tarmac apron outside it looked ridiculously new, clean, the paintwork gleaming. John knew quite a lot about the Mk XIV, not least since Celia had been flying them for some time. John walked around this example for a couple of minutes in the approved manner noting the differences from the Mk IX, the longer nose with extra blisters on top to accommodate the cylinder heads of the Griffon being the most obvious, apart from the cut down rear fuselage. He then climbed up the port wing root and clambered into the cockpit.

The Mk XIV was one of the latest developments of the Spitfire. The Merlin engine had been replaced by the Rolls-Royce Griffon, a direct descendent of the 'R' racing engines that had powered the Supermarine seaplanes that had won the Schneider Trophy fifteen years before and had so ignited John's love of flying as a boy. While the Merlin could be described as the nephew of the 'R' engine, the Griffon was the son. With a capacity of thirty-seven litres, ten more than the Merlin, and producing well over 2,000 horsepower, double that of the early Spitfires, this promised to be quite a ride.

Apart from the engine, there was another difference from the Spitfires he was used to. This version of the Mk XIV featured a cut down rear fuselage allowing for the installation of a tear-drop canopy. Rear vision was now unimpeded though, as he'd been warned, directional stability had suffered, particularly in the climb and dive.

Settling himself into the seat, he glanced at the data card hanging on the control column. What he must remember was the Griffon ran backwards compared to the Merlin, counterclockwise from the pilot's seat. The torque reaction on take-off would therefore be in the opposite direction to what he was used to. Getting that wrong would result in a very spectacular ground loop and wreck the undercarriage. Maybe him with it.

He requested and received take-off clearance from the control tower and began to make his final checks. There was something else he remembered. For the past several years Celia had taken to signing the aircraft she delivered on the inside of the cockpit door. A bright yellow chinagraph pencil. Occasionally, if the harmonisation of the controls was exceptional, she would add that as well.

John glanced at the door and to his joy saw her signature, 'Celia Ashby', and the comment, 'a lovely aeroplane'. The date was only a few days before. John doubted it had been flown since.

Boyishly thrilled, he started the engine and began to warm it, listening to the pops and crackles from the exhausts, a characteristic of the Griffon at low revs. As he began to taxi, John fancied he could smell the remains of Celia's perfume, however unlikely.

The torque effect on take-off was strong but easily corrected with a boot full of rudder as the Spitfire began to accelerate down the runway very, very quickly. He was airborne almost before he realised, listening to himself muttering, "Shit, that was quick." He held the Spitfire level, continuing to accelerate before easing the stick back. It climbed like a rocket, the huge five-bladed propeller clawing at the air. He kept climbing, only levelling off when his leg began to feel cold. 25,000 feet – it had taken barely ten minutes. Ridiculous.

So intent was he on flying the aircraft, he had temporarily lost track of where he was. Rule one: aviate, navigate, communicate. He trimmed the aircraft out then flew around in a circle calling up on the RT to get a fix on where he was. Approaching seventy miles west of Northolt.

For half an hour, flying between 300 and 350 knots, John indulged himself by flying every single manoeuvre he could think of. It was such a powerful machine. How different from the Mk II and Mk V he'd fought with in 1940 and '42. How useful it would have been then.

Northolt appeared on the horizon and John began a series of spirals down to land. As he did so he began to make comparisons. On balance, he preferred the Mk IX with the uprated Merlin. There were obvious similarities with the XIV but the Griffon engine made it a different aeroplane. But it was close. The difference between love and deep admiration. There were worse ways to celebrate his promotion.

***

In applying scientific and technological advances to the means of war, the Allies and the Germans had fundamental and totally different approaches.

From the outset, the Allies had recognised that weapons fit for purpose, produced in enormous quantities by utilising their great, and in the case of the Americans, astonishing manufacturing base, would be sufficient to win the war.

The Germans, seduced by the possibilities of future scientific advance, continuously pursued the magic bullet that would instantly transform their means of warfare. The V-1 and particularly the V-2 were exemplars of this philosophy. In doing so they absorbed vast resource that might otherwise have been used for more conventional weapon manufacture.

Through this pursuit of the esoteric, there were only a handful of scientific disciplines that the Germans were not ahead of the Allies. As Germany began to crumble, a race began between the British and Americans on the one hand, and the Russians on the other, to secure these scientific and technological assets, together with their associated personnel, for themselves.

Delivered promptly at nine in the morning, Luke signed for another thick parcel of documents. German originals with English translations attached.

Germany had conducted a quite enormous amount of weapon research and development since the early 1930s. Some of this had been very advanced and, in some areas, years ahead of the Allies. Whilst the scientific and engineering quality was excellent, nationally there had never existed and form of organisation to rationalise and structure these efforts to maximise their full potential. The Nazis had kept each group apart forcing them to work in ignorance of each other, that way the better to control them. Isolation and control of information being a feature of Nazi society. There had been little, if any, interchange between the various groups or the military who would be expected to use the weapons produced.

This was exactly the situation Henderson had feared for the nascent British activities in 1940. Through his efforts, and others, Britain had recognised this danger and had created methods and mechanisms to negate it. By combining the scientific and military efforts into a harmonious partnership quite spectacular results had been achieved; not least in the field of operational analysis by applying scientific technique and discipline to military practice.

Germany, most fortunately, had never achieved anything approaching this. Instead, there remained these disparate groups scattered across the country working in many cases in total ignorance of each other and particularly, what were the military priorities.

Prior to the invasion in June 1944, there had been much discussion and debate in intelligence circles as to how best to secure German research and development assets once Germany was defeated and the occupied territories liberated. To this end, Eisenhower issued an executive order in July 1944 instructing the formation of a special force, a task force, composed of both British and American specialists, supported by elite troops, to secure these German assets for the Allies. The British component became known as T-Force and eventually numbered around six hundred mixed personnel.

Over a period of many months large and extensive dossiers were produced detailing every known aspect of the German research and experimental establishments, manufacturing facilities and other centres of interest. This information was then codified into a series of large black bound manuals, inevitably known as the 'black books' which became the operational bibles of the T-Force units.

Following closely in the wake of the Allied advance, T-Force would identify and secure the targets of interest, preserve them from any further destruction or disturbance by looting or robbery, and hold them until such time as their examination by the nominated experts was complete and the removal of essential installations and documents was completed. Everything obtained was immediately shipped back to the UK for further analysis.

Thousands of documents and hundreds of tons of equipment began to flow back to the UK that, once categorised, was distributed around the country for further investigation.

Since the beginning of the year, Luke had received a constant stream of digests as the material reached the UK. He had cleared a filing cabinet, now rapidly filling up, to hold it. It was going to take years before the whole of it was processed and the information gleaned put to use.

But one thing had become very clear. This German research, much of which was extremely advanced, would direct British and American weapon development for years to come after the war.

*****

The Allies might have the most sophisticated suite of weapons the world had ever seen, while also having complete and utter dominance of the air, but their progress through Germany was being constantly stymied by one of the simplest of weapons imaginable: the German Panzerfaust.

A small, lightweight, hand-held anti-tank weapon, rocket-propelled and accurate up to around sixty yards. To look at it resembled nothing more than a long-sticked toffee apple, a large domed-shaped charge at the tip capable of punching through eight inches of armour plate. Easily carried and disposable with a simple line sight, it could be fired by anyone, including children, after a few minutes' instruction. Cheap and simple to produce, the Germans were making them by the tens of thousands.

A member of the Hitler Youth, with courage and good nerves hiding behind a wall or hedgerow, could destroy an Allied tank leading a column and bring a whole advance to an immediate halt.

The Panzerfaust was proving to be the most important and decisive weapon to frustrate the Allied advance and occupation of Germany.

As the weather had improved, the Allied bombing campaign had increased proportionately. Ranging over the whole of Germany, RAF Bomber Command and the USAAF were flying over 2,000 sorties a day, every day.

In support of the British and American armies, plus numerous requests from the Red Army as they approached Berlin, the raids were systematically laying waste to what remained of Germany's transport and logistic infrastructure.

Early April produced the latest batch of statistics from the Combined Bomber Offensive. In March 140,000 tons had been dropped on German soil. Over 6,000 acres of Berlin were now little more than crumpled rubble, in places estimated at 12,000 tons per acre. By way of illustration, the author commented that the equivalent area for London was four hundred acres.

John read the report, as he had so many others, without emotion.

As the Americans began the task of reducing the Ruhr pocket with multiple thrusts from either side, Bradley's 12th Army Group, now over a million and a quarter men, began to race towards the Elbe. To the north, the US Ninth Army advanced towards the Harz mountains, First US Army headed towards Leipzig while Patton's Third Army in the south were directed towards Chemnitz.

Resistance varied all along the fronts, from non-existent from the civilian populations, to fierce amongst groups of German soldiers faced with immediate execution by the SS should they attempt to surrender. Either way, it made little difference – the leading columns were advancing on average forty miles a day.

While the Americans continued their advance, so did Montgomery's 21st Army Group. One particular success had been achieved by a Scots Guards tank battalion. With American paratroops riding on their hulls as protection against German infantry armed with anti-tank weapons, they had advanced rapidly, reaching Munster on 3 April; fifty miles east of the Rhine. It was ironic that this final proof of the ability of British and American units to work together in harmony would come just as the final fracture between their senior commanders was occurring.

The Canadians, as they had been since Normandy, remained on the British left flank. II Corps began to force its way up the east bank of the river IJssel cutting off the German forces in Holland and blocking their escape route between the Zuider Zee and the lower Rhine. I Corps meanwhile concentrated on the east bank of the Rhine heading towards Arnhem.

The British armour, in the shape of XXX Corps, was also making good progress. Though pockets of strong resistance had been encountered, slowing them down, the pauses had been temporary. They had now reached the outskirts of Bremen. Beyond that was Groningen then Oldenburg and the ports of Emden and Wilhelmshaven opening the route to Cuxhaven at the mouth of the Elbe. The list read like the itinerary of a tourist coach trip.

John's map was now littered with a confusion of blue arrows as he tracked the advances of the Allied armies. On 11 April the US 67th Armoured Regiment became the first to reach the Elbe near Magdeburg having advanced over sixty miles in a single day. The mood in Norfolk House became ever more optimistic. Even the sceptics were becoming cheerful.

Then came the announcement that the American's beloved President Roosevelt had died.

The death of President Roosevelt came as a profound shock to the whole of the US personnel at Norfolk House. Americans identify with their president to a much greater extent that the British do with their prime minister. The loss was felt personally; strong men reduced to tears, black armbands in profusion.

That he was frail was obvious from the footage from Yalta but no one had suspected he was quite so ill. Under the American constitution the position of president was a combination of head of state and the head of the government; in British terms an amalgam of the prime minister and the king. Thus, to an American it was if King George VI and Winston Churchill had both died.

Immediately, Harry S. Truman, previously vice president, had been appointed president. Truman was something of an unknown quantity, but the change in leadership would have no immediate effect on the course of the war. It would continue as before.

111

In mid-April, Luke received the final definitive statistics on the V-Weapon campaigns.

Between mid-June 1944 and late March 1945, 10,492 V-1s were launched against London. Of these 4,261 were destroyed by the air defences. 2,419 had reached Greater London killing 6,184 people with 17,981 injured. In addition, 107,000 houses had been destroyed and a further million and a half damaged.

The V-2 attacks had occurred between September and March. 1,402 had fallen on southern England killing 2,754 and injuring 6,500.

Judged purely by the economics of war, it was a very poor return for such an enormous investment.

***

Plans for the reconstruction of Britain's cities, once the war was over, had been in hand for some time. Committees formed, working parties busied, particularly so for London. Quite why this summary report had appeared on John's desk was a mystery. Perhaps someone had just thought he'd be interested.

The summations and tabulations of the detailed survey reports of some of the worst affected areas were depressing. In some parts of London – the South Bank, Docklands, The Barbican – there was nothing left but burnt-out rubble. Three thousand tons of it per acre. Throughout the 30s, town planners had clamoured for the demolition and rebuilding of the swathes of London's slums. Now, the Luftwaffe and the V-1s and V-2s had obliged with the destruction phase. What remained promised to be a planner's dream, though where the money was to come from was anyone's guess.

Three thousand tons of rubble per acre. In Germany, where it had been estimated that forty per cent of all housing stock had been destroyed, figures around 12,000 tons were not uncommon. Bomber Harris's wind and whirlwind comment, prescient.

Learned estimates predicted it would take upwards of fifty years to rebuild London. That was easy to believe. The long-term effects of this war would last through the whole of John's lifetime and, he suspected, well beyond.

As the Western Allies continued their advance to the Elbe, behind them the Ruhr pocket began to disintegrate. By 18 April it had all but collapsed.

Whilst the Americans had estimated that it contained around 70,000 active German troops at the time of its encirclement, due to Hitler's standfast order, the true figure was closer to 370,000. It was an astonishing number, but deceptive. The quality of these troops was extremely poor. Rear service personnel, poorly lead, the ramshackle remnants of an army that had been out-thought and out-fought. Of these 370,000, 320,000 had surrendered, three times the number the Russians had taken at Stalingrad and dwarfing the numbers captured in Tunisia. As an army they were in a pitiful state. Only around twenty per cent had any infantry weapons while another twenty per cent had nothing but pistols. It had been an unequal contest.

This sudden influx of prisoners created a logistical nightmare. Huge open-air cages were constructed to hold and process them while continuous convoys of US trucks transported them westwards to the Channel ports for shipment direct to America.

The *Wehrmacht* in the west was broken and defeated. Now, the emphasis was shifting to the east, the Russians and the assault on Berlin.

On 1 April, Stalin had replied to Eisenhower's cable declaring his intention to halt the Western Allies at the Elbe. His response had been positive.

This plan, he said, complemented the opinion of the Red Army who now considered that Berlin had lost its previous strategic importance. That being so, only second-rate Russian forces would be directed towards it. The main thrust of the Red Army, expected in the second week of May, would be to the south in order to join up with the American Army.

No one at SHAEF believed him. Noting the date, Stalin's message had been dubbed Uncle Joe's April Fool.

Notwithstanding Eisenhower's declaration to the contrary, Stalin, paranoid as ever, still feared that the Western Allies, and the Americans in particular, would attack Berlin from the west. He therefore directed his armies to surround the city first before launching any serious assault towards its centre. It would keep the Germans in, and the Americans out.

The Russians had spent over two months planning their final assault on Berlin. They had assembled an enormous resource: in total 2,500,000 men of which one and a half million were committed to the attack; 42,000 guns and over 6,000 tanks and self-propelled guns. Four separate air armies containing thousands of aircraft. Zhukov's forces alone had a stockpile of over seven million shells.

The battle would begin with simultaneous attacks; Marshall Zhukov's 1st Belorussian Front from the east and the north, while Marshall Konev's 1st Ukrainian front would attack from the south. Further north of Berlin, Rokossovsky's 2nd Belorussian Front were still assembling; they too were to join the battle a few days later.

Berlin is a relatively small capital city. Though larger than Paris, London would comfortably accommodate it several times. The weight of ordnance about to fall upon it would leave little left standing. The Red Army had begun its assault on 16 April.

Someone in Norfolk House had opened a book on the date for the end of the war. When approached for his five shillings, John had asked which war?

He'd spent the morning reading the outline of Operation Downfall, the invasion of the Japanese home islands, and the preparations for it. It was going to be an enormous operation; several million US troops together with a sizeable British and Commonwealth contingent. And it would be a bloodbath. Not only would the Allies face the Japanese armed forces, but the whole of the civilian population, if need be, armed with sharpened sticks of bamboo. Massive levels of bombing and artillery bombardment would precede every attack together with the greatest firestorms the world had ever seen. Germany had been devastated. Japan, with its wooded houses, would be utterly levelled; nothing left. Since 1942, the Americans had only allocated ten per cent of its war capacity towards Japan. An invasion of the Japanese home islands would require the other ninety per cent and more.

For the German war, most had chosen to bet on a date in late April. John thought this overly optimistic. For want of a better choice, he plumped for 8 May. He might even be right. Time would tell.

From mid-April the weather had turned unseasonably warm; glorious spring days, lengthening evenings. The ache in John's left leg was becoming less and he had begun to walk from Kensington to Norfolk House in the mornings. This Friday morning, 20 April, was no exception.

It happened to be Hitler's birthday, his fifty sixth. John thought he would not see fifty-seven. Conscious of the date, the US Army Air Force and the RAF's Bomber Command sent their birthday greetings by way of particularly heavy raids on Berlin. Over seven hundred aircraft bombed the city centre and the eastern approaches in support of the Russian assault.

To the west, the US advances were continuing without serious hindrance. To the north, Montgomery's 21st Army Group were now established on Lüneburg Heath, a high plateau dominating northern Germany, and were closing on Hamburg. The Canadians, symbolically, had taken Arnhem the week before. The city, once home to over 100,000 people, was deserted.

The Dutch had suffered cruelly after the failure at Arnhem – not that it had been much better before. Viewing the Dutch as fellow Aryans who would be only too grateful to become part of the Greater Reich, they had been astonished by the hostility they encountered after the German invasion in 1940. The subsequent level of oppression reflected this. The Dutch railway strike at the time of Market Garden was also bitterly felt. The Dutch were made to pay, the population starved thereafter. The German occupation of the Netherlands, lasting almost exactly five years, was easily the most brutal in Western Europe.

Further south, the Americans were lining the western bank of the Elbe, had crossed the border with Czechoslovakia and were moving at speed into Bavaria. Meanwhile, the French Army was spreading out through southern Germany meeting little or no opposition. The war in the west was all but won. Everything now hinged on Berlin.

The Russians completed their encirclement of the city on 25 April as the lead elements of Zhukov's armies from the north met their counterparts of Konev's armies coming up from the south. They met at a point almost exactly due west of Berlin.

Coincidentally, on 25 April, south of Berlin at Torgau on the Elbe, the spearhead of the Russian 58th Guards Rifle Division met with the US 69th division.

The news that Germany was now cut in half was greeted with jubilation. Signals flashed up and down various chains of command. There was applause and cheering at Norfolk House.

The Red Army had immediately organised a lavish Soviet style banquet on the banks of the Elbe. It was, according to the reports John read, one glorious piss up.

*

It was a peculiar smell: odd, strangely sweet, thickening the air for miles, gradually increasing. In mid-April the British 8th Corps, while advancing in north-west Germany, stumbled upon a concentration camp at Bergen-Belsen.

A scene of biblical proportions, a horrific testimony to the inhumanity of man. Carpets of dead and dying, those alive barely recognisable. As medical teams were rushed forward to the site the British took immediate control. This included maximum publicity. The deeply shocked British troops began to bury 23,000 emaciated bodies while beginning the evacuation of a further 30,000 still clinging to life, many of whom subsequently died.

There followed numerous newspaper reports around the world. Pathé News showed an extended newsreel while Richard Dimbleby made a horrific and deeply moving broadcast for the BBC. Swan and Edgar in Oxford Street displayed large photographs in their shop windows.

An extended version of the Pathé report was shown at Norfolk House. There was no commentary: none was needed. Most of the women were in tears, so were many of the men. John watched it with a mounting sense of fury.

Later, sitting in his office, cigarettes and whisky, John thought of the Germans he had killed. It was not something he thought of very often. Now, he earnestly wished it had been more. Many more.

Eisenhower had issued a message to all Allied troops on the eve of D-Day. It said that they were about to embark on a great crusade. At the time, the statement had not been taken particularly seriously. The discovery of the German concentration camps and the horrors within, dozens more were found in the following days, proved Eisenhower's contention.

As he commented, "We are told that the American soldier does not know what he is fighting for. Now, at least, he will know what he is fighting against."

The Russian T-34 tanks fell victim to the Panzerfaust as readily as did the Shermans and Cromwells of the Americans and the British. To protect the hulls and turrets, the Russians had resorted to strapping steel-sprung mattresses from looted houses all around the tanks. It was a form of composite armour; the Panzerfausts would detonate prematurely, the hyper jet plume from the shaped charge would not be focussed and the armour's integrity would be retained.

While mattresses remained the favourite, the British and Americans had also used chicken wire with considerable success. Anything would do. Sandbags, even heavy furniture such as hardwood tables was being used. Anything to nullify the effect of the shaped charge.

As John recalled, there was a long history of the use of mattresses for defence. The Royal Navy's ships used them routinely for shell splinter absorption.

With Berlin now completely surrounded and isolated from any further reinforcement, the Red Army began to advance towards the centre from all sides: house to house, block by block, street by street. Vicious close-order fighting using methods they had learnt, at much cost, in Stalingrad.

To attack a street, two columns of tanks would slowly advance. Moving on the pavements, hugging the walls of the houses, they would direct their cannon and machine gun fire to the houses opposite, sweeping the frontages, concentrating on the windows and balconies.

As the tanks moved slowly forward, infantry assault groups worked their way through the houses on three levels: through the cellars, on the roof and the houses themselves. The assault groups were armed as in Stalingrad; grenades, sub-machine guns, knives and sharpened-edged short spades, wielded like axes in close-contact fighting. These initial groups were backed by reinforcement groups more heavily armed with machine guns and anti-tank weapons. These reinforcement groups were themselves backed by reserve groups, heavily armed, to thwart any counter-attacks. Such was the success of the technique it had become standardised, the procedure codified and formally endorsed by instruction manuals.

The standard method of breaking through a wall between terraced houses was by means of an explosive charge, then pick axes to enlarge the hole. This was hazardous because the defenders could fire back through the hole at the attackers before they could get a grenade through.

The Panzerfaust was not only an excellent anti-armour weapon, its shaped charge warhead was ideal for punching large holes through substantial walls. The Germans had produced them by the tens of thousands and the Red Army had captured a healthy supply. They also had the advantage of destroying everything in the room beyond the walls.

This procedure for advancing through buildings was named flank progress. That there were civilians mixed in with the defending troops made no difference to the Russians. Should they find any, women and children included, they were simply forced out onto the street. Their casualties, unsurprisingly, were enormous.

112

The last Monday in April and Luke was preparing to travel up to London by the early train. Still wet from the bath, he padded across the landing to his rooms. Hearing a noise, he glanced through the window down into the quad and caught sight of a fight between two of the now numerous feral cats.

Allegra's taste in cinema was nothing if not eclectic. The previous night's entertainment had included a wildlife documentary, mostly Africa, mostly large animals.

Entering his rooms he enjoyed the immediate warmth from the gas fire and began to dry himself off. That was the thing about nature. With an encounter there was only a choice of four possible responses. Feed, fuck, fight or flee. The four Fs.

As he dressed, he thought of their previous afternoon's cycle ride. Since the beginning of the war the wreckage of downed and crashed German aircraft had been collected, and after examination, subsequently dumped at a site at Cowley, just outside Oxford.

The wreckage, spread over many acres, made for an arresting sight. The remains of hundreds, thousands, unceremoniously dumped one upon the other. Weird and surreal. A cemetery of broken wings.

It was not a place to linger and soon they had continued onto the river.

By now it was a fine April morning; the sun was out and it felt warm, the promise of a spring confirmed.

Luke, as usual, walked from Paddington station. Five years now he'd walked over London – should he stop once the war was over, he would miss this.

Most of the bomb sites had lost their raw edge, eroded by weather and time. And the smells too had changed. London was smelling like a city again, not a battlefield. With the change of season everywhere was gradually turning green. The weeds, undisturbed amongst the rubble, were becoming spectacular. Wherever he looked, rosebay willowherb was thriving. Nature re-establishing, taking back her own.

***

John awoke suddenly, a sharp shooting pain in his left leg. Celia, deeply asleep, was lying across him, pressing down on his calf.

Gently, without disturbing her, he rearranged himself, curving into her back, around her bottom and down her thighs. Burying his head in her hair he listened to her breathing, matching his breaths with hers. It was immensely comforting, within her warmth.

The recognition of how much he loved her, and the impossibility of considering a life without her, had grown slowly. Now, he was sure, another warm and comforting feeling. And he was equally sure that Celia felt the same, though it might be just as well to ask her at some point. With the uncertainties of war, it had never seemed appropriate or sensible to look beyond it. Now, one just might.

He would wait for an opportune time.

Celia, as was her practice, had sprayed a little of her perfume on his pillow before she left. A consolation and a reminder in her absence.

There would be few heroes now. The Allied forces, British and American, were tired. Tired and weary of the continuous fighting. With the war in Europe so obviously won, their attitude had changed. They would fight when needed, but not seek it out. Self-preservation had become the overwhelming preoccupation. It was an attitude recognised and tacitly encouraged by all the British and American generals. Theirs were citizen armies, civilians in uniform for the duration.

Not so their opponents. Indoctrinated since the early 30s, few Germans could remember an alternative.

The Russians, fuelled by hate, had nothing of the Allied armies' inhibitions. Their intentions were simple. Kill as many Germans as possible, as quickly as possible. The Germans knew this. Fight or surrender they would be just as dead. No choice. And, if they did try to surrender, they were just as likely to be shot by the Gestapo. Fight or die, fight and die – no alternatives.

John read the reports of the accelerating disintegration of the remains of the German forces on the western front. The end had long passed beyond the if; what now preoccupied everyone was the when.

374

By the final week of April, the so-called thousand-year Third Reich had shrunk to an island of territory in the centre of Berlin ten miles long by three miles wide. Trapped within were around 40,000 German troops augmented by about the same number from the *Volkssturm*. Arrayed around this pocket were 450,000 Red Army troops, 13,000 guns, fifteen hundred tanks and over twenty thousand Katyusha rocket launchers. The Germans fought on as the remains of their capital city was systematically demolished to bury them.

South-east of Berlin lies the Spree Forest, a vast area of mature pine and close-packed young plantations. There were few roads and those resembled little more than tracks. Within its sprawl sheltered around 40,000 German soldiers, the scatterings of the *Wehrmacht*, mixed in with many thousands of terrified and fleeing civilians. All were attempting to move westwards, away from the Russians, towards the Elbe and the relative safety of the American armies. The forest area lay between the pincers of Konev's and Zhukov's advancing armies.

The Germans fought a series of desperate withdrawal actions centred on the large village of Halbe.

As with all fighting in forests, the battles were confused, vicious with huge casualties, particularly for the Germans. The Soviet artillery fused their shells to explode in the tree canopy to form thousands of wooden shards to act as shrapnel. The ground beneath, sandy, densely smothered in tree roots, offered little protection. The slaughter, soldiers and civilians alike, was fearful.

One report John read commented that the terrain was not dissimilar to that of the Ardennes, but with better weather. Of the 80,000 trapped within the forest around five thousand of the fleeing soldiers and civilians made it to the banks of the Elbe. The Russians slaughtered the rest.

There were camels in Berlin, hundreds, possibly thousands of them. Two American journalists had slipped away from the Torgau piss-up, crossed the Elbe on a Russian ferry and, with a mixture of bluff and bravado, had driven into the suburbs of Berlin. It was here they'd come across the camels. The Russians were using them as pack animals to transfer supplies and ammunition to the front-line assault teams. Camels could easily negotiate the destroyed buildings and rubble-filled streets reaching areas that wheeled transport could not.

Whilst the exploits of the two journalists was subsequently condemned by both the Russians and the Americans, and their despatches confiscated, their reports were nevertheless circulated around SHAEF.

Stalin had declared the Reichstag, the former seat of the German parliament, burnt out by Hitler in 1933, the heart of the fascist beast. As such, its capture had been nominated as the symbol of victory for the Red Army. Much had been promised to the troops who secured it.

Intent on its capture in time for the May Day parades in Moscow, the assault had begun at dawn on 30 April. There were far more defenders than the Russians had anticipated and their progress was slow; the fighting bitter, hand to hand, room to room. And there were a lot of rooms.

Two brave souls managed to raise the Red Banner on the ramparts of the building in the early hours of 1 May while the battle raged beneath them. But, being in the dark, the action was unrecorded. By the morning of 2 May the Russians had gained complete control of the Reichstag and its immediate surroundings. The raising of the Red Banner was carefully re-enacted, filmed and photographed, a significant piece of propaganda.

During the late evening of 1 May, the listeners to Hamburg radio were forewarned of an impending grave announcement. Solemn music; then Grand Admiral Dönitz addressed the nation. Hitler was dead. Dönitz himself had been nominated as his successor.

In the early hours of the following morning, the last functioning transmitter of radio Berlin announced, "The Führer is dead. Long live the Reich."

SHAEF, who had been monitoring German radio broadcasts continuously, made the announcement early in the morning. It was on the BBC eight o'clock news. It was the only topic of conversation on John's bus journey to Norfolk House.

Hitler had followed Mussolini. Summarily executed with his mistress near Lake Como, then hung by his heels from the roof of a Milan garage in front of a jeering crowd. Very Italian.

During the afternoon there was further good news. All German forces in northern Italy and southern Austria had surrendered unconditionally.

113

While the Russians reduced the remainder of Berlin to rubble and the Americans lined the west bank of the Elbe and advanced deep into Austria, Montgomery's 21st Army Group continued its campaign north towards the Baltic. Churchill feared that if the Soviet troops were to enter Denmark, they would then seal off any western access to the Baltic Sea.

Montgomery's Baltic campaign, Operation Enterprise, was launched on 30 April. Progress was swift, particularly after the announcement of Hitler's death, with few German soldiers showing any inclination to continue the fighting. While most surrendered immediately the British arrived, there were the occasional pockets of resistance, sadly mostly boy soldiers, some as young as twelve. Where resistance was encountered, the British columns simply stood off and pounded the area to rubble. There was no longer any patience left for subtlety. The choice was surrender, or be killed in the shortest possible time.

Lübeck was taken on 2 May, while Wismar, forty miles to the east, was taken on the same day, only hours before the first of the Russian forward patrols arrived. Denmark was safe. Hamburg and its substantial garrison surrendered on 3 May.

On the same day, a delegation headed by Admiral von Friedeburg, the newly appointed head of the *Kriegsmarine* by Dönitz, arrived at Montgomery's Tactical HQ on Lüneburg Heath. He had come to offer a surrender of all the German forces in the north, including those facing the Russians. Montgomery refused. He had no authority to act on behalf of the Russians but, he was prepared to take the unconditional surrender of all the German forces in Holland, the Frisian Islands, Heligoland, Schleswig-Holstein, Denmark and those parts of Germany west of the Elbe still under German control. Dönitz's wish to make a separate peace with the Western Allies before another with the Russians was not to be realised. It was to be a complete surrender, or nothing.

On 4 May, the delegation returned to Montgomery's HQ to formally sign the Instrument of Surrender as dictated by Montgomery. All hostilities on land, sea or in the air were to cease at 0800, British Double Summer Time, on Saturday 5 May 1945. 21st Army Group's war was over.

On 5 May, von Friedeburg was flown to Eisenhower' SHAEF Headquarters at Reims. Here he was joined by General Jodl on 6 May.

In the early hours of 7 May, Jodl, on behalf of Dönitz, signed the Instrument of Surrender. It was unconditional. General Susloparov, the chief Soviet liaison officer at SHAEF, signed on behalf of the Soviet High Command. This was not sufficient for Stalin who demanded another surrender ceremony to be conducted by the Red Army in Berlin for the following day. It made no difference. The war against Germany was over.

Significantly, and pointedly, Eisenhower had refused to meet any of the German delegation until the Instrument of Surrender had been signed. He then sent a short cable to the Combined Joint Chiefs of Staff. "The mission of the Allied force was fulfilled at 0241, local time, May 7 1945."

Norfolk House had begun its party early. Mid-morning found John sitting at his desk, coffee and a sandwich to his left, a large glass of whisky to his right. Before him lay a brief note, drafted more for himself than publication.

The telephone rang and he reached to answer it. Celia. She was at the flat having travelled up from Hamble in the early hours. Not unreasonably in the circumstances, John decided to award himself the afternoon off.

114

John and Celia rose late, both nursing moderate hangovers. Arrangements had been made during the previous afternoon for them all to meet in a pub off Piccadilly. Neither John nor Celia could remember its name, but they knew where it was. It would be the first time they'd all been together in one place in almost five years.

The streets were packed – happy people singing, dancing, drinking; everyone smiling, much laughter. If there was any public transport, they failed to find it and it was a tiring walk through the crowds to the pub taking them well over an hour.

They were the last to arrive. Camped out in a corner furthest from the bar, a couple of tables pushed together, were the others, two spare seats reserved.

The noise in the pub was deafening, conversation in shouted scraps. John glanced around the table, looking at them all. Matthew and Kirsty, Mark and Bridget, Luke and Allegra, Celia and himself. Recently he'd found a photograph of the four of them taken the week they'd gone up to Oxford; fresh young faces. They looked older now, worn. He caught Luke's eye and smiled as they mouthed something at each other, glasses raised.

Japan notwithstanding, he wondered where they all might be in another five years. Whether all the peacetime plans and hopes would be rewarded.

Matthew intended to join Kirsty's family farm in Scotland. Mark and Bridget were to stay on the south coast, close to the sea, and set up some sort of business. Luke would stay at Oxford, as would Allegra.

For himself there were the two choices. Stay in the RAF, drop two levels of rank and, after Japan, keep himself occupied and trained until the next war. Or, take his gratuity and leave. Ex Wing Commander Buchan DSO, DFC and Bar, AFC, unemployed and, from his perspective, unemployable. The only thing he knew was flying – flying Spitfires and fighting in them. That's how he'd been defined, how he'd thought of himself for the past five years. Fighter pilot. These days not an entirely unique capability.

As for the other choice, Celia's father had indicated that should he wish, his stock broking firm would make him very welcome.

There was, however, another thing he intended to do. And he would do it as soon as practicable. Marry Celia. John smiled to himself. That would do to be going on with. His smile faded as the thought struck him. He hadn't proposed yet.

Another glance around the table. Yes, they were older now, twenty-five. Hardly more than boys when it began, men now. The war had consumed their youth.

And there was something else, something fundamental. With the coming of peace in Europe, people had suddenly been relieved of that feeling of impending dread they had been living with since September 1939. It was an adjustment that, given time, would have unknown consequences.

Celia squeezed his hand and he told her what he'd been thinking.

She squeezed his hand again and smiled. It was a warm, open smile. And then another, ironic.

"I'll be thirty in a couple of more years," she said. "What an awful thought."

John squeezed her hand back.

"At least you'll be alive."

"God, I hope so."

Luke, like John, was looking around, enjoying the company, thinking. He'd had some recent news, a letter from Buck House a few days before. Whilst Henderson was to receive a Knighthood, Luke had been awarded the Order of the British Empire, an OBE. It was the highest award he was entitled to. Also, he'd been put on alert to join a delegation from the UK to visit Germany in several weeks' time as part of the T-Force operations. He wondered whether to mention it, but decided now wasn't the time. They'd all be in London for the next couple of days – there would be ample opportunity.

Meanwhile Elizabeth had joined them, a somewhat drunken and over-excited Julian in tow. Luke had met Julian a couple of times before. A left-wing documentary film maker whom Elizabeth had taken up with over the new year. Talented, certainly, and hailing from that peculiar thirties English tradition of well-heeled upper-class socialists. When sober he talked of nothing but film, when pissed he talked nothing but politics, interminably.

Luke could hear him, bending Allegra's ear.

"We own the future now. A new education system, a universal health service, all industry nationalised. It won't be like the last time. It'll be a real socialist government for equality. For the people by the people. It's going to be the people's time. The real people."

Allegra cast Luke a pleading expression and he moved to rescue her. Julian meantime continued with his political manifesto, oblivious to whether anyone was listening or not.

Patting Julian on the head as one might do an old pet dog, Elizabeth squeezed in beside Luke.

"Who's going back to the flat tonight?"

More dancing had begun at the end of the bar and she had to repeat the question to make herself heard.

Luke wasn't sure. "I think John and Celia intend to go back to Chiswick. As for the others, I've no real idea."

Elizabeth counted on her fingers. "Six then."

Luke smiled. "That seems about right."

"I'll go back to Julian's then. He should be able to walk that far."

The afternoon stretched into the evening and the evening into the dusk and the night. Since the beginning of May there had been light on the streets. No more blackout and, equally astonishing, it appeared so normal. How things should be.

Gradually, very gradually the celebrations began to wind down. It was approaching midnight before they prepared to leave – John and Celia to Chiswick, the others back to the flat. Promises to meet up the following afternoon.

John and Celia set off across Green Park. The spivs were moving amongst the couples stretched out on the grass hawking condoms.

"New johnnies five bob. Used half a crown."

John heard the call.

"Good God. How fucking desperate can you get?"

"Desperate for a fuck."

Celia smiled, a mischievous expression.

"I think one could make an argument for copulation as a patriotic duty on a night such as this."

John smiled in return. He knew where this was going. He caught Celia's expression, eyebrow raised, and laughed.

"We can discuss it further when we get back to Chiswick. Though we've got to get there first," he added, pausing to rub his leg. This seven-mile walk was going to take some time.

Reaching the bank of the Thames they began heading west. There were bonfires, it seemed, in practically every suburban street. Many buildings were lit up, searchlights across the sky and endless numbers of fireworks. Lights all along the Thames embankment.

What was the most striking was everywhere people had pulled back their curtains and lit up their rooms allowing the light to spill out over the streets. After almost six years of continuous blackout, this sudden illumination came as a sudden and profound shock.

As they continued walking John fretted. He knew what he wanted to say but was struggling to find the words to say it.

"We've been together almost five years," he said, as conversationally as he could manage.

Celia looked at him and smiled, but didn't comment.

"And, you could say we've come to a sort of agreement."

"You could say that."

"Is it what you want? I mean are you really sure you want to marry me?" John sounded earnest.

"Yes. I have been for as long as I can remember. But only if you ask me!"

They were alongside the Chelsea Embankment. John desperately sought an empty seat, failing to find one. Instead, he led her to the wall and leaning on it took both of her hands in his. He coughed, and then swallowed.

"Will you marry me?"

Celia waited before she answered – a suitable pause.

"Yes," she said, and kissed him. "And as soon as possible!"

Milton Keynes UK
Ingram Content Group UK Ltd.
UKHW031307061024
449308UK00001B/31